P9-DHF-868

It's her first case,
but she's his next victim.

"SUSPENSEFUL, COMPLEX,
COMPELLING...THIS THRILLER
TEEMS WITH CRISP,
REALISTIC DIALOGUE
AND ENGAGING CHARACTERS."
—*Publishers Weekly* (starred review)

PRAISE FOR LISA GARDNER

"**Gardner keeps us guessing to the finale.** She also keeps us on edge." —*Los Angeles Times*

"[Gardner] show[s] a flair for **lip-biting suspense.**"
—*People*

"Mary Higgins Clark practically invented the psychological suspense genre featuring a female protagonist who is both hero and victim, and Gardner . . . has mastered it."
—*Providence Sunday Journal*

"**Gardner serves up suspense at a furious pace.**"
—*Publishers Weekly*

"Gardner has firmly established herself as one of the hottest suspense talents around. Awesome!"
—*Romantic Times Bookclub*

"I love Lisa Gardner's hot, fast thrill rides. For my money, **when it comes to suspense, nobody does it better.**" —Jayne Ann Krentz

"Lisa Gardner knows how to produce a hair-raising mystery thriller. . . . **Gardner keeps the reader guessing with twist after ingenious twsit.**"
—*Charleston (SC) Post and Courier*

LISA GARDNER

THE
THIRD
VICTIM

BANTAM BOOKS

NEW YORK TORONTO LONDON
SYDNEY AUCKLAND

THE THIRD VICTIM
A Bantam Book

PUBLISHING HISTORY
Bantam mass market edition published February 2001
Bantam reissue edition / October 2004

Published by
Bantam Dell
A Division of Random House, Inc.
New York, New York

ISBN 0-553-57868-5

Printed in the United States of America
Published simultaneously in Canada

OPM   21 20 19 18 17 16

AUTHOR'S NOTE
AND ACKNOWLEDGMENTS

WHEN I FIRST PROPOSED this book to my editor, it was the winter of 1998 and nearly seven months since the last shooting—Kip Kinkel's May rampage in Springfield, Oregon. That tragedy had followed close on the heels of another, in Jonesboro, Arkansas (March 24, 1998), which had followed West Paducah, Kentucky (December 1, 1997), Pearl, Mississippi (October 1, 1997), and Bethel, Alaska (February 19, 1997). Like many Americans struggling to grasp five shootings in fifteen months, I wanted to understand why these mass murders had occurred and what could be done to prevent them.

After fine-tuning what would be appropriate to cover in a work of fiction whose goal must also be to entertain, I began researching this novel. One Monday, while wrapping up weeks of interviewing, I asked an expert if he believed that the rash of incidents indicated a new trend in juvenile behavior. While this point is controversial, the man did not hesitate to answer. "Absolutely," he said. "As for future shootings, the question is not if but when."

The very next day, Littleton, Colorado, joined the sad list of shot-up schools in a scope and scale that was staggering. I watched the news clips, and like people all around the world, I gave my thoughts and prayers to a community I had never met.

Each time one of these shootings occurs it is heartbreaking, but as Supervisory Special Agent Pierce Quincy tries to explain in the following pages, it does not have to be hopeless. With each tragedy, we have learned and are learning. In addition to Littleton, Springfield, and Jonesboro, there is Burlington, Wisconsin, where police responded to an anonymous tip in time to arrest three teenage boys plotting to assassinate a target list of "in" students, and there is Wimberly, Texas, where concerned students contacted police in time to foil a plot by five eighth-grade boys to blow up the junior high. People are learning to listen, and it does work.

In the end, I believe we owe an enormous debt of gratitude to each of the communities that has suffered this tragedy. By sharing their experience with us, and their sorrow, they are teaching us to be better people, students, families, and neighbors. May there come a day when white lilies and red roses are not piled against schoolyard fences. May there come a time when we are not haunted by the image of teenagers signing farewell notes on white caskets. May there be a future when our schools once again know peace.

The following people helped me tremendously with my research. I appreciate their help and patient explanations. Of course, all mistakes are mine, and some facts are subject to artistic license.

Dr. Gregory K. Moffatt, Ph.D., Professor of
            Psychology, Atlanta Christian College
Thomas Grisso, Ph.D., Professor of Psychiatry
            (Clinical Psychology), Director of Forensics
            Training and Research, University of
            Massachusetts Medical School
Steve Ellis, Officer, Amity Police Department

Rudolf Van Soolen, Chief of Police, Amity Police
    Department
Jonathan McCarthy, Paramedic, New Orleans
    Health Department
Amy Holmes Hehn, Senior Deputy District
    Attorney, Juvenile Division, Multnomah
    County
Stacy Heyworth, Senior Deputy District Attorney,
    Multnomah County
Michael Moore, Attorney-at-Law
Virgie Lorenz, teacher
Bruce Walker, computer whiz extraordinaire
Chad LeDoux, gun aficionado and fellow writer
Debra Dixon, author

THE THIRD VICTIM

ONE

OFFICER LORRAINE CONNER was sitting in a red vinyl booth at Martha's Diner, picking at her tuna salad and listening to Frank and Doug gossip, when the call first came in. She was sitting alone in the booth, eating salad because she'd just turned thirty-one and was beginning to notice that the pounds didn't magically melt away the way they had when she was twenty-one, or hell, even twenty-seven. She could still run a six-minute mile and slip into a size 8, but thirty-one was fundamentally different from thirty. She spent more time arranging her long chestnut hair to earn those second glances. And for lunches, she traded in cheeseburgers for tuna salad, five days a week.

Rainie's partner that day was twenty-two-year-old volunteer police officer Charles Cunningham, aka Chuckie. Known in the lingo of the tiny police department of Bakersville, Oregon, as a "green rookie," Chuckie hadn't yet gone to the nine-month-long training school. That meant he was allowed to look but not touch. Full authority would come when he completed the required academy courses and received his certificate. In the meantime, he got to gain experience by going on patrols and writing up reports. He also got to wear the standard tan uniform and carry a gun. Chuckie was a pretty happy guy.

Before the call came in, he was up at the lunch counter, trying to work some magic on a leggy blond waitress named Cindy. He had his chest puffed out, his knee crooked forward, and his hand resting lightly on his sidearm. Cindy, on the other hand, was trying to serve up slices of Martha's homemade blueberry pie to six farmers at once. One cantankerous old man muttered at the rookie to get out of the way. Chuckie grinned harder.

In the booth behind Rainie, retired dairymen Doug Atkens and Frank Winslow started placing their bets.

"Ten dollars says she caves," Doug announced, slapping a crumpled bill on the pink Formica table.

"Twenty says she dumps a glass of ice water over Romeo's head," Frank countered, reaching for his wallet. "I know for a fact that Cindy would rather earn good tips than Clark Gable's heart."

Rainie gave up on her salad and turned around to face the two men. It was a slow afternoon and she had nothing better to do with her time, so she said, "I'll take a piece of that."

"Hello there, Rainie." Frank and Doug, friends for nearly fifty years, smiled as a single unit. Frank had bluer eyes in his sun-weathered face, but Doug had more hair. Both men wore red-checked western shirts with pearl snaps—their official dress shirts for an afternoon spent out on the town. In the winter, they topped their shirts with brown suede blazers and cream-colored cowboy hats. Rainie once accused them of trying to impersonate the Marlboro Man. At their ages, they took that as a compliment.

"Slow day?" Doug asked.

"Slow month. It's May. The sun is out. Everyone is too damn happy to fight."

"Ahh, no juicy domestic disputes?"

"Not even a quibble over whose dog is depositing

what souvenirs in whose yard. If this good weather continues, I'm gonna be out of a job."

"A beautiful woman like you doesn't need a job," Frank said. "You need a *man*."

"Yeah? And after thirty seconds, what would I do?"

Frank and Doug chortled; Rainie winked. She liked Frank and Doug. Every Tuesday for as long as she could remember, she would find them sitting at that booth in this diner at precisely one P.M. The sun rose, the sun set. Frank and Doug ate Martha's Tuesday meatloaf special. It worked.

Now Rainie tossed ten bucks into the pot in Chuckie's favor. She'd seen the young Don Juan in action before, and Bakersville's young ladies simply loved his dimpled smile.

"So what d'you think of the new volunteer?" Doug asked, jerking his head toward the lunch counter.

"What's there to think? Writing traffic tickets isn't brain surgery."

"Heard you two had a little encounter with a German shepherd last week," Frank said.

Rainie grimaced. "Rabies. Damn fine animal too."

"Did he really charge Romeo?"

"All ninety pounds."

"We heard Chuckie 'bout peed his pants."

"I don't think Chuckie likes dogs."

"Walt said you took the shepherd out. Clean shot to the head."

"That's why they pay me the big bucks—so I can counsel drunks and shoot household pets."

"Come on, Rainie. Walt said it was a tough shot. Those dogs move *fast*. Chuckie indebted to you now?"

Rainie eyed the rookie, still puffed up like a rooster at the lunch counter. She said, "I think Chuckie's scared *shitless* of me now."

Frank and Doug laughed again. Then Frank leaned forward, a gleam in his old blue eyes as he started fishing for real gossip.

"Shep must like having more help," he said meaningfully.

Rainie eyed the bait, then refused the offer. "All sheriffs like getting people willing to work for free," she said neutrally. It was true enough. Bakersville's modest budget allowed for only one full-time sheriff and two full-time officers—Rainie and Luke Hayes. The other six patrolmen were strictly volunteers. They not only donated their time for free, but they paid for their own training, uniforms, vests, and guns. Lots of small towns used this system. After all, the majority of calls dealt with domestic disputes and crimes against property. Nothing a few good people with level heads couldn't handle.

"I hear Shep is cutting back his hours," Doug prompted.

"I don't keep track."

"Come on, Rainie. Everyone knows Shep and Sandy are having their differences. Is he working on patching things up? Getting more comfortable with his wife having a job?"

"I just write up civil incidents, Frank. No spying for the taxpayers here."

"Ahh, give us a hint. We're going to the barbershop next, you know. Walt gives free haircuts if you provide fresh news."

Rainie rolled her eyes. "Walt already knows more than I do. Who do you think *we* call for information?"

"Walt does know everything," Frank grumbled. "Maybe we should open up a barbershop. Hell, any kind of moron oughtta be able to cut hair."

Rainie looked down at the two men's hands, twisted from a lifetime of hard work and swollen by a decade of arthritis. "I'd come in," she said bravely.

"See there, Doug. We could also pick up chicks."

Doug was impressed. He began contemplating the details, and Rainie decided it was time to exit stage right. She swiveled back around in her booth with a parting smile, then glanced at her watch. 1:30 P.M. No calls coming in, no reports from the morning to be written up. An unusually slow morning in an already slow town. She looked at Chuckie, whose cheeks had to be aching from that smile.

"Wrap it up, rookie," she muttered, and drummed her fingertips restlessly.

Unlike Charles Cunningham, Rainie had never planned on becoming a cop. When she'd graduated from Bakersville High School, her first thought had been to get the hell out of dairyland. She'd had eighteen years of claustrophobia building up inside her and no family left to keep her chained. Freedom, that's what she needed. No more ghosts, or so she'd thought.

Rainie had boarded the first bus to Portland, where she'd enrolled at Portland State University and studied psychology. She'd liked her classes. She'd liked the young city brimming with cooking schools and art institutes and "alternative lifestyles." She'd gotten involved in a heady affair with a thirty-four-year-old assistant district attorney who'd driven a Porsche.

Nights spent taking over the wheel of the high-performance vehicle with all the windows rolled down. Putting the pedal to the metal and streaking up the sharp corners of Skyline Boulevard with the wind in her hair. Climbing higher, higher, higher, pushing harder, harder, harder. Searching for . . . something.

Then, when they finally crested the top of the hill, the city spreading out like a blanket of stars, pulling over and stripping off clothes as they furiously fucked amid gear-shifts and bucket seats.

Later, Howie would drive Rainie home, where she'd pop open a six-pack of beer alone, though she of all people knew better.

Rainie glanced at her watch again. "Come on, Chuckie. It's not like Cindy's going anywhere."

The radio on Rainie's belt crackled to life. Finally, she thought with genuine relief, some action.

"One-five, one-five. Calling one-five."

Rainie picked up the radio, already sliding out of the booth. "One-five here, go ahead."

"We have a report of an incident at the K-through-eight school. Wait . . . hang on."

Rainie frowned. She could hear noises in the background, as if dispatch had her own radio up very high or a phone next to the radio receiver. Rainie heard static and shouts. Then she heard four distinct popping sounds. Gunshots.

What the hell?

Rainie strode toward Chuck, turning him around just as dispatch came on again. For the first time in eight years, Linda Ames sounded frazzled.

"All units, all units. Reports of gunfire from Bakersville's K-through-eight. Reports . . . blood loss . . . blood in the halls. Calling six-oh . . . six-oh . . . Walt, bring the damn ambulance! I'm securing channel three. I think it's a school shooting. Oh my God, we're having a school shooting!"

Rainie got Chuck out of the diner. He looked pale and shocked. She waited to feel something but came up empty. There was a faint ringing in her ears. She ignored it as she slid into the old police sedan, buckled up, and reached automatically for the sirens.

"I don't understand," Chuckie murmured. "A school shooting? We don't have school shootings."

"Keep the radio on channel three. That's the designated channel, and all information will pass through there." Rainie slammed the car into gear and pulled out. They were on Main Street, a good fifteen minutes away from Bakersville's K–8, and Rainie knew that a lot could happen in fifteen minutes.

"We can't be having a school shooting," Chuckie continued, babbling. "Hell, we don't even have gangs, or drugs, or . . . or *homicides*, for that matter. Dispatch must be confused."

"Yeah," Rainie said quietly, though the ringing was growing in her ears. It had been years since she'd heard that sound. Years since she'd been a little girl, coming home from school and knowing from the first step into the doorway, the first note of foreboding in her eardrums, that her mother was already drunk and this was going to be bad.

You're a cop now, Rainie. You're in control.

Suddenly, she desperately needed to hold a bottle of beer.

The radio crackled again. Sheriff Shep O'Grady's voice came on as Rainie cleared the first light on Main Street. "One-five, one-five, what is your position?"

"Twelve minutes out," Rainie responded, weaving sharply around one double-parked car and barely squeaking by the next.

"One-five, switch to channel four."

Rainie looked at Chuckie. The rookie made the switch to the private channel. Shep's voice returned. He didn't sound as calm anymore. "Rainie, you gotta get here faster."

"We were at Martha's. I'm coming as fast as I can. You?"

"Six minutes out. Too damn far. Linda sent the rest of the officers scrambling, but most gotta run home for their vests and sidearms. Nearest county officer is probably twenty minutes away, and state a good thirty to forty minutes. If this really is a major incident . . ." His voice trailed off; then he said abruptly, "Rainie, you need to be the primary."

"I can't be the primary. I don't have any experience." Rainie glanced at Chuck, who appeared equally confused. The sheriff was always the primary on the case. That was procedure.

"You have more experience than anyone else," Shep was saying.

"My mother doesn't count—"

"Rainie, I'm not sure what's really going down at the school, but if it's a shooting . . . My kids are there, Rainie. You can't ask me not to think about my children."

Rainie fell silent. After eight years of working with

Shep, she knew his two children as well as a favorite niece and nephew. Eight-year-old Becky was horse crazy. Thirteen-year-old Danny loved to spend free afternoons at the tiny police station. Once, Rainie had given the boy a plastic sheriff's star. He'd worn it for nearly six months and demanded to sit beside Rainie whenever she came over to dinner. They were great kids. Two great kids in a building filled with two hundred and fifty other great kids. Not one above the age of fourteen . . .

Not in Bakersville. Chuckie was right: These things couldn't be happening in Bakersville.

Rainie said quietly, "I'll be the primary."

"Thanks, Rainie. Knew I could count on you."

The radio clicked off. Rainie hit another red light and had to tap the brakes to slow. Fortunately, cross-traffic saw her coming and halted right away. She was vaguely aware of the other drivers' concerned expressions. Police sirens on Main Street? You never heard police sirens on Main Street. They still had a good ten-minute drive, and now she was genuinely concerned that that might be too long . . . too late.

Two hundred and fifty little kids . . .

"Turn back to channel three," she told Chuckie. "Order the medics docked."

"But there's a report of blood—"

"Medics are docked until the scene is secured. That's the drill."

Chuck did as he was told.

"Get dispatch on. Request full backup. I'm sure the state and county boys have heard, and I don't want there to be any confusion—we'll take all the help we can get." She paused, sifting through her memory to classes taken eight years ago in a musty classroom in Salem, Oregon, where she had been the only woman among thirty men. Full-scale mobilization. Procedure for possible large-scale casualties. Things that had seemed strange to be studying at the time.

"Ask local hospitals to be on alert," she murmured.

"Tell the medics to contact the local blood bank in case they need to boost supply. Linda needs to request SWAT coverage. Oh, and tell the state Crime Scene Unit to be ready to roll. Just in case."

Dispatch returned before Chuckie could pick up the radio. Linda sounded shrill. "We have calls of shots still being fired. No information on shooter. No information on casualties. We have reports of a man in black at the scene. Shooter may be in the area. Proceed with caution. Please, please, proceed with caution."

"A man?" Chuck said hoarsely. "I thought it would be a student. It's always a student."

Rainie finally hit the rural highway on the edge of downtown and opened the car up to eighty miles per hour. They were on their way now. Seven minutes and counting. Chuck picked up the radio and ran through the list of orders.

Rainie started thinking of the other communities and schools she'd seen in the news without completely understanding. Even Springfield, Oregon, had seemed far away. It was a city, and everyone knew cities had their problems. That's why people moved to Bakersville. Nothing bad was ever supposed to happen here.

But you already knew better, didn't you, Rainie? You of all people should've known.

Chuckie was done with the radio. Now his lips moved in silent prayer. Rainie had to look away.

"I'm coming," she murmured to the children she could see clearly in her mind. "I'm coming as fast as I can."

ON TUESDAY AFTERNOON, Sandy O'Grady was trying hard to get some market-research reports done and was failing miserably. Sitting in a small corner office—a former bedroom of a converted Victorian home—she spent more time gazing out the window than at the stack of reports piled high on her scarred oak desk.

The day was beautiful, not a cloud in sight. A true

rarity in a state with so much rain that the locals affectionately referred to it as liquid sunshine. The temperature was mild too. Not as cool as it could be in spring, but not so warm that it started pulling in all the tourists and spoiling the mood.

The day was perfect, a rare treat for all of Bakersville's citizens, who endured all the other days too—the rainy autumns, the icy winters, the mudslides that sometimes closed the mountain passes, and the spring floods that threatened to destroy all the fertile fields. One good day out of a hundred, her daddy would have noted ironically. But he would've been the first to say it was enough.

Sandra had lived in Bakersville all her life, and there was no other place she'd want to raise her family. Nestled between Oregon's Coastal Range on the east and the Pacific Ocean on the west, the valley boasted lush, rolling hills dotted by black and white Holsteins and ringed by towering green mountains. The dairy cows outnumbered the people two to one. The family farm still endured as a way of life. People knew one another and took part in their neighbors' lives. There were beaches for summer fun and hiking paths for fall glory. For dinner, you could have freshly caught crab, followed by a bowl of freshly picked strawberries topped off with freshly made cream. Not at all a bad life.

In the end, the only complaint Sandra had ever heard about her community was the weather. The endlessly gray winters, the thick, pea-soup fog that seemed to weigh some folks down. Sandy, however, even loved the gray, misty mornings when the mountains barely peeked over their flannel shrouds and the world was wrapped in silence.

When she and Shep had been newlyweds, they would go on walks in the early morning hours, before he had to report for duty. They'd layer up in barn coats and black rubber boots and wade through dew-heavy fields, feeling the fog like a silky caress against their cheeks. Once, when Sandy was four months pregnant and her hormones were raging out of control, they'd made love in the mist, rolling beneath an old oak tree and soaking themselves to the bone. Shep had looked at her with such awe and wonder. And she had wrapped her arms tight around his lean waist, listening to his fast-beating heart and daydreaming about the child growing in her belly. Would it be a boy or a girl? Would it have her curly blond hair or Shep's thick brown locks? How would it feel to have a tiny life nursing at her breast?

It had been a magic moment. Unfortunately, their marriage had not seen many of those since.

A knock at her door. Sandy pulled her gaze guiltily from the window and saw her boss, Mitchell Adams, leaning against the old bull's-eye molding. He had his ankles crossed and his hands thrust deep into the pants pockets of a three-thousand-dollar charcoal-colored suit. Dark hair just brushed his collar in the back, and his lean cheeks were freshly shaved. Mitchell Adams was one of those men who always looked good, whether he wore Armani or L. L. Bean. Shep had hated him on sight.

"How are those reports coming?" Mitch asked. In spite of Shep's concern, Mitchell was one-hundred-percent business. He had not hired Sandy because she remained lithe and beautiful even at forty. He had hired her because he'd realized that the former homecoming queen had a brain in her head and a need to succeed. When Sandy had tried explaining this to Shep, he simply hated Mitchell more.

"The meeting with Wal-Mart is tomorrow," Mitch was saying. "If we're really going to convince them to move into our town, we have to have our numbers in order."

"So I'd better get the numbers in order."

"How far along are you?"

She hesitated. "I'm getting there." Code for she hadn't gotten a damn thing done. Code for she'd had another big fight with Shep last night. Code for she'd be staying late to get the reports done, and that would generate yet another argument with her husband, and she didn't feel as if she could win anymore. But she was too Catholic to do anything different, and so was Shep.

They just kept going around and around, and now Becky was spending all her time sequestered in her room with an army of stuffed animals she believed could talk, while Danny spent more and more time playing on the Internet in the school's computer room. He'd told Sandy that he was earning extra credit from Miss Avalon. But both Sandy and Shep suspected that their son didn't want to come home anymore. Then last month there had been the incident with the lockers. . . .

Sandy was unconsciously rubbing her temples. Mitchell took a small step into the room, then caught himself and moved back.

"By tomorrow morning," he said quietly.

"Absolutely. First thing in the morning. I know how important the meeting is."

He finally nodded, though Sandy could tell he wasn't satisfied. She didn't know what else she could say. That was her life these days. No one was completely satisfied—not her boss, her husband, or her kids. She kept telling herself that if she could just hang in there a little longer, things would work out. The meeting with Wal-Mart was something they'd been working on for nine months. Keeping late hours, burning the midnight oil. But if it went well, a lot of money would be pouring in. The commercial real estate company could finally hire more employees. Sandy would probably take home a nice-size bonus. Shep might finally notice she had real abilities and ambitions, just like him.

One forty-five P.M. Sandy got up and closed the blinds on her window, hoping that would help her focus. She poured herself a glass of water, picked up a pen, and prepared to get serious.

She'd just started reviewing the market data when the phone at her elbow rang. She picked it up absently, one half of her mind still processing numbers. She was not prepared for what she heard.

Lucy Talbot sounded hysterical. "Sandy, Sandy! Oh thank God I reached you! There's been a shooting, at the school. Some man, they claim he's run away. I heard it on the radio. There's blood in the halls. Students, faculty, I don't know who. People are running in from everywhere. You gotta get there quick!"

Sandy didn't remember hanging up or grabbing her purse or yelling to Mitchell that she had to go.

What she remembered was running. She had to get to the school. She had to get to Danny and Becky.

And she remembered thinking for the first time in a long time that she was glad Shep O'Grady was her husband. Their children needed him.

TWO

BAKERSVILLE'S K–8 LOOKED LIKE a scene out of bedlam. As Rainie came to a screeching halt half a block away from the sprawling, one-story building, she saw parents running frantically across the parking lot while children wandered the fenced-in schoolyard, crying hysterically. Fire alarms were ringing. Walt's 1965 ambulance siren as well, damn him. More cars came careening dangerously around the residential streets, probably parents called from work.

"Damn," Rainie muttered. "Damn, damn, damn."

She could see teachers gathering up their charges into small groups. A man in a suit—maybe Principal VanderZanden; Rainie had met him only once—took up a post by the flagpole and seemed to be trying to organize the chaos. He wasn't having much luck. Too many parents were running from group to group trying to find their children. Too many children were circling aimlessly in search of parents. A young boy with blood-soaked jeans staggered away from the whirling madness and collapsed on the sidewalk. No one seemed to notice.

Rainie jumped out of her car and ran. Cunningham was right behind her. As they cut through the sea of people, pushing toward the school's glass front doors, Rainie spotted Shep's patrol car, strategically parked to block off the west entrance of the parking lot. The sheriff himself, however, was not in sight.

The front doors had been thrust wide open. Rainie could just make out Bakersville's two volunteer EMTs, Walt and Emery, hunched down at the end of the wide hallway, where they were already ministering to a victim.

"Dammit," she swore again. The two men had no business being in the building before it had been secured.

A parent came running up, heading straight for the open doors. Rainie grabbed his arm just as he tried to push by, and she shoved him back forcefully.

"My kid," he started.

"Into the parking lot," she yelled. "No one enters the building! Hey you, you there in the suit. Come here."

Rainie snagged the younger man in mid-run. He had a look of authority about him, his olive suit nicely tailored and his black shoes freshly polished. He was frowning at Rainie, clearly anxious and in a hurry.

"Are you from the school? What's your name?" Rainie demanded.

"Richard, Richard Mann. I'm the school counselor, and I need to get to the students. We've had some injuries—"

"Do you know what happened in there?"

"There were shots. Then the fire alarm sounded; then everyone was running. One minute I was in my office doing some paperwork, the next minute it was chaos."

"Did you see who was shooting?"

"No, but someone said they saw a man run out the west side doors. I don't know."

"What about the students? Is everyone out?"

"We followed basic evacuation procedure," Richard Mann replied automatically. Then his face fell. He lowered his voice so only Rainie could hear. "Two teachers said they saw some students down in the halls. They had to attend to their own classes, though, so they didn't feel they could stop . . . and they didn't want their kids to notice. I've also seen some wounded children out here. I tried to grab the EMTs, but they were already heading into the building."

"Do you have any medical training?"

"I learned CPR from the Y."

"Good enough. Here's what you're going to do: Form a first-aid station on the school lawn. Gather up all the injured kids—I just saw a boy collapse by the sidewalk, so you need to send someone over there. Then ask among the parents. There's gotta be other people here who have some sort of training—CPR, animal husbandry, camping first aid, I don't care. Have them assist the kids and hold the fort the best they can. Walt looks to have his hands full inside, and we probably have another good ten or fifteen minutes before Cabot County's ambulance arrives."

"I'll do my best. It's just so hard to be heard above the noise."

Rainie pointed a finger at Shep's patrol car. "See that? In the backseat is a bullhorn. Knock yourself out. Now, once you get a first-aid area set up, I have another job for you. Are you listening?"

The young counselor nodded intently. His face was pale, and his upper lip was beaded with sweat, but he seemed to be paying attention.

"See all the people clogging the parking lot?" she said. "We need them all moved across the street. Tell the teachers to line up their classes and conduct a head count. When they're done, they can match up students with parents. But everyone except the wounded clears this parking lot, for safety reasons, okay? And nobody goes home until they've been dismissed by the police. Got it?"

"I'll try."

"Did you see Sheriff O'Grady?"

"He ran into the building. I think he was looking for his kids."

Richard Mann took off for Shep's car. Rainie eyed the sprawling white school building, which she gathered was still unsecured, then looked at her rookie, who was nervously stroking his gun.

Rainie took a deep breath. She had only classroom training in these things, and that had been years ago, but she didn't have any other choices. Walt and Emery were already in the school. Shep too. She and Chuckie might as well join the fray.

She turned to him. "Walk *right* behind me, Chuckie. Eyes open, hands off your gun. Walt's acting without authority, but he still doesn't deserve to be shot."

Chuckie nodded dutifully.

"There are just three things to remember at a crime scene: Don't touch a thing. Don't touch a damn thing. Don't touch a goddamn thing. Okay?"

Chuckie nodded again. Rainie glanced at her watch. 1:57 P.M. The parking lot was still a mess, and it was hard to think over the din of sirens and crying children. It was hard to look too closely, because now she was noticing the red spots on the sidewalk, the unmistakable trail of blood from the school into the yard. The injured children fleeing for their lives. And the others? The ones Richard Mann said the other teachers had seen?

Rainie couldn't think about that yet.

She had her Glock in her right hand and her backup .22 holstered at her ankle. She hoped that was enough. She gave Cunningham a reassuring nod, and entered the building with her walkie-talkie in her left hand.

The noise was louder in the building, the long hallways funneling the relentlessly pinging fire alarm and raining the sound down upon their heads. "Dispatch," Rainie yelled into her walkie-talkie. "One-five calling dispatch. Linda, come in."

"Dispatch to one-five."

"Get me Hank on the wire. I need to know how to turn off the damn fire alarms."

"Ummm, okay. One moment."

Rainie and Chuckie paused in the front lobby, wincing against the steadily increasing noise.

Ahead of them, the main hallway was surprisingly clean. No backpacks scattered, no books thrown across the vast white-tiled floor. To the right loomed the admissions office, where the glass windows were covered with pastel cutouts of paper flowers and the cheery word *Welcome!* Rainie still didn't see any signs of violence.

The walkie-talkie crackled to life. Rainie held it up against her ear to catch Linda's instructions. Inside the main office. A master panel. Rainie eyed the closed door. No telling what was on the other side. And impossible to hear. That was the whole problem.

She motioned Chuckie to the side. No time like the present.

Ducking low. Leading with her gun. Kicking open the door and rolling inside. Coming up . . . Nothing. Nothing. Nothing. Office secured.

She crossed to the main control panel, and a second later the fire alarms abruptly broke off.

Chuckie blinked sharply. The silence was stunning after the noise. Stunning, and eerie.

"That—that's better," Chuckie said after a moment, working on sounding confident when his face had turned the color of parchment.

"Major learning from Columbine," Rainie muttered. "The fire alarms obscured all sound. Made it impossible for the SWAT team to pinpoint where the shooters were in the building."

"You've been trained in school shootings?" Chuckie asked hopefully.

"No. I read *Time* magazine." Rainie jerked her head. "Come on. Keep your head on straight. Use your ears. You'll be okay."

They returned to the main hall, both of them holding their sidearms and moving gingerly. After the office, rows of blue lockers began, the doors closed. The shooting must have happened after all the students were back in class after lunch, Rainie decided. She wondered if that was significant. Then she wondered what she would find in the classrooms.

She noticed a few misshapen slugs on the floor as they moved farther in. Probably stray shots from the main area of incident, or maybe debris kicked into this area when people stampeded out. She stepped carefully around all the objects, though she had no illusion about the situation in front of her.

An officer's first priority when approaching any crime scene was to preserve human life. The second objective was to apprehend the perpetrator, if still in the vicinity, and secure the scene. Third was to detain witnesses and protect the evidence, for it was always the officer's job to look beyond the tragedy of the moment. In the days to come, the people of Bakersville would be clamoring for answers. They would want reconstructions of the day, who did what to whom. What had gone wrong. Who was to blame.

Rainie already knew that those questions would not be easily answered. The school was located in a residential area, and too many civilians had beaten officers to the building. Between them, the EMTs, and the students, the hallway was contaminated. And now here were Rainie and Chuckie, two armed and inexperienced officers at their first major crime scene. She was in trouble before she started, and she still had no choice but to continue.

Rainie could hear Cunningham breathing hard behind her, while Walt cursed fifty yards in front of her. "Goddammit, Bradley," the volunteer EMT was muttering. "Don't you cut out on me now. Hell, man, we got poker on Friday."

Rainie and Cunningham quietly came up behind Walt and took inventory. Custodian Bradley Brown lay at a main intersection of two wide hallways. From this vantage point, Rainie could see nearly a dozen classroom doors to the left. They were all shut, which immediately made the hairs on the back of her neck prickle to life.

She glanced at Chuckie, but the rookie was looking to the right, where the hallway led to two glass side doors, shattered and streaked with a dark substance that was probably blood. More lockers dented here, a great deal more damage. The primary area of incidence.

A body lay not far from the doors. Long dark hair, a flowing summer dress. Probably a teacher. Closer in, Rainie saw two more shapes. Smaller, motionless. Not adults.

Cunningham made a hiccuping sound.

Rainie turned away.

"Already looked," Walt said tightly from the floor.

"You shouldn't even be in here."

"They're kids, Rainie. Just kids. We had to."

Rainie didn't bother with any more chastising. Walt was a former army medic and an experienced volunteer EMT. He knew the considerations, and what was done was done. She turned her attention to the custodian.

Bradley was an older man, his gray hair bristly, his brown pants and blue chambray shirt well worn. He wore a modest gold watch, the kind you might get as a reward for twenty years of service. And he had been shot high in the chest: blood relentlessly seeped through the white gauze bandages.

"Others?" the janitor whispered.

"Everyone's fine, Bradley," Walt answered crisply. "Just gotta worry about your miserable hide. What are you doing, getting yourself shot like that?" Walt slipped an IV needle into Bradley's arm, trying to get fluids into the man as his own drained out.

"You're doing great," Rainie reassured the janitor, kneeling down beside his head and giving him a smile. "So what happened here, Bradley?"

"Got . . . shot."

"No kidding." She forced a chuckle, as if they were sharing a small story over lunch. "See who did it?"

"Came . . . around . . . the corner."

She nodded supportively. Bradley's skin was turning blue. He was going cyanotic. Then would come hypovolemic shock from blood loss, followed by unconsciousness. If the bleeding still didn't stop, he would die. Walt and Emery were working furiously, but bandage after bandage continued to turn red.

"Heard shots . . ." Bradley gasped. "Wanted . . . to help."

"You're a brave man, Bradley."

He grimaced. "Came around . . . boom. Never . . . saw . . ."

"What hit you?"

"Yeah." His breath escaped as a hiss. "Toured in 'Nam. Funny . . . thought it'd be . . . there."

Bradley's eyes suddenly rolled back in his head. Walt swore sharply.

"Dammit, I need more gauze. Emery."

Emery held open an empty kit. "We've hit bottom."

"Load and go," Walt directed, reaching for the gurney as Rainie scrambled out of the way.

"Won't do any good," Emery countered. "Hospital's too far away."

"Chopper?" Rainie asked.

"Called it in seven minutes ago. Probably got another five-minute wait."

"Well, shit," Cunningham cried from behind Rainie. "Stop the bleeding, do something for him. He's dying, can't you see?" The rookie looked at them all, then in a burst of movement ripped off the tan shirt he'd bought with pride just two months ago. "Here, here, use this."

"We need more," Walt said. "To bandage the wound up tight."

"The janitor's closet," Rainie exclaimed. "Right there. It must have something."

"Sanitary napkins," Walt declared. "They work like a charm!"

Chuck was closest. He grabbed the metal doorknob and pulled hard. The door was locked. He pounded it once with an open hand. When that didn't work, he leveled his gun.

"Jesus Christ!" Rainie hurtled herself at his outstretched arm and knocked the Glock .40 from his grasp just before he could fire. Then she turned on him with hard eyes.

"Goddammit. Don't you ever draw down like that! Not at a crime scene where you'd contaminate all the evidence, and not in a building where everyone is scared out of his mind. Half the parents out there would've come running in with their shotguns and blasted you to bits."

"We gotta get it open!" Chuckie yelled.

"Then throw your shoulder into it! You're not made of glass."

Chuckie's eyes lit up. He took a running leap at the closet as Rainie stepped to the side and prepared to cover. All those closed-up classrooms. Who took the time to shut a door when they were running for their lives? Who sealed up each room neat and orderly, as if they had all the time in the world? Not schoolchildren, she thought. Not teachers. Which left only one option.

The closet door split open. Cunningham crowed his triumph and plunged into the black depths before Rainie could stop him. Then he froze her heart with a cry.

"Oh my God! There's a kid in here!"

Walt and Emery rushed forward. Rainie pushed them back. "Let me check it out," she said tightly. "Jesus, Walt, you've already used up your nine lives."

She stepped into the walk-in closet, blinking three times as her eyes adjusted to the gloom. Cunningham was in a corner, leaning over a little girl who had scrunched herself into such a tight ball that Rainie could make out only her golden blond hair. Then the child looked up. Rainie knew her instantly.

"Becky O'Grady! Oh honey, are you all right?"

Rainie motioned for Walt and Emery to enter, then

holstered her gun and fell to her knees in front of Shep's youngest child. At first glance, Becky seemed to be fine. Rainie ran her hands down the little girl's arms, searching for any signs of injury. No cuts, no bruises. No signs of powder burns or bullet holes, or God knows what under these circumstances. Then she noticed the glassy look in Becky's bright blue eyes. Carefully, Rainie drew her forward, and the little girl collapsed bonelessly into her arms.

Rainie rushed Becky out of the closet and laid her out on the cool floor. Emery took over.

"Dilated pupils," he declared. "Lack of response. Can you tell me your name?"

Becky said nothing.

"Can you hear me?"

She remained silent, but when he snapped his fingers, she turned her head toward the sound.

"Shock," Emery said after a moment. "Probably caused by the trauma. She just needs time."

Rainie hunkered down in front of the child, less convinced and still worried. Becky had a smudge of dirt across her nose, cobwebs in her hair. She was wearing a green Winnie the Pooh T-shirt, with Pooh and Piglet dancing and a caption saying how merry it was to have a friend.

Rainie gently rubbed one of the sooty marks from Becky's cheek. She cupped a hand against the girl's pale face. "Honey," she said quietly. "How did you end up in the closet?"

Becky just looked at her.

"Were you hiding?"

Slowly, the girl nodded.

"Becky, do you know who you were hiding from?"

Becky's bottom lip began to tremble.

"Was it someone you knew?"

Becky looked down.

"It's okay, Becky. It's all over now. You're safe." Rainie glanced at all the closed classroom doors. "No one can hurt you anymore. I just need to know who did this so I can do my job. Can you help me do my job, Becky?"

Becky O'Grady shook her head.

"Just think about it, honey. Just think."

Minute passed into minute. The little girl remained silent, and finally she turned away from Rainie and rolled back into a ball. Frustrated, Rainie rose to her feet. Walt and Emery had loaded Bradley onto the stretcher. Chuck's shirt held a thick pile of sanitary napkins to the man's chest. Bradley's skin was still pale blue, but he seemed to be breathing more easily. Score one for the good guys.

Rainie looked around. The closet door was splintered. Walt had tossed half its contents into the hallway in his quest for sanitary napkins. He and Emery had tracked bloody footprints everywhere. The hall doors remained ominously shut, and Becky O'Grady was curled into the fetal position at Rainie's feet.

Then farther down the hall. The fallen teacher. The two smaller forms . . .

Jesus Christ, what had happened at Bakersville K–8?

Rainie pulled Chuckie aside and spoke quietly. "We need to get Becky out of here. Why don't you carry her outside and see if you can find Sandy? By now the other officers should be arriving. Have them set up a perimeter around the grounds. You tell them for me: Nobody gets inside the perimeter, and that includes the press, the mayor, and the richest parent in town. Then tell Luke he's in charge of the crime-scene log."

"Press will be here soon," Chuckie muttered, his face already scrunching with distaste.

"We'll let Shep deal with them."

"Okay." He was looking around the hallway now, the quiet, still hallway, with the shattered doors at the end. "Rainie? Why are all the classroom doors closed? I thought the counselor guy said they evacuated like a fire drill. Seems like none of the kids would close the doors or turn out the lights when they were running from the building. So who'd do such a thing?"

"I don't think it was the kids or the teachers."

"The man in black?"

"Would you take the time to close each door as you were fleeing from your crime?"

Chuckie's brow furrowed. "Probably not, but who does that leave?"

Rainie smiled at him wryly. "I don't know, Cunningham, but I guess I'm about to find out."

THREE

ANDY O'GRADY TOOK the S-corners of the residential street at forty-five miles per hour. The tires of her loyal Oldsmobile squealed their protest, but she didn't notice. Her hands were tight on the wheel. Her blue eyes were locked forward.

All around her, people were running. Sprinting out of their houses, charging down the neat little sidewalks, their faces white with shock, their mouths already yelling the grim news to their neighbors. They carried first-aid kits and blankets, towels and water bottles and anything else they thought might be of use.

Sandy screeched around the next corner, hit a speed bump hard, and finally had to brake. Just as well. Two blocks from the school the street was clogged with hastily parked automobiles and frantic parents. Sandy drove halfway up the sidewalk, slammed her Olds into park, and joined the fray.

So much noise. Walt's old ambulance braying. Children crying *Mommy, Daddy,* parents screaming children's names. She heard police sirens and revving engines. She heard a sharp, loud keening, as if the soul had been ripped from a mother's heart, and her own blood went cold.

This couldn't be happening. Not in Bakersville. Not

in her children's school. Oh God, couldn't someone make this all go away?

She waded through the sea of people and cars. She didn't know where to go. She just kept slogging toward the school, trying to get closer. Where were her children? Where was her husband? Wouldn't someone tell her what to do?

Up ahead, she saw a police officer in a Cabot County uniform. He seemed to be simultaneously ushering people away from the school building and asking who was in charge. No one had an answer for him. Parents just wanted to find their children.

Sandy finally arrived at the chain-link fence that surrounded the schoolyard. She pressed herself against it, peering into the parking lot, where she could now see children stretched out on the blacktop, some holding cold compresses to their heads, others lifting scraped elbows and knees to be bandaged. Five adults were manning the makeshift first-aid station, using emergency kits and towels as fast as other people handed them in. Sandy recognized Susan Miller, Johnny's mom and a nurse at Cabot Hospital. She saw Rachel Green, the head of the PTA and a stay-at-home mom, wrapping an eight-year-old's wrist. She saw Dan Jensen, the town vet, hunched over a boy whose jeans were caked with blood. Sandy could just make out the hole ripped through the tough fabric. The boy had been shot in the leg.

God, a bullet wound. The shooting was real. Everything was real. Someone had opened fire in Bakersville's school.

Sandy thought she was going to be sick.

Vice Principal Mary Johnson raced by. Sandy snagged her arm.

"Mary, Mary. What happened? How is everyone? Have you seen Becky or Danny?"

Mary looked frazzled, her normally neat hair in frizzy disarray, her faced covered with a sheen of sweat. Her expression was blank for a moment; then she recognized Sandy and clasped her hand.

"Oh Sandy, I am so sorry. We're doing everything we can."

"Has something happened to my children? Where are Danny and Becky? *Where are my kids?*"

"Shh, it's all right. I'm sure it's all right. I have to ask you to step away from the school. All the children were led across the street with their teachers. We put them in each yard in order of grade. So Becky's class is in the fourth yard down. Danny's would be four yards down from there."

"You've seen them? They're okay?"

Mary Johnson hesitated. Something flickered in her gaze. Sandy felt her breath catch in her throat again.

"I don't know," Mary said. "There have been so many children—"

"You haven't seen them."

"We evacuated most of the children from the school. It's just taking us a bit to get it all sorted out."

"Oh my God, you haven't seen my children."

"Please, Sandy—"

"Are there fatalities? Just tell me. *Are there fatalities?*"

Mary Johnson tightened her grip on Sandy's hand. Then Sandy saw it all in her somber gaze, the news the vice principal didn't want to say out loud, the news they would all be struggling with for the next few days, months, years: Children had been shot and killed.

It really was happening here.

Sandy couldn't breathe, couldn't think. She wanted to turn back the clock six hours, when she had been at home, pouring bowls of Cheerios for her children before kissing them on the head. She wanted to turn back the clock to ten hours before that, when she had been tucking their wiggling forms into bed and reading stories of little boy wizards and magical spells. That was what their lives were supposed to be like. They were just children, for God's sake. Just children.

A shout rose up from the crowd. Sandy and Mary turned toward the school doors just in time to see Walt and Emery come racing out with a stretcher.

"Move, move, move," Walt was shouting.

The Cabot County officer yelled at people to clear the street. A car was in the way. No one seemed to know who owned it. The officer opened the door and popped the car into neutral. Two young men ran over to help push the vehicle out of the way. People cheered the small victory. Walt was already firing the ambulance to life.

Then Sandy saw Chuckie Cunningham running across the parking lot with a towheaded little girl wrapped tight in his arms.

Becky.

Sandy leapt forward before Mary Johnson could stop her. She raced across the parking lot and opened her arms just as Becky saw her and cried, "Mommy!"

And then her little girl was in her arms. Sandy was holding her close, inhaling the sweet scent of apple shampoo. She was squeezing her tight, tight, tight, and Becky was holding her neck so hard it hurt.

"My baby, my baby, my baby."

"Mommy, Mommy, Mommy."

"My baby."

She raised tear-filled eyes to Chuckie, who she now realized was half naked and streaked with blood.

"Danny?" she asked hoarsely.

"I don't know, ma'am."

"Shep?"

"I'm sorry."

Sandy sank to her knees. She had one child with her, one child safe. But it wasn't enough. The foreboding was grabbing hold of her again. Something cold and dark flowed through her veins. She raised her head pleadingly to the sky.

"Where is my son? Oh God, *where is Danny?*"

ALONE IN THE SCHOOL, Rainie gripped her Glock .40 with moist palms. Her breath came in shallow gasps. She could feel her heart pounding unnaturally in her chest. She did her best to ignore the sensations as she walked to the far left side of the school—the end farthest from the bodies—and prepared to conduct a methodical search of classrooms she was already sure weren't empty.

She turned her mind to dim memories of lessons learned in police courses taken years ago. Some kind of acronym thing. ACCESS . . . AGILE . . . ADAPT. That was it. ADAPT.

A: Arrest the perpetrator, if still at the scene.
(Was the perpetrator still at the scene? The reports of a man in black. All these closed doors.)

D: Detain and identify witnesses and suspects.
(The herd of students who'd already raced out of the building. Bradley Brown, still fighting for his life. Witnesses maybe, but other people's responsibilities now.)

A: Assess the crime scene.
(The clean halls and untouched front office. The dented lockers farther in, the spent shells on the floor. Don't overlook the obvious, that's what they said in class. What was obvious in a school shooting? The dead on the floor?)

P: Protect the scene.
(Rainie winced. The EMTs, the battered closet, the shells Cunningham had kicked across the floor. The parents who'd taken over the parking lot. The state Crime Scene Unit was going to arrive, and her career would be over.)

T: Take notes.
(Rainie stared at her gun. She thought of the spiral notepad in her breast pocket. She wondered how she was supposed to hold that and the gun.)

• • •

FORGET TAKING NOTES. She had to focus on step one, arresting the perpetrator if possible. God knew what it meant that she was doing things out of order. At least she was doing them and trying the best she could.

Her mind moved forward. She was searching a particularly large and complex crime scene for a suspect. She had a vague recollection of a lecturer explaining how to work a grid at a large site. Start in, spiral out, slowly expanding the area searched. She couldn't remember much more beyond the theory and decided she would have to approach this scene as a horizontal strip. She would work left to right. Quiet, calm, prepared.

Rainie put her back to the wall, tucked her chin against her chest to make herself a smaller target, and led with her gun.

Stay calm, stay professional. Do your job.

The first room was the hardest. The top half of the closed door was glass but decorated with so many cutout pictures of bunnies and tulips that she couldn't see inside. The lights were off as well, as in all the rooms in the school.

Rainie slowly twisted the doorknob with her left hand. From the crouch position, she pushed the door open into the room. Shadows, long and gray, in the back of the room. Sunshine, bright and fierce, in the front. She rolled across the threshold and came up with her Glock held in the two-handed Weaver stance. Right. Left. Front. Back. Nothing.

Rainie finally rose to her feet in the empty room. She turned on the lights and propped the door wide open to keep the premises exposed. And then she prepared for the next room.

Bit by bit she worked her way down the hall. Then she was at the intersection, where bloody gauze still covered the floor and the dents on the bright blue lockers grew worse. She saw more blood splatters. A big dent on a bottom locker, where a body must have careened into it hard. Casings were scattered across the white-tiled floor as if someone had flung a handful down the hall.

She could picture things now. The loud crack of gunshots, followed by the panicked screams of school-children. Little girls and little boys streaming from classrooms as the fire alarm sounded; teachers begging them in shaking voices to remain calm. The chaos of bodies running for the front doors, pushing, shoving, tripping, falling. Blood in the halls.

She took a deep breath, forced her pulse to slow.

Stay professional, Rainie. Do your job.

She checked out the fifth-grade classroom, then the sixth. Next the library, big and sweeping with endless rows of books. Nothing.

Finally she was at the end of the hall, where shattered glass was strewn across the floor from the broken doors, where three bodies lay quiet and still.

Rainie didn't want to look at the victims, especially not the children. She understood that the sight would hurt her, scar her someplace deep, where even tough guys like her were vulnerable. She knew it would make her think of other times, too, after she had worked years to forget those scenes.

But this was bigger than her. It had needs that had nothing to do with her own. It was about the rights of the victims and the needs of the parents outside, though she knew that from here out nothing anyone did for three sets of parents would ever be enough.

The first victim, a little girl, lay on her side. Rainie felt for a pulse, though Walt had already warned her and blood stained the entire front of the girl's shirt. Rainie swallowed hard and moved on, trying not to disturb the scene.

The second victim was also female. Looked approximately eight years old. She had also received multiple bullet wounds to the chest. She was lying just ahead of the first victim. Their arms stretched out toward each other, their fingers nearly touching. Had they been holding hands walking down the hall? Best friends giggling together? Rainie wanted to brush back the little girl's hair. She wanted to whisper to her that it would be all right.

Her vision blurred, tears burned hot in her eyes. She couldn't afford that.

Be professional. Move on.

She noted positioning. She noted victimology. She crossed to the third body.

Lying just outside the computer-lab door, this victim, also female, appeared to be a teacher. Three female fatalities—coincidence or plan? She had long dark hair and exotic features. She was also young, her smooth skin making her appear as if she were simply sleeping. Then Rainie noticed the small, neat bullet hole in her forehead.

Small-caliber weapon, Rainie thought. Probably a .22. Christ, the teacher didn't look a day older than herself. Late twenties maybe. Early thirties. No wedding band, but beautiful enough that you had to think some man would be sitting alone tonight, holding her picture with shaking hands while trying to forget the future that would never be. Christ.

Rainie had to take another deep breath. Only three more doors. All near the epicenter of violence. All dark and waiting. Time to get on with it.

Rainie backed up against the wall and sat in a crouch until her hands stopped shaking.

Only the teacher had a head wound, she thought. A single-entry shot, dead center, delivered with a great deal of precision. The two girls sported a multitude of wounds, high, low, left, right, as if they had walked into a firestorm. But the teacher . . . the teacher was different. Perhaps the intended target? Shooter went for her first, then encountered the two girls walking down the hall?

Or maybe he started with the girls in the hall, and

upon hearing the noise the computer-lab teacher opened her door. She would've been right in front of the killer. Had he gotten up his courage by then? Decided it wasn't that different from a video game? Figured why waste bullets if he could do it with a single shot?

Either scenario bothered Rainie. For the little girls to have so many wounds and the adult victim only one. There was something to that. She just didn't have the time to think about it now.

Suddenly, she heard a noise. The faint screech of a metal chair slowly being pulled across the floor.

Rainie scrambled across the hallway. She threw herself against the wall next to the classroom door just as the metal handle turned and the door eased open.

"Don't do this," a man said. "We can still fix everything. I swear to you, son, there's nothing that happened today that we can't handle."

Shep O'Grady came into view, tan uniform stretched tight over his burly frame. His buzz-cut hair glistened with moisture, while his bulldog features were unnaturally pale. From her angle, Rainie could see that he'd managed to unsnap his holster, but he'd never had time to draw his weapon. Now his hands were held in front of him in a gesture of submission. He worked frantically to plead his case.

"I'm sure it's all a big mistake. A misunderstanding. These things happen. Now we gotta work together, clear things up. You know there's nothing I wouldn't do for you."

Shep took another step back, his hands still up, his gaze focused ahead. Being forced into retreat? Rainie didn't know. Then she glanced fifteen feet behind Shep, where the three bodies lay. Shep was being herded into the scene of carnage, she realized. And when he got there . . .

It was amazing how steady her hands felt, how calm her nerves had become. Shooting was something she'd done all her life. Never in the line of duty, but Shep was her boss, her friend. They went way back, had a history together few could appreciate. Everything felt natural after all.

One last thought: commit to the shot, for hesitation was the number one killer of cops.

Rainie pivoted sharply away from the wall and simultaneously shoved Shep out of the doorway. Her gun went level, her legs braced for recoil, and her fingers found the trigger just as Shep screamed, *"No!"*

And Rainie found herself face-to-face with thirteen-year-old Danny O'Grady, pale as a sheet and bearing two handguns.

FOUR

OREGON STATE HOMICIDE DETECTIVE Abe
Sanders had just sat down to a late lunch, a
big Italian sub with double pepperoni and
double cheese. His wife would yell at him if
she saw him, lecture him about jeopardizing his health
and turning her into a cholesterol widow. Most of the
time he agreed with her, and at the ripe old age of
forty-two, he had the trim waistline to prove it. But not
today. Today was just one of those days.

Margaret Collins, an attractive blonde who manned
the department phones, came walking by his desk and
did a double take. "Wow, Abe. Next thing we know,
you'll be drinking beer."

"They were out of turkey," Abe muttered, and unconsciously held his Italian sub closer to him, as if he
feared someone would take it away.

"The Hathaway case turned sour, didn't it?" Margaret deduced sagely. She was a true-crime buff and
often had better instincts than any of the detectives.

"Damn judge," Abe said, and took a huge bite of
sandwich.

"Inside a drawer isn't plain sight."

He chewed busily, too polite to talk with his mouth

full. After a choking swallow, he declared, "The drawer was already open."

"By another homicide cop."

"Damn cop," Abe said, and took a bite of cheese.

Margaret laughed. She winked, making him momentarily forget his wife, then sauntered away, leaving him alone with his feast. Abe chewed down another bite, but his heart wasn't really in it. Brown deli mustard had dripped onto his desk. He shook his head and set down the sandwich in favor of a napkin.

Truth was, he always ordered indulgent food when cases went bad, and he rarely ate any of it. He'd fantasize about just what he'd like to order, salivate while in line, and get the largest size possible. Then he'd take it out, think about the calories, the fat content, the cholesterol level, and set it aside. Decadence just wasn't in him. He was a type-A control freak to the core, even when confronted with a loaded Italian sub or a plateful of double-chocolate brownies. He'd even been known to put the lid back on a pint of Ben & Jerry's chocolate-chip cookie-dough ice cream after only one bite.

When Abe Sanders was young, he'd been the Boy Scout with all the merit badges, the student with the good report card, and the track star with the fastest time. He'd read the classics "just for the hell of it." He'd gotten the girl every guy had wanted. And he'd bought a four-bedroom ranch in an older, "nice" section of Portland with an impeccably manicured lawn.

Then he'd finally shocked his family. He'd become a cop.

His parents joked that their neat-freak son had decided to clean up the whole world. His two brothers, one older, one younger, told him he suffered from an overdeveloped hero complex. His chess buddies gravely informed him that the entire accounting community had wept the day he headed for the academy, that spreadsheets would never be the same.

Abe himself never really talked about why he

became a cop. Maybe he simply understood better than most that life was messy, even for type-A control freaks. There was his wife, whom he loved and adored and who finally discovered, after five years of trying, that she could never have children. There was the tidy house they'd chosen as their home in the early eighties, only to have gang-bangers and crack addicts move in down the block. There was Abe himself, anal, precise, obsessive–compulsive, learning that his planned path as a CFO simply couldn't hold his attention.

He wanted a sense of accomplishment, a sense of change. Hell, maybe he did just want to make the whole world as orderly as his desktop files.

Didn't matter in the end. Detective Sanders was a damn good cop.

Other detectives rode him hard. They shook their heads at his manicured hands, told jokes about his polished loafers. Tried to drive him nuts by replacing his expensive, personally purchased black stapler with a cheap gray government issue that always jammed. One day they even rotated the tires on his car to see if he'd notice (he did).

Then they worked with him.

Abe Sanders with a case was a man obsessed. Abe Sanders with a case was passion and drive and, for reasons not even he could explain, anger. Pure rage at the injustices of life and the goddamn shit-faced pea-for-brains numbnuts who took away good, honest, hard-working lives.

Maybe other detectives didn't understand the value of a good stapler, but all cops knew rage. It was the common denominator no one ever spoke about and everyone understood.

Abe carefully rewrapped his sandwich, placing it in the middle of the triangle-shaped paper, folding in the corners, and rolling it tight. He dabbed at the mustard on his desk with a wet napkin. Then he threw everything away.

The Hathaway case had burned him. Not that it was

really the judge's fault. Snickers had written the search warrant too loosely, so the cops had had to improvise. That never worked anymore. Lawyers ran the world, and smart cops had to learn to anticipate the fine print. That was just the way of things.

Abe could count on one hand the number of warrants and arrests he'd had problems with. Being anal was good.

He got up to go wash his hands, and his lieutenant stuck his head out of his office.

"Sanders? Need a word."

Abe walked in curiously. He sat on the edge of the hard plastic chair in his lieutenant's office. And a moment later he heard about a small town called Bakersville, two hours southwest of Portland, that didn't even have its own homicide force. He sat, quiet and stunned, as his lieutenant described what they believed to be the second school shooting in Oregon in just a matter of years. Already reports of casualties. Crime Scene Unit was on its way, county officers on their way, and state officers rushing in. No word on the shooter yet and, oddly enough, no one could locate the sheriff.

"The call has come down from the governor," his lieutenant said. "This case is high profile and, by all accounts, already out of control. The brass wants a good front man, someone with experience, solid organizational skills, and the ability to coordinate city, state, and—most likely—federal resources."

"Absolutely."

His lieutenant looked at his neatly tailored gray suit and strong, trim figure. "Someone who looks good to the media."

Abe smiled wolfishly. He liked the press. He knew just how much to feed them and then he devoured them alive. It made him happy. "Absolutely!" he said with more enthusiasm.

"You'd have to be on the road. Probably two to three weeks straight at the beginning, then all the return trips."

"Not a problem." It wasn't. Sara hardly noticed his presence these days. He'd finally given in to her pleas and gotten her a ten-week-old puppy. Now she was busy coddling the pup and feeding the pup and chucking it under the chin. One day he was going to come home and find the dog decked out in baby clothes and a bonnet. The damn thing would probably grin and take it, too; so far, the sheltie seemed remarkably even-tempered.

Sometimes Abe found himself petting the creature. The little guy's downy coat was remarkably soft to the touch. Not that he wanted to get that close to anything that had no bladder control, for chrissakes.

"Then you're on the case," his lieutenant said. "Tackle it as if you'd gotten there yesterday. And Sanders . . ."

Abe halted at the door.

"The EMTs reported at least two children dead. It's gonna be a tough one, for everyone."

"Is the shooter a kid?"

"No word on the shooter yet."

"But most of them are kids."

"We're assuming that's the case. Play it tight. And quick. That would be best for everyone."

Abe understood. When kids were harmed, people went a little nuts. Sometimes, cops did too.

Sanders commandeered a car. He phoned ahead for a hotel room, as he always did, grabbed what little information the department had on the still-evolving scenario, and hit the road.

"One measly sheriff and two semitrained officers," he muttered as he headed home to pack his bags. "Kids killing kids, and not even a homicide department to manage the mess. Good thing I'm heading out there, 'cause these yokels have got to be shitting their pants."

RAINIE JERKED HER FINGER off the trigger just before she pulled it back.

"Danny," she gasped.

The boy stood, shell-shocked. His right arm was extended halfway, pointing the .22 somewhere around Rainie's kneecaps in a sure grip. He held a .38 in his left hand, down by his side, and for a moment Rainie wasn't certain where to look.

She kept her weapon trained on him, then Shep took a step toward her.

"Stop!" she yelled to no one, to all of them. Shep was still armed, and though she trusted him as a friend, she couldn't count on his actions as a father. If he thought Danny was threatened or if Danny felt threatened . . .

Rainie could feel the situation spiraling dangerously out of control. She reined in her panic.

"You," she said to Shep, keeping her gaze on Danny. "Are you okay?"

"It's a mistake," Shep said desperately. "All of this is one big mistake."

"Fine, but until this mistake is over, keep your hands where I can see them."

"Rainie—"

"Danny, I want you to listen to me. You must put down your guns. Okay? I want you to move very slowly and place your weapons on the floor."

Danny didn't move. His gaze swung wildly from side to side, and Rainie could nearly smell the panic roiling off his skin. He was dressed in black jeans, a black T-shirt, and white running shoes. She couldn't see any more weapons on him, but it was hard to be sure. He came from a house loaded with firearms, and she knew Shep had taken him hunting from the time he could walk.

"Danny," she said in a more commanding voice. "I'm going to count to three, and then you are going to place your weapons on the floor."

"Rainie—"

"Shut up, Shep. Danny, are you with me?"

"He didn't do anything!"

"*Shut up,* goddammit, or I'm going to make you flatten out on the floor too!"

Shep shut up, but it was already too late. Danny's expression had grown wilder, and his right hand was beginning to tremble. Rainie shifted her stance for better balance. She slid her finger back on the trigger, just in case.

"Danny," she said more loudly. "Danny, are you listening to me?"

The boy turned his head slightly toward her.

"This is pretty intense, isn't it, Danny?"

He nodded shortly, both his hands shaking now.

"I think you'd like this to end, Danny. I know I'd like it to end. So I'm going to tell you what we're going to do. I'm going to count to three. You are going to slowly lower your weapons to the floor. Then, when I tell you to, you're going to kick the guns over to my feet. Then you simply lie down with your hands and feet spread. That's it. Everything will be over, Danny. Everything will be all right."

Danny didn't say anything. His gaze flickered past her, to where the two girls were sprawled with their hands still outstretched toward each other. He seemed to notice the teacher as well, and a deep tremor snaked through his thin frame.

Christ, he was going to go. Shoot himself or suicide by cop. Rainie didn't know which, but the end would all be the same. Dead bodies. Dead kids. Jesus, no.

"Danny," Rainie said desperately.

It was too late. His right arm lifted.

"No!" Shep sounded wild.

"Don't do it, Danny!" She had no choice, her finger pulling back on the trigger.

And Danny turned his gun toward his head.

"*Goddamn!*" Shep hurtled toward his son. Rainie jerked her gun up and blasted her shot into the ceiling, just as Shep sent himself and his boy tumbling to the ground. Danny's handguns disappeared from view, trapped between two bodies. Then one came sliding out from between them. Rainie kicked it away and looked in time to see Shep grab the .22 in Danny's right hand. He squeezed hard. His son cried out. Shep jerked the weapon free and flung it down the hall.

That quickly, it was over. Danny collapsed on the floor, the fight gone out of him, as his father sat up. The burly sheriff was breathing hard and tears streamed down his cheeks.

"Goddamn," Shep gasped. "Goddamn, goddamn. Ah, Danny . . ."

Belatedly, he tried to pull his son into his embrace. Danny pushed him away.

Shep's head fell forward. His big shoulders continued to shake.

Quietly, Rainie took control. She rolled Danny onto his stomach eight feet from where three people would never move again. She spread his arms and legs and patted him down. Finding no additional weapons, she curved his arms behind his back and handcuffed his wrists.

"Daniel O'Grady," she said as she hauled him to his feet, "you are under arrest. You have the right to remain silent. Anything you say can and will be used against you in a court of law—"

"Don't say a word," Shep ordered roughly. "You hear me, son? Don't say a thing!"

"Shut up, Shep. You can't invoke silence for your child, and you know it. Do you understand these rights as I've said them to you, Danny? Do you understand that you're under arrest for what you did here at school?"

"Don't say a word, Danny! Don't say a word!"

"Shep," Rainie warned again, but it didn't matter.

Danny O'Grady didn't even look at his father. He stood with his shoulders hunched, his oversize black Nike T-shirt too big on him, his features haggard. He said finally, "Yes, ma'am."

"Did you do this, Danny?" Her voice softened. Rainie heard her own confusion, her need for reassurance. She'd known this boy most of his life. Good kid. Used to wear her deputy's badge. *Good kid.* She said more firmly, "Did you shoot these people, Daniel? Did you hurt these little girls?"

And he answered, in a faraway voice, "Yes, ma'am. I think I did."

FIVE

RAINIE AND SHEP remained silent, each trying to process what they had just heard. Shep didn't argue with Danny's statement, didn't try to say it was a misunderstanding, didn't try to remind her that Danny was just a kid. He appeared too overwhelmed.

Rainie herself couldn't think of anything more to say. She was a cop; she had heard a rough confession. Her duty was clear.

Rainie led her handcuffed murder suspect to the front doors of the school, where a dozen flashbulbs promptly went off in her face. The media had arrived. Shit.

She backpedaled furiously, yanking Danny away from the glare of hot lights and frenzy of shouted questions. He looked at her in dazed confusion, meekly submitting to her will. She wished he wouldn't look at her like that.

"You can't be seen walking out with us," she told Shep after a minute, the three of them pressed against the hall walls like fugitives.

"I'm not leaving you alone with him."

"You don't have any say in the matter. I can interrogate him without you, and I can sure as hell stick him in jail without you, and you know it."

Shep absorbed this with a scowl. Oregon law didn't give much special consideration to juvenile murder suspects. As long as Danny was at least twelve years of age, he could be held criminally liable for his actions and would be eligible for waiver to adult jurisdiction. His rights were the same as those of any person under arrest, and his parents had no say in things. The best Shep and Sandy could do was hire a good lawyer for their son. And be happy that he wasn't fifteen years old, in which case he'd fall under Measure 11 and automatically be tried as an adult. And be happier still that Oregon didn't have so-called CAP laws, which would hold Shep or Sandy criminally responsible for allowing guns to fall into Danny's hands.

"What do you want to do?" Shep asked.

"Take off your shirt."

Shep glanced at his son, followed her train of thought, and unbuttoned his sheriff's uniform. Underneath it was a plain white T-shirt, worn in places and bleached white by Sandy every Sunday when she did the laundry. The sight of him in just his undershirt made him look all too human and tore at Rainie's emotions a little more. She resented that.

Shep carefully draped his shirt over his son's head, as if his boy were made of glass and Shep couldn't bear to break him.

"It will be all right," he whispered. He looked at Rainie again, humbled and waiting for her next command.

"Go find Luke," she said, her voice coming out unsteady. She jerked her head toward the east exit. "Have him bring the patrol car around to the side."

"I want to ride with Danny."

"No. Luke's going to find a state guy, someone we don't know, and he's going to interview you. Don't look at me like that, Shep. You know it has to be done. You and Danny have been alone together. He's your son. . . . We have to know what he said to you. What he did. Why you entered a crime scene alone, and"—

she smiled thinly—"why you appointed your second-in-command the primary officer the minute you got the call."

She met Shep's gaze and, for the first time, saw him flush. "You didn't think I'd picked up on that, did you? Or were you hoping I'd let it go?"

He didn't say anything.

"Did you know, Shep? Did you hear the news and already know?"

"It wasn't like that."

"I don't even believe you and I'm your friend. Dammit." Rainie was suddenly fed up. She *was* the primary. She had hours of work ahead of her, processing a thirteen-year-old boy, testing his hands for gunpowder residue, demanding to know why he'd shot up his school. Then she'd return to the crime scene, wade through it again and again in order to get into a mass murderer's head. Finally, worst of all—tomorrow morning, most likely, or evening at best—she would personally attend the autopsies of two little girls who'd died holding hands. She would have to listen to the inventory of the trauma to their bodies. She would have to imagine once again what their last moments had been like. Then she would have to contemplate that another child, one she'd known personally, one she'd been proud of, had done that to them.

"Get out of here," she told Shep. "Find Luke and get this show on the road."

"I need to find Sandy first," Shep said stubbornly. "We have a friend . . . a lawyer. She can give him a call."

"Get out of here!"

Shep finally relented. He gave his son one last glance. It looked like he wanted to say something more but couldn't find the words.

The sheriff turned and walked out the front doors. Flashbulbs flashed. A roar rose up from the crowd at the sign of fresh activity. Then Rainie caught a new sound—the faint beating of helicopters bearing down upon them. The medevac choppers had finally arrived to carry the wounded away.

And Rainie couldn't help thinking that it would be much later before the ME's office came for the bodies.

OFFICER LUKE HAYES was thirty-six years old, balding, and shorter than most women. His trim build, however, was a compact one hundred fifty pounds that turned many ladies' heads and became useful in a fight. In Rainie's opinion, however, Luke's biggest asset was his steely blue eyes. She'd seen him stare down drunks twice his size. She'd seen him hypnotize enraged housewives into lowering their favorite knives. Once she'd even watched him reduce a growling Doberman to a groveling mass with a single, relentless look.

Shep was smoke and steam. Rainie got restless and moody. Luke balanced out their tiny department with his steady presence and slow, curving smile.

Rainie had never seen him ragged. Until today.

Leading Danny to the east-side exit—the one opposite the area of incidence—Rainie caught up with Luke just outside the door. His head was covered in sweat and he'd soaked his uniform through. For the last fifty minutes, he'd been trying to keep panicked mothers from rushing the school building, while collecting names and witness statements, and the strain showed on his face.

"Are you okay?" he asked Rainie immediately.

"Good enough."

His gaze flickered to Danny, and his strong shoulders slumped. Rainie understood his thoughts. Luke and Rainie playing with five-year-old Danny in the one-room sheriff's department while Shep took care of something or other. Let's play cops and robbers. *Rat-a-tat-tat.* Or maybe cowboys and Indians. *Bang-bang-bang.*

"*You know why big cities have so many problems,*

Rainie? 'Cause they can't do anything like this. Can't bring their kids to the office. Don't have others helping them out. No wonder our jobs are so slow in Bakersville. We're too busy taking care of our own to have time for trouble."

"We need to get going," Rainie said softly.

Luke sighed, nodded slowly, and squared his shoulders. He was ready.

Luke took up the post on the right side of Danny's hunched form. He looped his hand through the boy's bound arm. Rainie did the same on the left. On the count of three, herding Danny between them, they ran the gauntlet to the waiting patrol car.

Compared to the relative quiet inside the school, the sounds and sensations of the outside yard hit Rainie as a one–two punch. Reporters yelling questions as they spotted two cops hustling a cloaked person out of the school. EMTs shouting orders as they frantically loaded up the next injured student. Children crying, crying, crying in their parents' arms. A mother, alone on her knees on the ground, weeping hopelessly.

Rainie and Luke kept their attention focused ahead as other officers rushed to assist them.

"Move, move, move," someone was yelling. Rainie thought that was stupid. They were all moving as fast as they could.

"Clear out, clear out. Come on, people, back off!"

The reporters were closing in, photographers fighting maniacally for the front-page shot.

Rainie heard a new scream and made the mistake of turning her head. Shep had found his wife. She was holding Becky tight against her chest and turning toward the running police line.

"No," Sandy cried, took a step, and was caught from behind by her husband. "No, no, *nooooo!*"

A muffled sound emerged from beneath the shirt. Danny had heard his mother and started to cry.

Finally, they arrived at the patrol car. Rainie hastily

stuffed Danny in the back, the shirt still wrapped around his head. The reporters were shamelessly trying to jostle in, but the officers forced them back.

Rainie rounded the driver's side. Luke jumped into the passenger's seat. With two slams of the car doors, they shut out the chaos and were alone with their murder suspect. Shep's shirt had slipped down. Danny didn't seem to care, and it was too late to fix it now.

Luke turned on the sirens. Rainie pulled away from the curb.

A moment later they hit a wall of people clogging the street. Rainie prompted them with the horn and they reluctantly parted, all craning their necks to peer at the suspect in the back of the car. A few people looked stunned and saddened.

Others already appeared murderous.

"Damn," Luke murmured.

Rainie stared in the rearview mirror at her young charge. Danny O'Grady, suspected murderer of three, had just fallen asleep.

SIX

RAINIE WORKED ANOTHER six hours.

Together, she and Luke formally processed Daniel O'Grady for aggravated murder. They took his fingerprints and photograph. They tested his hands for gunpowder residue (GSR) and had him exchange his clothes for an orange corrections-department jumpsuit that was twice his size. Later his clothing would be tested at the state crime lab for gunpowder, hair, fiber, and bodily fluids—anything that would further tie him to the crime.

With the Cabot County DA present, they conducted a ten-minute interview before a lawyer, Avery Johnson, showed up and coldly put a halt to further questions.

He berated them for interrogating a child, informed Rainie that his client was obviously not in a stable frame of mind, and demanded that Danny be immediately moved to the county's juvenile facilities, where he could be examined by a medical doctor and treated for shock.

During this whole exchange, Danny sat listlessly and appeared to be a million miles away from the sheriff's office where he had once played after school.

Luke and Cabot County DA Charles Rodriguez

made arrangements to drive Danny the forty-five minutes to the juvie facilities. Rainie had to return to the school grounds, where the CSU had finally arrived and some state homicide detective named Abe Sanders was ordering everyone about as if he owned the place.

She exchanged one last batch of nasty stares with Avery Johnson. He told her she would be hearing more from him. She told him she could hardly wait. He told her this was a travesty of justice. She just stared at him harder, because she knew what her next line was supposed to be and her heart wasn't in it.

She sent the lawyer on his way and, with Danny in Luke's custody, headed back to the scene of the crime.

For the next five hours, Rainie walked the scene with the technicians from the state CSU. She reviewed with them what she knew of the EMTs' intrusion on the scene, as well as her own activities, which had left gunpowder residue and ceiling plaster in the key incidence area. The technicians were not amused. They took her Glock .40 to compare GSR found on it with GSR found at the scene. Then Rainie helped collect more than fifty-five spent cartridges from a shooting that had left three dead, six injured, and an entire town devastated.

Police officers recovered four empty magazines for the .22 and three speed loaders for the .38 revolver. None of the cops liked finding the rapid loaders—they were a tool designed to make a police officer's life easier, and it reminded them that this crime hit close to home.

At eight P.M., Rainie held an impromptu briefing out in the playground. She introduced herself as the primary officer and related her experience capturing Danny O'Grady in the afternoon. She thanked the various state and county officers who'd responded to the call and stayed for hours after their shifts had ended to assist with the case.

Then Detective Sanders, the state liaison, took over, discussing the theory of the crime, which they were developing as they processed the scene.

It appeared to be a blitzkrieg style of attack, he said,

occurring shortly after one P.M., when the students had returned to class. According to the third-grade teacher, the two girls, Alice and Sally, had asked for a bathroom pass. Shortly after they stepped into the hall, everyone heard the first sounds of gunfire.

It was unclear whether they had been the first victims or if that had been the computer-science teacher, Melissa Avalon. She had been alone in the computer lab, so no one knew if she stepped out after hearing the shots or if she was shot first, then the girls. It was doubtful the medical examiner could shed any light on things, as time of death wasn't an exact science. What they were working on now was figuring out the exact path the shooter had walked and the trajectory of the shots so they could extrapolate a logical sequence of events.

No material witnesses? Rainie asked.

None, the other officers agreed. Most students registered the sound of gunshots, then started running toward the exits with no clear idea where the shots were being fired. Six students reported seeing a man in black, but these were the younger children and none of them could be more specific. Where had this man come from? Where had he gone? How tall? How short? Fat, thin? Asked to be more exact, the kids quickly grew confused.

Two officers had followed up at the houses immediately around the school grounds. Those neighbors hadn't spotted any strange man cutting across their yards.

"Ergo," Sanders concluded, "this man-in-black thing is a dead end. Probably just the boogeyman, conjured up in traumatized minds. It happens."

"Wait a minute," Rainie said. Sanders shot her an annoyed glance. She could already tell he was assuming control of the case. He was the state guy with a pretty suit and a bigger police shield than hers. He obviously had no use for small-town cops or small-town theories. The big-city guys never did.

"There's still the issue that six children reported seeing a strange man," she said firmly. "That must mean something."

"That hysteria is contagious," Sanders said.

"Or that they saw something out of place, *someone* out of place. Look at the shootings. You're saying it's a blitzkrieg attack. Most victims are sprayed with bullets and we got holes all over the school to match. But then there's Melissa Avalon. Single shot to the forehead. That's a very precise wound for a random attack."

"Maybe he had it in for her. Do we know about Danny's relationship with the teacher?"

Officers flipped through their notebooks. No one had followed up on the victim's background yet.

"Look," Sanders said graciously, obviously deciding that Rainie wasn't a complete idiot, "the Avalon angle does appear interesting. I'll make note of it. And tomorrow, when we start getting the case team assembled, I'll assign a couple of guys to check it out. Hell, there's still plenty of footwork to do. This is just the stuff off the top of my head."

"Then off the top of my head, I don't think we should be dismissing anything yet."

Abe rolled his eyes. "Yes, ma'am." Then he muttered, "Of course, you were the one who arrested the kid."

Rainie stiffened. She'd had a long day; she didn't need this kind of bullshit. The anger that welled up in her chest was dangerous. It was also out of proportion, not just because Abe Sanders was obviously some kind of putz, but because she'd arrested a kid she knew and, dammit, she *liked*.

You stupid, selfish little boy, how could you be so cruel?

Abe Sanders was still looking at her, waiting to see if she'd take the bait. If she ranted and raved, she'd look unprofessional and he could feel better about things. Rainie had no intention of giving him that kind of satisfaction.

She said, "We need to have a conversation tomorrow."

"Yep."

"First thing in the morning."

"Absolutely."

"Seven-thirty?"

"Seven."

"Fine. See you then."

They returned to the CSU technicians still working the school. The building was now ablaze with lights, covered in a swath of yellow crime-scene tape and littered with plastic strips from Polaroid film. In the hallway, sections had been cordoned off to form a grid. The most "active" areas were handled by men in white space suits with special vacuums to suck up every last particle of dust. In other places, technicians scraped blood off windows into tiny vials or sprayed down walls with Luminol in hopes of bringing more carnage to light. Officers stood by, carefully recording all findings into a crime-scene log that would probably fill three binders by morning.

Rainie walked into a classroom and, with a magnifying glass, resumed combing the walls.

She didn't leave for another two hours, and then the feel of the pine-scented air against her cheeks was shocking, and the stars appeared almost too white in the clear night sky.

She needed to do at least two reams of paperwork. The DA wanted to file charges by noon tomorrow and would need the first wave of police reports. Rodriguez would be taking an aggressive stance. Five counts of aggravated murder for three deaths. A crime so heinous, Daniel O'Grady should be immediately waived to adult court to stand trial. The thirteen-year-old was a menace to society. He had killed little kids. He had betrayed his community. He had reminded his neighbors that evil could be the person next door. Let's lock him up for the rest of his life.

Never to date, attend a prom, fall in love, get

married, have children. To be alive until he was eighty or ninety years old, but never to live.

Rainie didn't go to the office. She drove home, where she could sit on her back deck beneath the clear night sky and listen to the owls hoot. She went home, where she could strip off a uniform that smelled of death and grab a cold beer.

She went home, where, finally free from prying eyes, she rested her forehead against the neck of the cold beer bottle, thought of those two poor little girls, of the schoolteacher, of Danny, of herself fourteen years ago.

Police Officer Lorraine Conner went home and, alone at last, she wept.

NOT THAT FAR AWAY, a man watched.

He was dressed completely in black and held a pair of high-powered binoculars to his eyes. The binoculars were a recent purchase, made when the need to see her face, her expression, her clear gray eyes, had become too much to bear. Now the view made him giddy. He could see everything on her back deck, every nuance of her slender body, backlit by the moon and topped off by the porch lights. She was *crying*. Crying.

In all the times he watched, he'd never seen such emotion from her.

It excited him.

It was hard to imagine, but all those years ago when Bakersville had first captured his attention, it had had nothing to do with Officer Lorraine Conner. He'd been reading an article on the Internet, "Small Dairy Community Destroyed by Floods, Promises to Rebuild." The journalist began with a melodramatic litany of rising river waters, torrential downpours, and thundering mud slides that descended upon a tiny coastal town during one week in February. How neighbor banded with neighbor to drive their cows to higher ground. How the water kept rising, deluging the lower farms, lifting entire houses off their foundations, and still rose, heading up the rolling hills.

Doe-eyed cows, trapped for days in frigid chest-high water, bawling in fear. Entire trailer trucks, bravely trying to reach more cattle, swept off inundated roads. Pinch-faced wives and children, finally retrieved by boats from their huddled last stands on metal barn roofs. Stoic dairymen, shooting their own herds to put the fragile beasts out of their misery.

As the journalist assured all the readers, here was a town that had met the wrath of God.

And then rebuilt. Bake sales, bingo drives. Innovative programs such as Adopt-a-Cow, which encouraged city kids and large corporations to support individual cows with money for food and shelter. Half a dozen operations, built on higher ground and spared the flood, opening their barns, hay-lofts, and milking parlors to their neighbors for as long as they needed. The town was making a comeback.

At the end of the article, the mayor was quoted as saying, "Of course we're helping each other. This is Bakersville. We're strong here. We care about our town. And we know what's right."

The man had known then that Bakersville would be next. A perfect little place, with perfect little people extolling their perfect little values. Where everyone loved everyone, and everyone was a friend. He wanted them all dead.

He was a patient man. He understood better than most the importance of planning. Good reconnaissance, his father had always barked. A smart soldier does his homework.

His father was a shit-for-brains asshole. But the man did his homework. He identified his target. He researched. He learned. Politicians, school officials, reporters, major organizations. Sheriff's department. He planned. He had all the time in the world, as far as he was concerned. What was more important was doing things right.

He would show this town the wrath of God. He would show them the wrath of him.

Then Officer Lorraine Conner. The first time he saw her in person, casually walking by during one of his many recon visits, he'd nearly stopped in his tracks. High cheekbones, an uncompromising chin. Bold gray eyes that possessed a hard, direct stare. Not pretty, but striking. Arresting, if you were into puns.

Here was a woman who knew how to get things done. Not a trace of stupidity, which he'd come to expect in small-town cops. Not even a wide girth or beer gut to show how she really spent her Friday nights. She was fit, fighting trim, and supposedly hell on wheels with a rifle.

Then he heard the rumors.

Her mother. Fourteen years ago. The brutal slaying that had never been solved. The woman drank, you know. Used her daughter as a human punching bag. Shameless, the old biddies hissed, their eyes bright as they imagined their own hands connecting with firm, young flesh. Everyone knew Molly Conner would come to no good.

They say the shotgun blast ripped off her whole damn head. Not a trace of flesh left above the neck. Just some headless torso in cheap, four-inch heels, clutching her bottle of Jim Beam. Told you she'd take the booze with her to the grave. Chortle, chortle, chortle.

Young Rainie came home from school and found the mess. Least that's what she told the cops. Came inside to find the body, walked back outside to see a squad car pulling up to the drive. That young deputy—you know, Shep, before he became the sheriff—he was the first at the scene. Reported Rainie had brains dripping down her hair, all over her back. Handcuffed her right away and took her in.

Later they dismissed the charges. Experts claimed the fact the brains were dripping down proved they'd fallen from the ceiling, that she walked in when the scene was still fresh, not that she'd pulled the trigger, which would have caused the gore to blow back onto her body in horizontal streaks. Or some such nonsense.

Let me tell you, no one can get convicted in this damn state. I mean, the girl's covered in fresh guts and somehow that ain't enough? Lawyers. That's the problem. Lawyers.

'Course, Rainie turned out all right in the end. Sure as hell a damn sight better woman than her mom. She's not even that bad a cop.

The man agreed with them there. A few taps on the keyboard and he'd learned quite a bit about Rainie Conner. Had received a bachelor's in psychology from Portland State University. Upon returning to Bakersville, she'd become the first female officer in the sheriff's department. She'd passed her academy courses the first time around. She had a file of excellent reviews. She stayed fit by jogging three to four times a week, and she always read the current issue of the *FBI Law-Enforcement Bulletin* the minute it arrived. She was dedicated, thorough, and, according to various drunken rednecks, she moved fast for a girl.

The man had also learned things about Rainie's intensely private personal life. She did date men (which was subject to some debate within town) but always from an outside community. She didn't go out often, nor did she keep any one man around for long. She never let her dates pick her up or bring her home. Instead, she would meet them at the chosen restaurant, possibly return to their house, and rise and depart long before they even woke up in the morning.

She seemed to have some basic need for sex but never for sharing. That fascinated the man.

She also had another quirk. Every day when she came home from work, she opened a bottle of Bud Light. And every evening before she went to bed, she emptied the full bottle of beer off the back of her deck. An ode to her dead drunken mother, the man figured. Did she picture Molly Conner dead then? Remember the headless torso and gray matter on the ceiling?

It was one of the reasons he'd bought the binoculars. Because sometimes her lips moved as she poured out the booze, and he was beyond general interest now, beyond objective reconnaissance. He desperately, desperately needed to know what she said.

Up yours, Mom?

Fuck you?

The man was enamored with Rainie Conner. She had become his personal hero. And she had added something to his particular venture. She was the police officer destined to find him out, he'd decided. She alone could recognize his genius, his mastery. Finally, ten years later, here was an adversary worthy of his talents.

In the beginning, his plans for Bakersville had been modest. They had changed since then.

Now the man carefully retreated into the cover of low-growing shrubs. He put away his binoculars. He took one last, admiring look at his gun and allowed himself the luxury of remembering how good it had felt. . . .

Then he moved on. He still had many more things to do before the long drive back to his hotel.

SEVEN

Wednesday, May 16, 8:00 A.M.

INTERVIEW OF DANIEL JEFFERSON O'GRADY
May 15, 2000

This is Officer Lorraine Conner, conducting an interview of Daniel Jefferson O'Grady, who is suspected of murdering three people at the Bakersville kindergarten-through-eight school, on Tuesday, May 15, 2000. Assisting me is Officer Luke Hayes. Also present is District Attorney Charles Rodriguez. O'Grady has been advised of his rights and has refused counsel. The time is 4:47 P.M.

CONNER: Danny, can you tell us what happened today at your school?
Silence.
CONNER: Danny, are you listening? Do you understand my question?
Silence.
CONNER: What day is it today, Danny?
Pause.
O'GRADY: Tuesday.
CONNER: Very good. Is Tuesday a school day?
O'GRADY: Yes.
CONNER: Did you go to school today?

O'Grady: Yes.

Conner: When did you go to school, Danny?

O'Grady: This morning.

Conner: With your sister? With Becky?

O'Grady: Yeah. My mom drops us off. Becky doesn't like the bus. It ran over a cat.

Conner: That's sad. Becky likes animals, doesn't she?

O'Grady: Yes. She's freaky.

Conner: Are these the clothes you wore to school today? The black jeans, black T-shirt?

O'Grady: Yes.

Conner: Do you wear a lot of black clothes?

O'Grady: I don't know.

Conner: Is there a special reason you wore all black today?

Silence.

Conner: Did you go to class this morning, Danny?

O'Grady: Yes.

Conner: You're in seventh grade, aren't you? Who's your teacher?

O'Grady: Mr. Watson.

Conner: Is he a good teacher? Do you like him?

O'Grady: He's all right, I guess.

Conner: What did you study this morning?

O'Grady: We have English in the morning, then math. Then we were going to have a geography game this afternoon. Map games, the capital cities . . .

Conner: The game didn't happen this afternoon, did it, Danny?

Silence.

Conner: Do you bring a backpack to school?

O'Grady: I have a backpack.

Conner: What did you have in the backpack today?

Silence.

Conner: Danny, did you have two guns in your backpack? Did you bring guns to school?

Pause.

O'Grady: I guess so.

Conner: Where did you get these guns? Are they yours?

O'GRADY: No. *(pause)* My father's.

CONNER: Did you take them out of a drawer?

O'GRADY: The gun safe.

CONNER: The safe? It wasn't locked?

O'GRADY: The safe was locked. My father always locks the safe.

CONNER: Then how did you get the guns out?

O'GRADY: I'm smart, all right? I'm very smart.

Pause.

CONNER: All right, Danny. You're smart enough to open the safe, get two guns, and bring them to school. Then what were you smart enough to do, Danny?

Silence.

CONNER: Did you fire your guns at school? Did you start shooting in the hallway?

Silence.

CONNER: Danny, I'm trying to help you. But to do that, I need to know what happened this afternoon. Those little girls and that teacher are dead, Danny. Do you understand dead?

Pause.

O'GRADY: My grandma died. We went to the funeral. That's dead.

CONNER: And did your parents cry? Did it make them very sad? As sad as they were today? You saw your father cry, Danny. Do you understand why he was crying?

O'GRADY: Yeah. *(barely audible)* Yeah.

CONNER: What happened this afternoon, Danny? What did you do? Were you just so mad, was that it?

Silence.

O'GRADY: I'm smart.

CONNER: Danny, did you kill those girls? Did you open fire on your classmates?

O'GRADY: I'm smart. I'm smart, I'm smart, I'm smart!

CONNER: *Did you kill those girls, Danny?*

O'GRADY: Yes! Yes, okay? I'm *smart*!

CONNER: *Why,* Danny? Why did you do such a thing?

Sound of door bursting open.

JOHNSON: My name is Avery Johnson, and I'm here to represent Daniel O'Grady. This interview is over.

CONNER: Why, Danny, why?

JOHNSON: Don't answer—

CONNER: Tell me why! *Why did you kill those little girls, Danny?*

O'GRADY: I'm scared.

ON THE BOEING 747, Supervisory Special Agent Pierce Quincy finally took off the headphones and set aside the tape recorder. He'd listened to the interview of America's newest mass murderer three times since taking off in Seattle. Now he took a moment to jot down his thoughts in a notebook he had hastily purchased at Sea-Tac airport. On the outside of the red spiral book he had written: CASE STUDY #12, DANIEL JEFFERSON O'GRADY. BAKERSVILLE, OR.

The stewardess came up, took his empty cup to give him more room, and smiled charmingly. Quincy returned the smile automatically, then broke off eye contact before she would be tempted to start up a conversation. He was still preoccupied with schoolboys and the forces that drove them to kill.

Over the years, Quincy had received many charming smiles from flight attendants. At the age of forty-five, he had dark hair that was graying at the temples, but he was tall, lean muscled, and well dressed. He also carried himself well. He'd been there, done that, knew where he was going, believed in always being polite, and had absolutely no patience for fools. He made his living flying to four different U.S. cities in five days and hunting down the worst predators the human race had to offer. And he had a direct, probing gaze that people found either deeply compelling or completely intimidating.

Especially on business trips, when his briefcase was filled with crime-scene photos of some of the most brutal slayings on earth. After fifteen years in the business, Quincy was prone to shuffling the photos like playing cards, an act that made him both proud of his objectivity and saddened by his callousness.

It had been pure coincidence that Quincy was on the West Coast when Quantico called about the Bakersville shooting. In theory, Quincy was on personal leave from his job of researching killers and teaching homicide-investigation classes at the FBI Academy in Virginia. Last week, however, he'd received word of a strangled prostitute's body found along Interstate 5 in Seattle. Local police were concerned the case might have connections to another string of murders committed in the eighties by the notorious Green River Killer, who was never caught. Quincy had revisited that case last year as part of a project to close out cold-case files. Unfortunately he'd not found any fresh leads. Then the new murder.

The FBI's deputy director had personally given Quincy the news and told him to stay home.

"These are the times when you need to be with your family," the deputy director had said. "We understand that. This case is probably unrelated. I don't want you worrying about it."

Quincy had thanked the man for his concern. Then he had gone to Dulles airport, purchased a ticket to Seattle, and boarded the plane. His youngest daughter was returning to college the next day, his ex-wife had no intention of speaking to him even if he did stay, and as for his daughter Amanda . . . There was nothing Quincy could do anymore for Amanda. What was done was done, and frankly, Quincy needed his work.

Before transferring to a research role with the Behavioral Science Unit five years ago, Supervisory Special Agent Quincy had earned his stripes as one of the Bureau's finest profilers. Each year, he'd taken on roughly one hundred and twenty serial rapists, murderers, and child kidnappers. He'd pursued men with IQs well above genius level and ensnared them in traps of their own making. He'd analyzed crime scenes awash with blood and found the case-breaking clue. He'd saved lives and he'd made mistakes that sometimes cost lives.

He knew how to handle that kind of stress. In fact, his ex-wife, Bethie, routinely claimed he didn't know how to live without it. According to her, his world had become as dark as the murderers he analyzed, and without a brutal slaying to unravel, he simply didn't know what to do with himself.

Quincy didn't care for that image of himself, but neither did he refute it. His line of work did take its toll. He spent so much time enmeshed in cases of extreme violence, it was easy to lose perspective. All county fairs became places where child molesters lay in wait for new victims. All basements housed human remains. All charming, good-looking law students were secretly psychopaths.

Frankly, Quincy would never, ever take a ride in a Volkswagen Bug, the vehicle of choice for many serial killers. He just wouldn't do it.

Nor, he had found, could he watch his daughter die.

In Seattle, the prostitute's murder turned out to be a one-off crime, eventually traced to a trucker passing through the area. Quincy had gone so far as to peruse homicide's cold-case files, ostensibly to offer fresh perspective but really to delay going home, where he would no longer be Super Agent, capable of capturing even the most vile of villains, but instead Helpless Parent, resigned to waiting by a hospital bed like any other person for the inevitable to occur.

Then a young boy had walked into his Oregon school and opened fire. And Quincy, in a matter of speaking, had been saved.

Like most Americans, Quincy had only peripherally noticed a small but tragic shooting that occurred in November 1995 at Richland High School in Lynnville, Tennessee, leaving two dead and one wounded. The tiny town, population 353, seemed too remote to have any connection with Quincy's life, and the small murder spree seemed an isolated occurrence. But just three months later another shooting occurred: Frontier Junior High, Moses Lake, Washington. Three killed, one wounded, by a fourteen-year-old student. Almost exactly a year later a new shooting, in Bethel, Alaska. Two killed, two wounded, by a sixteen-year-old gunman who had lined up a gallery of friends to watch his rampage. Eight months later sixteen-year-old Luke Woodham murdered three people and wounded seven in Pearl, Mississippi. Two months after that three more students died at Heath High School, in West Paducah, Kentucky. The pattern was clear. Jonesboro, Arkansas; Springfield, Oregon; Littleton, Colorado; Fort Gibson, Oklahoma. Other schools, other tragedies seared into the national consciousness.

Headlines screamed of an epidemic of violence sweeping across America's youth. Video games, some cried. Too many guns, not enough parents. Or maybe it was Hollywood or Capitol Hill or Jerry Springer. But something had to be done to stem the tide. Ban guns, censor cartoons, install metal detectors, enforce dress codes, something.

In the FBI's Behavioral Science Unit, researchers such as Quincy were less certain. Were the shootings a genuine trend or a statistical anomaly? Were these "normal" children motivated by outside forces such as the media, or did this point to a deeper, developmental issue?

What really drove teenagers to kill, and how could shootings be prevented?

Even at Quantico, the leading criminal experts didn't have ready answers.

And that frightened them, for they had children too.

Six months ago Quincy had begun a major research effort to dissect the minds of juvenile mass murderers and identify ways to help them, as well as to prevent future shootings. The goal was to devise a system that would help identify potential mass murderers for school officials and law-enforcement agencies. Also, Quincy hoped to formulate action steps to help parents and teachers deal more effectively with potentially violent teens.

Identifying future shooters, however, was easier said than done.

Unlike serial killers, mass murderers were not a homogeneous bunch. People went postal because they'd had a bad day, because they were mentally unstable, because someone influenced them, because they were high/drunk/stoned, because they were in love/out of love/confused by love, because they sought glory, because they sought revenge, because they sought death. Mass murderers could be young, old, rich, poor, well educated, poorly educated, well adjusted, or loners. Their attacks could be random or well planned.

In addition, many mass murderers ended their rampages by taking their own lives, making it difficult to get more information. What had brought that person to the breaking point? What had the shooter been thinking during his rampage? Would he repeat his act given the chance, or was it a onetime homicide spree? Most of the time, no one ever knew.

The best experts could do currently was a "risk assessment" of individuals, a checklist of behaviors statistically found in mass murderers. Mass murderers:

1. had a history of violence, e.g., wife-beating, child abuse, brawls, etc.

2. inspired "subjective fear" in people. After shootings, there were always a few neighbors or coworkers who had a "bad feeling" about the person. They avoided the man at work, didn't let their children play with the boy, were sure never to be alone with the guy, etc.

3. exhibited antisocial behavior, either a loner-type personality or someone who deliberately violated societal rules.

4. had poor social skills.

5. liked to make threats, realistic or idle.

6. lacked a support system, e.g., came from a fractured family, had few friends, etc.

7. felt wronged—by life, the corporation, peers, spouse, etc.

8. were under severe situational stress, e.g., recent job loss, impending divorce, death in the family, etc.

Quincy felt that the checklist was not a bad tool. Human resources departments of many major corporations routinely used it to identify potentially dangerous employees. In the wake of school shootings, school counselors across the country had also requested the information for their offices.

Unfortunately, the checklist was proving too vague when applied to youthful offenders. What was "situational stress" for an eleven-year-old? Getting braces, having a pimple, breaking up? What was a "history of violence" for a grade-school boy? Throwing rocks, tearing wings off flies, engaging in rough sports?

Add to that the significant number of children who came from broken homes, and that every teenager worth his salt felt deeply and grievously wronged by life, and a statistically improbable number of youths emerged as future homicidal maniacs—hardly an encouraging thought.

Children were simply too hard for adults to understand or predict in the best of circumstances. Their coping skills were limited, they were a bundle of hormones, and they generally believed everything must happen now, today, immediately, with no thought of long-term consequences.

Finally, juveniles were highly motivated by peer pressure, a rare factor in adult homicide. Children were also proving more susceptible to media images and outside influences such as cults and hate groups.

In short, the more Quincy learned, the more he realized how much he had left to learn. This would be a long assignment. Years, he was beginning to think, of spending quality time with kids who killed kids.

He was both intrigued by the task and repelled by it—in other words, his general state of mind.

The fasten-seat-belt light came on. The plane was preparing for descent. Quincy gathered up Danny O'Grady's interview tape and notes. His brow furrowed.

He did not have much information on the case yet, but already there were a number of elements that bothered him. The shooting of the teacher seemed so exact, for one thing. He wanted to know more about her and Danny's relationship. Then there was the timing of the shooting. Why when all the students had gone back into class? That struck him as an attack strategy devised to *limit* the amount of damage, as if the shooter didn't want many people hurt.

Finally, there was the interview. Judging by the tone of the child's voice, Quincy would bet he'd been in a state of shock, not the best time for a thorough interrogation. Plus, while the investigating officer had done a nice job of trying to open the boy up by resorting to simpler questions, she had used too many leading questions. That was always dangerous with children, as they were prone to giving the answer they thought the adult desired, instead of the right answer. Danny's repeated reference to being smart bothered Quincy as well. Something else needed to be asked.

He wondered what the chances were of the boy's lawyer agreeing to an interview. Then he wondered what the chances were of the local police welcoming his assistance with the case.

Supervisory Special Agent Pierce Quincy smiled.

A local police officer welcome a fed with open arms? Hardly. He was already placing bets on which expletive Officer Lorraine Conner would use first.

EIGHT

YOU LITTLE SHIT. Go behind my back to the DA one more time, and I'll tie you up, take you out into a field, and personally introduce you to Bakersville's home-grown cow pies. Got it?"

"I simply needed some information—"

"You tried to yank my case!"

"Only when it became clear that you weren't qualified to handle it."

Rainie's eyes bugged open and she nearly foamed at the mouth. She was having a bitch of a morning, which had already included one very terse conversation with Abe Sanders at seven A.M. Apparently that had not gotten the job done, however, because here it was just after eleven and she was going to have to take her scissors and cut him down to size. How dare he ask the DA to remove her as primary officer on the case! How dare he try to claim state jurisdiction of her homicide!

Didn't he know better than to mess with a woman who'd gotten only four hours of sleep?

Rainie moved out from behind the hastily erected desk—actually a piece of plywood laid atop two sawhorses—that had just been placed in the brand-new "op center" for the Bakersville case team. Sure, the command post was really the attic of Town Hall, stifling and dusty and hot, but she'd managed to commandeer a coffeepot and a water cooler from the mayor's office. Already, that made these quarters luxurious compared to the twenty-by-twenty headquarters of the sheriff's department.

Rainie had been working her damnedest this morning. Up at four-thirty to burn the knots out of her muscles with a good, hard run, she then typed up the police reports from the night before, met with the mayor about getting more space for her case team, and prepared for her first meeting with Abe. She'd thought they'd made the ground rules perfectly clear at that time. The case would require state and local cooperation. Abe would serve as point man for the state's resources, handling the physical evidence, managing the CSU, and adding his own considerable experience to the investigative efforts. Rainie's department would provide the ground troops—herself, Luke, and three volunteer officers—to conduct interviews and pull records. They knew the people in their town the best and would get more cooperation from the school and parents than state officers would.

Abe was welcome to process the crime scene and commandeer the school computers in search of further evidence. Rainie knew she needed help. But she would not, could not, should not, give up jurisdiction of the case. End of story.

Or so she'd thought at seven this morning.

"You messed up," Sanders said now, obviously worried she hadn't gotten the message the first time. "You're inexperienced and it showed."

"I secured the scene and arrested a murderer. Shame on me."

"You trampled the scene," he corrected with a grimace. "My God, you let in the EMTs. Haven't you ever seen what they do to a place? Why not just invite the fire department and throw a party?"

"I ordered Walt docked. He chose to violate those

orders. Something Bradley Brown is still very grateful for."

"He might have lived anyway."

"Might have lived? Are you guys paid by the body or what?"

Sanders remained unswayed. "EMTs ruin scenes, simple fact of life. So do concerned parents running after their children and school bureaucrats trying to do head counts—"

"We got there as fast as we could. Geography is another simple fact of life, and geography places that school in the middle of a residential area and us fifteen minutes away. Can't stop what we aren't there to manage."

"Fine, what about once you were there? Discharging your weapon? In the middle of the scene?" He raised a brow.

"An armed murder suspect drew down on me!" Rainie snapped. "Value a crime scene. Don't plan on dying for it."

"Oh, now I get it. You were afraid for your life, so you shot up the ceiling. I stand corrected, Officer. That makes perfect sense."

"You insufferable—"

Rainie fisted her hands at her side. She counted to ten a second time and noticed that another man had just appeared in the doorway, also wearing a sharply pressed suit. God help her, the state men were multiplying.

She forced her fists open and managed in a more reasonable tone of voice, "As I wrote in my report, Detective—which you have no doubt read, edited, and found fault with the font size—at the last minute the suspect's father threw himself in front of me, forcing me to alter my fire."

"So you're trigger-happy? That's how you want to go on record?"

"Hey, have you ever pulled your weapon on the job?

Have you ever been in the line of fire? What the hell do you know about being trigger-happy?"

Sanders scowled. Apparently, Mr. Perfect never had been at the front lines. Look who was the inexperienced one now? Rainie's triumph, however, was short-lived.

"Well," the state detective said briskly, "that brings us to all the problems with the arrest."

"What?"

"First off, the confession. Have you talked to the DA yet about the confession?"

"Hell, I called Rodriguez in to listen to the confession. Everything was by the book."

"Apparently not everything. O'Grady's lawyer is already seeking to have the confession tossed—"

"You thought he'd ask to have it entered into evidence instead?"

Sanders ignored her sarcasm. "He claims the boy was in shock at the time and in no state of mind to waive his rights. He also points out that your questions were leading, which is inappropriate when interrogating a minor. He has a score of experts lined up to contend that you put words in Danny's mouth, getting him to say exactly what you wanted to hear."

"Like I wanted to hear that my boss's son killed three people," Rainie grumbled, then waved her hand in a dismissive motion. "Fine. It doesn't matter. We still have the positive GSR results and the two handguns. We can build one helluva case off that."

Sanders smiled thinly. For the first time, Rainie understood that they really were in trouble.

"Yes. The gunpowder residue found on Danny O'Grady's hands and clothing." Sanders adopted the demeanor of a thin-lipped defense attorney. "Is it true, Officer Conner, that you discharged your weapon at the scene?"

"Yes, as I explained—"

"Isn't it true that anytime a gun is fired, it emits gunpowder residue?"

"Sure, but I was hardly standing over Danny—"

"But it would get on your hands, wouldn't it, Officer? And then didn't you pat down the suspect, Danny O'Grady? Didn't you touch his clothes, his arms, his hands as you searched for weapons, as you twisted his arms behind his back for the bracelets? In fact, couldn't all that gunpowder found on his person really have come from *your* hands from discharging *your* weapon?"

Rainie was stunned. Christ, she hadn't thought of that. Everything had happened so fast. First trying hard not to kill Shep or his kid. Then needing to get Danny immediately restrained. What was she supposed to do? Tell a murder suspect to stay there like a good boy while she ran to the lavatory to wash her hands?

"The lab can do more tests," Rainie mumbled desperately. "There are different kinds of gunpowder. They could prove what's from my weapon, what's from his."

"Oh, they're trying to," Sanders assured her, resuming his normal punching tone. "We don't know yet if it's possible, however. Looks like Danny was using his father's ammo, and wouldn't you know it, Shep does his ordering for the department and for himself all from the same manufacturer. Tricky, huh?"

Rainie had a headache. She almost rubbed her temples, then realized she couldn't afford to give away that much. Plus, that man was still standing in the doorway, taking everything in with no apparent regard for their privacy. If he was a reporter, she would have to kill him.

"Do we at least have the murder weapons?" she asked Abe, since he was the one in charge of evidence.

"ATF took the weapons for ballistics testing. We don't have results yet."

"But what else could they be? If all else fails, we've got Danny's prints on the guns. That's something."

Abe said, "No prints on the guns."

"*What?* No way. I *saw* him holding those guns. I

made Shep leave the building before me. There is no way the weapons were wiped clean."

"Not wiped clean—smeared beyond lifting one clean print. Such as what might happen when an experienced police officer pretended to wrestle a handgun from his child's grip."

"No," Rainie said.

"Why not? Because Shep is your boss? Because you feel indebted to him?"

"Don't go there. That has no bearing on anything."

Sanders, however, had no learning curve. "Everything has bearing. In the hands of a good defense attorney, Conner, the Andy Gibb poster you kissed every night when you were twelve can have relevance. I asked around. You were arrested for murder fourteen years ago, at the tender age of seventeen. Arresting officer, one Shep O'Grady. And the man who worked to have the charges cleared, one Shep O'Grady."

"Because he realized he made a mistake."

"Who cares? Fact remains that you work together, you have dinner at his house, and fourteen years ago he helped you out of a bind, then six years after that gave you a job some people still question. You think that won't come up during trial? Shep's got loyalty to Danny; you've got loyalty to him. And you three are alone at the scene. Face it, chain of custody on this case is screwed."

"Nothing inappropriate happened in that building, Detective. You weren't there. You don't know how things went down."

Sanders was silent for a moment. Then he said quietly, dangerously, "No, I don't think *you* know how things went down. Shep made you the primary officer before ever arriving at the scene. Why? When you arrive at the school, Shep's car is there, but for forty-five minutes there's no sign of him. Where's the sheriff? What's he doing?"

"He already stated that Danny was holding him hostage in that classroom."

"Do you know that? Do any of us really know that? From where I'm sitting, you search this whole school without them ever peeking out their heads. Then, when you're due to enter that classroom anyway, they finally show themselves. Next thing you know, you're front-row center for a little display that magically makes you discharge your weapon—obliterating a key piece of evidence—while giving Shep O'Grady a chance to handle the other two key pieces of evidence. Damn convenient if you ask me."

Rainie was incredulous. "You think Shep staged an *armed* confrontation between a police officer and his son on the off chance it would eliminate some of the evidence against Danny?"

"He didn't stage it for *any* officer, Conner. He staged it for you. You've known Danny for eight years. Hell, according to everyone in this town, you and Luke helped raise Danny O'Grady, watching him every afternoon in the office. What were the chances you'd open fire?"

"Shep is a good cop. He wouldn't tamper with evidence."

"He's a father. Don't kid yourself."

"I was there, I saw it go down. I know what happened."

"Yeah, well, Shep's already going all over town claiming there's trouble with the evidence and that he's certain his kid will walk. Who do you think pointed out that you'd discharged your weapon before frisking Danny? Who do you think is claiming the scene is FUBAR? Shep's got his own agenda. You just don't want to see it, and that's why you need to hand over the case. To someone who is perfectly objective. To someone who has experience."

"To someone who loves looking good in front of a camera."

Sanders shook his head. He appeared disgusted. "Conner, I got a ninety percent conviction rate. Hate me if you want to, but show me a little respect. You're the one keeping the case out of ego. I just want to push it ahead to conviction, so everyone can get on with their lives."

"Then you're an idiot," Rainie told him flatly. "You really think locking away a thirteen-year-old kid will make us feel better? Give us a sense of closure? Personally, I'll be driving by that school for the rest of my life, wondering what really happened yesterday afternoon. And all the parents and teachers will be wondering the same thing. What drives a boy to kill? Why did two little girls have to die? Why *didn't* we prevent this from happening?

"More than an arrest, my town needs an explanation, and I'm going to get it for them. Now get out of my office, Detective, and the next time you talk to Rodriguez, pull that stick out of your ass. It's really not helping."

Rainie returned to her desk and sat down. A moment later she had the satisfaction of hearing Sanders storm away. It didn't improve her mood, however. She was already growing weary of their battles.

And disheartened. Sanders was right: she had fucked up yesterday. She'd done her job earnestly, and that meant nothing in the criminal justice system. She had captured a suspect but destroyed the evidence. Soon she'd only be fit for a job with the LAPD.

And her credibility would come into question. People still whispered. Of course, it was a small town. If people didn't whisper through the long, rainy winters, everyone would lose their minds.

Rainie Conner's tough. Gotta watch out for her. Killed her own mother.

Rainie sighed, then became aware that the man in the navy blue suit was still standing there, watching.

"Can I help you?" she asked sharply.

"Officer Lorraine Conner?"

"I don't know. Who's asking?"

The man smiled, a wry tilt of one corner of his mouth. The gesture crinkled the corners of his eyes and momentarily startled Rainie. Lean hunter's face. Penetrating blue eyes. She did a quick double take before she caught herself. Then she was embarrassed. Whoever the man was, she already wished he'd turn and walk away.

He said, "I'm Supervisory Special Agent Pierce Quincy of the FBI."

"Ah shit."

He smiled dryly again. And it got to her again, even now, when she definitely knew better. She wished for a bottle of beer.

The agent moved into the room and, without waiting for an invitation, took a seat. "I take it that gentleman is with the state?"

"Mr. Perfect is a state homicide detective. God help us all."

"A ninety percent conviction rate is impressive."

"So is his spelling ability. You still want to deck him after a five-minute chat."

"Problems with the case?"

"I screwed it up royally," she assured him.

"And now you're resting on your laurels?"

"Hardly. I'm planning my next line of attack."

The corner of the man's lip twitched. Rainie was happy to see that she had amused him, but she still wasn't in the mood for a chat. She sat forward and cut to the chase. "What do you want, G-man? I'm tired, I have a triple homicide to investigate, and I'm not giving up jurisdiction of my case. Just so you know."

"I'm here to help—"

"Bullshit."

"Okay, I'm one more bureaucrat placed on this earth to mess with your mind and question your abilities."

"Finally, some honesty in law enforcement."

"I also want to talk to Daniel O'Grady."

Rainie leaned back. That answer she believed. She just wasn't sure what it meant.

She tilted her chair onto its back legs, absently placing one foot on top of her desk, then crossing her other foot over it. Her legs still ached from running this morning. She stretched out her calves while she gave Supervisory Special Agent Pierce Quincy another appraising stare.

Experienced, she thought, well established in his career. Probably in his forties, graying slightly at the temples. Worked well with his short-cropped hair and distinguished suit. Added to his power. She was willing to bet money Supervisory Special Agent Pierce Quincy consciously did a lot of things to add to his image of power. He didn't need much help, though. It was all in his eyes—that piercing, steady stare. This man had seen some things on the job. He'd taken on a few things more. Nothing overwhelmed him anymore, and for a moment Rainie was envious.

"You a profiler?" she asked, though she already knew the answer.

"I do some profiling. I also teach classes and research various subjects for the Behavioral Science Unit."

"You study serial killers."

"Serial killers, rapists, and child molesters," he said with a straight face, then added, "It makes for very pleasant dreams."

"What do you want with Danny? He's a suspected mass murderer. That's different from a serial killer."

"Very good, Officer. Plus, he's a juvenile mass murderer, which is distinctly different as well. Unfortunately, we don't understand these distinctions, hence my new research assignment."

Rainie's brows shot up. "You're researching school shootings?"

"Correct."

"You're going from town to town, investigating kids murdering other kids?"

"Yes."

Rainie shook her head; she didn't know whether to be amazed or appalled. "Traffic accidents I can handle," she told him. "Drunken brawls, stabbings, even the occasional domestic incidents. But what went down in that school yesterday . . . How can you focus on something like that full-time? How can you keep from waking up screaming every night?"

"With all due respect, Officer, I have a bit more experience with violent crime than you."

Rainie grimaced. "Thank you. Words I haven't already heard twelve times this morning." She straightened up in the chair and let her feet hit the floor. "Well, sorry to break it to you, Agent, but I doubt you'll get to speak with Danny. His parents got him a crack defense attorney who's placed him off-limits to all interviews. Despite the fact that Danny has confessed twice and was found holding the murder weapons, he's pleading innocent."

"Do you think he's guilty?"

"I think I have a case to put together."

"That's a careful answer."

She smiled at him wolfishly. "I may be inexperienced, SupSpAg, but I learn quick."

"Soup Spag?"

"Supervisory Special Agent, in local law-enforcement terms. We're not big on titles, you know."

"I see." Quincy appeared a little dazed. Rainie had a feeling he wasn't sure what to make of her yet, or how to handle her. The thought pleased her. She liked keeping the feds guessing. In the end, it might be the only thing she had to show for her day.

So she supposed she should've known. She'd no sooner started feeling smug than the FBI hunter went on the attack.

He said calmly, "I don't think Daniel O'Grady shot up his school. And I don't think you're certain of it either, Officer Conner. I think we're both still wondering what really happened yesterday afternoon. And better yet, how we can prove it."

NINE

RAINIE DROVE QUINCY to the school.

Quincy sat in the passenger's seat, gazing out the window with what he was afraid must be an incredulous stare. He had not been to Oregon in many years and had forgotten its stunning beauty. They drove through rolling verdant pastures liberally sprinkled with black and white Holsteins and topped by red farmhouses with bunches of yellow pansies. He could smell freshly mown grass and the salty tang of ocean air. He could see towering mountains ringing the valley, their summits carpeted in dense Douglas fir.

King-size cab trucks whizzed by, their powerful V-8 engines gunning. People waved to Rainie as they passed, and about half a dozen black Labs lolled their tongues as they panted merrily out the window. Up ahead, everyone slowed for a John Deere tractor that was laboring down the road. No one honked at the aging farmer or yelled at him to pull over. They simply waited and waved politely when they finally had room to pass. In answer, the farmer touched the brim of his faded red baseball hat.

"That's Mike Berry," Rainie said, as they swung wide around the green tractor, breaking her silence for

the first time since they'd gotten into the patrol car.
"He and his brother own the two biggest dairy farms
around here. Last year they bought out three family
farms that were destroyed by the floods. One belonged
to Carl Simmons, who's sixty years old and has no
family left. Mike arranged for a living trust, so Carl
can stay in his home until the day he dies and never
worry about a thing. The Berry brothers are good
people."

"I didn't think there were many places like this left,"
Quincy said honestly.

Rainie turned to look at him. "There aren't."

She went back to driving. Quincy didn't bother her
again. He could tell that her mood had turned pensive,
and in truth he was growing troubled himself. For all
his talk of objectivity and professionalism, it was difficult to look at such beautiful countryside and contemplate the savagery that had gone on in the grade
school. So far, few things in Bakersville were as he'd
anticipated.

That included Officer Conner. All PC platitudes
aside, most female cops he'd known were broad-
shouldered, thick-waisted, and, frankly, butch. He
would not use those terms to describe Officer Conner.
Her five-foot-six figure appeared fit and pleasantly
curved. Her long chestnut hair, worn unapologetically
loose, framed a startling, attractive face with wide
cheekbones, firm jaw, and full lips.

Then there were her eyes. Not blue, not gray, but
somewhere in between. Quincy imagined that the color
shifted with her mood, becoming soft flannel when she
was contemplative, icy blue when enraged. And when
she was intrigued? Her head tilted slightly, her lips
parting in anticipation of a kiss?

Quincy skittered away from his thoughts and shifted
uncomfortably in his seat. It wasn't like him to think of
a police officer that way. Business was business. Especially these days.

He moved his analysis to her qualities as a cop. She

was inexperienced. Her handling of the crime scene and the suspect proved as much. But he didn't think she was dumb. In his thirty-second appraisal, she had struck him as stubborn, smart, and naturally analytic. He already understood she was fiercely loyal to her community and, at times, proud to a fault. He suspected she lived for her job, had few close friends and few outside interests. This, however, was cheating. He was drawing heavily on the profile of the surviving child of an alcoholic, which could go one of two ways—an underachieving drunk or an overachieving workaholic. Since Rainie obviously wasn't the former, he imagined she was the latter. She had yet to prove him wrong.

All in all, she was a different sort of police officer from what he'd expected. Probably different from what Detective Abe Sanders had been expecting as well, and thus they were butting heads. With all due respect to Bakersville's sheriff's department, most small-town police officers had good people skills but weren't the brightest bulbs on the Christmas tree. They made roughly twenty thousand a year. Their cases were routine. They had a tendency to settle into ruts as masters of their tiny domains, and what analytic abilities they did have atrophied as they patrolled Friday night football games.

Of course, Quincy was an arrogant federal agent, paid extra to look down at all other forms of law enforcement—especially those mental midgets in ATF.

Rainie turned off the rural route, and farmland gave way to a neighborhood. Minutes later a sprawling white school building came into view. Yellow crime-scene tape roped off the parking lot, and mounds and mounds of wrapped flowers threatened to bury the chain-link fence.

Rainie pulled the patrol car over.

"You haven't been here yet today, have you?" Quincy asked quietly.

She shook her head, still looking at piles of flowers,

balloons, and teddy bears. Two feet deep, stretching along a good ten feet of fence. Loose roses and pink ribbons and tiny, tiny crosses. Handmade signs saying *We love you, Miss Avalon*, and a large red carnation heart reading, *For my daughter*.

Rainie's eyes had grown overbright. She sniffled roughly, and Quincy knew she was fighting hard not to cry. He turned to the makeshift memorial.

"It's one of the amazing things," he said after a moment. "On the one hand, these incidents are so tragic, they make us fear the worst about humanity. What kind of society produces children who attack other children with assault rifles? On the other hand, these incidents *are* so tragic, they bring out our humanity. The small acts of courage that get the kids through the day, from the EMTs entering a war zone to the teachers risking their lives to tackle a shooter. From the brother who protects his sister with his own body, to the mother who administers first aid, setting aside her fear for her own child to help someone else's. And all around the globe it strikes a nerve—people feel a need to send flowers, poems, candles, anything to let your town know it's not alone. Bakersville is in their thoughts and their prayers."

Rainie wiped the corner of her eye, then blinked a few times. "Yesterday," she said thickly, "the call went out that the hospital needed more blood to handle the casualties. The Elks immediately opened up their lodge to the Red Cross. Next thing you know, there was a line of people extending four city blocks waiting to give. The grocery store sent out their bag boys with free lemonade for everyone. A couple of older ladies set up play stations for the kids. There were people in that line for two or three hours and they never complained. Everyone just said it was the least they could do. That was the story the *Bakersville Herald* carried today on the front page. The news of the shooting was in a smaller box in the lower right-hand corner. Not everyone agreed with that prioritization, but I thought they might have a point."

"The shooting is about an individual. The aftermath is about a town."

"Something like that." Rainie unfastened her seat belt. "If you don't mind, Agent, I spent most of yesterday in that building, and now I'd just like to get this over with. Not being an experienced profiler type, there are many things in that school it hurts me to see."

Quincy followed her into the school. He already had his notepad out and his mind working overtime.

Earlier, in her office, Officer Conner had agreed to walk Quincy through the crime scene for his notes, as well as to refresh her own. He would not say that they were working together, more that Rainie shared his concerns about Danny's innocence. Thus, she was allowing him to tag along as a quasi-observer, quasi-expert. Of course, she'd told him frankly, the minute he tried to claim the case as his own, she reserved the right to cut him off at the knees. At the time, she'd looked at his kneecaps quite seriously.

Quincy had the feeling that Officer Conner was not known for playing nice with others. Perversely enough, he liked that about her.

Now they walked down the yawning hallway toward the back of the school. Quincy noted the floors dusted with printing powder, the small sections of cutout tiles that must have been spotted with blood and been carted away to the lab.

According to Rainie, the CSU had finished up round one of processing the scene this morning. There would be future visits as the task force sought to finalize a thorough "walk-through" of the events on that day. Then there were the mounds of evidence it would take months to sort through. Quincy estimated that a school of this size would yield hundreds of footprints to sort and thousands of fingerprints to match. The crime-scene log would probably grow to six or seven volumes.

"This is where I found Walt and Emery assisting Bradley Brown," Rainie said, pointing to a bloody area at the intersection of two main hallways. She looked at him expectantly.

"Was Brown conscious?"

"Yes. I asked him if he'd seen anything, and he said no. He heard the shots, came running up this hall, turned right, and boom."

Quincy turned right, where the level of violence was clearly depicted by the outline of three bodies on the floor. "Everything happened down there?"

"That's what we think."

"In the hallway, not a classroom."

"That's correct."

"How did Danny end up in the hallway?"

"According to his teacher, he never returned to class after lunch. Mr. Watson said he'd wondered what was going on, but Danny was hardly ever late, so he figured there must be a good reason he hadn't returned yet."

"What time was that?"

"The school runs three lunch periods. Danny's is the last, ending at one-twenty. Students have five minutes to get to class, signaled by a bell at one-twenty-five. Danny wasn't in his classroom at one-twenty-five. At one-thirty-five, dispatch received a call about shots fired."

"So Danny skips his class. And the girls are in the hallway because?"

"Alice needed to use the rest room. Sally was her buddy—in the third grade, you travel in pairs. Their teacher gave them a hall pass."

"What about the other fatality, Melissa Avalon. She's alone in the computer lab?"

"Yes, it's her lunch break. She keeps the lab open for students to use during cafeteria hours, then closes up shop at the one-twenty bell."

"And that's scheduled, correct? At one-twenty, she's always alone in the lab?"

Rainie nodded, easily following his train of thought. "It's looking more and more like she was the target, isn't it? Sally and Alice just happened to be at the wrong place at the wrong time."

"That's my assumption at the moment, but let's not jump ahead." Quincy moved to the janitor's closet, arching one brow at the mess. "I take it Officer Cunningham is one big boy," he murmured.

Rainie grimaced. "He was doing his best at the time. Things were intense."

"Becky O'Grady was hiding in the back of the closet?"

"Yes, all the way in the back. Curled up in a ball. She appeared to be suffering from shock, and I couldn't get her to answer many questions. I understand that Sandy took her to the emergency room, but the doctor said she just needed time."

"Do you think she saw what happened?"

"I don't know. Luke talked to her teacher this morning. She claimed Becky was in the classroom right up to the time of the shooting. Mrs. Lund thinks she got separated from her class during the mad dash to exit the building. It was a good thirty or forty minutes before Mrs. Lund even realized Becky was gone."

"So now we have two questions." Quincy ticked them off on his fingers. "First, what happened to Danny O'Grady between the end of lunch—one-twenty P.M.—and when you finally confronted him at . . ."

"Two-forty-five-ish."

"Over an hour unaccounted for." Quincy frowned.

Rainie smiled thinly. "Not completely unaccounted for. Shep was with him. He claims he arrived at the school a little after one-forty-five. Students had already fled the premises. He went inside to offer help and encountered Danny, dazed and confused and picking up the guns."

"Picking up the guns? Oh, I like that. As if the boy simply stumbled upon them."

"You don't believe Shep either, do you?"

"He's not the most objective witness," Quincy observed. "I'll stick with my analysis for now: we don't know what Danny did between one-twenty and two-forty-five. The next question we have is what happened to Becky O'Grady from roughly one-thirty-five to your arrival at around one-fifty." He frowned again. "I don't like the fact that the two students unaccounted for just happen to be brother and sister. I don't believe in coincidence."

"You don't think Becky's part of it, do you?" Rainie was startled. "For heaven's sake, she's eight!"

"Has someone followed up with her yet?"

"Luke Hayes and Tom Dawson are going to try to interview her this afternoon. I'm not optimistic, though. Shep and Sandy are pretty hostile right now, and we don't have the right to question her away from her parents. I doubt anything will come of it."

"You could ask the DA to subpoena her as a witness for the grand jury."

Rainie shrugged, then surprised him by saying, "I looked into that this morning. According to Rodriguez, there's still no way of enforcing testimony. Her parents could simply coach her to say she doesn't remember, and that would be that. My guess is that if we hope to get anywhere with her, we need to play nice. Who knows? Shep and Sandy have to be wondering what really happened yesterday. Maybe sooner or later they'll be willing to let Becky talk. Perhaps they'll even let Luke ask her questions this afternoon. I'm just not betting on it."

"How well do you know them?" Quincy asked.

"Well."

Quincy nodded and let her move away. He didn't think she was aware of it, but she had wrapped her arms tightly around her middle, as if she was trying to block out the scene. The stance made her appear younger, more vulnerable. She was looking at the outline of Melissa Avalon's body. By all accounts, Miss Avalon had also been beautiful, compassionate, and dedicated to her job.

Wordlessly, they moved down the hall to the shattered doors. Quincy stopped at the door across from the computer room.

"Danny came out of this classroom?"

"Yes. He was backing Shep through the door at gunpoint."

"Holding both the .22 and the .38?"

"Yes."

"How did he seem?"

"Agitated. Wired." Rainie's brow furrowed as she contemplated his question further. "He seemed hostile toward his father."

"Holding him at gunpoint would appear hostile."

Rainie shook her head. "There was more to it than that. Shep was telling him that everything would be all right, then he was trying to tell him not to speak to me. But everything kept coming out as a command, and that made Danny withdraw even more. I think he has a big chip on his shoulder regarding his father. Shep rides him hard."

"How so?"

"Shep was a big football star in his high school days. Superjock. Danny . . ." Rainie shrugged. "He's small for his age, not good at sports. I think Shep believes he just needs to try harder, and I think Danny wishes his father would leave him alone."

"Have you ever heard Shep call his son stupid?"

Rainie shook her head. "You're talking about the interview tape, aren't you? Danny's obsession with being smart. That's the oddest thing. See, Shep's not the kind of father to worry that much about grades. Bad day on the football field, yes. Bad day on the report card, hey, these things happen. I don't know where that was coming from."

"Does Danny have any close friends?"

"We're still working on that."

"We'll want a complete list of all students absent yesterday, plus notes on whether they knew Danny O'Grady and can account for their time."

"Alibis for children," Rainie muttered, and rolled her eyes. "Why the ones who were absent?"

"Because no one says the shooter had to be in attendance that day. Plus, they still might be involved. In several of the shootings, other students played a role, either encouraging the main suspect's actions or enjoying the show."

"*What?*"

"Bethel, Alaska," Quincy said. "Evan Ramsey did the shooting, but two fourteen-year-olds encouraged him. One went so far as to teach him how to use the shotgun. Both assembled some of their other friends to join them in the cafeteria for a 'show.'"

"Wonderful."

"Luke Woodham also appears to have been influenced by other kids," Quincy reported. "In this case, I'm wondering if that's where Danny's obsession with 'I'm smart' is coming from. It sounds rehearsed and overly vehement. Either it's a phrase he's using to compensate for genuine doubts about his intelligence, or it's a cover for something else. Something that's still too frightening or overwhelming for him to say. How did he seem after the shooting?"

"Distant. Withdrawn. He sobbed a little when he heard his mother's voice. Then he fell asleep like a baby in the back of the patrol car."

Quincy nodded, not surprised by her description. "He's dissociating, keeping himself distanced from the events until he's able to deal with them. That's a normal reaction to any kind of trauma. The question becomes, how long will the dissociation last, and how will he react when his mind does start to process what happened."

"He's on suicide watch," Rainie volunteered. "I understand that's standard procedure for a case like his."

"It's not a bad idea. Unfortunately, Danny is probably suffering from post-traumatic stress disorder and now will go through its various symptoms. One day he might talk about everything very matter-of-factly, then collapse, weeping, the next day. He might sound cold at times as he repeats the day's events over and over again. He will probably refuse to call victims by name. All of this can be interpreted one way or another by well-meaning people. And none of it means he's guilty. It simply means he's experienced a trauma, whether as a perpetrator or a witness, and his mind is struggling to cope. That fact, however, can get quickly lost."

Rainie sighed. "I don't know," she said. "Maybe we're making this too complicated. On the one hand, some things don't make sense about the shooting. On the other hand, what shooting makes sense? And who else could've done it? All the students present that day were in class when the shots were fired, so they're accounted for. The only two students with time lapses are Danny and Becky, and neither choice is appealing. Maybe in the end it's just too hard to believe a child did it, so I focus on the question because it's easier than the answer."

"It's good to focus on questions," Quincy said. "It's your job."

"Well, it's not a good job today, Agent. Maybe tomorrow it will be, but I'm not particularly enjoying it today."

She headed for the side doors, obviously disturbed again. Quincy wasn't surprised when she stopped by the broken windows and gazed out on the rolling green hills and afternoon sun. Recharge, he thought. Sometimes he had to do that himself.

He bent down and inspected the shooting area more closely. He noted the way the bodies had laid and tried to picture in what direction they'd fallen. Then he explored the door frame around Melissa Avalon's computer lab for telltale holes.

Ten minutes later he was done making notes. Now he had many questions for the medical examiner.

He turned back to Rainie, who was still standing by the broken doors. She was no longer looking outside, however, but staring at the outline of Melissa Avalon's body. Her gray eyes were impossible to read, her features stilled.

Quincy wondered how few hours of sleep Rainie Conner had gotten last night. And for just one moment, he was tempted to ask her. To step over the line and into her space, because once upon a time he'd been the inexperienced agent with a homicide and he understood how some images stayed in your head long after you turned out the lights.

Some nights he did wake up screaming.

But that was neither here nor there.

He said, "I'm done now."

Rainie led him from the building.

TEN

OUTSIDE, RAINIE AND QUINCY encountered Principal Steven VanderZanden. A slightly built man with an expressive face and twinkling eyes, he now appeared subdued as he surveyed bloodred roses piled against the chain-link fence. The wind ruffled his dark, thinning hair and pressed his gray suit against his frame. He didn't seem to notice. He walked the fence line, adjusting arrangements so that names showed more clearly, then pushed back two teddy bears to reveal a framed portrait of Melissa Avalon.

Rainie and Quincy walked up to him quietly. Principal VanderZanden and his wife were relatively new to Bakersville, having moved into the area three years earlier when VanderZanden accepted the job at the K–8. Not having kids, Rainie had never met him until last summer, when they'd rubbed shoulders at a town function. VanderZanden had impressed her then with his enthusiasm for his students and his rapport with their parents. No project was too big in his eyes, no student too small for his attention. He had been giggling like a schoolgirl over having secured the federal grant for Bakersville's first computer lab and could barely wait to surf the Web himself.

He also seemed a little bit flirtatious, but he had a few glasses of wine under his belt when she'd run into him, and, frankly, the whole crowd was pretty loose by then.

"Principal VanderZanden." Rainie shook his hand. She could tell he was preoccupied. Yesterday evening he'd returned to the school to survey the damage and inquire as to when he might have the building back. With only one month to go before school was out for the summer, no one knew what to do about classes. They could bus the kids to neighboring Cabot, but that town was nearly forty minutes away, and after everything that had happened, parents wanted to keep their kids close to home.

"How are you, sir?" Rainie made the introduction between VanderZanden and Quincy. She still wasn't sure what she thought of the federal agent's presence, but so far he was proving less annoying than the state detective. There was something to be said for that.

"Are you an expert?" VanderZanden homed in on Quincy's credentials. "Can you tell me what happened in my school?"

"I don't think there's any such thing as an expert when it comes to these crimes."

"Maybe we should've gone with metal detectors." VanderZanden turned back toward the building. "After the Springfield shooting, Oregon educators were warned. But even then I thought of it as an issue for the high schools to address. We have kindergarten students here. I didn't want them starting their educational experience passing through giant security stations and being patted down by armed guards. What kind of message would that send?"

"Personally, I don't believe in metal detectors," Quincy said, but added before the principal could be too encouraged, "They would simply make the students better targets by creating long lines in front of the building."

"Oh, this is ridiculous!" VanderZanden shook his head and expelled a gust of pure frustration. "I've been up all night with calls from frantic parents, wanting to know what to do. The teachers are frightened, the school board overwhelmed. On top of all that, Alice's parents asked me to give the eulogy at her funeral. Of course I'll do it, I'm honored. But still . . . You go into education, you fantasize about watching your students grow up, maybe even attending their wedding or admiring their firstborn child. You certainly don't expect to give the eulogy at their funeral. Did you know that Sally's and Alice's parents are going to pay the burial expenses with money from their college funds?"

VanderZanden obviously didn't expect an answer. He turned away to adjust another bouquet. Quincy and Rainie exchanged looks. They would just let the man talk. Apparently, he had a few things to say.

"The flowers started arriving first thing this morning," VanderZanden added after a moment. "I've seen pictures of the flowers sent to the other schools, so I expected something like this. Still, to see it. Notes and cards from all over the country. Teddy bears and balloons from hundreds of strangers." He turned to them, sounding angry again. "I received calls from two other principals who've been through this and half a dozen child experts who are experienced in this area. It's like we joined some club. I don't want to be part of a club! I wish we were alone. I wish we were the only place this had ever happened. Instead, we're what? The eleventh, twelfth, thirteenth school to go through this? Dammit, we should've known better!"

He pinched the bridge of his nose, clearly trying to pull himself together and not having much luck. His gaze returned to the picture of Melissa Avalon. He pinched his nose harder.

"I'm sorry. It's been a long twenty-four hours."

"It's okay," Rainie said. "Take your time."

"I needed time last night. Now I need a vacation.

Well, that's neither here nor there. I'm sure you have more questions, though I already told Detective Sanders the little I know about things."

"Detective Sanders?" Rainie inquired sharply. Warning lights went off in her head. She didn't ignore them. "What did you tell Detective Sanders?"

"Not much." VanderZanden shrugged, obviously caught off guard by her tone. "I was in my office when I heard the shots. I came out to the main entranceway to see what was going on and heard someone scream. The next thing I knew, the fire alarms went off and everyone began running for the door. At the time I figured it was something minor. A student had fired a cap gun in the halls and the smoke had triggered the alarms. Or someone had lit a few firecrackers as a prank. These things happen.

"The first time I realized it was serious was when I saw the face of Mrs. McLain, the sixth-grade teacher. She was white as a sheet; her hands were shaking. I told her to calm down, it was just a drill, and then she *looked* at me. She looked at me and she said, 'I think some students have been shot. I think someone just shot at us. I think he's still there.' Even then it wasn't until I saw Will's bloody leg in the parking lot that I realized she'd been right—someone had opened fire in our school."

"Did you hear anyone say Danny's name?" Quincy asked.

VanderZanden shook his head. "I heard Dorie screaming about a man in black coming to get her. Of course, Dorie is only seven years old, and we've had problems with her imagination before. Once she had the entire second-grade class convinced they couldn't go to the bathroom because little trolls hid inside the toilets to snatch children for lunch. You have no idea how messy it can be when twenty-one seven-year-olds won't use the rest rooms. I had parents calling me for weeks."

"Were a lot of children around when she was going on about the 'man in black'?" Rainie asked.

"Everyone was around. We'd evacuated the whole school into the front parking lot, as specified in our fire-drill manual."

Rainie blew out an exasperated breath. "Well, that explains that batch of interview answers," she muttered to Quincy. "One hysterical girl, two hundred and fifty impressionable minds." She returned to Principal VanderZanden. "Are you sure none of the teachers saw anything? What about Mrs. McLain? I can't believe someone was shooting a gun in the hallway and no one noticed."

"I don't think the shooter was standing in the hallway. One of the teachers said that it sounded like the shots were coming from a room at the end of the west wing. Maybe the computer lab. I know that from where I was standing in the main entranceway, I couldn't see a thing."

Rainie glanced at Quincy. He nodded faintly, sharing her thought. The killer started with Miss Avalon, then turned to see Sally and Alice. Shot them as well, then ducked into the now-empty computer room as all hell broke loose. It would explain the lack of witnesses as well as the random firing pattern.

"What can you tell us about Danny O'Grady?" Quincy asked VanderZanden. "Was he a good student? Did he get along well with others?"

"Danny's a fine student. He's made the honor roll several times. He was hardly ever sent to my office with discipline issues. Melissa—Miss Avalon was just telling me the other day that she'd never seen anyone so good with computers. He has a natural talent for it."

"What about enemies?" Quincy pressed gently. "Was Danny picked on by other students? Was he considered popular by his classmates—or was he often a target of their unwanted attention?"

Rainie nodded her head at this question. She

should've thought to ask it herself last night. Rightly or wrongly, most school shooters felt painfully persecuted by their peers. Rainie had even read somewhere that these homicides weren't that different from teen suicide—the less popular kid felt an unbearable amount of pain and decided to do something about it. In the case of a school shooting, however, the kid didn't just plan to end his own life but to take some of the offending parties' lives with him. That's the thing with teenagers—they came up with sentences that didn't always fit the crime.

VanderZanden seemed to be struggling with Quincy's question. He finally shook his head. "I wasn't aware of anything," he said, then added more reluctantly, "I'm an adult, however, and an authority figure. In other words, while I try to be in touch with my students, I'm still probably not the best judge of what really goes on among twenty adolescents during a thirty-minute recess."

"What about close friends of Danny's who might be able to tell us more?"

"I don't think Danny has close friends. He's quiet, keeps to himself." A thought seemed to strike Vander-Zanden all at once. "You know, there was this incident, not too long ago . . ."

Quincy and Rainie perked up.

"There's this older boy, Charlie Kenyon. Do you know him?"

"Oh, sure." Rainie supplied for Quincy: "Charlie's the son of our former mayor. Nineteen now, a bit too much money, way too much free time. He was sent off to military school back east four years ago, but he returned last spring no worse for the wear. Now he fancies himself some kind of minor hood. Hangs out where he's not wanted, drives under the influence every other weekend. We've brought him in half a dozen times, but it's always misdemeanor stuff and his father's quick with bail money and high-priced lawyers. I don't get the impression Charlie's feeling a need to reform anytime soon."

VanderZanden nodded his head with real emotion. "That's Charlie. About two months ago he started hanging around our school after hours. Teachers would see him lounging outside the fence, talking to kids on the playground. As long as he was on the street side of the fence, however, there was nothing we could do. Then one day Mrs. Lund saw Charlie hand Danny a cigarette through the fence. She immediately took the cigarette away from Danny and wrote him up, but there was nothing she could do about Charlie. He told the boy not to sweat it. 'Detention is when all the fun stuff happens,' or something like that. We sent a note home to Danny's parents, and we never caught him smoking again, but we'd still see Charlie around. I don't know why he insisted on bothering us at the K-through-eight. You'd think he'd be more interested in the high school."

"Did Charlie know Miss Avalon?" Quincy asked.

"I don't think so. She moved to town just last year, when we got the federal grant. Then again . . ." Principal VanderZanden flushed. He looked at Rainie with something akin to embarrassment.

"She was very pretty," Rainie filled in for the tongue-tied principal. "Very, *very* pretty."

"She's a very good teacher," VanderZanden added immediately, but his dark eyes appeared wistful. Melissa Avalon had been beautiful.

"How old was she?" Rainie inquired.

"Twenty-eight."

"Young enough and pretty enough to attract a nineteen-year-old," Rainie concluded, and looked at Quincy. He appeared deep in thought.

"Miss Avalon moved to Bakersville recently?"

"Last summer. We hired her in August. Frankly, we'd given up on getting the grant, and then boom. You know the feds. Obviously."

"Where did Miss Avalon come from?"

"She'd just gotten her master's from Portland State University."

"Was this her first job?"

"Her first full-time teaching position. She subbed in Beaverton's school district before that. That's one of the reasons we hired her." VanderZanden gave them the apologetic look of a veteran civil servant. "We have a very tight budget here, and new teachers are cheaper than experienced ones."

"Do you know anything about her private life?" Rainie asked. "Where her family lives, anything?"

VanderZanden hesitated. He looked self-conscious again and wouldn't meet Rainie's gaze. "I believe she has parents in the Portland area."

"What about past relationships? Maybe an old boyfriend she left behind? A current beau who wanted more of her time?"

"I think . . . I think you should ask her parents about that sort of thing. It's not appropriate for me to be commenting on the private lives of my staff."

"Principal VanderZanden, we don't have a lot of time."

"Phone calls are fast, Officer," he said firmly. "It's the advantage of modern life."

Rainie frowned, not liking the principal's sudden lack of cooperation, but before she could push harder, Quincy pissed her off by taking over the interview.

"What about Danny's relationship with Miss Avalon? Did they get along well? Did he have any problems in her class?"

"Oh no," VanderZanden said emphatically. "That's the crazy thing about yesterday. I would've sworn Miss Avalon was Danny's favorite teacher. Certainly he loved being in the computer lab and was one of our most adept students on the Internet. Before school, during lunch, after school. It seemed he was always in the lab. Sometimes Miss Avalon even stayed late just for him."

"On the Internet?" Rainie jumped in. "Do you know what he'd do on the Web, where he'd go?"

"I'm not sure. Visit Web sites, look things up."

"Did he go into chat rooms?"

"Probably. Miss Avalon had it set up so students couldn't access X-rated sites—she had one of those filters installed. Otherwise, students were free to roam. The whole point was to encourage them to be more computer savvy."

"Did he play computer games?" Quincy asked. "Any specific ones?"

"I don't know. In all honesty, the only person who would is Miss Avalon."

Rainie nodded, chewing on her bottom lip. Danny loved the Internet. That put a new spin on things. An adept user could go just about anyplace, learn just about anything. The Springfield shooter, Kip Kinkel, had used the Internet to learn how to build bombs and rig booby traps. Right before they were murdered, his parents had even commented to friends that they were happy to see their troubled son take an interest in computers. Finally, something nonviolent . . .

It also meant Danny could've been exposed to any number of crackpots and loose cannons. Forget just Charlie Kenyon. Danny was a young, troubled boy whose family was going through a hard time. His vulnerability would've been boundless.

"We need to search those computers," Rainie muttered.

"Detective Sanders already has them. Didn't he tell you?"

"Oh, you know Detective Sanders. He's such an efficient little— It must have slipped his mind." Rainie smiled sweetly for VanderZanden, though her sarcasm was not lost on Quincy.

"Did Danny often stay late after school?" Quincy returned to the original line of questioning.

VanderZanden glanced at Rainie. She shrugged. "It's a murder investigation. Everything is going to come out sooner or later."

VanderZanden sighed. He appeared tired and worn again. A man due to have many more sleepless nights and ethical struggles over how to best serve his students. He said quietly, "Danny's parents have been having marital difficulties."

"Sandy got a new job," Rainie told Quincy bluntly. "She likes it, but it's a lot of hours. Shep didn't want her to work in the first place, let alone if it came in the way of getting dinner ready."

"Are they separated?"

"Nah. They're Catholic."

"Oh, got it."

"Sandy came in one day to meet with Danny and Becky's teachers," VanderZanden explained. "She expressed that there was a great deal of tension at home and she knew it was hard on the children. She wanted their teachers to understand what was going on and keep an eye out for the kids. Becky has certainly been more withdrawn this year. And Danny has had a few . . . issues."

"The smoking," Rainie prompted. "And . . ."

"Three weeks ago Danny came to school agitated. He couldn't remember his locker combination, and something in him just went. He started pounding on the door with his fists and yelling how much he hated the locker and the school and how was he supposed to remember anything when everyone knew he was stupid—"

"Stupid?" Quincy interjected. "You heard him say he was stupid?"

"Oh yes, I was there, Agent. It took both myself and Richard Mann to subdue him. Danny was yelling 'Stupid, stupid, stupid' over and over again. I was very worried about him."

Quincy looked at Rainie. She shrugged. She didn't know where this was coming from either, but Danny seemed to have an issue with his intelligence.

"He was on the honor roll?" Quincy asked the principal again.

"Yes."

"You considered him a good student? His teachers were pleased with his performance?"

"Yes. He wasn't the best in some subjects, but, then, when something interested him . . . I don't think there was anything he couldn't do on a computer."

"Principal VanderZanden, did you ever hear his parents call him stupid?"

"Sandy? Never. She loves those kids. As for Shep?" VanderZanden arched a brow. "Let's just say he was more concerned about the size of his son's muscles than the power of his brain."

"Did Danny do many after-school sports?"

"Shep made him try out for football. He got on the team, but sports aren't Danny's forte. He's small for his age, a bit awkward. Unfortunately, his father can be rather . . . forceful. He wanted his son to play football, so Danny played football. In all honesty, however, Danny mostly warmed the bench. He just wasn't any good. You know, you really should talk to the school counselor, Richard Mann, about these things. He met with Danny a few times after the locker incident and would know a lot more about his state of mind."

"We'll be sure to do that," Rainie told the principal. She remembered Richard Mann from yesterday. He'd been very efficient in setting up the first-aid station and clearing the parking lot. She also remembered him as being on the young side, and that made her immediately wonder about him and pretty Miss Avalon. More food for thought.

"We're going to need a copy of Danny's school records from you," Rainie told the principal. "His report cards, incident slips, everything."

"I'm not sure—"

"We can get a subpoena if we have to. I'm just asking you to save us all some time."

"All right, all right. There's just so much to do. . . ." VanderZanden looked at his school building. The front doors were closed, the interior seeming shadowed and foreboding from this distance. Yellow crime-scene tape still roped off the parking lot and wove through the chain-link fence, while dark red stains spotted the school sidewalk—blood from the wounded students who had clutched neighbors' hands while waiting for the medevac choppers to arrive. It was impossible now to look at the building and not think of death.

"I understand that Columbine had to completely refurbish the inside of the high school," the principal murmured. "After the shooting they ripped out the carpet, repainted the walls, redid the lockers. They even changed the tone of their fire alarm, which had sounded for hours that day. And their library—that poor, tragic library—simply doesn't exist anymore. They covered up the entrance with a new bank of lockers and brought in a trailer to house the books."

He looked at Rainie and Quincy. There were no twinkling lights in his eyes. "I'm not sure what I'm supposed to do here," he said honestly. "The damage isn't that extensive, and yet it is. I want the children to feel safe again, but in this day and age, schools can be scary places. I want the building to be welcoming, but I don't want to pretend nothing happened. I want us to move on, but I don't want us to forget.

"I don't know how I'm supposed to do all that. When I was training to be a principal, the biggest threat we could imagine was an earthquake. They certainly hadn't started the duck-and-run drills in the L.A. schools for drive-by shootings. Nor had they ever envisioned that schools would become war zones for rival gangs and street disputes. Now we have teachers and students dying in the halls. Small towns, big towns, black, white, upper class, lower class—it doesn't seem to matter. And the human in me wants to rail against that, wants to live in denial, while the principal in me knows I can't do that. I have an obligation to my students. If this is the world we live in, then this is the world I must prepare them for. But how do I do that?

I'm not sure *I'm* prepared for this world. I know Miss Avalon wasn't."

"Have you arranged for grief counseling?" Quincy asked gently.

"Of course. Several child psychologists are coming into town."

"I didn't mean just for the students. I meant also for you and your staff."

"Of course, of course." Principal VanderZanden's attention drifted back to the memorial. It rested on the poster that said, *We love you, Miss Avalon.*

His figure swayed. He suddenly looked small to Rainie. A slight, vulnerable man growing old in front of her eyes.

"She really was trying to help him," VanderZanden said to no one in particular. "She really cared for her students, especially Danny. If you could've seen the time she spent with him, all those hours after school because she knew he didn't want to go home. She helped him learn basic programming, she laughed with him over Internet jokes. She was so patient, so caring. . . . Sometimes I hate Danny O'Grady. And that makes me feel worse. What kind of principal hates a student? What kind of man fears a child?"

Principal VanderZanden obviously didn't expect any answers. He squared his shoulders. He walked back to his car while clouds finally moved over the sun and the first drops of spring rain began to fall.

After a moment Rainie said, "I think he needs some help."

"You would, too, if you'd just lost the woman you loved."

"Principal VanderZanden is a happily married man!"

And Quincy said, "Not when he was with Melissa Avalon."

ELEVEN

SANDY O'GRADY KEPT THINKING that Danny was dead.

Small communities had their rituals, their established ways of dealing with the major passages of life. Almost all involved food. Someone was getting married—bake the bride's favorite bread and tape the recipe card to the baking tin for her future kitchen. Someone was having her first child—pile up the homemade sugar cookies cut into the shape of little booties. A graduation barbecue—bring Mama's award-winning three-bean salad. The yearly race to bale hay before the Oregon rains ruined the crop—bring fresh corn and tomatoes from the garden, plus bags of sugar and rock salt for the ice cream maker. Maybe include a package of chocolate chips.

Someone died—bring out the casseroles. Dad's ham and potato surprise. Grandma's seven-layer taco supreme. Bake a ham, baste a turkey. Make it big, hearty, and rich. And deliver it with plenty of Kleenex and a shoulder for the widow to lean upon. Then return two days later with a pan of brownies or a couple of apple pies. Sooner or later even the most stoic survivors turned to sugar for solace. It's simply a way of life.

Yesterday evening, on the O'Grady front doorstep,

the first casserole had appeared. It was accompanied by a note that said *Deepest sympathies.* No name attached. Sandy realized then how bad the days would be. Neighbors understood their torment. Some even sympathized. But in these circumstances no one knew what to do.

When Danny had been transported to Cabot County's juvenile detention hall, he'd been wearing a bulletproof vest.

The police had spent the evening in the O'Gradys' home. Men Sandy and Shep had never seen before, wearing grim expressions and navy blue windbreakers emblazoned with the letters CSU, cordoned off Danny's room. They pulled apart his bed, disemboweled his closet. They tore into his desk, dismantled his furniture, and boxed up everything he had ever touched. They shredded Danny O'Grady's bedroom, dusted it down with fingerprint powder, then left as somberly as they came.

Becky hid in the coat closet.

Sandy's parents came over. They hugged Sandy and wept. They pulled Becky from the closet and cried harder. They looked at Shep stonily, so he would know that whatever had happened, it was his fault. Then Sandy's mother moved into the kitchen and started baking. Her father sat on the couch and did his best to look strong.

The parish priest had paid a visit. He sat with Sandy and Shep. He reminded them that the Lord gave no burdens that could not be borne. He assured them faith would get them through this time of sorrow. He took to speaking of Danny in the past tense, which at once seemed natural and nearly drove Sandy out of her mind.

Danny was not dead. Danny was not a burden. He was a confused and frightened boy, lying now in an institutionally gray juvenile hall with bars on the windows. He was in a state of shock, the doctors told Sandy and Shep when they tried to visit this morning.

Curled up tight with his arms wrapped around his knees, as if he was so exhausted by life he was trying to return to the womb.

No, they couldn't see him yet. He needed more time and more sleep. Maybe tomorrow.

Sandy didn't want to leave. She didn't want to return to a house that magically produced casseroles and to a mother who was turning out row after row of pies as if a properly fluted crust was the secret to managing life. She didn't want to spend another minute with the priest who had married her and Shep and who now looked at them with the solemn compassion usually reserved for lepers. She didn't want to stare at her garage, where early this morning someone had scrawled *Baby Killer* with dripping red paint.

Danny was not a stone-cold killer. He was a child. He was *her* child, and she wanted her family back! She wanted to be a warrior mom, slayer of all dragons for her children.

Except no one could tell her which dragon to slay. No one could tell her what had happened yesterday afternoon to turn her eight-year-old daughter into a silent ghost and her thirteen-year-old son into a mass murderer.

Now their lawyer, Avery Johnson, was speaking with them in their kitchen. They had just returned from the preliminary hearing in front of the juvenile-court judge, where Sandy had been shocked by the informality of the proceedings. The room had looked little different from a high school classroom, with its plain white walls and linoleum-tiled floor. The judge, wearing a dark robe, clearly was surprised to see two lawyers in suits. His opening comment had been "You guys don't come here often, do you?"

In this very simple room with very simple proceedings, the county DA, Charles Rodriguez—a man Shep had worked with for years, a man Sandy had invited to her house for dinner on numerous occasions—formally filed a petition for waiver to adult court given the "heinous nature of Daniel O'Grady's crimes against the community."

He'd charged their son with five counts of aggravated murder, one count for the first victim and two counts for each additional victim as they were part of a multiple homicide. If found guilty in adult court, Danny could receive five consecutive thirty-year-to-life sentences. He had gone into the care of the county yesterday evening. He would never come home again.

Sandy kept thinking that Danny was dead.

"Now, you have to look on the bright side," Avery Johnson was saying. "Danny's only thirteen years old. He has statistics on his side."

"Statistics?" Sandy asked weakly. She was mangling a piece of freshly baked apple pie. Her mother had served it with a giant scoop of vanilla ice cream just ten minutes ago. Sandy watched the ice cream melt into little flowing rivers, then she formed dams with bits of baked apple. After a moment Shep took her plate and ate the pie himself. In times of crisis, he always gained an appetite while she lost hers.

"In the upcoming hearing," Avery was saying, "we must argue what's in the best interest of the child and the community. Basically, a waiver hearing focuses on two key aspects of Danny's personality: Does he pose too great a risk to others to be sufficiently handled by the juvenile system, and is he amenable to rehabilitation? Naturally, the DA is going to argue that Danny's act proves he's a dangerous felon beyond all hope of rehabilitation, thus he falls outside the jurisdiction of juvenile court. The judge should cart the child away to adult court, which has the means to handle a master criminal.

"Our job is to prove otherwise, and the good news is that the statistics are in our favor. The majority of children who commit violent acts won't reoffend in adulthood. Furthermore, and we must emphasize this, studies show that there is a *higher* chance of recidivism with a child who is incarcerated with adults than with a child who is held in juvenile facilities. Thus, it is in the state's own best interest to keep Danny in juvenile jurisdiction, where he can be rehabilitated and then start over on his twenty-fifth birthday as a productive member of society."

"You're assuming Danny is guilty," Sandy said shortly. "Why are you assuming that my son is guilty?"

Avery, an older man with wire-rimmed glasses and expensive suits, gave her a faint smile. He had eaten his pie within minutes, then gently patted his upper lip with his paper napkin as if it had been made of the finest linen. Sandy wasn't sure if she liked him yet. She thought he might be too pompous, too rich and oozing of success for her taste. But Shep had been taken with him since they first met at some law-enforcement function where Avery was the keynote speaker. Shep went so far as to call him a "friend," though Sandy knew that wasn't really true. Avery Johnson moved in circles beyond them. He lived in a gorgeous home in Lake Oswego and was hardly taking this case out of the goodness of his heart. Sandy imagined the man charged five hundred dollars an hour and was racking up billable time even as he ate their pie.

She did not know how they were going to pay him. She had no idea what kind of lies Shep must have fed the man about their financial circumstances to even get him to show up. She just knew that Shep wanted Avery Johnson. He was the best there was and Shep wouldn't hear of anything less for his son. That was his idea of fatherhood, and it both enraged Sandy and broke her heart.

"Sandy, you can rest assured that I will never let a jury think your son is guilty." Avery smiled at her again. "But we're not at a jury trial yet. Six months from now it will be Charles Rodriguez and myself 'discussing' Danny's future with Judge Matthews, who, frankly, is a miserable old fart who would like to bring back corporal punishment to public schools. He probably does think Danny is guilty. He probably thinks

Danny should hang. Fortunately, that's not germane to the hearing. At this point we're simply addressing which court should have jurisdiction over the case. So I need to argue that, guilty or not, Danny's—and the community's—interests are best served by keeping this case in juvenile court."

"Because even if he's a mass murderer now, when he grows up he'll be magically cured?"

"Exactly. And there's nothing magical about it. I've been reading articles on juvenile crime all night, and the experts call it 'desistance phenomenon.' From ages twelve to eighteen, male teens exhibit a spike of criminal activity as their rise in hormones and developmental changes outpace their coping skills. Then at eighteen, as they become adults, get jobs, and find more permanent relationships, they settle down. Criminal activity falls off, and even teens once described as 'troubled' go on to lead normal lives."

"So if Danny is innocent, he's innocent. But if he's guilty, he's merely going through a phase? That's what we're going to argue in court?" Sandy's voice was becoming shrill. She couldn't help herself. It sounded ludicrous. It sounded insane.

Shep shot her an impatient stare. "For God's sake, Sandy, what do you want to hear? He just told you his job is to keep Danny out of adult court, and this is the way he can do it."

"Sandy—" Avery began soothingly.

Sandy cut him off. "I don't know what I want to hear! Maybe that my only son is not capable of killing three people. Maybe that my firstborn child is not a murderer, it's all been a big mistake." She slammed her hand down on the table.

"Look at you two, discussing legal theory as if it makes a difference. This isn't a ball game. It doesn't boil down to who wins or loses at the end of the night. This is our son! This is our community! How are we going to walk down the streets if Danny is found guilty? What are we going to tell Becky? My God,

Shep, didn't you see what they wrote on our garage? They're going to kill him. Our neighbors hold Danny responsible for the murder of two little girls, and sooner or later someone is going to kill him. Dammit. Dammit, dammit, *dammit*!"

Sandy pushed back from the table. She got up, paced four steps around the tiny kitchen, then realized she was crying uncontrollably. Shep did not get up to console her. Last night he had tried to come to her bed after months of sleeping on the sofa. His voice had sounded ragged. He'd told her he just wanted to hold her. Maybe they could put aside their differences for a while. Once, they'd been good friends.

Sandy's anger had been too tight in her chest. She had looked at her husband, the father of her children, raw and vulnerable with his big shoulders sagging, and all she could think was that if Danny had been driven to murder, it was Shep's fault. He pushed the boy too hard. He had never appreciated that Danny was different, more intellectual, more like her. Instead, Shep had tried to force him into his arrogant, macho world.

He had broken their son. He had broken their family. Sandy hated him.

And then, as abruptly as the emotion had overcome Sandy, it ripped through her body and she had nothing left. She stood in their kitchen empty, exhausted, and swaying on her feet.

She turned toward the doorway and there was Becky, watching her with somber blue eyes.

"Don't let the monster get you, Mommy," Becky said. Then she turned and walked back into the family room, where Sandy's parents were watching TV.

Sandy returned to the table and had a seat.

"I know this is an emotional time for you," Avery began.

"Jesus fucking Christ," Sandy said.

Shep sighed heavily, got up, and cut himself a third piece of pie.

"Look," Avery said briskly, "let me walk you

through the whole process. Maybe by the end it will be clearer to you what we're trying to accomplish. The next six to twelve months are going to be crucial to Danny's future."

Sandy held up a hand. "Why do we have to wait six to twelve months?"

"Because it's going to take that long for everyone to prepare for the waiver-motion hearing. It's not a small thing."

"But Danny can't come home, can he? You said there's no bail for juveniles accused of murder. So what is this? My son isn't even on trial yet, isn't even found guilty of murder, and he's going to spend at least six months locked up in a juvenile detention hall? For God's sake, how can that be legal?"

"It's the way the system works."

"Well, fuck the system!" Sandy was beyond reason and knew it.

Avery Johnson gave her that small, soothing smile again. Then his voice got sharp. "Mrs. O'Grady, I know you don't want to hear this, but there is a good chance that Danny committed these crimes. He was found holding Shep at gunpoint. He brought your family's guns to the school, and, furthermore, he confessed *twice*."

"He's in shock. You said so yourself. He doesn't know what he's saying."

"The guns, Mrs. O'Grady. The guns. How did two handguns get from your safe to the school?"

Sandy looked at Shep helplessly. He stabbed the air with his ice-cream-covered fork. "My son didn't do it," he said stoically.

For the first time, Sandy felt a rush of warmth toward her husband.

Avery Johnson said sternly, "You're a police officer, Shep, and not even you can prove your son's innocence—"

"I will—"

"You can't—"

"I got six months."

Avery Johnson sighed. He clearly thought they were both in denial. He tried again:

"Even if you manage to explain away how *your* guns came to be at *that* crime scene, why *your* son held *you* hostage, and why *your* son confessed twice to *three* murders, the fact remains that Danny is a troubled boy. He obviously has issues. Thus, all legal necessities aside, as parents you should be able to see the value of the next six months as an opportunity to get Danny the help he needs. He'll be examined by child-development experts. He'll take a battery of psychological exams. He'll have his childhood, his family, his friends, all thoroughly explored. While I'm sure it may be awkward at times, the result should be a better understanding of who Danny is and what problems he's facing. Does that make sense?"

Sandy finally considered the matter. She glanced at Shep, who was rolling a bite of pie around in his mouth in a manner that indicated he didn't really taste it. She could tell the lawyer's words had depressed him; his shoulders had slumped again. Danny had problems. Danny had issues. It was Shep's way to deny all things he didn't like to hear, but he had no more words left. The lawyer's comments had struck too close to the secret doubts in their hearts. What if Danny was troubled? What if they had turned their little boy into a monster?

There were such dark shadows beneath her husband's eyes. Sandy had to look away.

She knew that after leaving her room last night, Shep had lain down on the floor next to Becky's bed. Their little girl had refused offers to sleep in her parents' room, instead building a wall of stuffed animals around her bed. Big Bear, her favorite doll, was reserved for special bodyguard duty. Hannah the horse was positioned at the door. Twelve Beanie Babies cordoned off the windowsill. Pugsley the dog was handed over to Sandy, just in case she needed protecting too.

Becky whimpered many times in the middle of the night. Once, around three A.M., Shep caught her leaping out of bed and running for her closet. When he tried to shake her awake, she whimpered harder, so he finally carried her back to bed with Big Bear. Becky mumbled for him to look out for monsters before falling more deeply asleep.

At six A.M. Shep moved to the couch in the family room. At seven A.M., when Sandy went to check on Becky, she found her curled up in the far corner of the closet, four dresses pulled down to hide her gleaming blond hair.

Becky still hadn't said anything about what had happened yesterday, and the doctors predicted she never would. Whatever she had experienced was too traumatic for her eight-year-old mind, and she was now working resiliently to lock it all away. Sandy and Shep were instructed to make their daughter feel safe, while being careful not to sound dismissive of her fears. Whatever that meant.

Sandy had the feeling she and Shep were aging exponentially these days. She would dearly love to pick up the phone to speak with Margaret or Liz or Margie about it, the way the four mothers had been comparing notes on their children for the last six years. Except she couldn't do that. Her children might be suffering, but her son was supposedly the cause of everyone's pain. It was now her job as his mother to pay his dues.

"What . . . what if Danny did do it?" Sandy ventured for the first time, staring tremulously at the rich, successful Avery Johnson, who held their future in his hands. "What if all the experts study Danny and conclude that he is a killer?"

"This is what I've been trying to explain. The point of this trial isn't to say that Danny is a killer; it's to evaluate whether he will kill again. Juvenile court is going to appoint a forensic psychologist to evaluate Danny, his personality, past behavior, violent tendencies, et cetera. There is a whole range of parameters this psychologist will analyze, hence it takes some time. When he's done studying Danny, the expert will write up a report. In this case, given the seriousness of Danny's alleged crime, the forensic psychologist will probably make two statements. One will say, presuming Danny did commit mass murder, he has X percent chance of killing again. If he didn't commit mass murder, he has Y percent chance of being rehabilitated."

"I don't understand. If Danny didn't do the crime, then he should have a one-hundred-percent chance of leading a normal, healthy life. How can there be a second statement?"

"The forensic psychologist is looking beyond this moment, Mrs. O'Grady, to Danny's entire life, not just this one act, which he may or may not be guilty of."

"Danny has always been a very good boy," Sandy said automatically.

Avery Johnson looked at her sympathetically but firmly. "Danny suffers explosions of violent rage. He spends a lot of time with guns. He has a reputation for being antisocial. These things are going to come up, Mrs. O'Grady. The forensic psychologist will be looking at all sorts of factors, including tensions in your family and other sources of stress."

Shep bowed his head. Sandy knew what he was thinking. Their crumbling marriage. Shep's raging temper—not a great model for dealing with aggression, though Shep, God bless him, had never lifted a hand against her or the children. The furniture, however, was not always so lucky.

Shep finally spoke up. "What if we don't like the expert's findings? Can't we get our own shrink?"

"Absolutely. First thing tomorrow morning I'll petition juvenile court for our own forensic psychologist. They'll still appoint the expert, but he'll work for us."

"What does that cost?" Sandy asked hesitantly. "I mean . . ."

She glanced at Shep; she could tell he was angry

she'd brought up money. But she couldn't help herself. Sheriff paid only twenty-five thousand a year, and Sandy barely made nine dollars an hour at her job. She'd been hoping for more, she'd been hoping to be salaried after this new deal with Wal-Mart closed, but that already seemed a million years ago. She'd run out of the office and never looked back. In the evening Mitchell had left her a very nice message telling her to take all the time she needed, but she could tell he was disappointed. He needed help for the meeting now. With her gone, he'd have no choice but to find someone else. That was business.

"The juvenile court pays for the experts. It comes out of the court's funds."

"It won't cost us anything?" Sandy asked.

Her husband growled. Avery Johnson assured her it wouldn't. For the first time she saw some compassion in his eyes. He probably understood a great deal more about their finances than she'd thought.

"The advantage of having our own expert is that he'll be subject to patient-client confidentiality. Danny can be perfectly honest with him, and if we think that's too damning in the end, we simply won't have our expert testify. No one will be the wiser."

"But us," Sandy said.

"If you have the information, you can get Danny help," Avery said calmly.

"If you keep him out of adult court," she countered.

"That's the challenge," he agreed. "For a thirteen-year-old boy, adult court spells doom."

They were all silent for a moment, contemplating the road ahead and the young life at stake. Sandy rubbed her aching temples.

"Danny didn't do it," Shep said stubbornly. "I'm going to prove it."

The phone rang. Shep automatically picked it up. He said hello, then his face froze and he slammed the phone down.

"Wrong number," he muttered, but they all knew he

was lying. The phone had been ringing all morning. Disembodied voices yelling, *"I hope they rape the bastard good. I hope in prison they fucking tear him apart. Baby killer, baby killer, baby killer."*

Sandy had lived in this town all her life. She had loved it with her whole heart.

She turned back to Avery Johnson. "What are our chances? Tell me honestly. What happened to the other boys accused of mass shootings?"

"Nearly all are in jail for life. But most of the shooters were sixteen, which made them fall automatically under the jurisdiction of adult court."

"But not everyone? There's been an exception?"

"Jonesboro. Those two boys were too young, and Arkansas didn't have a statute for sending juveniles to adult court."

"They remained in juvenile custody?"

"I believe they were ordered held until their twenty-first birthdays."

Sandy felt hopeful for the first time. "And did that work out, Mr. Johnson?" she asked anxiously. "Are they safe, productive members of their community now?"

"Nobody knows yet, Mrs. O'Grady. Nobody knows."

TWELVE

THE MAN'S FAVORITE service provider was AOL. He liked the way it grouped headline news and made it easy to jump from story to story. Double-click on news summary, *Sheriff's Son Suspected in Small-Town Slayings.* Two paragraphs later, double-click again for the *in-depth* report. Whole world mourns. Three families devastated, president cries out for greater gun control, yada, yada, yada. A sidebar gave him additional options. He could chat with others on the subject. See a timeline of all the recent school shootings. Read an interview of other school-shooting survivors discussing how each new incident reopened their wounds and ripped out their hearts. He read that article. Open wounds, bleeding hearts. God, he loved journalism these days. For that matter, he kept the December 20, 1999, edition of *Time* magazine under glass. Anything for inspiration.

Two hours before he'd downloaded the most recent articles on the Bakersville story. Not as much coverage as he'd hoped. Only three dead, that was the problem. Front-page news had become a lot more competitive than when he'd first started. He'd have to remember that.

Six P.M. The man pushed away from his laptop. Damn, he was hungry.

This motel didn't offer much in the way of amenities. He'd hoped for a larger hotel, a nice innocuous chain. No such luck within driving distance of Bakersville. He'd had to go with a cheap, privately run place. On the one hand, the owner seemed overly interested in his guests. On the other hand, there wasn't a large staff working all hours of the night to notice the man's activities. Win some, lose some.

The man's stomach grumbled again. He decided to try the local bar.

Fifteen minutes later, coat and hat in place, he journeyed down the tiny main street into a dimly lit tavern. Three local men, clustered around the single TV, looked up curiously. The lone, balding bartender gave him a small nod of greeting. The man took a seat in front of three silver keg levers and ordered a beer.

"Anything good on the news?" he called down to the other men.

"Senate wants some new gun law. Hold the parents accountable for whatever damage their kids do with guns."

"About time," the man's friend mumbled. "As they say, the apple never falls far from the tree; these kids had to get their ideas from somewhere."

The third man eyed the first two levelly. He had an old, weather-beaten face from a lifetime spent riding a John Deere. He said quietly, "Shep's a good man."

The other two shrugged and almost immediately began studying their feet. Apparently they felt in no position to argue.

So the man at the bar drawled, "Shep's a good sheriff, sure. But a father—don't you think a father is a separate thing?"

The three men turned away from the TV. For the first time, they truly studied him. The older man, Ruddy-Face, spoke first. "I don't think we caught your name."

"Oh, I'm just passing through. Business, you know. Generally I love traveling down the coast. Pretty countryside, nice people. But this time . . . A thirteen-year-old boy shooting two little girls. Then murdering that poor teacher . . . Such a beautiful woman, such a horrible waste." He turned back to the bartender, whose welcoming demeanor had already disappeared. "Can I get an order of buffalo wings? Extra hot. Extra blue cheese."

"Nobody knows if Danny O'Grady did it," Ruddy-Face said stiffly. The bartender nodded.

"Come on, Darren," one of his friends said softly. "My wife heard it straight from Luke Hayes's mother that Danny confessed."

"And I'm telling you that the O'Gradys are good people."

"Any other suspects?" the man at the bar asked casually.

"Some kids reported seeing a man in black," Ruddy-Face said instantly.

"Come on, Darren, no one believes that. They're kids. They're frightened and they got a big imagination."

"Doesn't mean it's not true."

The other men frowned but once again deigned not to argue.

"I heard the O'Gradys have marital problems," the man at the bar said next.

Ruddy-Face tried his cold stare on him. He was large, barrel-chested and thick-armed even now, from a lifetime of work. The man at the bar was not impressed. Old men like Ruddy-Face didn't engage in bar fights. They used their age and position to shame their opponents into silence. Well, he'd finally met his match. The man at the bar had no shame.

"I'm just saying what I heard," he said evenly.

Ruddy-Face took a step forward. One of his companions caught his arm.

"Leave him alone, Darren. Man's got a right to his opinion."

"Last summer," Ruddy-Face said in a clipped voice,

"I drove to Bakersville for the weekly auction. Damn if I didn't blow out a tire on my trailer and nearly kill us all. Shep O'Grady was passing by in his patrol car, his son sitting in the passenger seat. They pulled over and helped me out. And Danny didn't just sit there. He got out of the car, helped line up the spare, and worked on tightening the lug nuts like a fine young man. When I thanked them both, he told me, no problem, sir, and shook my hand. I don't know what happened in that school. But I wouldn't be too quick to judge a boy, or two parents, the rest of you have never met."

The man at the bar said, "Really, that's interesting. 'Cause I heard Danny O'Grady has a nasty temper. Hangs out with the wrong crowd, trashed his own locker. My client has a son at Bakersville K-through-eight, and he said everyone knew Danny O'Grady was not right in the head."

Ruddy-Face drew his bushy white brows into a thick, thunderous glare. His friend once more caught his arm.

"Face it," his friend said in a placating voice. "Tragedies like this aren't meant to make sense. Makes me wonder sometimes if each generation don't need a war, simply to have a way to vent."

"You think war makes for better youths?" Ruddy-Face asked incredulously.

The friend shrugged. "I remember shooting up Germans and Koreans, but never our schools."

"That's a load of horseshit, Edgar."

"I'm just saying—"

"Drug addictions and double amputees, that's what you're saying. Yeah, war works wonders for young men."

"Well, what do you think is going on, Darren? These shootings keep happening! Jee-sus, how many has it been now!"

All the men fell silent, even the one at the bar, who was fighting not to grin.

Ruddy-Face said shortly, "I guess we'll just have to see what happens."

Edgar snorted. "If anything happens. Bakersville doesn't even have a sheriff anymore. I hear that woman's in charge."

"Officer Lorraine Conner," the man at the bar said, and the bartender eyed him curiously.

Edgar nodded. "Yeah, that's right. She's taken over the case, and God knows she's barely old enough to vote."

"They also brought in a fed," the man at the bar offered. "Some expert in school shootings."

"The feds got an expert in school shootings?" The bartender spoke up for the first time.

The man grinned at him. "Interesting, isn't it?" he said. "Now we just have to find out if the man is any good."

EIGHT P.M. THE STREETS of Bakersville had descended into dusky shades of gray, and Rainie's mood had grown tense.

After speaking with Principal VanderZanden, Rainie and Quincy had paid a visit to Melissa Avalon's tiny apartment, hoping to learn more about her life. By all appearances, Melissa Avalon was specifically targeted in the shooting. Perhaps she'd even been the only intended victim, and Rainie was having a hard time believing Danny O'Grady would purposely shoot the one teacher who'd been kind to him. Which raised the question of who Melissa Avalon was and, better yet, who might have wanted her dead. After hearing Quincy's suspicion of an Avalon-VanderZanden romance, Rainie was starting to lean in the principal's direction. Or maybe his betrayed wife . . .

Quincy, on the other hand, wasn't convinced of anything yet. He seemed to buy Melissa Avalon as the primary target, but he didn't think that meant the shooter had to know her. He'd murmured something about plenty of strangers having murdered plenty of young pretty women simply for being young pretty women. Rainie really didn't want to know what the agent read at night.

Unfortunately, Sanders had halted their investigation cold by getting to Avalon's apartment first. Drawers were rifled, the kitchen dismantled, the bed ripped apart. The crime-scene technicians had even pawed through the woman's tampons.

Rainie would have to wait for the state's report on the evidence or beg Sanders for information about her own damn case. It didn't leave her feeling amused.

She had stormed back to the task-force center with Quincy just in time to meet Luke Hayes and Deputy Tom Dawson. They had hoped to interview Becky O'Grady before dinner. They had failed. Avery Johnson had been at Shep's house. He had demanded to be present for the interview, and Sandy and Shep had insisted on sitting in as well. That had put an eight-year-old witness in a tiny family room with five scrutinizing adults.

Becky did the logical thing. She held her stuffed bear tight, curled up in a ball on the sofa, and fell asleep.

After fifteen minutes Luke and Tom headed for the door. Shep didn't see them out. The lawyer took care of that, after informing the officers that the O'Gradys would be changing to an unlisted number immediately due to harassing calls. Also, he wanted patrols to guard the family's safety. Hadn't they seen what some hostile redneck had written on the O'Gradys' garage?

The graffiti had really bothered Luke. He took two Polaroids for their files. Then he drove straight to the hardware store, where he purchased one bucket of primer and one bucket of white paint. He and Tom had spent the last hour personally repainting Shep's garage. Neither Shep nor Sandy ever came out to thank them.

Rainie didn't know what to say. Tragedies brought out the best in towns. But they could also bring out the worst.

Luke and Tom had no sooner left than the mayor paid Rainie a visit. He'd just received a call from Sally Walker's parents. What was this about the autopsies being pushed back until the next day? Why couldn't the families get their daughters' remains back so they could get on with the funerals? The parents were furious.

Also, had Rainie managed to catch George Walker on the five o'clock news? That's right. The father had appeared on camera stating to anyone who would listen that Danny O'Grady was getting away with murder. He'd killed three people, and the Bakersville sheriff's department would never go after him because he was Shep's son. Favoritism plain and simple, so all you mothers out there had better round up your children and lock the doors. One day soon, Danny O'Grady would be back in town.

All afternoon long there had been a run on rifles at the sporting-goods store. Not just in Bakersville but also in neighboring Cabot County.

People were frightened, the mayor stated bluntly. People were angry. So Rainie had better wrap this case up quick. Or there would be a hell of a lot more violence in these small-town streets.

Right after the mayor left, Rainie got out a new box of number-two pencils. She sat across the sawhorse desk from Quincy and methodically broke every single one in half. Then she broke the halves in half. Then she composed her thoughts.

It did her no good. Day two of the investigation and she had nothing but a longer list of questions. Why had Danny shot the one teacher who had apparently been trying to help him? Had Charlie Kenyon influenced Danny to act? Or maybe someone Danny met on-line? It seemed far-fetched to think that a stranger could influence a teenager to kill, but by all accounts Danny was a vulnerable kid and, God knows, stranger things had happened.

The single, small-caliber shot to Melissa Avalon's forehead. The scattered wounds on the others.

It seemed as if she ought to know more by now, but instead she had no answers, and she had worked herself into a state where the mere sound of Quincy's pen scratching against paper made her want to grab his notebook and beat him over the head with it. He'd laughed when she broke the pencils in half. The fed guys never knew how to have any fun.

He wasn't so bad, really. Cool in his detached FBI sort of way. Curious in how he kept staring at his cell phone, as if he was both expecting an important call and dreading it. And intense. More intense than she would've guessed this morning.

There was something about the way he had moved through the scene at the school, something about the way he had meticulously picked through Melissa Avalon's ravaged apartment, as if every bit of information was going into his brain and by sheer force of will he'd make the pieces fit. She had the impression that Quincy might be a little bit bright, and a little bit serious, and a little bit *strong*. That made her stomach tighten, which was something she needed right now about as much as a hole in her head.

Damn FBI agent. Damn state detective looking to prove a point. Damn Danny O'Grady. And damn a bunch of drunken fools who'd decided the only answer to violence was more violence. Christ, didn't they know how much paperwork they were going to cause her?

Rainie glanced away from the window and the night descending upon Bakersville's streets. She looked down at her new sawhorse desk, found that her hands were still fisted at her sides, and knew that her jumbled thoughts were all just noise. She could handle an FBI agent and a state detective. She honestly didn't give a rat's ass about what the mayor wanted for some press conference, and she wasn't afraid of a few local boys full of too much beer and not enough common sense; she'd dealt with that before.

What she didn't know, what she genuinely feared, was tomorrow morning at five A.M., when she would drive to Portland to watch the chief medical examiner cut open two little girls.

The thought of it unnerved her. She didn't want to see Sally and Alice again. Not now, when she knew their names and their families and that they had been best friends from birth. She didn't want to think of their final walk down that hall or the single cemetery plot that would now hold twin coffins.

Last night, for the first time in over five years, Rainie had dreamed of her mother's death. The blood and brains on the wall. The smell, the godawful stench of seeping human fluids and fresh gunpowder settling into the carpet. The headless body slumped on the floor, looking so strange and alien Rainie wouldn't have known it was her mother except for the bottle of Jim Beam still clutched in her lifeless hand.

And as she'd been staring, seventeen years old again, gray matter dripping down onto her hair, Danny O'Grady had come walking out of the kitchen and calmly handed her the smoking shotgun.

"I only did what you wanted done," he'd said, then exited out her front door.

Rainie had woken up in a cold sweat at four in the morning, shivering uncontrollably. She forced herself to walk into the tiny living area, where the brown carpet and gold-flowered wallpaper had long ago been replaced. She studied every single aspect of the room—new, modern, fourteen years later—and she could've sworn she saw blood on the ceiling.

Rainie went back to bed, but she knew from the trembles in her hands when she woke up an hour later that her dreams had still been unkind.

This case was getting to her. She hadn't expected that after all these years. It frightened her. And it made her mad.

"I want dinner," she stated abruptly, standing up at the crude desk and beginning to gather her things.

Quincy looked up from his notebook. His expression was mild, but he'd discarded his jacket, rolled up his sleeves, and loosened his burgundy tie. It made him look more approachable. It also emphasized the dark circles beneath his eyes. Apparently, superagent hadn't been sleeping much even before arriving in Bakersville.

"They have food in this town?" he asked with feigned surprise. "And here I'd thought we skipped lunch out of necessity."

"Lunch is for sissies," Rainie said. "Come on. I'll take you to Martha's Diner. Best chicken-fried steak in town."

Quincy raised a skeptical brow, maybe questioning Martha's claim to fame, maybe already anticipating his arteries hardening. Either way, he grabbed his navy blue jacket and followed.

Martha's Diner was quiet at this hour. Most working folks had already eaten, and most farmers would soon be in bed. Nothing like several thousand cows to ruin a town's nightlife. Rainie recognized the credit union's president, Donald Leyden, eating alone after his divorce. Then Rainie spotted Abe Sanders.

Sitting alone in a corner booth, Sanders was holding his cell phone with one hand while picking at a skinless chicken breast with the other. In between comments on the phone, he chewed raw carrots from a Ziploc bag. Then Rainie noticed the Tupperware container of lettuce. The state detective traveled with salad. If she hadn't known before, she definitely knew now—Abe Sanders was the Antichrist.

"Yes, I hear the puppy," he was saying with some exasperation into the cell phone. "No, Sara, you don't need to put him on the phone. No, no. Hey—" His voice suddenly changed to a higher pitch. "Hi there, Murphy. Yes, you're a good dog. You're such a good dog. Now put your mom back on the phone. Really, put your mom—Sara. Sara, there you are. Yeah, yeah, I said hi, but he's a dog, for chrissakes. He doesn't understand the modern miracle of AT&T.

"Wait a minute. Is he whimpering now? Why is the puppy whimpering? What happened? What? Really?" Sanders sounded surprised, then sheepishly pleased. "Murphy goes around the house each morning looking for me? He misses me. Huh. I'll be damned. He really is a smart little guy."

Sanders finally noticed Rainie and Quincy staring at him.

He sat up quickly, looking caught red-handed, and hastily said good-bye. He was still blushing when he snapped shut his flip phone.

"New puppy," he muttered. "My wife . . . she's kind of nuts about the thing. You know how it is." He swallowed, then nodded toward the empty side of the booth. "Want to have a seat? I got some news."

Rainie already felt wary, but she slid into the red vinyl booth while introducing Quincy to Sanders. The two had obviously heard of each other, and the handshake was perfunctory.

"So what brings you to Bakersville?" Sanders asked after Quincy blew off Rainie's suggestion of chicken-fried steak and ordered a Caesar salad. Rainie shook her head to let him know he was making a mistake, then ordered the steak, mashed potatoes, and an extra helping of gravy. She hadn't eaten all day, and she'd be damned before she was shamed by two men into eating salad. She was still trying to decide if a chocolate malt would be overkill, when Quincy answered.

"I'm researching school shootings for the Behavioral Science Unit. Naturally I'm interested in this case."

"You're observing?"

Quincy looked at Rainie. "Something like that."

"We don't need federal help," Sanders said bluntly.

Quincy smiled. "Don't worry, Detective. I wouldn't dream of stepping on Officer Conner's toes by claiming jurisdiction over the case. I hear she has very strong feelings on the subject—and that she's very good with her sidearm."

Rainie grinned at the unexpected compliment. Sanders scowled.

"Well," the state man said briskly, wiping his hands on his napkin, "the whole thing will probably be moot by morning. As a matter of fact, I'm pretty sure I wrapped up the majority of the case today."

"Really?" Rainie gave him a dubious glance. "And here I thought I'd destroyed the case just this morning."

"Sometimes the evidence comes together in spite of an officer's best intentions," Sanders assured her.

"I'll remember that. What new evidence?"

"Oh, didn't I tell you?" Sanders feigned surprise. "Got some info back from ATF today. Tracing Danny's .38 revolver and .22 semiauto was simple. Both registered to one Shep O'Grady. Furthermore, the CSU recovered five .38-caliber slugs from the area of incidence last night. Today the ME confirmed that blood and fiber on the slugs are consistent with the two juvenile DOAs, and—drum roll here—ballistics determined that rifling on the slugs matches Danny's revolver. You were right, Conner, we got at least one of the murder weapons."

"So the .38 was used to kill the two little girls," Rainie said with a frown. "That still doesn't prove Danny was the one who pulled the trigger."

"Yeah, but we also got Danny's prints on all the casings recovered at the scene. A good lawyer will still argue that only proves Danny loaded the guns, not that he fired them, but at this point the circumstantial evidence is overwhelming. We can tie Danny to the murder weapon. He has no alibi for the time of the shooting, and we have a witness—you—who places him in the school immediately after the shootings, holding his father hostage. Even if we can't get his confession entered into evidence, I think we have enough for a jury to connect the dots."

"What about Melissa Avalon? So far, the evidence ties him only to the girls."

"Don't know about Avalon yet. It appears she was shot once in the forehead with the .22 semiauto. No exit wound, of course, so we have to wait for the ME to retrieve the slug during tomorrow's autopsy. Cases like this generally aren't promising, though. Twenty-two-caliber slugs are only forty grains and made out of soft lead. Most of the time they're too deformed from ricocheting around the skull to yield any rifling marks. We'll have to see. On the other hand, I learned some dirt today when I got my hair cut. According to the rumor mill, Avalon and the principal were really tight . . . if you know what I mean."

"Big deal," Rainie said. "Quincy figured that out after a ten-minute chat with the principal. Go, fed."

Quincy shrugged modestly. Sanders looked chagrined. "You knew he was stepping out on his wife?"

"His reaction to Miss Avalon's death seemed overly intense for the circumstances."

"Huh." Sanders scowled, grabbed a fresh carrot stick, and then recovered. "It doesn't matter to the investigation," he said firmly. "I checked with the administrative staff, and Principal VanderZanden was in his office when the shots were fired. From what I can tell, Danny is the only one unaccounted for at the time. Something else to put in our reports."

"There are still the students who were absent yesterday to consider," Rainie said.

"Twenty-one students out sick," Sanders reported. "Sixteen already have alibis in the form of anxious parents. I bet you the other five are cleared by tomorrow afternoon."

"What about the computers?" Quincy asked. "Principal VanderZanden said Danny spent a great deal of time on-line. I'm curious about that."

Sanders looked at him shrewdly. "You're thinking outside influence," he said.

"It's been a factor in several of the shootings. And I

am surprised by Danny's sophistication in breaking in to what I would presume to be a state-of-the-art gun safe."

Sanders grunted. "Don't know enough yet about the gun safe to determine how hard he had to work to get into it. I do know Shep had a helluva gun collection. We're lucky Danny went with two small handguns instead of the rifles. God knows what kind of damage he could've done then."

"Do we know why he chose the .38 and .22?" Quincy asked.

Sanders looked at Rainie. She shook her head. "He didn't comment and I didn't think to ask. I guess I assumed because they were easier to fit into a backpack. Concealment."

"But Danny was a hunter, wasn't he?" Quincy asked.

"Sure. Since he was very young."

"Did he spend a lot of time with handguns as well?"

Rainie had to think about it. In the meantime, their dinners arrived. Quincy's salad looked fresh and crisp—the advantage of being in farm country. Rainie's chicken-fried steak, on the other hand, was smothered in thick gravy, with a pat of butter melting on top. The smell made her stomach growl, but when she picked up her fork, she discovered that the conversation had already destroyed her appetite.

"Shep generally tells hunting stories," she said after a moment. "I know Danny has some marksmanship awards, but I think they were with a .22 rifle."

"First place, junior division," Sanders confirmed. "We seized the trophy from his bedroom."

Rainie grimaced. She didn't want to think what it must have been like for Sandy and Shep to watch their son's room be boxed up by Crime Scene Unit personnel. Or what kind of impression that must have made on Becky.

Quincy was talking. "So Danny's most comfortable with a rifle but selects two handguns. He has a love-hate relationship with sports but goes after the teacher of the computer lab, whom he supposedly adores. He hides in a room so nobody will see him but never leaves the building after the shooting. Interesting." He turned to Sanders again. "About the school computers . . ."

"Techies are examining them now," Sanders said. "Looks like a main computer and three workstations. The school had a firewall server, so the good news is that it probably has a record of which workstation visited which Internet sites at what time. In theory, the lab rats will have a complete rundown for me of all the sites visited by the end of the week. I did get a call this afternoon saying that the computers have been messed with—the cache file purged, the Web browser's history file deleted, et cetera—so it appears that someone made an effort to cover their tracks. The techies weren't too concerned. Something about probably being able to find things in the cookies, or God knows what. They were going to start work on it in the morning."

"If there are any problems, we have excellent recovery agents at the Bureau," Quincy mentioned casually.

"Yeah, yeah, yeah." Sanders definitely had no intention of parting with his evidence. He waved his hand dismissively. "I'm sure we'll be fine. We already got a lot of evidence in place. At this point, the computer stuff will just go to state of mind."

"We don't have anything connecting Danny to Melissa Avalon," Rainie pointed out.

"Then the DA just pursues the charges for killing the girls. That's fine by me. There are only so many consecutive life sentences a man can serve."

"A boy can serve," Rainie said absently, giving up on her dinner altogether and stealing a piece of Quincy's lettuce. "Only so many consecutive life sentences a boy can serve."

Sanders rolled his eyes. "Like age has anything to do with it these days. We're about to be overrun by an entire generation of juvenile psychopaths. Isn't that right, Quincy? Dual-income families have turned out a batch of superpredators who have no sympathy or remorse. Blast 'em up on Nintendo; blast 'em up on the streets. Murder pregnant women; run home to watch Bugs Bunny on TV. *The New York Times* ran a whole article on it."

"I wouldn't believe everything you read," Quincy said.

"Why not? I read that article in the early nineties and we've had how many school shootings since then?"

"Half a dozen, I'm sure," Quincy said mildly, "but we still had one of the safest school years on record in 1998."

Sanders gave Quincy a dubious look. The FBI agent returned it levelly. "In the 1992–1993 school year," Quincy said, "a time frame I'm sure that article quoted, there were fifty-five fatalities. As you point out, however, this is before we experienced the rash of school shootings. In the 1997–1998 school year, we saw three school shootings. And yet, total fatalities for that year were only forty, nearly a thirty-percent decline. The truth is, violence in schools is a lot like airline crashes—tragic and shocking and headline-grabbing, but by no means indicative of the whole sector. Children are still safer at school—and in planes—than in the family's minivan."

"But then again, these incidents aren't magically going away," Rainie countered. She stole a crouton from Quincy's salad and gave him her own version of his hard, direct stare. "In the beginning, maybe you could dismiss this as a phase, but it's been years now. One shooting is scary. Seven are downright terrifying."

"We face troubling issues," Quincy agreed, "but we shouldn't lose perspective. Overall juvenile criminal offenses have declined in the last five years. And as we've cracked down on drugs and gangs, schools have become safer. That's the good news.

"On the other hand," he added as he saw their growing skepticism, "*some* teenagers are shockingly violent and lacking in remorse. And, unfortunately, the media distorts that fact. *Normal Boy Kills Ten. Perfect Family Murdered by Fourteen-Year-Old Son.* It leads us to rampant paranoia and, if we're not careful, fear of all children. The truth, however, is that the overwhelming majority of children who commit these shootings aren't, quote unquote, normal. Several have suffered from recognized mental disorders and were supposed to be on medication. Even the ones who weren't under a doctor's care probably had a strong degree of attachment disorder, making it easier for them to contemplate murder."

"What's attachment disorder?" Sanders asked.

"It's the failure to bond," Rainie said instantly, then shrugged and helped herself to more of Quincy's salad. "I studied psychology in college. I remember a thing or two."

"Very good," Quincy assured her, then frowned and pulled his salad protectively to him. She stole another crouton. He gave up.

"Everyone needs to bond," Quincy explained to Sanders. "In theory, as children we bond with our parents. We cry, our parents respond to our cry by feeding us, and we decide our parents are good people and love us—we bond. As we grow older, this bond extends to the rest of society, helping us be good friends, neighbors, husbands, et cetera. Unfortunately, not all children form bonds. The baby cries and is hit. In that case, instead of learning to trust or care about others, the child becomes egocentric, lying compulsively, manipulating others, being incapable of feeling empathy. For the most part, we see this phenomenon in abused or abandoned children. Lack of bonding, however, can happen in 'good' households too. It's just not as common."

"Good parents have bad kids?" Sanders asked, and rolled his eyes to show his opinion. Quincy wasn't fazed.

"Absolutely. A mother suffers from severe postpartum depression and is unable to meet her infant's needs. Or the newborn suffers from a painful medical condition and it's not in his mother's power to meet his needs. Or the newborn simply isn't amenable to bonding. No matter how hard the mother tries, the baby pulls away. It's rare, but it happens. So yes, good parents can end up with one child who is very social and one child who is very antisocial."

Sanders gave Quincy another dubious look. "I don't buy it," he said bluntly. "You're saying these kids are little freaking psychopaths from birth. Well, if that's the case, why doesn't anyone notice? Why do all the headlines read *Normal Boy Kills Ten*?"

"Think Ted Bundy," Rainie offered conversationally. "Everyone thought he was a handsome, charming man. Only problem was that he raped and murdered young girls as a hobby. Oops."

"Exactly," Quincy said, and gave her an approving nod. Rainie found herself smiling back. The fed had warm blue eyes when he smiled like that—dazzling, Paul Newman eyes.

"Still sounds like psychobabble to me," Sanders was harrumphing. "The kids are murderers. End of story. The best solution is to lock them up and throw away the key."

"Age doesn't matter?" Quincy asked mildly. He was still looking at Rainie. Belatedly, they both returned their attention to the salad.

"Nope," Sanders said. "If the kid is capable of doing the act, he's capable of paying the price."

Quincy shrugged, obviously less convinced. He stabbed another bite of salad, then surprised both Rainie and Sanders by saying, "Maybe. God knows I've seen some things." He paused. "Some kids are dangerous," he said finally, more forcefully. "Some of the youths I've interviewed probably are beyond all help, let alone our ability to imagine. But not all of them are like that. And our legal system is based on the philosophy that we'd let a hundred guilty men go free before sending one innocent man away. It seems clear to me, then, that we have an obligation to try to identify which youths are amenable to rehabilitation. Not to simply lump all offenders together, then ship them out of sight."

"Can you really help a kid who's committed murder?" Rainie asked curiously.

"Sometimes. The younger the child is, the better the chances. Also, attachment disorder is a range. Some of the kids I've interviewed represented the extreme end of the spectrum. To put it in Sanders's terms, they are 'little freaking psychopaths.' And I'll agree with him there— it's safer for us all to lock those ones up and throw away the key." Quincy smiled dryly at the state detective. Then his voice dropped. He appeared more somber. "However, that's not the case for all of our teenage offenders. As we discussed before, Officer Conner, mass murderers are not homogeneous. Some of the school shooters were definitely more followers than leaders. They were troubled, they were vulnerable. They let themselves be manipulated into performing a violent act, because they were hurt and disturbed and didn't know how to deal with that. They did what they did, but afterward they also felt remorse and regret. I think these kids probably could be reformed. Given their ages, it seems a shame not to try."

"And if we're wrong and they kill again?" Sanders quizzed. "You gonna be the one visiting the family's home to tell them how your failed science experiment murdered their wife, sister, mother? You gonna be the one on TV trying to explain why we thought it was such a great idea to let a known killer loose on society?"

Quincy gave him a faint smile. "It happens. Some of our more prolific serial killers—Kempner, for example—are graduates of the juvenile system. Killed young. Were sentenced to rehabilitation. Came of age. Killed even more people."

"At times like this, I'm glad I don't have a kid," Sanders said.

Quincy finally sighed. He set down his fork and seemed to lose interest once and for all in the salad. "Things are becoming more complicated," he murmured. "Do you know we're now using our serial-killer profiling techniques in high schools?"

Rainie arched a brow. Sanders exclaimed more eloquently, "You're shitting me."

"I shit you not, Detective. In the wake of the recent shootings, several school districts have implemented 'student profiling.' School administrators have a checklist of 'suspicious' behavior to use to evaluate each student's potential for violence. Things like animal cruelty, abusive language, writings containing graphic violence. A few of our agents are now teaching classes in behavioral science and psychological profiling to teachers."

"What happens if a student is profiled as potentially dangerous?" Rainie asked with a frown. "Do they call the cops, pat him down, and confiscate his video games?"

"Most districts have a policy to notify the parents, then the student can be sent to counselors or be expelled. It's being taken quite seriously."

"So were the Salem witch trials."

"Yes, but the witches never killed thirteen people. Schools are under pressure. Three years ago Principal VanderZanden rejected the notion that a shooting could happen here. How much do you want to bet he's regretting it now? And if the school board hears of profiling next week, how much do you want to bet your teachers will be searching for future homicidal maniacs in between grading papers?"

They all grew silent. Sanders shook his head. "Man, I could not be a teacher," he said vehemently. "I see two to four homicides a week, nice fresh kills, and still the thought of what's going on inside the classroom scares me to death. Half of these teachers are being bullied and harassed by their own students, and now they're supposed to actively wonder which little boys are cold-blooded killing machines. Yeah, they'll sleep well at night."

Rainie shrugged. "Teachers should be used to it by now. When was the last time the PTA called for better parenting? It's always the school's fault. No matter what happens, my God, why aren't schools doing a better job of raising our kids?"

Quincy smiled dryly. "Spoken as two people who don't have children."

"I wonder what did it for Danny O'Grady," Sanders mused out loud. "He doesn't seem so different from the other school shooters to me. Bit of a loner, spends all his time in a computer lab, and can't cut it on the football field. I haven't found a teacher yet who knows of any close friends. Then you throw in the fact that his father seems to have a God complex, his parents are fighting all the time, and little Danny pretty much cut his teeth on a hunting rifle. . . . Hell, maybe profiling would've saved the school from him. Seems like it was only a matter of time."

Quincy shook his head. "I don't think profiling would've identified Danny O'Grady. He was a good student, polite with his teachers, diligent in his studies. We've heard no stories of torturing pets and not even a fascination with fire. Danny is angry. But there's still no evidence that he's homicidal."

"Oh, the kid did the deed," Sanders said confidently. "Conner caught him red-handed with the murder weapons, and he's confessed twice. Case closed. Now we just got to wrap everything up before this whole frigging town explodes. Redneck assholes. There oughtta be an IQ requirement for owning a gun."

Rainie didn't say anything. It was after nine-thirty, the diner was nearly empty, and in spite of Sanders's big words, they all appeared pensive.

"Food for thought," Quincy said in the hushed solitude of the restaurant, wiping his hands on his paper napkin and getting ready to stand. "All of the school shooters craved notoriety. They walked openly into their schools and pulled out their guns in plain sight. They wanted their classmates to know it was them. They wanted full recognition of their vengeance. But Danny O'Grady managed not to be seen by a single person. In fact, one of the teachers claimed the shots were fired from within the computer lab, as if the killer was deliberately seeking to remain unnoticed."

"He panicked, he was scared," Sanders said.

"Second thought. School shootings are about displaced rage. Now, by all accounts, Danny has a domineering, intimidating father. I imagine he does have some displaced anger. So why didn't he target the football coach, a macho man like his father, or star athletes, who would represent the kind of boy his father wants him to be, or the school principal, a classic father figure? Why would he deliberately seek out Melissa Avalon—young, female, and an expert at the subject he loved the most? What about her would incite his rage?"

"Maybe he developed a crush on her. She refused his attentions and he snapped."

"Third thought. Most shooters go after as many victims as possible. Overkill and inciting terror in their peers is part of their fantasy. They want to feel powerful. So why did Danny wait until after lunch, when everyone was back in their classrooms? And why choose smaller handguns when he's comfortable with rifles and they'd inflict more damage?"

"Maybe it wasn't a real school shooting," Sanders said with a scowl. "Maybe he just wanted to get back at Miss Avalon because she hurt his feelings or looked at him the wrong way and it was more than he could take. So he snaps, plots his revenge against her, and the other two girls simply get in the way."

"Not a bad theory, Detective, but you have one problem."

"What?"

"You can't tie him to Melissa Avalon's death. You're

saying that she's what this was all about, and yet she's the one victim you can't prove he killed. How do you explain that?"

Sanders finally spluttered to a halt. He was wide-eyed and thinking hard.

Quincy's lips curved into an ironic half smile. "I don't know what happened yesterday afternoon in that school, Detective, but I think there's more to it than meets the eye. We need to keep our minds open at this point. And we need to know what's in those computers. Especially after what your technicians said."

"What did my technicians say?"

"That somebody tried to erase the Web browser history and cache files. You don't erase what isn't important."

"Shit," Sanders said.

Quincy smiled again, but the shadows were darker around his eyes.

They all rose from the table. Rainie reached for money, but Sanders surprised her by picking up the tab.

Then they were outside, where the night air smelled of pine needles and fresh spring rain. No one had anything more to say. Sanders walked back to his car. Rainie and Quincy remained standing alone. She studied his face again, his blue eyes that could be both warm and hard. She wondered if he was right about Danny, and the fact they still knew so little frustrated her.

She wanted answers for her community. She wanted answers for Shep and Sandy. She wanted answers for herself, so she could finally get visions of the school out of her head and the night would stop closing in on her.

The fed was watching her, the look on his face hard to read. She studied his hands again. Those hard-earned calluses. The absent wedding ring.

"I need somewhere to sleep," Quincy said at last.

She said, "I know just the place."

THIRTEEN

Wednesday, May 16, 10:03 P.M.

GINNIE'S MOTEL HOTEL wasn't seedy. The mattresses were twenty years old and the scarred maple dressers had been picked up at garage sales, but the flowered curtains were hand-sewn, the worn white sheets freshly laundered, and the rugs vacuumed vigorously each day.

Ginnie ran the front desk, her gray hair in pink sponge curlers and her massive frame covered by a dark blue muumuu with an orange-flowered print. She explained to Quincy that she had opened the Motel Hotel ten years ago when her fourth husband, George, had passed away. After so many years of taking care of men, she'd decided to run a business where she could have a new man over every night. She winked flirtatiously when she said this. Quincy hoped she was joking.

Ginnie went through her spiel. She served home-made muffins every morning, Toll House cookies every night. She'd wash your laundry for two bucks a load; please leave the dirty clothes piled by the front door. Finally, the Motel Hotel was not as rustic as it seemed. She'd installed state-of-the-art data lines so she could check her stock portfolio every hour on-line.

She slapped a laminated list of access numbers for

local Internet providers on top of the desk. Then she invited Quincy to visit her site at BigMama.com.

Rainie suppressed a smile. Quincy began to back away slowly from the muumuu. Moments later he and Rainie were in the parking lot, where the tiny string of rooms spread out in a pink-painted V.

"Where the hell have you brought me?" Quincy asked Rainie as he found his door and fumbled with the key.

"Local color," Rainie told him. "Only tourists stay at the Motel 6."

"Can't I be a federal tourist?"

"Of course not. Ginnie knows the best gossip in Bakersville—after Walt, of course. Show up for breakfast tomorrow morning. Down a few bran muffins. You'll be amazed how much you'll learn."

"And how clean my colon will be," Quincy muttered, and shoved the old door open.

Inside, Rainie watched as Quincy set his duffel bag on the single queen-size bed, placed his computer beneath the pine table, and identified the location of the phone jack. She imagined that she was observing a ritual the agent had performed in hundreds of hotel rooms in hundreds of small towns. He checked the closet, grabbing the extra pillow for the bed, then hung his jacket neatly on the back of a chair. Next he entered the tiny bathroom, inspecting the stock of soap and shampoo. Finally he returned to the front of the room, studying the window and the door locks.

A single curved latch, which appeared older than dirt, held the window shut. Quincy grimaced. The door cheered him up about as much. One chain, easily snapped. One bolt lock that could be jimmied by a two-year-old. He shook his head.

"Is anyone around here aware of basic safety?"

"And spoil our small-town charm? The city council would never hear of it. Besides, what kind of idiot robs a fed?"

"I'm going to need a broom handle to jam this

window," he said seriously. "And a chair to stick under the door."

"Don't you carry a gun, SupSpAg?"

"Yes, but requisitioning sticks involves less paper-work."

Quincy went outside, found a suitable twig to jam the lower window casing, and jury-rigged the room the best he could. Apparently, he did take safety seriously. Then again Rainie had caught a glimpse of the photos he carried in his computer bag. She supposed if she did nothing but stare at murder victims all day, she would be obsessed with bolt locks and window guards as well.

Finally, Quincy dusted off his hands. He'd done all he could do with his accommodations. Now his gaze drifted to the phone. Rainie watched him quickly look away. Unfortunately, there was little else in the room to hold his attention. Ginnie didn't believe in TV.

The night was thick outside. The room filled with shadows. Nothing left to do but say good night and hope they didn't wake up too many times, dreaming of little boys armed with assault rifles and little girls flee-ing down long, dark hallways.

"Rainie," Quincy said after a moment, "can I buy you a drink?"

Rainie was startled. She hadn't seen the offer com-ing. She stared at him harder and tried to decide what it meant. A drink. Just a drink? With smart, capable Supervisory Special Agent Pierce Quincy. He struck her as the kind of man who lived his life by certain rules. But his gaze was softer now. Not an agent anymore, she thought. A man addressing a woman.

She honestly wasn't sure what to do with that.

She felt restless, edgy. She'd seen too much death, and tomorrow morning she would rise at the crack of dawn to examine it some more. She should be alone. Sit on her back deck, cradle an icy bottle of beer, and listen to the hoot owl mourn. But she wanted to go to a bar. Someplace where the music was loud and the dance floor crowded and all the women were pretty, while all the men had a gleam in their eyes. She could pick a date. She could pick a fight. On nights like this, she wasn't sure which she preferred.

She just knew that sometimes she was her mother's daughter, and she never trusted herself when she was in this kind of mood. *Go home, Rainie. You know the drill.*

She studied Quincy instead. The firm set of his lips. The strong line of his shoulders. That blue, blue gaze of a man who knew what he was about.

Goddamn him.

Thirty minutes later, she'd changed into civvies and they were sitting at a bar.

Tequila's was a happening place. Plank floor covered in peanut shells. Tiny booths covered in scarred brown vinyl. Pitchers of beer that went for a buck fifty on Wednesday nights and all-you-could-eat mozzarella sticks during happy hour. The jukebox belted out country favorites. On the dance floor, half the couples moved easily to the rhythmic steps of line dancing. Deeper in the shadows, other couples moved to other rhythms in perfect time.

Rainie yelled her order for a bottle of Bud Light over the din. Quincy surprised her by ordering the same. He struck her as a Heineken man, but live and learn.

For a while they simply sat, watching the dance floor, absorbing the noise and loosening up until the lessons of Bakersville's K–8, and Danny O'Grady, seemed far away.

"Nice place," Quincy said shortly.

"Fun," Rainie said.

"Come here often?"

"Careful, SupSpAg. Next thing you know, you'll be asking my sign."

Quincy grinned. It was a good look on his face, especially with his shirtsleeves rolled up and his silk tie loosened. He took a long pull from the beer bottle.

"Nice and cold," he said. "How's yours?"

"Don't know. I'm an alcoholic, Quince. Came from an alcoholic mother. Probably had an alcoholic father. I'd know if my mother had sobered up long enough to remember his name."

He gave her a curious look. "We didn't have to come to a bar."

"Not a problem. I've been sober ten years. I know what I'm doing."

"But you still order a beer?"

"Yep. I like holding the bottle in my hand and knowing I can set it down again. It's the sense of power, I'm sure. Plus"—she slipped him a wink—"beer bottles are a goddamn phallic delight."

Quincy burst out laughing. She grinned back at him. She bet he didn't laugh often, which was too bad. He sounded good laughing. He looked good too.

"And you?" she asked, setting down the bottle. "Tell me the truth, SupSpAg, what really brings you to Bakersville?"

"The job, of course. So much crime, so little time."

"Travel a lot?"

"Three or four cities a week. I'm either a federal agent or a rock star."

"Hell on relationships," she said casually.

His lips curved at one corner. She hadn't fooled him. "I was married," he said. "Lasted fifteen years, which was probably seven more than I deserved. I used to carry a photo of her in a silver frame in my briefcase. Every hotel room I stayed in, the first thing I would do was place her picture on the table. Unfortunately, that didn't match her idea of quality time. We divorced. I learned to work without her photo on my desk. And you?"

"I don't do relationships. Have a strict policy against them. I figure if half of the American people are getting divorced, that's good enough for me."

Quincy gave her a skeptical look. She could tell he was trying to evaluate her statement for truth versus bravado. "You're young, intelligent, beautiful. What about starting a family?"

"Oh no. I don't do children. They're small, needy, easily destroyed. Let's be honest. I've come a long way from my family history, but I'm still the child of an abusive alcoholic and we don't make great parent material. For the Conners, the cycle ends here."

"You shouldn't underestimate yourself, Rainie."

"I don't underestimate myself. I'm simply honest."

She watched him take another swig from his beer. He was definitely interested. She could see the light in his eyes. He was reluctant, bemused, but interested. Call her a fool, but it made her smile.

She leaned forward, sweeping her long hair to one side as she prepared to get serious. "So tell me more, Quincy. We're here in a bar, a long way from crime scenes, and you're almost through your first beer. Tell me all the baggage. I like starting with the junk out in the open. It saves time later."

"I don't have interesting baggage."

"Everybody does."

"No, I just have typical law-enforcement stuff. The ex-wife. The two grown children who barely know I exist. Too much dedication to the job, not enough attention at home. The usual mistakes."

"Yeah? So why are you avoiding phones?"

He jerked, caught off guard. Then he gave her a more measured stare. It pleased her to surprise him. She was beginning to realize that with an academic like him, it was a form of flirtation.

"I didn't realize it was that obvious."

"Pierce?"

"Don't call me that. Only my ex-wife uses my first name. Everyone else calls me Quincy, like the medical examiner from the old TV show. Serial killers and their sense of humor," he murmured.

She kept looking at him. He finally set down his beer.

"One of my daughters," he said abruptly, "is in the hospital."

"Is it serious?"

"She's dying. No, that's not true," he corrected himself. "She's dead. She's been dead for four weeks. Twenty-three years old and involved in such a bad automobile accident that the front windshield carries an imprint of her face. I know. I made the police show it to me." He looked off in the distance a moment. Rainie was struck by how haggard he appeared. Then how exhausted.

"Now she lies in a hospital room," he said quietly, "where machines breathe for her and pump her heart and feed her food, while the rest of us sit by her side day after day, desperate for some miracle to save her. Except that her brain is dead and the machines can't fix that. The miracles of science take us so far, and yet not nearly far enough."

"Jesus. Shouldn't you be there?"

"Yes."

"Well, why aren't you?"

"Because if I had to spend one more minute sitting in that room, watching that mockery of human life play out in front of me, I was going to lose my mind." His eyes suddenly glinted with moisture. He brushed it away with the back of his hand and looked at her almost impatiently. "Rainie, my daughter doesn't have a *face* anymore. Her vehicle hit a telephone pole going thirty-five miles per hour without her seat belt on. Do you really want to hear how the force of impact pushes a body not just forward but up in the air? That steering-wheel columns are designed to collapse so they won't crush a person's chest or internal organs, but that they also can't halt all the G forces once they've been unleashed? How the body keeps going forward, keeps going up. How the person's skull now slams into the metal frame of the windshield, which isn't designed to collapse, which isn't designed to give way? And then comes the nose and face, slamming into the windshield, shattering all those bones, while the skull is driven deeper into the person's brain. . . .

"My daughter doesn't have a head anymore. She has a pulpy mass carefully held in place by staples and thread and miles of fluffy white gauze. The only reason she was even put on life support was that the doctors were waiting for permission to harvest her organs. But now she's there, a grotesque doll animated purely by machines, and my ex-wife, Bethie, keeps mistaking that for life, so she won't let go. And I don't think it's right. I don't think there's any . . . dignity . . . in that. And I don't think my younger daughter, Kimberly, should have to sit at her sister's side and listen to her mother and me fight over when to pull the plug. My feelings on the subject are clear. Now it's up to Bethie to figure out when she can let go."

"So you arrived, you gave your expert advice, and you left."

Quincy blinked several times. "You know, you could at least pretend not to see through me," he said at last. "Particularly when you're sober at the time."

He took another swallow of beer, looking as if he needed it now. His bottle was nearly empty. The waitress stopped by to ask him if he wanted a second. He hesitated, his gaze clearly thirsty, but then shook his head.

"Surprised you didn't go to whiskey," Rainie commented.

"I did, for a week. Then I had to give it up due to irony. Amanda was killed by a drunk driver."

"Ah."

"I tried eating. Potato chips, candy bars, Gummy Bears. Anything that came out of a hospital vending machine. But I kept forgetting to chew, and that made things difficult. I resumed jogging. That seems to do the trick. You?"

"Twelve miles, four days a week. Bet I could run you into the ground."

"I'm nearly fifteen years older than you, Rainie. I bet you could run me into the ground."

"Quincy, you're not that old."

The space between them sparked again. He looked away first.

"Now it's your turn," he said abruptly. "Tit for tat."

"All right." She brought up her chin gamely and got a good grip on her Bud Light. "My mom was a drunk. A mean drunk. A promiscuous drunk. Trailer trash, you know the type. She got into a lot of brawls, hung out with men who beat her, and, following the trickle-down theory of family management, returned home to beat me. Except one day when I came home, she'd been decapitated by a shotgun blast to the head. And unfortunately for me, I was the first person at the scene."

"Did Shep O'Grady arrest you?"

"Yep." She shrugged. "I would've arrested me too. The whole town knew what she was doing. Now here she was dead, and I had her brains in my hair. I made a great suspect. But I was the wrong one."

"And who was the right one?"

"Officially, it's still unsolved. Unofficially, they're pretty sure it was her man of the moment. A neighbor saw him at the house right before she heard the gunshot. Maybe it was some kind of lover's quarrel, or maybe he was just too drunk to think straight. My mother didn't exactly date rocket scientists. He was a trucker, I think. They put out an APB, but no one ever saw him again. Just some guy passing through. And now it's been so many years I don't even remember his name." Rainie shrugged again. "Given the way my mother lived, I don't think the story could have ended any other way."

"And for you?" Quincy said quietly. "After all that, I'd think you would've left Bakersville for good."

"I tried. Went to Portland. Enrolled in the university. Got drunk. For four years. Then joined AA. When I finally graduated, I decided I might as well go home, because for all of my running I was ending up in the same place I began. Besides, I like it here. I inherited my mother's house, all paid for, which is good when you're making fifteen grand a year."

"You still live in the house where you grew up?" He gave her a skeptical look.

"I don't mind. It's the deck I like the best anyway." She gave him a funny smile. "Honestly, I like small-town police work. I get to deal with people, not paper. And Bakersville is a good community. We have a lot of nice folks."

"Excluding the neighbors who never said a word about your mother beating you each night. And excluding the neighbors who still believe that you're a murderer."

"Oh, the ones who think I killed my mother don't mind. In their opinion, what goes around comes around."

"But you don't think that, do you, Rainie? And these last two days, staring at Danny O'Grady—that must have been very difficult for you."

She stiffened. Her hands tightened around her Bud Light. "Don't psychoanalyze me."

"I'm not," he said evenly. "I can't help noticing, however, that today you gave an instant explanation of attachment disorder. Combine that with the fact you grew up in an abusive household, in circumstances not that different from those experienced by most violent kids. These issues aren't new to you. You've given it some thought. Long after this case is over, you'll still be giving it some thought."

"Well, at least my interest is personal and not some misplaced hero complex."

She had lashed out reflexively. It did not occur to her just how bitter and vicious she sounded until she saw him wince.

"Touché," he murmured.

Rainie promptly looked down, embarrassed. It was in poor taste to ask a man to share his troubles and then hold them against him. She wanted to be a better person than that, but she knew she wasn't. She had a quick temper and a bristly personality. Apologies came hard to her.

"I don't mean to make you self-conscious," Quincy said quietly.

"Danny bothers me," she said abruptly, before she changed her mind. "I saw his eyes. Trapped. Angry. Confused. I know that stare, and I looked at those bodies and I wondered . . . Everyone says kids can't be that angry, homicidally angry, but I know they can be. Sometimes it's hard not to be. To be young and helpless and defenseless . . ." Her voice broke off. She sat there, holding the rest of the words in and feeling her heart beat against her chest like a trapped bird.

"You worry you could've been Danny O'Grady?" Quincy asked.

She didn't say anything.

"You're not Danny," he said firmly.

"I know that! I'm a woman, and women don't displace rage. We don't become mass murderers or serial killers. We focus our anger instead, going after whoever hurt us, or self-destructing. It doesn't matter, though. That's not what this is about. It's the violence, I think. Because it's a shooting and not an automobile crash or combine accident. I'm not sure. But it's bringing it back. Everything. Like it happened yesterday. And everyone was just so busy wondering that day if I'd killed her or not, no one bothered to ask me how I felt. I'm not sure I even bothered to wonder how I felt. All those times, all those nights, the screaming fits. But she was my mother, and it took so much bleach to get the blood out of the ceiling. I think I scrubbed for days and still you could see the pink stains and she was my *mother,* for God's sake. The only family I had."

"Rainie, are you okay?"

"Yes, fine. Dammit, I need to shut up." He had taken her hand at some point. She didn't remember when, and the fact she hadn't noticed such a thing jolted her. She always noticed when she was touched. All these years later, she was very careful about physical space. She took her hand back, raking it through her hair and discovering that she was more agitated than she'd realized. Quincy was looking at her again with concern. It made her want to laugh flippantly, but that would do no good.

"I'm sorry," she said shortly. "I accuse you of treating me like a patient, then I treat you like a shrink."

"I'm not your therapist," he said evenly. "Let's keep that straight."

"Of course not. I don't need a therapist!"

He raised a brow. She grew more flustered. He took back her hand.

His gaze was reassuring. "Rainie, listen to me. What you're going through is very real. It's called post-traumatic stress syndrome. Fourteen years ago you suffered a major trauma. And even though you've dealt with that trauma on many levels, it still affected you. Now you're going through a similar situation and that's bringing the first one back. It happens to everyone. When the Gulf War happened, the Veterans Administration had to set up hotlines for the Vietnam vets who were suddenly experiencing flashbacks to twenty-year-old firefights. Sadly, every time one of these school shootings happens, it puts all the other families in all the other communities through the wringer again. Flashbacks, nightmares, anxiety attacks. All part of the drill."

"I'm a professional. It's my job. Will attend homicide. Won't bat an eye."

"You're human." His fingers squeezed hers. "You're an intelligent human. Your brain is going to work in spite of you."

"Well, take this brain back. It's stuck on instant replay and I've had enough."

He smiled faintly. "The older the trauma, the sooner it will fade. In the meantime, it might help to talk to someone. Does the sheriff's department provide any mental-health resources?"

"Our department doesn't even provide coffee."

"Perhaps some of the professionals flying in to help the kids."

"Yeah, perhaps." But her tone of voice told them both she'd never go. Seeking out a real professional would be too much like admitting a weakness. She didn't do that anymore.

"It's getting late," Quincy said.

Rainie looked around. The music was dying down and tables had cleared out. He was right; they should both be going. Separate rooms, she knew. She had said too much, and you couldn't hook up for a one-night stand after baring your soul.

She rose on her own. After a moment Quincy followed suit.

"Quincy . . . Sorry about your daughter."

"Thank you. It doesn't help, but it does."

"I know." She hesitated. "I'm also sorry for what I said earlier. The misplaced hero complex. I'm not the best at playing nice with others."

"And here I thought it was part of your charm."

Quincy placed his hand on the small of her back and guided her toward the door.

Outside, the night was cool and Rainie was back to watching him expectantly. His hand still rested on her back. His body was close. She could smell his aftershave, subtle and expensive. She didn't know what it was about him. He was strong, intelligent, sophisticated. She'd never tried finding someone who challenged her. She'd always just gone with the unquestioning young stud, the kind who wouldn't ask too many questions. It was safer.

Now she studied the exposed hollow of Quincy's throat, where a light smattering of dark hair rippled across it. Now she gazed at his other hand with those long, deft fingers. Now she looked up into his face and peering blue eyes that saw too much.

She took an instinctive step back, confused and suddenly spooked. His head had already dropped forward and his lips brushed her cheek.

"I'm not your therapist, Rainie."

"I know."

His lips brushed her other cheek, warm, firm, dry.

"I don't know what I'm doing here. I have policies about these things." His lips fell to the hollow of her neck. Her head had fallen back. She knew better, but she didn't. The kiss was light. It teased her.

"No fraternizing?" she murmured.

He raised his head. "No one-night stands. No passing through. I'm too old for that shit, Rainie. I've been to too many towns, spent too much time studying the worst that men can do. I've tried marriage and I've tried fatherhood and I have all the things I'm proud of in my life and all the things I wish I'd never done. I don't believe in one-night escapism anymore. I don't see the point."

She tried to open her mouth to argue, but he cut her off by brushing his lips over hers. She startled in surprise. He stopped, lingered, his mouth moist, seeking. His hands were splayed across her back. He held her lightly, giving her plenty of room, and that made her both grateful and disappointed.

She had just started to lean forward when he broke off the kiss.

"I'm interested in you, Rainie," he murmured against her ear. "You're not what I expected. You're smart. You're complicated. And I already know you won't go home with me tonight."

"I won't," she whispered.

"You're going to torture yourself with the drive to the ME's office tomorrow. You're going to dream of your mother and dead little girls."

"Don't—"

"I'm not your therapist, Rainie. I'm simply a man who's been there."

His hands fell from her back. He stepped away and

she felt the night intrude bitterly. Her arms grew cold. She shivered as she watched him walk over to his car, but she didn't call him back. She had her own vehicle to drive home. One of her rules. One of her many, many rules designed to keep herself safe.

Supervisory Special Agent Pierce Quincy drove away.

And, after another moment, Rainie went home alone.

FOURTEEN

SHEP WAS WAITING FOR Rainie on her back porch when she got to her house. Judging by the pile of empty beer bottles at his feet, he'd been there a while, and the wait had done nothing to improve his mood.

"Where the hell have you been?" he demanded when she finally walked through the sliding glass door.

Rainie eyed him for a minute. It was late, well past midnight, and she didn't have the patience for this conversation. On the other hand, she supposed she should've seen it coming.

She loosened the cuffs of her worn chambray shirt. "Go home, Shep."

"Aren't you meeting with the ME first thing in the morning? Christ, Rainie, this is a murder investigation. What are you doing running around till the small hours of the morning?"

"I believe I'm acting as primary on the case. Now get the hell off my back deck."

Shep pretended not to hear her. He set down his beer and stood authoritatively, as if he was still acting sheriff. The fact that he swayed on his feet didn't help. Rainie shook her head.

"We gotta talk about this case."

"You're drunk, you're not thinking straight, and if anyone sees you here, George Walker will have even more ammunition to take to the five o'clock news. Suspect's father cavorting with police."

"Danny didn't do it!"

"We got his prints on the casings, Shep."

"Not all of them."

"What the hell does that mean?"

"Oh, Sanders didn't tell you, did he?" Shep got a smug glow in his eyes. He pounded his chest. "I got my own contact at the state crime lab. When I talked to him this afternoon, he told me they'd found prints on the shell casings from the .38 and the .22—except for one .38 casing. A single casing with no smudges, no dirt, no prints. In other words, wiped clean. And get this, there's something odd about the shell casing. My contact couldn't tell me what, but he'd sent it out for further analysis. So there you go. Something's odd about the evidence, Rainie. Something else went down in those halls, and this proves it."

"Oh, Jesus Christ, Shep. Not all shell casings will yield prints and you know it. Now, for the last time, go home."

"One casing wiped clean, Rainie! I'm telling you, someone else was at that scene. This proves it. Maybe Danny helped. Okay, okay? I can see that much. He got the guns, maybe he thought that he was helping a friend. But someone else pulled the trigger. You gotta help me with this, Rainie. You gotta believe me."

"I don't have to do any such thing."

"What does that mean?"

Rainie looked her boss in the eye. She said crisply, "First you appoint me primary, Shep. Not even at the school yet, and you already know something's up. Then there's that whole confrontation with Danny. You get me to discharge my sidearm. You manage to get your prints all over the guns. Thirty seconds later most of the physical evidence is destroyed. And you made sure everyone knew it. Officer Conner screwed up the case. Danny will walk away scot-free. What the hell went down in that hallway, Shep? You want me to help you, you tell me what was really going on that afternoon."

"Rainie, I swear to you—"

"Bullshit! Cut the crap." Her temper went. She was suddenly bone-weary and deeply resentful of Shep. He'd made her part of this tragedy. And now he was on her back deck, begging for her help, after playing her like a fool. How dare he do that to her? Especially when she'd considered him a friend.

"You knew what was going on, Shep. You suspected Danny. *Why?*"

"Don't you yell at me, Lorraine Conner. I may not be on active duty, but I'm still sheriff of this town!"

"What the fuck happened, Shep? What did you do?"

"This is no way to treat me! Didn't I help you out all those years ago? All those questions I could've asked. All those questions that have still never been answered about what went down that day. I never followed up. I let sleeping dogs lie. Now it's your turn to do the same."

"Get off my property!"

"He's my son! Goddammit, Rainie, he's my son. . . ."

Shep's shoulders suddenly convulsed. He stood on her porch, surrounded by half a dozen empty beer bottles, and wept into his hands for his child.

Jesus Christ. Rainie went into her house. She fetched two fresh bottles of beer from the fridge. Back outside, she wordlessly handed one to Shep. The other she cradled in her hands, waiting for that feeling of power, of control. It didn't happen tonight. Jesus Christ.

After a moment Shep pulled himself together. He wiped his face with the sleeve of his shirt. He twisted off the cap of the bottle and downed half the contents in a single swallow. Then he downed the other half.

"How'd you get here, Shep?"

"Drove."

"You're not driving home."

"I know."

They stood in silence. Rainie looked up at the night sky. It was clear following this afternoon's rain. The stars were like pinpricks of silver against black velvet. She loved this kind of night. Perfect for sitting on her deck, listening to the owls and imagining the waves crashing against the rocky shore. The inside of her house might hold all the bad memories of her childhood, but the outside held the few precious things that had been good. The land and the trees and the sky. The knowledge that no matter what happened, she was only a small part of it in the end and the stars would be here long after she was gone and the last tears had dried.

Maybe other people were overwhelmed to think of their tiny size in relation to the cosmos. She was comforted by it.

"I gave Danny the combination for the gun safe," Shep said quietly. "He asked for it two weeks ago, and I gave it to him."

"You went to all the trouble to get a state-of-the-art gun safe and then you gave your child the combination?"

"Sandy's gonna kill me."

"Shep, you're in such a world of hurt."

"I didn't know! Danny said he wanted practice breaking down handguns since he'd already mastered his rifle. Hell, I was happy he was interested. You gotta understand, Rainie, guns are about all Danny and I have left. I tried football—he's just no good. I tried basketball, baseball, soccer. The boy has no athletic ability. He just wants to read or surf the Web or some such garbage. . . . You don't know what it's like to be a father, Rainie, and realize one day that you got the son you always wanted and, somehow, he turned out to be his mother."

"Did you know the pistols were missing?"

Shep was silent, which was answer enough.

"Jesus, how can you be so smart and yet so dumb?"

"Don't you think I just got punished enough?"

"No, I think George Walker got punished enough. I think Alice Bensen's parents got punished enough. Dammit!"

"I didn't *know,* Rainie. Three days ago I checked the safe for the pistols. They still weren't there. So I asked Danny about it. He said he hadn't gotten them back together yet, that was all. The minute he reassembled them, he'd put them in the safe. I didn't think about it again."

"Until you got the call."

"But Danny didn't do it! I swear to you, Rainie, that boy doesn't have a single aggressive bone in his body. Hell, if he was more like me maybe I could imagine it. But he's his mother's son. He wouldn't hurt a fly."

"What did you find when you got to the school, Shep?"

"It's just like I said in my report. When I arrived, the building was already evacuated. Someone said they saw the shooter run from the building. Someone else said there were still wounded kids inside. So I went in. And in the computer lab I found Danny holding the revolver and semiauto—"

"Holding them? Not picking them up. Holding them."

"He'd just picked them up—"

"Shep!"

"All right! He was holding them, dammit. Holding both guns and looking faint. The minute I said his name, he pointed them at my head."

"And that doesn't tell you anything?"

"He was panicked, Rainie! Frightened and, ah hell, he'd been crying. I swear to you, there were tears on his cheeks. For chrissakes, this is Danny. Danny who used to wear your deputy's badge. Danny who liked to play under the desks. Danny who always wanted to sit by you at dinner—"

"Shut up! I don't want to hear it anymore."

Rainie walked away from him. She stood at the edge of her deck, her arms wrapped tight around her middle for warmth. In the distance, she saw a flicker of light, as if the moon had caught a piece of glass. It troubled her, and she was trying to focus in on the source, when the trees rustled abruptly and a large bird took flight.

"If Danny's involved," Shep said from behind her, "it's only because someone else got him into it. He's been . . . troubled lately. And maybe he's impressionable. At thirteen all young boys are impressionable."

"We know about the lockers, Shep. And we know about Charlie Kenyon. The Danny in my mind is a sweet little boy, and just yesterday morning I would've agreed with you, but I'm not sure anymore. There is a lot more to him than meets the eye. And these kids . . . they're always somebody's sons, Shep. They're always somebody's children."

Shep's head fell forward. Rainie had told him the truth with the best of intentions, but she couldn't stand to see him look so defeated.

She offered quietly, "We're trying to learn more from the school computers. Maybe if we can find a record of him talking to someone on-line . . . hooking up with an outside influence . . . I don't know."

"Good, good." Shep's voice had picked up. "That's the thing. Find out who really did all this."

"You really want to know what happened, Shep, let us talk to Danny. The FBI agent, Quincy, he's a trained psychologist and an expert in mass murderers. He'll know how to handle Danny. He'll get to the bottom of this."

"No."

"Shep, you want me to help Danny, but you don't. Make up your mind."

"No interviewing him! He's confused right now. Maybe he even wants to take credit for things—some kids are like that, you know. But I don't want my kid spending the rest of his life in prison because he felt a need to brag."

"What about Becky? She might have seen something—"

"The doctors say she's in shock."

"Quincy's an expert."

"Since when did you start thinking so much of an outsider? Wait a minute. That's where you've been, isn't it? You went out with the fed!"

"Well, tie stones to my feet and drown me in a river."

"That's not funny."

"Shep, if you want answers, give me some help. At least let Quincy interview Becky."

"Our lawyer will never go for it."

"It's not his call."

"I can't. I don't—I gotta talk to Sandy first. Let me talk to Sandy."

"Thank you, Shep," Rainie said seriously. "Sandy has a good head on her shoulders. She'll do the right thing."

Shep, however, didn't look convinced. He said wearily, "I got a son in juvenile detention for murder. I have a daughter sleeping in closets, and I have neighbors spray-painting *Baby Killer* on my garage. The right thing? I don't know what that is anymore. I already heard from the mayor that we're not allowed to attend any of the funerals. He thinks it'll upset people too much. For God's sake, this is my town, Rainie. I know George Walker. I used to bowl with Alice's uncle. Now—now it's come down to *this*."

Rainie didn't say anything. She didn't have the words to comfort him.

"Someone else pulled that trigger," Shep said tiredly, stubbornly. "Mark my words. And you gotta help me prove it, because a state detective and a federal agent aren't going to care. They don't live here. They don't know Danny the way we do. So it's just you and me. The way it was fourteen years ago. Just you and me again."

"You didn't do me any favors fourteen years ago, Shep."

Shep's gaze simply fell to the deck.

Rainie sighed. She moved over to the deck railing and dumped out her bottle of beer. She said what she needed to say, soft, so no one could hear.

Shep didn't pry. He knew better after all these years.

After a moment she turned back to him. "Come on, Shep. I'll drive you home."

CROUCHED BEHIND A DENSE cover of trees, the man finally released his breath. It had been no good. She always ducked her head when she spoke, so even with the binoculars he couldn't see clearly enough. Maybe if he brought a video camera one night. He could record her actions, then play them back for someone who specialized in lip-reading. An expert might be able to see enough.

But that would be sharing. He didn't want to share. Rainie was special. His.

He planned to keep it that way.

The man rocked back on his heels, pursing his lips as he considered his options. His head was buzzing a bit. He'd stayed in the bar long enough to have two beers, even though he shouldn't have. But Ruddy-Face had still been standing there, looking down at him all stern and tough. It had punched buttons better left alone and he'd found he couldn't back down. So he'd stayed, drinking down beer he couldn't taste and feeling that measured, hateful stare.

Then he'd simply started to laugh. The whole thing was too damn funny for words. Old men thinking war would be good for kids. Give 'em a Hitler and they won't have to kill one another.

The man had started to laugh, and he was still laughing when he left the bar, watching old Ruddy-Face shake his head. Fuck Ruddy-Face. Fuck 'em all. If only they knew . . .

The first time the man had picked a town for one of his projects, he hadn't been anxious. More like curious about what he could do. He'd had a vision. It started as a dream late at night, a way to pass the hours when he was alone and no one cared. Then it took over his waking hours. It became an obsession, a fierce, burning need gnawing away at his gut.

Show the old man. Show up the old man. Fucking show up the old fucking man. He'd head out to the cemetery, guzzling hundred-dollar bottles of the fucker's precious brandy and feeling the fury beat like a drum in his veins. *You think I'm weak? You think I'm dumb?*

Well, let me show you. . . .

The first time he'd been very careful. No ties between himself and the community. He'd selected the town by computer, researched it by computer, approached the players by computer. When it had finally been necessary to conduct some on-site activities, he'd worn disguises and used only cash. The three *P*s of a successful mission: Patience, Planning, and Precautions. *See, I was* listening, *you old* fuck.

In the end, it had been easy. Screams and smoke and blood. Beautiful, fantastic death.

Not a tremor in his hand, not a care in the world.

But then it had been over. Police came, investigated, arrested, moved on. Case closed. He returned to everyday life, visited the cemetery again, guzzled another bottle of brandy.

Who's weak now, old man? Who isn't feelin' very smart?

And then . . .

Nothing. Story faded from the news. Town got on with things. People moved on with life. And he was alone again, feeling his power, knowing the things he knew, and . . . bored.

Time for a second strike. Raise the stakes, prove his point, elevate the game.

He picked the next town more carefully, spent longer reconning in the area, studying the rhythms of life. Still lots of patience and planning. Still many, many precautions. Computers were a wonderful tool.

Then one day everything was in place. Screams and smoke and blood. Beautiful, fantastical death. This time he lingered afterward—from a ways away, of course, using binoculars—but still he lingered, adding an extra zing.

Cops arrived on scene. Dull, unimaginative small-town yokels. Saw what he wanted them to see, thought what he wanted them to think. Made their arrest, felt good about themselves.

In fact, everything went so well, the man decided not to go home right away. He hit upon the hotel plan—in a separate city, of course, though frankly he wasn't convinced even that precaution was necessary. He rented a car, drove back into town. Hung out in the local bars and listened to the local folks talk. He had so much fun, he even went to the funerals and watched the mothers cry.

Who's smart now, you old fuck?

Five days later it was all over and done. Reporters packed their bags. Lawyers worked out some deal. He returned to the ordinary world of his "acceptable life," and eventually this film also faded from his mind.

He needed something more. His plans worked, but the thrill was lacking. From what he could tell, he was too smart (*Hear that, old man?*). He could make the cops dance on a pinhead and they'd fucking thank him for the floor space.

He needed a place more challenging, a target more riveting, and an opponent more worthy. He needed to expand the playing field.

Bakersville had come to him like a goddamn wet dream.

The perfect place, the perfect target, and the perfect cast of Keystone Kops hot on his trail.

Finally, he was having some fun.

Big, burly Shep, crying over his son. Smart, pretty Officer Conner, worrying about her town. And now

Supervisory Special Agent Pierce Quincy. Quantico's best of the best.

Finally, he had a game worth playing. Which was good, because as far as he was concerned he was no longer producing a single-act play. This game was just beginning.

Do you remember what it felt like when you pulled the trigger, Officer Conner? Do you still dream about the wet sound of your mother's exploding head?

Someday I want to hear all about it.

But not tonight. Tonight he had to drive to Portland. He still had work to do.

THE FIRST TIME Becky O'Grady fell asleep, she dreamed she stood up to the monster in her school. She planted her feet in the hall. She yelled, "Bad, bad monster. Leave my brother alone! Don't you hurt my friends!"

The monster was ashamed. He crawled away. Then Alice and Sally hugged her and cried. Pretty Miss Avalon kissed her on the cheek and told her she was very brave. Everyone was happy, including her mommy and daddy, who never fought again, and Danny, who gave her a kitty.

The second time Becky fell asleep, she dreamed she stood up to the monster and he bit off her head.

At five in the morning, Becky O'Grady crawled to the hall closet and piled coats on top of her shoulders. But she knew it wouldn't do any good.

The monster was coming. She had not saved Danny, and she and the monster both knew it. Soon he would come for her. Soon it would be her turn.

Becky whimpered for her mother. But mostly she cried for Danny, because when he had needed her most, she had not saved him.

FIFTEEN

SANDY STOOD AT THE kitchen sink, washing the same flower-bordered plate over and over again. Outside, the sun was shining. She had cracked the window to let in the fresh morning air, and now she could hear the sounds of her neighborhood preparing for a new day. Somewhere down the street a lawn was being mowed. Probably Mr. McCabe. He was a retired school principal who took religious care of his yard. In June, people drove in from miles around just to admire his roses.

A dog barked three or four houses over. Then came the sounds of a mother yelling for her child. Andy? Anthony? Maybe Andrea, the Simpsons' four-year-old daughter. Last Halloween she'd dressed up as a cowboy—not a cowgirl, she'd told everyone, a cow*boy*. Sandy really liked the child, even if she insisted on calling her Mrs. O'Grady, which made Sandy feel old.

She turned the plate in her hand and rhythmically washed the back.

When she and Shep had first moved into this neighborhood eleven years ago, they were one of the few couples with kids. Since then the neighborhood had grown and so had the families. There must be five toddlers on this block alone. Two of the girls in Becky's class lived just four blocks over. There were a number of boys as well, though most of them were too young for Danny. Sandy had always thought that was a shame. It was so easy for Becky to find someone to play with, whereas Danny had to be driven to someone's house. That took planning. That took having a parent home to serve as chauffeur.

Danny had never complained, though. He seemed content to read books or stay at school or play on the computer. Later in the evenings she'd sometimes go on walks with him around the neighborhood. They'd wave at the other families. Danny would check out houses with DirecTV. Or sometimes she'd walk and he'd ride his bike around her and show off stunts like riding no-handed for her amusement.

She'd always liked those walks. She'd felt safe, passing through their modest community where everyone worked hard and knew one another's name.

This morning Sandy didn't feel comfortable enough to step outside to get the morning paper. She was too afraid people would stop and stare. And she wasn't sure which bothered her most, the looks of anger or of pity.

She stayed in her kitchen, a prisoner under house arrest, and scrubbed her appliances until they sparkled. Then she attacked the kitchen floor, all the while pretending it was just another day in the neighborhood and her life hadn't really ended two days ago.

This morning Sandy had called the detention center at promptly seven A.M. It had been forty-eight hours since she'd last spoken with her son, and she desperately needed to see him. Was he frightened, was he scared? Did he understand what was happening to him? Did he miss her or call out her name in the middle of the night?

What if he was having nightmares? What if he wasn't getting enough to eat or the blankets scratched or the sheets itched? For God's sake, she was his mother and she needed to be with her son!

The head of the detention facilities, a Mr. Gregory, had firmly but politely informed her that Danny had already begged them not to let his mother in. The director had located Danny in the cafeteria first thing this morning to mention that his parents wanted to visit. Danny had immediately grown so agitated that staff members had had no choice but to return him to his room.

It appeared he was too traumatized to deal with his parents. Maybe in a week or two.

Sandy had never heard of anything so ridiculous. If her son was traumatized, all the more reason for her to come. She could bring his favorite toy, bake his favorite cake. Please, something, anything . . .

Don't leave me on the outside like this. Don't leave me feeling so helpless.

Mr. Gregory informed her that her son was still under suicide watch. And they'd had to return Danny to his room because, at the mention of seeing his parents, he grabbed a fork from another youth and tried to puncture his own wrist.

She and Shep were not to visit. Period.

The sound of the lawn mower stopped. A sharp bang as Mr. McCabe removed the clippings bag. He was probably dumping the grass on his flower beds. Sandy had seen him do it a hundred times. Churning the grass clippings into the beds to replenish the nitrogen. Working the soil tenderly with his old, gnarled hands.

She finally set the plate in the drying rack. The dishes were done. Her countertops sparkled, her floor was freshly mopped. She'd even cleaned the stove and wiped down the microwave. Now it was eight in the morning and Sandy didn't know what to do.

She turned toward Becky, who was eyeing her somberly from the kitchen table.

"Would you like more cereal, honey?"

Becky shook her head. The bowl of Cheerios placed

in front of her fifteen minutes ago still appeared to be untouched.

"What about some fruit?" Sandy coaxed. "Or what about pancakes? I can make you chocolate chip pancakes!"

Sandy regretted the words the moment she said them. Chocolate chip pancakes were Danny's favorite.

Becky shook her head.

Sandy resiliently turned toward the refrigerator, searching for more options. Becky hadn't eaten in nearly two days.

"I know," Sandy said brightly, "how about some salad!"

She eagerly pulled out the clear glass bowl. The salad had been among four dishes that had arrived on their front porch yesterday. The others had contained macaroni and cheese, a ham-and-potato dish, and some kind of mystery-meat surprise. This bowl had impressed Sandy, however. The mixture of strawberry Jell-O, apples, bananas, walnuts, and whipped cream was a favorite children's salad, and it touched her that others were thinking of Becky. God knows, the little girl was suffering too.

Sandy held up the brightly colored salad for Becky's inspection. Becky had always loved Jell-O and whipped cream. . . .

A slight hesitation, then finally Becky nodded. They had a winner!

Sandy dished up a large bowl for her daughter, humming slightly to herself in honor of having scored a victory. She poured a glass of orange juice to go with Becky's breakfast. After another thought, she poured a glass of juice for herself as well and joined her daughter at the table.

From the living room came the sound of Shep snoring. He'd been out most of the night and returned at some small hour of the morning, reeking of beer. Sandy knew without asking where he'd gone. Rainie's house.

Whenever he was troubled, whenever he had something on his mind, he always went there.

Once Sandy had entertained wild notions of what must be going on at the Conner residence. Everyone had heard stories of Rainie's mother and what kind of woman she'd been. Sandy had imagined her husband and his deputy rolling around in a torrid embrace. She had fantasized about them laughing together and giggling madly over what an idiot pretty little Sandy Surmon must be not to suspect a thing.

One night in a fit of jealous rage, she'd hightailed it over to Rainie's tiny home in the middle of the soaring woods. She'd driven up the dirt driveway at full steam, already formulating a bold confrontation in her head.

She'd discovered her husband and Rainie sitting on the huge back deck in complete silence, each just staring out into the woods and holding a beer.

Sandy had gone back home without ever saying a word.

Over the years she'd come to realize that she simply couldn't fathom her husband and Rainie's relationship. She didn't know what caused the long silences between them or the unspoken exchanges. She didn't understand how Shep could sometimes seem to belong more to Rainie than to her, when Sandy had borne him two children and, as best as she could tell, Rainie only handed him bottles of Bud Light.

Whatever bonded them was deep, but at least it wasn't sexual. So Sandy did her best to fight her nagging, painful wish that Shep would come to her when he was troubled, instead of heading to another woman's house for hours of companionable silence.

"Mommy, what happened to school?"

Sandy looked at her daughter, genuinely startled by the question and the sound of her daughter's voice. Becky had barely spoken since the shooting, and when she did, it was generally a one-word statement. "What do you mean, honey?"

"There's no school today."

"No, Becky, there's no school today."

"Tomorrow?"

"You don't have to go to school tomorrow either, sweetheart. I don't want you to worry about school. It's all done for a bit."

Her daughter continued to eye her intently. "Are the other kids going to school?"

"You mean your classmates? No." Sandy was trying to pick her words carefully. "They're all done with school for a bit as well."

"It's not summer."

"It's almost summer."

"Mommy, it's not summer."

"Becky . . . You know something bad happened at school, right? You understand that?"

Becky nodded.

"Well, that bad thing has made everyone sad. You're sad, aren't you?"

Becky nodded again.

"I'm sad," Sandy said softly. "Daddy's sad. And the other kids, they're sad too. So for a little bit, because everyone is so sad, there's no school."

"But someday?"

"Someday, Becky, yes, there will be school. But it's okay, honey! It won't be until you're ready, and we'll make sure the school is very safe. So the bad thing—"

"The monster."

Sandy hesitated. "Yes, so the monster can't happen anymore."

Becky stared at her. Her eyes were big and serious. Sandy hadn't realized until now just how old her little girl had become. Then Becky returned her attention to her bowl of whipped cream and Jell-O. Sandy understood. Becky didn't believe her. She already assumed her world wouldn't be safe again. Not in a time when monsters could go to school.

Sandy returned to the kitchen sink, downing the last of her orange juice and then carefully, methodically washing the glass. The light on the answering machine blinked madly at her, but she'd already heard the message yesterday. Mitchell trying to find her, before Shep had changed their phone number to end the relentless calls. Mitchell, so sorry to disturb her at a time like this, but he was desperately trying to get his hands on the Wal-Mart reports. Could she please give him a quick buzz and tell him where he might find the files?

Sandy knew what he was looking for. She could picture the files perfectly in her mind. But she hadn't picked up the phone and called him back.

Maybe Shep was right. Maybe she'd been working too much, putting her own needs in front of the children's. If she'd been home more, paying more attention . . . If Danny had felt safer, more important, more loved . . .

If . . . if . . . if . . .

Sandy shut off the water. Her hands were shaking on the faucet; she had tears in her eyes.

Mommy, what happened to school?

I want to make the world safe. Oh God, honey. I wish I could make the world safe for you.

"Mommy."

Sandy turned back to Becky. For a moment, she thought she saw blood on her daughter's face and she nearly screamed. Strawberry Jell-O, her mind filled in belatedly. Strawberry Jell-O.

But then she saw the tears in her daughter's eyes.

"My tongue hurts."

Sandy rushed across the kitchen. She looked at her daughter's mouth, and to her dismay, she realized it was bleeding. Poor Becky's tongue was bleeding.

"What happened? Did you bite your tongue? Ah, honey, let me get you a washcloth and an ice cube. Hang on a second."

She picked up the salad, carrying it over to the sink. It wasn't until she was running a fresh washcloth under the tap that she looked in the bowl and noticed the way light glinted off fragments of Jell-O.

Very slowly, Sandy got out a spoon. She dug through the salad. She pulled out five shards of glass.

Baby killer. Baby killer. Baby killer.

It's a children's salad! Even if you hate us, what kind of animals put shattered glass in a fucking children's salad!

She returned to Becky with surprising calmness. She wiped off her little girl's face; she gave her an ice cube to suck on. Already the bleeding appeared to have stopped. The glass shards were small. Maybe they hadn't done much damage.

Tenderly Sandy feathered back Becky's fine blond hair. "How are you feeling, honey?"

"Okay."

"Did you eat much?" she asked lightly.

Becky shook her head. "Not hungry."

"If your tummy hurts, you'll tell me, won't you?"

Becky nodded. Sandy decided to let it go. Becky seemed fine and Sandy didn't want to frighten her with another trip to the emergency room.

"I know," Sandy said briskly, "let's make some snickerdoodle cookies! I'll bring out all the ingredients and you can help me measure everything. How does that sound?"

Becky shrugged.

"Wonderful. Let me just clean this stuff up and we'll be on our way."

Sandy gave her daughter a bright, reassuring smile. She kept her chin high and her features composed. Then she returned to the kitchen sink, where she spooned all the Jell-O salad and the three other casseroles into the garbage disposal while she swore to herself that she would not, would not, *would not* cry.

"Don't let the monster get you, Mommy."

"Becky, I would never dream of doing any such thing."

SIXTEEN

Thursday, May 17, 6:33 A.M.

QUINCY DID NOT DREAM of his daughter. In the gray hours of the morning, he tossed and turned in the pink Motel Hotel, caught in a case that had happened nearly a decade ago. Thirteen-year-old Candy Wallace, with the pretty blond hair and hundred-watt smile. Beautiful, sunny Candy Wallace, who was raised a devout Baptist and had no idea of the true evil that lurked in men's hearts.

She was snatched on her way home from school on a normal Wednesday afternoon. One minute she was walking down the street. The next, a pile of books was all that remained.

But Candy's captor hadn't really wanted Candy. He wanted Polly, her sixteen-year-old sister, and getting the wrong sibling angered him. So he took to calling the Wallaces' home. He would put Candy on the phone. And then he would do things to her while her sister and parents listened.

After the first phone call, Quincy was brought in to listen as well. They considered him to have expert ears.

Now, in the throes of his dream, he did not remember Candy Wallace's screams or the agonized face of her mother. He did not recall her sister Polly begging for the man to stop, to please come take her instead.

She would willingly go with him if he would just let her little sister go. Please, please, please. . . .

Mostly, Quincy remembered Candy's last words, after five days of endless agony.

"Please don't be sad, Mom and Dad. It'll all be over soon and I know I'm going to a better place. God loves me and will take care of me. I'm going to be fine. I love you. I love even this bad, bad man. My heart is true."

Quincy woke up with tears on his cheeks.

He lay in his bed for a long time, thinking of the strength of a thirteen-year-old girl, thinking of God and faith and the things he'd left behind after too many years on the job.

A day after the last phone call they found Candy Wallace's body, naked, bruised, and mutilated. Three weeks after that they arrested the man who did it, an unemployed handyman who had once worked on the air-conditioning unit at the Wallaces' home. He said Candy had insisted on telling him that God loved him, so he'd cut out her tongue. Quincy had thought that there was nothing they could do to this man that would ever be enough.

He'd flown back to Virginia feeling isolated and worn to the bone.

He'd entered his home but walked away from his family, because he'd never learned to go from a crime scene to the people he loved. At times like this, he couldn't look at his daughters without seeing all the horrors that could befall them. The handymen, the drifters, the charming law students. He couldn't look at his family without seeing pain and suffering and death.

Now Quincy got out of bed. He called the hospital to learn that Amanda's condition hadn't changed. His ex-wife was asleep in the room if he wanted to speak with her. Quincy told the nurse not to wake her. His other daughter, Kimberly, was not at the hospital. She had probably returned to school. Like him, she seemed to have accepted that her sister was gone, a defection to Quincy's camp that Bethie couldn't bear.

Of course, things between his ex-wife and their younger daughter had been tense ever since last year, when Kimberly had announced she was studying sociology at New York University. Someday she wanted to be a profiler with the FBI. Just like her dad.

Quincy pulled on an old pair of running shorts and a gray FBI T-shirt. He hit the street, inhaling sharply at the cold sting of morning. Then he was off and running, still thinking of a young girl's dying screams and unfailing love. Still thinking of his own daughter, and the tragedy he hadn't protected her from after all those years of trying to make the world a safe place.

And then he was thinking of Rainie and her shadowed gray eyes and strong, stubborn chin. The way she took her punches. The way she still got up for the fight.

Once he'd made the mistake of thinking that isolation was protection, that focusing solely on his work would make a difference for people, for his family. He had listened to a young girl die, but he had not heard what she was saying.

Quincy was old, but he was learning.

He ran for a long time, with the mountain air cool and clean against his cheeks. He greeted a beautiful morning in a lush, coastal valley and he understood why Rainie Conner still lived here, perfectly.

SHORTLY BEFORE ONE, Quincy showed up in the tiny task-force center in the attic of city hall. He hadn't expected Rainie to be back yet from the autopsies scheduled in Portland, but she was already sitting at her sawhorse desk when he arrived. She didn't look up right away, scribbling intently on some piece of paper.

He took a moment to study her. Her face was paler than yesterday, the shadows deeper under her eyes. Another sleepless night, he presumed, coupled with a brutal morning. Autopsies were never easy, particularly when they were of children.

Judging from her focused movements, however, Rainie still had no intention of slowing down.

She reminded him of someone else. It took him a moment to place the name. Tess. Tess Williams. Another case, years ago, but with a better ending. Tess had made the mistake of marrying the perfect man, the kind other women always said was too good to be true. In Jim Beckett's case, they were right. The handsome, dedicated police officer had had a small sideline activity. He pulled over beautiful blondes for speeding, and then he murdered them. Tess had been the first person to figure out her husband's evil doings, and she'd slowly gathered the evidence against him while still sharing his bed.

Jim Beckett did not go down without a fight. He cut a long, bloody swath through the task-force team, including putting some fresh scars on Quincy's own chest. But Tess proved to be tougher than anyone had suspected. When Beckett hunted her down after he escaped from prison, Tess made sure the Massachusetts taxpayers never had to pay for his room and board again.

Quincy hadn't thought of her in years. He tried to do the math on how old her daughter Samantha would be now. Ten years old? It had been a bit. He wondered how she and Tess were doing.

He never followed up on the people in his cases. Even in the ones that went well, he was still a reminder of a dark time. Somehow, it didn't seem appropriate to be sending out Christmas cards.

"Are you going to stand there mooning all afternoon?" Rainie asked from her desk, still staring down at her paper.

"Just admiring the view."

She looked up long enough to shoot him a hard glance. "Oh, please."

"The autopsies went that well, I see."

"Everything I ever feared, plus ten. For heaven's

sake, either get in the room or shut the door. I can't stand people loitering in the doorway."

Quincy took his time entering, eyeing her more cautiously. She was more ragged than he'd expected. When she spoke, her voice carried the edge of someone teetering on the brink of a dark place. He would bet she hadn't let herself cry. That was a bad sign. Sometimes you had to cry after autopsies. It was the only way to release the pain.

"Writing up the report?" he asked neutrally.

"Nope. Writing up a list. What do you think of the mysterious man in black?"

"Pardon?"

"The man in black, the figure various kids reported seeing at the school. Fact or fiction?"

"I don't know."

"What if he exists? Could a stranger be involved in shooting up a school?"

"You would be amazed at the things a stranger can do," Quincy said slowly, "even one met over the Internet. Witness all the young kids currently being lured from chat rooms into real-life meetings with pedophiles."

"Fine." She scribbled furiously. "Man in black. Connection to Danny through the Internet, then tries to cover tracks by erasing the hard drives of the machines. Except then we're back to Melissa Avalon. Why one precise gunshot to her head? I hate that fucking wound." Rainie caught herself, blew out a breath of air, and briskly started writing again. "We can work on that angle later. Next up, school counselor Richard Mann."

"What about Richard Mann?"

"He's young, thirty-three according to his file, though he doesn't look a day older than fifteen if you ask me. If we go back to assuming that Melissa Avalon was the intended target, he could have motive. Maybe he had a thing for Melissa Avalon and didn't like learning about her private staff meetings with

VanderZanden. Plus, as a counselor, he'd know what buttons to push to drive Danny over the edge. That takes care of means."

Quincy finally got it. "You're working on a list of other possible suspects."

"Yes, the fed can be taught."

Quincy arched a brow. She wasn't just edgy this afternoon, she was brutally cutting.

"May I ask who you have listed?"

"Charlie Kenyon, Principal VanderZanden, the mysterious man in black, and now Richard Mann."

"I thought the principal had an alibi."

"At first glance, but you never really know until you start applying pressure."

"Charlie Kenyon makes sense," Quincy mused after a moment, deciding it would be most productive to play along. "An older, influential kid. We already know he has trouble with authority and likes to hang around the school. I'm less convinced about the principal. Even if it was a love affair gone awry, I have a hard time seeing him shooting two students and an even more difficult time seeing him coerce Danny into taking the blame."

"Strong authority figure. Danny can't stand up to his own father, so why should he be able to stand up to the school principal? Plus, you heard his last words in the interview. The kid's scared. When you're in elementary school, who seems more all-powerful and all-knowing than your principal?"

Her logic wasn't bad. "But then there is Vander-Zanden's reaction to consider. He appears genuinely grief-stricken."

Rainie granted that. Then her eyes lit up. "What about his *wife*?"

Quincy exhaled slowly and watched her scribble it down. Her movements were feverish. She was trying too hard.

"Rainie, why are you making this list?"

"Focus. This investigation lacks focus."

"You already have a suspect in custody. That appears very focused to me."

"Yes, but we don't know if he's the right suspect."

"His fingerprints on the casings haven't convinced you?"

"They didn't convince you."

"I'm paid more to be skeptical."

Rainie set down her pen. She paused long enough to look him in the eye, and Quincy was startled by the sight of her pale skin stretched taut over her gaunt face. Apparently she was forgoing food as well as sleep. It was only a matter of time, then, until she crashed.

"Shep visited me last night," she said abruptly.

"Ah," Quincy said. Things became much clearer for him. "Laid on the personal guilt."

"Of course. What are friends for? Even better, he contacted the crime lab himself through a friend. Turns out Abe Sanders has been holding out on us."

"I can hardly wait."

"There's a problem with one of the .38 shell casings. Not only does it completely lack prints or smudges—as in it appears to have been wiped clean—but ballistics found something strange about it. When I followed up this morning, I learned that it had some kind of residue inside, probably a polymer."

"Plastic? As in perhaps threads of polyester fabric?"

"Who knows? But *inside* a shell casing is a weird place to find traces of fabric, plus Danny was wearing one hundred percent cotton when I brought him in. They're conducting further tests, of course, but we're back to having more questions than answers."

"You're going to kill Detective Sanders, aren't you?"

"Yes. At three this afternoon. You're welcome to watch." Rainie smiled tightly. "Then I had the most fascinating chat with the ME at seven this morning. She conducted Avalon's autopsy late last night so we could get straight to the girls this morning. Lucky me. And get this: the .22 slug that killed Melissa Avalon was not deformed. In fact, the damn thing traveled in a nice straight line through the center of her brain and stopped at the base of her skull. No ricocheting. Nice, recoverable slug with an intact base. Should yield plenty of rifling marks for ballistics. Except it has none."

"No rifling marks? Is the ME thinking a smoothbore gun?"

"I don't know what the hell Nancy Jenkins is thinking. The woman is definitely intrigued and, unfortunately for me, coy. Let me see if I can get her exact words right. Something like 'The slug would appear to have come from a .22, but I don't think it has.' "

"She doesn't think it has?"

"Turns out Nancy Jenkins is a gun buff. She's not commenting officially until she gets the ballistics report back, but there's something funny about the slug that killed Melissa Avalon. And she's pretty clear it's not your average funny. It's your smart, clever funny."

"Too smart and clever for a thirteen-year-old boy?"

"Now you're getting it."

"And the bullet came to rest at the base of Avalon's skull?"

"Exactly. At the base of the skull. As in a downward trajectory. As in how can a four-foot-ten boy shoot down at a five-foot-six woman?"

"Who was not on her knees," Quincy filled in for her, "considering how the body fell."

Rainie nodded angrily. "So there you have it. At this point it looks like there's something rotten in Denmark. At the very least, it's doubtful that Danny killed Melissa Avalon, which also raises questions about Sally and Alice."

"There was probably someone else present and a murder weapon we have yet to identify."

"Yep. A murder weapon we have yet to identify and a motive. Why Melissa Avalon? I can't get it out of my head. Why young, beautiful Miss Avalon?"

"And now you're building the new theory of the case."

"Since I am primary officer, I thought I'd give it a shot."

"Rainie, can I make your day?"

"By all means, give it a whirl."

"I have a one-thirty appointment with Richard Mann to ask him about Danny O'Grady. Come with me, Rainie. I'll be good cop, you be bad cop. Together, we'll ambush him."

A feral gleam came into Rainie's eyes. The satisfaction in her face was enough to make him smile. And unfurl something slow and tender in his chest.

"I get to be bad cop?"

"You are the most qualified."

"SupSpAg, I could kiss you."

"Promises, promises," he said lightly, and led his favorite law enforcer from the room.

SEVENTEEN

Thursday, May 17, 1:28 P.M.

THEY MET RICHARD MANN in his office at the battered school, which had finally been opened up to staff members. He'd told Quincy he needed to catch up on paperwork, and Rainie's impression of the young counselor was of someone deeply disheartened. His face was pale, his eyes bruised. He'd made an effort to dress up for the meeting in tan khakis and a sage-colored sweater, but he maintained a certain rumpled air that spoke of sleepless nights and unanswered questions. Did he wonder if he should've seen the shooting coming? In the dark hours after midnight, did he think there was more he should've done?

Rainie didn't know much about the man. She'd asked a few parents, all of whom said he seemed very nice. Inexperienced, a few commented, but hardworking in an earnest sort of way. Tuesday, when things had been hairy at the school, he'd certainly stepped up to the plate and done what she'd asked. There was something to be said for that.

But Rainie still wondered about him and Miss Avalon. Even tired, Mann had that clean-cut, all-American look going for him. Trim figure. Short-cropped brown hair. Blue eyes. In a high school he would've inspired half a dozen juvenile crushes. And at Bakersville's K–8?

"Officer Conner," Mann said with obvious surprise when she showed up in the doorway alongside Quincy. "How nice to see you again." He smiled at her, clearly not alarmed by her presence, and held out a hand.

"Mr. Mann." Rainie accepted his handshake. Weak grip, she thought. Definitely young. Then added, unnecessarily, not at all like Quincy.

"Oh, call me Richard. Mr. Mann is my father."

"I know the feeling." She and Quincy took seats. Located off the admissions office and next to Vander-Zanden's room, Richard Mann's space was small but tidy. The main attraction was one large window overlooking the side of the school parking lot, which let in lots of sun. The floor was blue Berber, the walls stark white, and the multitude of filing cabinets industrial gray. Except for two plants and one poster of cartoon faces demonstrating different human emotions, there wasn't much in the way of decorations. Definitely a bachelor's office, Rainie decided. She'd bet his apartment looked equally utilitarian.

At the moment, empty cardboard boxes and discarded files littered the floor.

"Cleaning house?" Quincy inquired.

"Going through old files," Mann confessed. He waved his hand apologetically over the pile. "We're starting to run out of room, and most of these files are from before my time."

"That's right. You're new here."

"It's been a whole year. I don't feel so new anymore."

"Bakersville is a big change from L.A.," Rainie observed.

"That's what I was looking for."

"Small-town life?"

"Someplace with no drills for drive-by shootings." He smiled weakly. "Of course, that didn't work out quite like I had planned."

"Where were you when the shooting started?" Rainie asked.

"In my office. It was my lunch break."

"You don't eat during normal lunch hours?"

"No. I have an open-door policy for the kids. You know, anyone can walk in if there's something they want to talk about. That sort of thing."

"We understand Melissa Avalon also left her door open for the kids during lunch."

"That's right." He nodded.

"So you both took lunch at the same time." Rainie narrowed her eyes suggestively and watched Richard Mann grow confused. He'd been expecting an interview about Danny O'Grady, not his own activities on the day of the shooting.

"Yes, I believe so," he said with less certainty. On his lap, his hands were already beginning to fidget. This, Rainie decided, was going to be like shooting fish in a barrel.

"You two ever do lunch together?"

"Well, we *were* coworkers—"

"We understand Miss Avalon liked to get to know some of her coworkers."

"I don't understand . . ."

"She and Principal VanderZanden. Or didn't you know about that?" Rainie hardened her voice, and Richard Mann squirmed in his seat.

"I thought we were going to talk about Danny."

"How well did you know Melissa Avalon?"

"We worked together, that's all."

"She was very beautiful."

"I suppose . . ."

"Young, about the same age as yourself?"

"Yes, I guess."

"Also new to the area. Come on, Mr. Mann, don't tell me you two didn't have anything in common."

"Wait a minute. You think Melissa and I—" Mann made a little gesture with his hand, looked at them with shock, then vigorously shook his head. For the first time since the start of the interview, he visibly re-laxed. "I'm sorry, Officer, but if you guys think I was involved with Melissa, then you don't know much about her."

"What do you mean?" Quincy asked smoothly.

"Melissa had issues—Freudian issues."

"You mean with her father?" Rainie demanded sharply.

"I don't know all the details," he replied, "but she mentioned once that she was estranged from her fam-ily. Her father was a hard man, she said, very demand-ing and not very forgiving. Then you consider that she took up with VanderZanden in a matter of weeks and the man's nearly twice her age . . ."

"A substitute father figure," Quincy filled in.

"That was my analysis, yes," Mann said, and flashed Quincy a grateful smile. He was obviously pleased to have a chance to show off his own psycho-logical training to a big-shot profiler.

"The father ever visit?" Rainie pressed.

"I don't know."

"What about her mom?"

"I don't know."

"For someone you worked with for a whole year, you don't know a lot about her, do you?"

"She was very private about her family!"

"Not with Principal VanderZanden."

"I was *not* involved with Melissa Avalon," the coun-selor said through clenched teeth. "We were coworkers, that's all. If you people are so concerned about her private life, talk to Steven. Or, better yet, call her father. I've heard a rumor he hasn't even bothered to claim her body yet."

"We'll be sure to do that," Quincy said.

"So what about Danny O'Grady?" Rainie pounced. "We understand you'd been seeing him as a counselor."

"Only for a few weeks—"

"Oh yeah? And precisely how long does it take to figure out that a boy who trashed his school locker has problems managing rage?"

"His parents are going through a rough time. There was no reason to think Danny's anger was anything more than an adjustment phase. When marriages turn sour, kids get mad."

"Where were you again when the shooting happened?"

"In my office!"

"Do you have witnesses?"

"How dare you!" Richard Mann lurched out of his chair, his handsome face beet red and his expression injured. "I did everything I could to help those kids, Officer. Don't you remember? *I'm* the one who arranged the first-aid center. *I'm* the one who got the parents cleared out of the parking lot so the emergency vehicles could get through. And now *I'm* the one fielding dozens of calls from parents whose children are waking up screaming. So how dare you imply that I had something to do with this? My God, this is breaking my heart!"

"Officer Conner doesn't mean to imply anything, Mr. Mann," Quincy said calmly, holding up his hands in a soothing gesture. "It's simply her job to ask these kinds of questions. Of course we appreciate the help you gave on the day of the shooting."

Mann turned to Quincy, obviously still unsure. Quincy smiled warmly.

"I just thought we were going to be speaking about Danny," Mann said after a moment. "I wasn't expecting this kind of . . . attack."

"Police interviews can be intense," Quincy said diplomatically. "Of course, we consider everyone innocent until proven guilty."

Mann looked pointedly at Rainie. She lifted one shoulder in a negligent shrug. Pretty boy had no alibi and got really defensive really fast, she thought. Then again, the student he'd been counseling had allegedly murdered three people. It probably didn't let him sleep well at night.

"Back to Danny O'Grady," Quincy encouraged.

"I don't know what I can tell you there," Mann said sulkily. "Some of it is privileged."

Quincy beamed at him. He said with a saccharine sweetness that nearly made Rainie roll her eyes, "Of course, I would never ask a psychologist to violate his oath by breaching client confidentiality. Even general information would be helpful."

Mann had to think about it. He finally sank back down into his seat, steepled his hands in front of him, and regarded the FBI agent more intently. "I honestly don't know much," he said at last. "I'd just started talking to Danny a few weeks ago, and the first few sessions were small talk. You know, establishing trust, building a rapport. We hadn't had a chance to get into things."

"These things take time."

"We talked a little bit about Danny's interest in computers," Mann offered. "Danny really loved surfing the Net, playing around with programming. He never flat-out admitted it, but I got the impression he might be involved with hacking. The computer was exciting to him, but also a challenge. He might have been pushing the envelope a bit."

"Maybe going places he wasn't supposed to?"

"Maybe. I think it's obvious to everyone that Danny has issues with self-esteem. His father is too hard on him. He berates Danny, tries to force him into doing things he doesn't want to do. He's hardly a model of support."

"He makes Danny feel dumb?"

"Dumb, inferior, weak, helpless. Honestly, I think people should be required to get a parenting license before they're allowed to have children."

"Shep may not be the perfect parent," Rainie interjected with a frown, "but he loves his son and wants the best for him."

"Fine, but that and a quarter still won't get Danny a cup of coffee." Mann waved his hand to silence her next round of protests. He was back on sure footing, and the parents had been right—his earnestness was compelling. "Look, Officer. I'm the one in the trenches, and I can tell you wholeheartedly that intentions don't matter in parenting. Kids don't understand what you mean. They understand what you do. And most of the things Shep does make Danny feel powerless and incompetent. Computers, on the other hand, make him feel strong."

"Did he ever talk about people he might have met on-line? Places he might have gone?" Quincy pressed.

"I can't comment on that."

"Hey, Mann—" Rainie began impatiently.

He cut her off primly. "Danny is my patient and I won't violate privilege."

"Can you really exercise privilege if you're only a school counselor?" Rainie asked Quincy.

He gave her a look that clearly told her not to take the bad-cop thing too far. Mann was getting edgy, and they needed to get more information from him.

"You should try the computers," Mann said abruptly. He leaned forward, saying in almost a whisper, "I want to help, but I can hardly start my career by breaking confidentiality. On the other hand, Danny was using the school computers. Now, I'm not a computer person, but I thought cops had the ability to trace anything these days. . . ."

Quincy and Rainie exchanged glances. Mann had done everything but the wink, wink, nudge, nudge. So they were back to the computers. Okay.

"Is there one person Danny mentioned a lot?" Quincy tried probing. "Maybe a new friend he'd made recently?"

"Everyone knows about him smoking with Charlie Kenyon."

"But what about someone on-line? Maybe an adult figure from a chat room or e-mail loop. That sort of thing?"

Mann hesitated again. His gaze went from Rainie to Quincy to Rainie again. What the hell. She let her features relax and gave pretty boy a smile.

"It would be helpful, Mr. Mann. Coupled with what you did in the school parking lot on Tuesday, how quickly you helped manage the situation—that would make you something of a hero in this whole affair."

Hero, apparently, was the right word.

"There was someone," Mann confessed. "Danny thought it was another kid, a fellow hacker he'd befriended on-line. I read a few of the e-mails, and the language seemed more sophisticated, though. I was betting it was really an adult male passing himself off as a teenager."

"And you weren't concerned by this?" Quincy asked.

"Oh, I was concerned," Mann told him vehemently. "That's why I asked Danny to start bringing me the e-mails. I know the things that can happen on-line— child molesters, pornographers, terrorists. The Internet isn't any safer than a walk through New York City at night. But what Danny showed me was harmless. They were friendly notes, admiring his accomplishments on the computer, sharing information about other programs to try, Web sites to visit. On the other hand . . ." He paused. "I've heard rumors that Danny said something right after the shooting. That he was saying over and over again that he was smart."

Quincy glanced at Rainie. She gave up that information with a nod.

"The notes Danny got, they always ended with this guy telling Danny how smart he was. Stuff like *I can't wait to see what the whiz kid does next. You're so smart.*" Mann shrugged helplessly. For the first time, Rainie thought he looked miserable. "That strikes me as coming from this guy. So maybe there were other notes, other things that Danny didn't tell me. I don't know . . ."

Mann's voice faded. Then he said more quietly,

more somberly, "I really wanted to help Danny O'Grady. I was concerned about the Internet relationship and concerned about his parents' marital problems, but I thought I could reach him. Even reading the e-mails, I didn't see it coming. I thought . . . I thought kids who did this sort of thing were supposed to have a history of violence. Torturing household pets, starting fires, playing violent video games. Danny didn't do any of those things. To me, he seemed to be a decent boy going through a hard time. I honestly had no idea. I swear, I had no idea. . . ."

Richard Mann's shoulders slumped. He simply sat there, shaking his head.

Quincy leaned forward. "Mr. Mann, do you happen to have a copy of any of the e-mails?"

"Danny wouldn't let me keep them. He worried he was already violating the person's trust by even showing them to me."

"Do you remember anything about them? A name, a chat room, an e-mail address?"

"I don't—wait a minute. The e-mail address. I remember trying to understand what the guy meant. Something about no fires. Volcanoes. Lava. That was it: No Lava. Isn't that odd for a signature?"

"No Lava. No Lava what? Do you remember the carrier, the Internet provider?"

"One of the major ones, I think. AOL maybe, or CompuServe. Something like that."

Rainie scribbled it down. She looked at Quincy.

"We have some federal agents who specialize in undercover Internet operations," he said. "We could send someone on, pretending to be a teenage boy, see if No Lava takes an interest."

Richard Mann sat back. He ran a hand through his short hair and expelled a pent-up breath. "I really am trying to make things right. Sally and Alice were sweet girls. And this . . . it just shouldn't have happened here."

"We'll see."

Rainie rose. She handed Mann her card and gave him the usual spiel to call the sheriff's office if he thought of anything else, though she seriously doubted he'd be in the mood to talk to her anytime soon. As she opened the door of the office, however, he spoke up again.

"Officer Conner." Rainie halted, and the counselor motioned to the space behind her, which housed a large desk for the school's secretary. "As you can see, my office is directly off the main administrative space. While I might have been eating lunch alone at the time of the shooting, there is no way I could have left without someone noticing. Ask our secretary, Marge. I'm sure she can confirm that I took one roast beef sandwich into my office at the start of the period, and I hadn't gone anywhere by the time the first shot was fired. Just so you know."

Rainie nodded. She knew when she was being put in her place. Then her gaze fell to the old files strewn across the floor and she read the two names on top. *Sally Walker. Alice Bensen.* Of course. They wouldn't need permanent records anymore.

Richard Mann had followed her line of sight. His expression had become equally subdued.

"I should take those," Rainie murmured after a moment. "For the victimology reports."

Mann gazed at her curiously. Was he startled by how she could think that way? Or was he wondering, as she was, when she had learned to be so cold?

He picked up the two files. He handed them over to her.

After that, there was nothing left to say.

EIGHTEEN

B

Y THE TIME RAINIE and Quincy grabbed lunch at Dairy Queen and headed back to the task-force center, Abe Sanders was waiting for them. The state detective was sporting a sharply pressed gray suit and shiny black shoes, making Rainie suspicious that the man who traveled with salad also packed an iron and a shoe-polishing kit. Just what did he do for fun in his spare time?

He had made himself at home behind Rainie's desk and was reading a fax. Rainie snatched the paper out of his hands without preamble.

"I doubt that's for your eyes."

"You mean we're not all part of one big happy family?" he drawled innocently.

Rainie skewered him with a glance, then scanned the fax. It was from the law offices of Johnson, Johnson, and Jones. Those office Christmas parties must be a hoot. The fax informed her that she and her deputies were not to contact Shep, Sandy, or Becky O'Grady without legal counsel being present. If any member of the task force insisted on violating this order, a harassment suit would be filed against the Bakersville sheriff's department. Sincerely, Avery Johnson.

"Wonderful," Rainie muttered. That conversation between Shep and Sandy had obviously gone well. Or had Shep mentioned her interest in interviewing Becky to Avery Johnson as part of his desire to do everything absolutely right for Danny? You would think an experienced sheriff would know better.

"Looks like we won't be interviewing Becky O'Grady anytime soon," Sanders commented.

"We'll see," Rainie said. She handed the fax to Quincy, who appeared unconcerned.

"Routine," he said.

"Just the beginning," Sanders agreed, speaking with the confident air of one experienced officer to another. "By the end of this case, the whole town will be swimming in lawyers representing, protecting, and suing the masses. I'm surprised George Walker hasn't already filed a notice to sue the sheriff's department. God knows he thinks this whole thing is Shep's fault."

Rainie chewed her bottom lip. She hated to admit this with Sanders present, but she was out of her league. "You think I'll be sued?"

"Sure," Sanders said matter-of-factly. "The Walkers and the Bensens will probably launch civil suits against the sheriff's department for either not warning the community about Daniel O'Grady or botching the investigation against him. That, of course, will involve you. Then they'll probably file a civil suit against the O'Gradys personally, just in case things don't work out in criminal court. I wouldn't be surprised if Melissa Avalon's parents do the same. Finally, you have all the kids who were injured, though none of them sustained wounds that are that serious. They'll probably fall into two camps: those who would just as soon put this all behind them and those who will pool their resources and go for blood."

"But why sue a sheriff's department?" Rainie asked with a scowl. "We're so broke most of our officers work for free. And the money we do have comes straight from the city, which means people are just suing their neighbors in the end."

"The city and department carry liability insurance," Sanders explained. "Those policies run into the millions, so a good lawyer will argue that there's money to be had with only the insurance companies to be hurt."

"But the premiums go up, and taxes go up, and again all the neighbors foot the bill."

"You're thinking too logically, Rainie. Kids got hurt. The system let people down. Now they want someone to blame. Didn't you learn anything in the nineties? Law enforcement is both the first line of defense and the best scapegoat in town."

Rainie shook her head. She hated lawyers. They took everything and made it too complicated. And they seemed to think that money healed all wounds. Don't just mourn your child, cash in on the loss.

Rainie crossed behind her desk, nudged Sanders to get the hell out of her seat, and did her best to focus on the matters at hand.

"So," she said shortly, folding her hands in front of her and regarding both men. "I met with ballistics, as well as the medical examiner in Portland this morning. Sanders, is there anything you've been meaning to tell me, or should I shoot first and ask questions later?"

The state detective shrugged. "Oh, you mean about the so-called mystery casing."

"What the hell, let's start with that."

"Ballistics has an odd duck, that's all. One casing that has no prints on the outside and some kind of substance on the inside."

"A polymer," Quincy said.

Sanders shot him a look. Then he gave Rainie a stare of disgruntlement. He obviously didn't like her sharing information with the fed. Rainie couldn't care less.

"Yeah, a polymer," Sanders said finally. "I didn't tell you about it, though, because we don't know anything yet. They need to run more tests. Until then we don't have any new information."

"Sanders, a strange casing is information—"

"Conner, a case of this size with this much evidence has a million and a half things like a strange casing. We got debris that can't be categorized, footprints we can't match, and bodily fluids out of place. It goes with the territory. If I tell you about every single question that comes up, you're gonna go nuts."

"I'm the primary officer, Sanders. Going nuts is my problem, not yours."

"All right, all right." Sanders held up two hands in a gesture of peace. "I was honestly trying to be helpful."

"Bullshit. You just want to keep this case quick and simple."

"Yes! Quick and simple is better for everyone. For God's sake, this whole town is knee-deep in firearms."

"All the more reason for us to be making sure we get at the truth. And right now I'm really not sure Danny did it."

"Because of a stupid casing?"

"Because of a stupid casing, a stupid slug, and a stupid trajectory that indicates Melissa Avalon's killer was at least a few inches taller than her!"

"What?"

Abe Sanders appeared genuinely startled. Rainie also drew up short. Then she got it. The detective didn't know about the medical examiner's report yet. He'd only been communicating with the crime lab, not the ME's office.

"Didn't you know?" she couldn't help drawling in mocking imitation. "The .22 slug followed a downward trajectory from the victim's forehead to the back base of the skull. In other words, an undersize thirteen-year-old boy did not shoot a standing grown woman."

Sanders looked stunned, then perplexed, then thoughtful. Rainie could see him turning over the facts in his mind. Was there any way Danny could've reached up with his arm and held the gun at a downward angle? What if Danny had been standing on something? What would he have stood on, and why?

She understood Sanders's mental musing, because

she'd gone through it all herself at seven this morning. The ME and her assistant had even demonstrated the logistics to Rainie. The only way they could re-create the approximate trajectory of the slug was if someone at least the same height fired the shot.

"Shit," Sanders said after a moment.

"Exactly. So now this mystery casing isn't as unimportant as you thought. Plus we have the issue of a .22 slug with no rifling marks. In short, none of our evidence matches anymore."

"Wait a minute, wait a minute," Sanders said quickly. "Let's not throw out the baby with the bathwater. We recovered a .38 revolver at the scene, which was used to kill two victims. We have Danny's prints on the majority of the .38 shell casings, plus three rapid loaders. I don't know about Melissa Avalon, but we still have a case against Danny for Sally and Alice."

Rainie stared at the state detective incredulously. "This doesn't change things? We have a major hole in the case and it doesn't change anything for you?"

"It raises some questions we need to answer," Sanders said levelly, "but no, it doesn't change the case for me."

"How can it not change everything?"

"Because everything isn't changed! Look, I know this is your first homicide, Conner, but the truth is, they don't all wrap up in neat little boxes. You end up with questions and sometimes the evidence is a mess. Our job is to make a case, and we still have enough to argue that Danny killed two girls. Now, maybe he didn't kill Melissa Avalon, maybe there was somebody else at the scene or someone who decided to take advantage of the chaos for his own agenda, but from where I stand, Danny O'Grady killed Alice Bensen and Sally Walker, case closed."

"No," Rainie insisted vehemently. "Case is not closed. The minute we get a mystery person at the scene, case is shot to hell. Enter defense lawyer Avery Johnson. See Avery Johnson argue that Danny procured the guns and Danny loaded the guns but that somebody else—say, the five-foot-eight man on the grassy knoll—pulled the trigger. Watch jury lap it up like a cat at a creamer. The minute we have a mystery person at the scene, our case, as it were, is officially dead in the water."

Sanders scowled. He opened his mouth to argue, then shut it, then started to speak again, then finally settled for scowling harder. It was obvious he genuinely believed that Danny had done the shooting. But he also couldn't fault Rainie's logic. A mystery person provided reasonable doubt; they no longer had enough for the DA to make his case.

Sanders turned to Quincy. "Feel free to step in at any time," the state detective growled.

Quincy shrugged. "I thought Officer Conner was doing a nice job."

"Well, you're the expert, dammit. Tell us what we're missing."

"Honestly, I believe we're back to investigative basics. It seems to me we have a number of key questions. One, why Melissa Avalon? Her murder bears unique elements, so one theory would be that she's the linchpin behind what happened. We know that she and VanderZanden were probably involved. According to Richard Mann, she had fractured relations with her family, particularly her father. Now, I wonder if her father has access to a computer."

"Luke Hayes is in charge of the victimology reports," Rainie said. "I can ask him to focus on Melissa Avalon for now and try to have something for us tomorrow."

Quincy nodded. "Second area of focus: the school computers. We know Danny spent a great deal of time on-line, possibly talking to someone called No Lava. Who is this person? And what was his agenda when he contacted a thirteen-year-old boy? Learning what's on the computers should help us with a second possible theory of this case, that the man in black is a stranger who Danny met on-line."

"Speaking of which," Sanders interjected gloomily. Both Rainie and Quincy turned to stare at him. He focused on Rainie, saying defensively, "I was going to tell you. There just hasn't been time."

"Spit it out, Sanders."

"I got a call from our technicians this morning. They're having problems recovering data from the school computers."

"What kind of problems?"

Sanders smiled tightly. "You'll like this. As I mentioned before, there were some signs that Danny—"

"That someone," Rainie corrected.

"Fine, that someone made an attempt to clean the machines. The history file for the Web browser had been deleted and the cache file had been purged. But that's pretty obvious stuff that most computer-literate people know how to do, so the techies weren't that worried."

"I gather it gets worse."

"In a nutshell. I guess anytime you visit a Web site, the site puts a small piece of information in the computer's 'cookie' file so that the next time the user visits the site, the site can 'remember' information about the user. A good technician can bring up the cookie file from the hard drive and get fairly complete records of every place the user has been. Nope. On all four computers, the cookie files had been deleted as of six P.M. Monday, May fourteenth. The only cookies present are new ones from Tuesday morning, and they're a hodgepodge collection of eToys.com and various Pokémon sites, probably from the kids that morning."

"What about e-mails?" Quincy pressed. "I know I can go on-line and retrieve old e-mails, even ones I've read and deleted."

"Generally yes. *Someone*, however, cleaned out the old and the saved e-mails, then compacted the files so they're unrecoverable. Finally, the person accessed the firewall server and deleted all the data logs. In short, the four computers are wiped clean."

"I want them," Quincy said simply.

"You can have them," Rainie agreed.

"Wait a minute," Sanders protested. "We have good people—"

"The FBI has better."

"Dammit, our technicians have already started work—"

"Then the FBI's data-recovery agents will be all that much faster at finishing."

"It's true," Quincy told Sanders, who looked ready for a full-blown snit. "Even after everything you've described, the information is somewhere on the computers. When a file is deleted, the computer generally only deletes the directory reference to the file, not the actual data. So unless our infamous someone thought to use a Department of Defense–approved deletion program that overwrites the data with zeros, the information is on the machine. We need this information. Whatever Danny was doing on-line with No Lava is highly relevant to what went down Tuesday afternoon. So let our data-recovery agents handle it. We'll get answers sooner versus later."

"We can get the information too," Sanders insisted curtly. "I can put a rush order on it. There's no reason for the FBI to get involved."

"Too late," Rainie said.

"Dammit, it's just an excuse to steal jurisdiction—"

"I don't give a rat's ass!" Rainie yelled back. She slapped her hand against the top of her desk. "Someone else was in the school. Someone else shot Melissa Avalon. I want to know who, goddammit, and for the last time, Sanders, it's *not* your call."

Sanders fell back into steely silence. He crossed his arms over his chest. He muttered, "Man, what I'd give for a hot fudge sundae right now."

Rainie glared at him harder. They all fell silent. The seconds ticked off. After a moment Quincy said, "Third action step."

He looked at them both. Rainie nodded to show she was paying attention. Sanders returned to the conversation more grudgingly.

"We go back to what you were doing this morning, Rainie—a complete list of other possible suspects. VanderZanden, Charlie Kenyon, Richard Mann, Melissa Avalon's father, this computer person, No Lava."

"I'm working on that. I just don't have a lot of manpower."

"Fine," Sanders interjected crossly. "Let's divvy it up between us. What the hell, we can pretend cross-jurisdictional investigations really work. I'll take VanderZanden. The fed can have No Lava, since he's stolen my computers. Luke Hayes has Melissa Avalon's father—"

"I'll take Charlie Kenyon and Richard Mann," Rainie volunteered.

"Perfect," Sanders said flatly. His eyes met Rainie's with open challenge. "That just leaves us with one last suspect: Shep."

"No way! He's the sheriff—"

"Whose time at the school is completely unaccounted for! We know he's got problems at home. We know he's an older man, which makes him exactly Melissa Avalon's type. And we know he goes way back with you, Conner, which makes this whole damn case even more interesting."

Rainie decided to ignore that last comment. She said tightly, "Shep called me from his radio after the shots were fired, meaning he was in his patrol car, not at the school."

"Or he did the deed, returned to his car in the parking lot, and made the call."

"Shep would not frame his own fucking son!"

"We don't know that he did! Come on, the evidence is all over the place. Danny did it. Wait, no, a second person's present, maybe he did it. You said it yourself, Conner, Danny's got the perfect defense right now—

the man on the grassy knoll. Looks to me like he's about to walk. Meaning Shep's either really clever or really lucky."

"You," Rainie said hotly, "have been watching too many Oliver Stone movies."

"I'll do it," Quincy said calmly. They both looked at him belatedly, as if just now remembering he was there. "I'll look into Shep," he repeated, then quickly cut off Rainie's objection. "It's due discipline, Rainie. There are too many things about this shooting that don't make sense. Until they do, everyone must be a suspect—mysterious men in black and, yes, the town sheriff."

Rainie sat back. She wasn't happy, but there was no more point in arguing. Quincy returned to the general conversation.

"One last thing," he said. "If the UNSUB is a stranger, we need to cast a wider net because chances are that he's still in the area."

"You mean in Bakersville?" Rainie asked incredulously.

"No, this town is too small to hide in. He'd look for a neighboring town, maybe a larger tourist resort. Someplace where he could go to bars and local establishments and watch all the news coverage. He's probably following the investigation very closely and asking others about it. It's his way of reliving the moment, of still having fun. We should make contact with neighboring police departments. Have their officers ask hotel workers and bartenders. Any new faces showing a lot of interest in Bakersville's tragedy? Any mid-twenties to mid-forties white males who've been mouthing off on the subject or asking a lot of questions? That sort of thing."

Sanders nodded. "I can make a few calls," he said, then shrugged dubiously. "I don't want to lose my own men to a wild-goose chase, though. You guys may like the notion of some mystery man, but I keep coming back to the victim's injury. I've seen a lot of homicides, and a single gunshot wound to the forehead—that's a targeted victim any way you look at it. Maybe it wasn't Danny, but *somebody* specifically wanted Melissa Avalon dead."

Quincy didn't argue. Neither did Rainie. It did seem to come back to Melissa Avalon, and the fact that they still couldn't understand why made them all very uncomfortable.

"Well, at least we have one lucky break on our side," Quincy said finally.

Sanders and Rainie exchanged startled glances. Sanders did the honors. "We have a break?"

"The recovery of the .22-caliber slug. You said it yourself, Detective. Most .22s become too deformed for a ballistics test. My guess is our shooter knew that too. So he tells Danny to bring a .22. Chances are, his slug will ricochet inside the skull, obliterating trajectory and rifling marks. Given all other circumstantial evidence, Danny will be blamed for Melissa Avalon's death as well. Except the bullet doesn't ricochet. It holds a trajectory that immediately lets us know the shooter must have been another adult. And it keeps enough of the base intact to reveal its little secret—it's perfectly smooth, indicating a unique weapon. One 40-grain slug later, we know something else happened at that school."

Rainie slowly nodded. Without the slug and its trajectory, there would never have been any reason to look beyond Danny O'Grady. Especially with the boy confessing each and every chance he got.

Sanders, however, was frowning. "I don't get it. You're saying someone asked Danny to bring a .22 to cover for his own .22. But why the hell would he do that? Why wouldn't he simply use Danny's gun?"

Rainie stopped. Stared. She looked at Quincy, who for once appeared completely flummoxed.

"The .22 slug is smooth," she murmured. "It definitely didn't come from Danny's gun. And that poses another question: If the shooter brought his own weapon to kill Melissa Avalon, why a .22? It's not that powerful, particularly for a head shot. Frankly, many people survive that wound. And yet he fired only one shot to her forehead with his own gun. Risking her living to tell the tale. Risking someone seeing him armed. I don't understand. . . . Something here doesn't make sense."

They all looked at one another. No one had an answer. A preselected victim. A mystery slug. An unidentified man who had cajoled a thirteen-year-old boy into taking part in murder.

They had come a long way from a mindless act of rage, and now, suddenly, Rainie didn't know where they were going anymore. She thought about her small, peaceful town. She thought about the towering trees and the gentle rolling hills. She thought about Danny, so scared and frightened and determined to take credit for murder. She thought of the school halls, still streaked in blood.

And for the first time in fourteen years, Rainie was frightened.

NINETEEN

DANNY SAT ALONE in his eight-by-eight room, staring at a spider that was slowly working its way across the thin-carpeted floor.

The door was open. Every morning at 6 A.M., the doors were flung wide by burly staff members who yelled, "It's that time, boys and girls." The doors stayed open all day, joining a series of look-alike rooms to a main hallway until nine o'clock at night, when everyone prepared for bed. More staff people—not guards, Danny was told, but *guides*—came by and locked everyone in from the outside. At ten o'clock came lights-out. Danny would find a face peering in through the Plexiglas window, making sure he followed the rules.

Danny followed the rules. He didn't make any trouble. He got up when he was supposed to. He let the *guide* escort him to the cafeteria. He stared at his tray. He let another *guide* lead him to a classroom, where twenty boys, ages ranging from twelve to seventeen, pretended to be studying under the eyes of some chipper lady who insisted that they could be whatever they wanted to be. Later they were allowed to *socialize*.

Danny always came back to his room, where he sat alone. No one cared. Cabot County's Juvenile Center was a newer facility. It operated as a giant, beige-colored dorm, unlike the other places kids whispered about. Old prisons converted into youth facilities where the walls and floors were slabs of concrete and everybody got to watch everybody pee. Cabot County wasn't anything like that. Some of the kids got to wear their own clothes as long as they didn't sport gang colors or offensive T-shirts. The social room had lots of Plexiglas windows and real live plants. If kids earned enough merit points, they could watch TV or even rent movies for the VCR.

For the most part, the guides led them through their days, a careful schedule of meals, classes, and rec time. As long as you did what you were told and went where you were told, no one made a fuss. You could even be alone during the social time. Sit in your room. Stare at your blue hospital scrubs. Watch spiders. Didn't matter.

The whole point was that you were never going to make it any farther. The nice rooms had Plexiglas windows for a reason. And all the outside doors were inch-thick steel. Then there was the ten-foot-high fence ringing the yard and topped with coils of barbed wire. The searchlights. The guides who had keys to rifles loaded with rubber bullets.

When Danny first got there, the older kids had been fascinated by him, and they told him stories of juvies who'd run for it. Kids who had been flattened by mattresses, gassed with pepper spray, or, rarely, if they made it beyond the fence, hunted down by growling Dobermans. If the dogs catch you, they're each allowed one bite as a reward, kids said. The guides pick the place.

Danny thought the kids were full of shit, but he didn't say anything. Since the day he'd come in, that had been his motto. Don't give up a word.

I'm smart, I'm smart, I'm smart.

I'm scared.

Now he watched the spider laboriously climb toward the barred window, thirsty for sunlight or maybe the wind in its hairy little face.

Danny fingered his scrubs—no laces, no buttons, no belts for a kid under "SWatch"—and tried to get his mind to shut up.

The lawyer came to talk to him yesterday. Danny hadn't wanted to see the man. He had a fancy gray suit and an expensive watch and Danny knew he must cost a lot of money, which made him feel worse. His mom would be stressed about that, trying to figure out how to pay. His father would yell at her that it didn't matter, because good old Shep didn't get how the world worked. He was still lost in his football fantasies where he and/or his son were scoring the winning touchdown during the big homecoming game.

Danny hated worrying his mom. He knew she had cried. He'd heard her himself. Late at night he tried to cover his ears with his hands to block out the sound, but then he'd have to move his hand and stuff it in his mouth to keep from whimpering.

The lawyer made small talk. He told Danny what a lawyer did and what a trial was about. What his role would be and what Danny's role would be. He spoke as if Danny was four years old, and Danny let him. He stared at a point just beyond the lawyer's ear while the man babbled for an hour.

Danny wasn't supposed to talk to the counselors, he was told. They technically worked for the detention center, so it could be argued that they were law enforcement and anything he told them might be used against him at trial. To be on the safe side, Danny should ask for a chaplain or a pastor or a rabbi if he felt like spilling his guts. Priest-penitent privilege was absolute.

Danny didn't talk. He knew absolutely he could not talk, could not trust anyone, even during the quiet hours of the night when the words bobbed up inside him and lodged as a fierce, hard knot in the center of his chest. That's when he saw what had happened again, clearly but somehow distanced, as if it had all been a dream and had nothing to do with him. Then he'd raise his hand, see that he wasn't even trembling, and want to scream and scream and scream.

The lawyer told him two experts would be visiting him as well. There were more rules about talking. One of them couldn't be trusted. Danny was to be careful. The other—Schaffer, maybe?—worked for his parents. He could tell him everything. Maybe he should think about telling him everything. Maybe he would feel better about getting it off his chest.

The lawyer looked at him kindly.

Danny thought about Miss Avalon. The expression that had washed over her face. The way she had turned toward him. Her last words, not understanding.

"Danny, run! Run, run, run*!"*

The spider reached the window. Danny watched it race happily over the warm, unbreakable glass.

So many things in his mind. All these images, but so far away. Blood. Noise. Smells he'd never imagined. Hot guns in his hands. But so far away. Maybe just a dream. *Snap,* open your eyes and it's gone. Maybe a bad TV show. *Click,* turn it off, go to bed.

Sally and Alice and Miss Avalon. Sally and Alice and pretty Miss Avalon.

"Run, Danny, run!"

Danny got up. He raised his hand and slammed it down on the spider. Smash. He had happy spider guts all over his hand. He studied his fingers. They still wouldn't tremble. He stared at his hand and he willed it to shake. Nothing.

Danny, the stone-cold killer.

He went back to his bed.

RAINIE SWOOPED DOWN on Charlie Kenyon like a bat out of hell. She'd had four run-ins with the nineteen-year-old, and this time around she didn't have the patience. She spotted him riding a small Huffy dirt bike down a bumpy logging road on his father's wooded estate, she flipped on her lights, and she went after him.

Quincy was riding shotgun. He didn't blink an eye at the display of sirens, lights, and billowing dust as Rainie pulled Charlie over to the side of the road and fishtailed to a stop. She got out of the car with her hand resting on the top of the baton in her heavy utility belt.

"Off the bike, Charlie."

"Holy shit, Officer, was I speeding?" Looking cool in a black leather jacket and too-tight jeans, Charlie remained standing over the dirt bike. He gave her a mocking grin. Rainie worked on not smashing in his face. She needed to get more sleep. Even for herself, she was short-tempered these days.

Charlie's gaze flickered behind her, to where Quincy was climbing out of the car.

"Who's the suit?" Charlie asked.

"None of your business."

"Breaking in a new partner? Shouldn't you have told him about the dress code? Man, I've seen guys killed for wearing silk ties in these parts."

Rainie ignored his comments. "Whose bike, Charlie?"

"Why? Gonna make me an offer?"

"Whose bike, Charlie?"

"Mine—"

"It's sized for an eight-year-old."

"I'm nostalgic."

"Really? And here I thought you were just a lying piece of shit. Get off the bike, Charlie, and put your hands in the air."

Charlie finally dropped his James Dean routine long enough to scowl and whine. "Hey, I won the bike fair and square. It's not my fault the kid never learned to dodge left in a fight."

"I said *now*."

"I'm on my father's property—"

"*Now!*"

Charlie finally went quiet. He stared at her. He stared at Quincy. Then he grudgingly swung a leg over the bike and let it drop to the ground. "All right, all right, don't get your panties in a wad."

"Hands in the air. Turn around. Place them against the tree trunk. Spread your legs."

"You're gonna pat me down? Over stealing a bike?"

"Who said this had anything to do with a bike?"

"What the—"

He was too late. Rainie had already gotten close enough to hook her foot around his. She twisted him straight into the tree trunk, planted his hands above his head, and frisked him. A minute later she was the proud owner of a corkscrew, a switchblade, two hundred dollars cash, and a roll of quarters.

Quincy helped himself to the coins. He hefted the roll in his hand, fisted his fingers around it, and admired the weight. Charlie Kenyon knew how to pack a punch.

"Slow nights, Mr. Kenyon?" he asked Charlie.

Rainie released her pressure on the teen's back. He turned around unhurriedly, making a big show of shaking out his arms and fussing with the collar of his leather jacket. After smoothing back his brown wavy hair, he gave Quincy a disdainful stare.

"I'm sorry," the teen said with bracing sarcasm, "but I didn't catch your name."

"Supervisory Special Agent Pierce Quincy. FBI."

"Ah shit," Charlie said.

Rainie finally smiled. "Funny, your father said the same thing when I spoke to him this afternoon. It appears it's one thing to tangle with the locals, but not even your father feels like messing with the feds."

"You can take the bike."

"No kidding. Charlie, tell us about Danny O'Grady."

"What?"

"You heard me. We want to know everything you ever said to Danny. And if I were you, I'd give us absolute cooperation, because a few eyewitnesses have already told us enough to book you as an accomplice to murder. You're nineteen, Charlie. You end up aiding and abetting a mass murder, and there's nothing your pissant ex-mayor father can do to help you anymore. You graduate to a whole new league of adult delinquency. We're talking hard time, and not even at one of those lovely country-club prisons. You'd get the real thing."

"Hey, hey, hey, hey." Charlie held up two hands and made a big show of backing off. "You think I was involved with hurting those girls? No way, no how. I got an alibi." He gave Quincy a look. "And she's real sweet, if you know what I mean."

"Why were you hanging out at the elementary school? Are high school kids too tough for you? Bigger, stronger, might actually put up a fight?"

"I don't know what you're talking about. I just got a thing for jungle gyms."

"I'm getting angry, Charlie. I'm not getting a lot of sleep these days, and the mayor told me this morning to do whatever's necessary to solve this case, so I wouldn't make me angry right now."

"I got a federal witness," Charlie said promptly.

Quincy looked at the sky. "Where?"

"Shit, I thought you guys had standards."

Quincy eyed Rainie balefully. "I guess that explains Waco."

Charlie flinched. "This just burns me, man."

"My heart's breaking," Rainie assured him. "Why were you at the elementary school, Charlie?"

" 'Cause I get bored, okay? 'Cause there's nothing to do in Bitchville, U.S.A., and sometimes I need a little distraction."

"Is that what Danny O'Grady was to you? Distraction?"

Charlie shrugged. "Danny was interesting. Real potential, if you know what I mean."

"No, I don't. He was a good student, smart, stayed

out of trouble. The only potential I saw in him was to get a lot further in life than you ever will."

Charlie turned away from her. He looked at Quincy slyly. "You know what I mean, don't you, fed? I've heard about you. You're some big-shot profiler. Best there ever was, put away the infamous Jim Beckett. Dazzle me, fed. It's damn slow around here. I need someone to say something interesting just so I can stay awake."

"I think you should keep doing the talking," Quincy said evenly. "Us law-enforcement types have a hang-up about hearing things in your own words. Besides, I'm sure you love to listen to yourself speak."

"You're no fun."

"It's a job requirement."

"Charlie, what were you doing with Danny?"

"*Nothing*, okay? Exercising our First Amendment rights. You come down on me for that and I'll sic the ACLU all over your small-town ass."

Rainie turned to Quincy. "This isn't working for me."

"He seems very belligerent," Quincy agreed.

"I think we're going to have to do something about that."

"Harm a single dead-skin cell on my head and my father will sue you back to the Stone Age."

"At this point, your father would have to get in line." Rainie turned back to Quincy. She said thoughtfully, "I'm thinking hair or jacket."

Quincy carefully scrutinized Charlie's black biker jacket and meticulously styled hair.

"Jacket," he said.

"Okay." Rainie stepped forward. Charlie saw her coming and tried to duck right. She countered, found a sleeve, and neatly spun Charlie around. A second later she held the black leather jacket and Charlie stood stunned.

Rainie smiled at him. She was in such a dark mood these days. She didn't want to deal with punks. She was sick of kids who wielded guns and switchblades with no real concept of death.

"We're going to play a game, Charlie. I'm going to ask questions. You're going to answer. Quincy, the expert, is going to evaluate your answers for truthfulness. If he doesn't like what you say—or you make me angry again—I'm going to start slicing up your coat. You give me lip, your jacket loses a sleeve. Got it?"

"It's just a dumb jacket. I can buy a new one."

"Okay." Rainie opened his switchblade and found the collar.

"Wait, wait, wait, wait, wait!" Charlie was panting. His gaze was locked down on the collar, and perspiration beaded his upper lip. The jacket was old and sported a biker gang's symbol on the back. The kid could deny it all he wanted, but Quincy and Rainie had him pegged. The jacket was part of Charlie Kenyon's costume, and he felt overexposed without it. They might as well have snatched Superman's cape.

"First question, Charlie. Why were you hanging out with Danny O'Grady?"

"Because he was cool, all right?"

"Danny is a computer geek. How is that cool?"

"No, no, no." Charlie was shaking his head. "You don't get it. You had to look in his eyes. He was *old*, man. And ... and ... angry. At his father. I know these things."

"Danny's a kindred spirit?" Rainie asked dryly.

"Something like that."

"What about Melissa Avalon?" Quincy interjected. "What was she?"

Charlie's answer was more forthcoming. "She was hot! Jesus, fed, did you look at her? Whoa, mama."

"You ever approach her?"

"Sure, I tried." He shrugged, his hands digging into his pockets. He was definitely self-conscious without his jacket. "She, uh, was intimidated by my good looks. Besides, I heard later I violated her age rules. Avalon had a geezer fetish."

"Was she a kindred spirit?"

"What d'you mean? Oh, was she angry? I don't know. Didn't seem angry to me. You should ask Danny. He was the one spending so much time with her."

"Did he ever mention his feelings for Miss Avalon to you?"

"Didn't have to. The boy was lovesick for her. You could see it all over his face."

"Did Avalon know this?"

"Probably. I don't think puppy crushes were new to her."

"How did she treat Danny?"

"I don't know. I hung around the school grounds, not the freaking computer lab."

"Did Danny know about her 'geezer fetish'?"

"Sure, I told him. What, you guys think Danny killed her in a jealous rage? Nah, you don't get it." Charlie shook his head, sounding honest for the first time. "Danny's smarter than you think. He knew he liked her, but hell, she was a teacher. He understood what that meant. Worship from afar, end of story. He wasn't imagining white picket fences or the mother of his children. The kid's thirteen, for chrissakes."

"What about the other two girls?" Rainie asked. "Sally and Alice?"

"Couldn't pick them out of a lineup if I tried."

"Are you going to go to the funerals, Charlie?"

He shrugged. "The old man's making me."

"Do you think it's sad that they're dead?"

"Don't know them. Don't care."

"You're a real hard-ass, aren't you, Charlie Kenyon?"

"You're the one threatening my jacket."

"Did you ever talk to Danny about killing people?"

"We talked about lots of stuff."

"Charlie." She held up the switchblade, then his jacket.

Charlie's jaw hardened. She thought he was going to freeze up on her. Then she moved the blade closer to the collar and he surrendered again.

"Yeah. Sure. You wanna know? Sometimes I dream

of blowing this whole freaking town off the map. I dream of getting my hands on a big motherfucking nuke and saying *sayonara,* babe. You know, plant life grows back bigger and stronger after a nuclear holocaust. Maybe that's what this town needs."

"You told all this to a thirteen-year-old boy?"

"Only after he told me he wanted to hack his father into twenty different pieces and run him through a blender."

Rainie stared at him. A muscle worked in her jaw. She said with more anger than she wanted to give away, "A child tells you he fantasizes about murdering his own father, and you didn't think to go to the police?"

"Who am I going to go to? Shep, his dad? Or, better yet, you?" Charlie chuckled unkindly. "Isn't that a pretty picture? Half this town still talks about what you did to your mother. What would you have done with Danny? Mail him a shotgun?"

"I never harmed my mother," Rainie said hotly. "And if I had done such a thing, I'd be in prison where I'd belong, not standing here talking to you."

But Charlie had that sly look back on his face. "I know, I know," he said with a conspirator's wink. "The fed's here. You don't want to blow your cover. That's all right. But you don't have to lie to me, babe. I'm telling you, I can see these things. And you're a member of the cool-kids club too. Hell, around here, you're probably the charter member."

"One last question," Quincy interjected quickly, because the shotgun comment had pushed Rainie to the brink and they all knew it. "Did Danny ever mention an on-line friend to you? Someone named No Lava?"

"Computer geek? Yeah, maybe. Danny was always into something. I didn't know how one person could spend so much time staring at a screen."

"Did you ever see any of the e-mails?"

"What the hell would I want with them?"

"Danny really liked No Lava. Maybe you were jealous."

"Look, I've never even heard of this No Lava, and frankly, the name sounds like an impotent dude to me. Danny liked mail, okay? Six months ago, eight months ago, I don't remember, he was all excited about someone he'd met on-line. He was always having to go check his frigging e-mail. That's all I know."

"You encouraged him," Rainie said softly. "Danny was troubled and you helped push him over the edge. Now three people are dead, and some of that's on your head, Charlie. You're going to have to live with that."

"Who gives a fuck? Legally, I'm free as a bird. Now, give me my jacket back. As much fun as this has been, I got places to go and people to see."

"Sure," Rainie said. She smiled at him. Then she raised the switchblade and sliced the collar clean off his coat.

Charlie shrieked. Quincy took a shocked step forward.

Rainie retrieved the severed piece of leather. A moment later she squeezed the long plastic bag of white powder from the collar onto her palm.

"Heroin. About three ounces of it, which would make a little more than simple possession. Congratulations, Charlie. Legally speaking, your troubles are just beginning."

"Goddamn cunt! How dare you! You're no better than me! You're no better than any of us!"

"Sure I am, Charlie. There are two choices for angry people in this world, and only one of them wears a badge."

Charlie shrieked again. Rainie enjoyed loading him into the car.

TWENTY

IT TOOK RAINIE four hours to process Charlie Kenyon. She had to catalog the heroin into evidence. Then she had to store it in the safe that passed as the department's evidence locker. She'd just finished fingerprinting Charlie when his father's lawyer arrived and tried to tell her she'd used entrapment to find the drugs. Rainie volunteered an FBI agent as her corroborating witness. FitzSimons turned downright abusive. She'd had no right to search Charlie Kenyon, no justification for mutilating his jacket, and she'd violated every constitutional law ever envisioned by the forefathers and then some.

Rainie took it in stride. It amazed her how comforting the drug bust felt after the relative chaos of the past three days. She knew Charlie, she knew FitzSimons, she knew Charlie's dad. All the usual suspects, all the usual paperwork, all the usual crimes. She could've done this arrest in her sleep.

She spent two hours carefully wording the arrest report and building the file against Charlie. Then the paperwork was done and she returned to the task-force center, where the shadows had grown long and the attic office was eerily quiet. Well past ten o'clock; another long day in a long, strange case.

Luke Hayes had gone to Portland, where he would hopefully interview Melissa Avalon's parents. Sanders was out doing God knows what Sanders did. Maybe arranging the soup cans in the grocery store or crashing a Tupperware party for more stay-fresh seals. Quincy was following up on No Lava. Or maybe he'd started in on Shep. Whatever he found, she'd probably be the last to know. She was both frustrated by that and grateful.

Now there was just her and the hum of the old computer and the buzz of all the thoughts still crowding her head.

Charlie had rattled her today. Not just with his accusations against her. Rainie knew what people thought and said. She accepted that salacious rumors would always be more appealing than cold, hard fact. It didn't get to her.

He had spooked her with his comments about Danny.

"Only after he told me he wanted to hack his father into twenty different pieces and run him through a blender."

Rainie couldn't let the statement go. So much violence. So much rage. She knew these things happened. God knows, some nights . . . Huddled in the closet, bruised and shaking and still tasting the blood on her split lip. Wishing it would go away. Wishing she'd have the strength to make it stop.

The fantasies. That she'd rise up and her mother would finally cower before her. That just once she'd strike back, maybe slap her mother hard, and then her mother would repent, weeping, "I never knew how much it hurt. I swear I never realized. Now I know and I'll never do it again."

Maybe that was the difference. Through all of her pain, Rainie never forgot that Molly was her mother. And the kernel of her fantasies was still about love and forgiveness. That her mother would realize what she was doing. That she'd give up the bottle. That she'd take her little girl in her arms and swear never to hurt her again. That for once Rainie could relax in her mother's embrace and feel safe.

Even at the worst of it, she had not wished her mother dead.

It had taken a great deal more than that to push her over the edge.

Rainie paced the tiny attic. Her body ached and her mind ached and she couldn't stand being alone with her own thoughts anymore. She needed sleep, a decent meal, a good hard run. It was too late to jog, she had no appetite, and she was honestly afraid to close her eyes.

"What would you have done with Danny? Mail him a shotgun?"

No, she would've told him that she understood. She would've taken him to her back deck, where the mountain pines towered above them and owls hooted deep in the shadows and it was difficult to take yourself seriously when you were so small in the general scheme of things. She would've let him talk. Get it all out, angry child to angry child if that's what it took. Then maybe she would've talked. Perhaps she would've told him things she'd never told anyone else. Sitting on her deck with the trees around them and the clean mountain air fresh on their faces.

Maybe she would've saved Danny O'Grady.

But she hadn't done any such thing. She'd seen him just two weeks before the shooting. She'd thought he was pale and jumpy and curt with his father. And in the next instant she'd shrugged it away because, just like everyone else, she thought it was a phase. Trouble happened only in bad families. Not to a nice, ordinary kid like Danny.

She, a kindred spirit, had failed him. And she didn't know yet how she was going to live with that.

QUINCY WAS HUNCHED over his laptop in his cramped hotel room when knocking sounded at the door. He'd been working for two hours, scouring various on-line carriers for any record of a member named No Lava. His eyes were blurry. His shoulders carried knots the size of small boulders. Every time he shifted to get more comfortable, the rickety desk threatened to collapse and take his laptop with it. Thirty minutes ago he'd started cramming crime-scene photos under the uneven legs for better support. He did not want to know what this said about his life.

The knocking came again.

Quincy pushed away from the table, rubbed the back of his neck, and self-consciously checked the mirror. His white shirt, pressed crisp just this morning, was now a wrinkled mess. His tie was somewhere on the floor. His cheeks sported a five o'clock shadow, and his dark hair was rumpled from running his fingers through it over and over again. If memory served, this look had worked for him in his thirties, when it made him sexy in a dark, brooding sort of way. He was in his mid-forties now. He thought he simply looked tired.

Some decades were definitely better than others, he thought. What the hell.

He checked the door's peephole and was not surprised to see Rainie standing there.

He opened the door, and for a moment they simply studied each other.

She'd changed out of her officer's uniform. Now she wore faded straight-leg jeans and a loose hunter-green sweater with a turtleneck collar that framed her face. Her chestnut hair was down and freshly brushed, gleaming gold and red beneath the hotel's outdoor lights. She didn't appear to be wearing a drop of makeup, and Quincy liked her that way. Her pale skin fresh and untouched. No barriers between his hand and the feel of her cheek, or his lips and the corner of her mouth.

He had spent the latter part of the afternoon learning things about Lorraine Conner he had not anticipated. Certainly he was starting to understand that her past held a great deal more than met the eye. Maybe nothing, but maybe something. He doubted she would tell him the whole truth yet, and he wondered about the dangers of learning it all at the last minute, when it might be too late for both of them.

He should be careful. He was a smart, logical man who knew better than most the dark potential of human nature. The warning did him no good. She was here, at his hotel room, and he suspected his face now held a giddy smile.

"Hey," she said after a moment.

"Good evening, Rainie."

"Working?"

"Just finishing up."

"Really?" She stuck her hands in her back pockets and studied the pavement. She was clearly self-conscious, and that touched him.

"I was just about to order take-out Chinese," he said politely. "Would you like to join me?"

"I'm not that hungry."

"Neither am I, but we can pretend together."

She entered his hotel room. He made an effort to clear his paperwork off the bed, since the room was small and there was no place else for her to sit. She studied his laptop while he shoved manila files back into his black leather briefcase/computer carrier.

"Looking for No Lava?" she asked.

"Yes. Most Internet providers have member directories where you can enter your on-line name and vital statistics. Lots of people fill out the forms, so I thought I'd see if we could get that lucky. Unfortunately, we're not that lucky. Next step is to get a subpoena and contact the carriers directly."

"Did you run a background check on Shep today?" she asked.

Quincy stopped, still holding four files, and blinked. She wasn't wasting any time. He put the files in the bag, zipped it shut.

"Do you like lo mein?" he asked lightly.

"Order whatever you want."

"Lo mein it is." He picked up the batch of take-out menus Ginnie had left next to the phone and sorted through them until he found one for the Great Wall of China. He placed an order for lo mein and green tea. Rainie was still studying him.

"I don't think we should have this conversation," he said presently.

"That means you found something."

"No. It means I have professional standards and this is a clear case of conflict of interest. Shep is your friend. You and he go way back." He regarded her steadily.

"I never slept with Shep," Rainie said matter-of-factly.

"You know most people think that you're the reason his and Sandy's marriage is falling apart."

"We're not involved. Never have been, never will be."

"He spends a lot of time at your place."

"I know."

"Rainie—"

"People talk. Don't you get that yet? It's a small town, it rains eighty percent of the year, and the cows outnumber the people two to one. Most of the time there's nothing else to do around here but talk. That's just the way it is."

"Why didn't you tell me about the shotgun, Rainie? The shotgun that killed your mother had your prints on it until it disappeared from the police evidence locker. Then one day it was magically back in custody, but completely wiped clean. Why didn't you tell me it disappeared from evidence?"

Her face went cool, her chin coming up, her gray eyes turning the color of slate. He recognized that expression. Her fighter's stance.

"Do you think I killed my mother?"

"No."

"Do you think I shot her in cold blood? Came home

from school one day and blew off her goddamn head? I'm just a female version of Charlie Kenyon. No better than Danny O'Grady?"

He said gently, "No, Rainie, I don't."

"Then what does it matter, Quincy? It was fourteen years ago and I didn't do it, so just let it go. It's one thing to deal with all the stares and rumors from my neighbors, but I don't expect that from you!"

"Give me some credit," he countered sharply. "I'm not a small-town deputy you can snow under with a few loud words. I know something happened, Rainie. Something happened, Shep helped you with it, and that's what binds you, isn't it? I still don't know what. Maybe I don't need to know, but there *is* something between you and Shep. And it's beyond professional ties and it makes the fact that you were alone in the school with Shep and Danny very shaky. Sanders was right. You should've surrendered jurisdiction over this case. And I suspect you know that as well."

She fell silent, her lips thinning. He'd caught her off guard. He had wondered in the beginning what a woman as smart as Rainie was doing working such a limited job, and today he'd gotten his answer. Because it kept her in control. She worked with nice people, but none of them was the type to pry. He suspected she dated men of more brawn than brains and kept the relationships short. No one could question her too much. No one could get too close. She had turned protecting herself into a way of life.

"I couldn't give up jurisdiction," she said abruptly.

"Because you promised Shep you'd be the primary in the case?"

"Yes." She hesitated. "I owe him that much."

"Just how much do you owe him, Rainie?"

"Shep had faith in me. He's been a good friend and I feel loyalty toward him. But I have professional standards, too, Quincy, and I don't compromise them. We all go through life making our choices and we're all responsible for what we've done. If Danny shot those girls, then by God, he needs to be held accountable for that."

"You're sure of that?"

"Of course I'm sure! Covering up doesn't do him any favors. Why don't people realize that? We have a basic human need to make restitution in order to absolve our guilt. Letting kids walk away scot-free or shielding them from the consequences of their actions doesn't help them. A moment's mistake, a moment of bad judgment could fester into a lifetime of hatred and self-loathing and destructiveness. Until it's become a dark spot you can't forget and can't let go and it builds and builds—"

She broke off. She was breathing hard. Her gaze had become locked on the blue floral bedspread and her hands were fisted at her sides.

"The nightmares are worse, aren't they?" Quincy asked quietly.

"Yes."

"You're not eating."

"I can't."

"You're too smart to be doing this to yourself."

"I can't seem to stop."

"Why did you come here tonight, Rainie?"

She looked at him with frustrated, troubled eyes. "I think I need to talk."

"Then talk. But say something new, Rainie, because I no longer have the patience for lies."

The Chinese food arrived. Quincy split the lo mein, though he suspected she wouldn't eat. She didn't. She set the white container aside but accepted a cup of tea. He took a bite of his own dinner. He wasn't that hungry either, but he'd learned a long time ago that letting himself get run-down during a case, especially a very difficult case, didn't do anyone any favors.

"Sally and Alice's funeral will be held tomorrow afternoon," Rainie said shortly. "The mayor just called and told me. The bodies were retrieved from the ME's office this evening, and the families don't want to wait. Everyone thinks it would be best to get this behind us."

"That will be a rough afternoon."

"Yeah. We've called for backup from Cabot County. Extra patrols both during the funeral and afterward. Patrol cars stationed outside of the bars, you know."

"Emotions are already running high, add to that a little booze . . ." Quincy trailed off. They both knew what could happen. Young men and guns, vigilante justice.

"We'll be doubling up the guard around Shep's house," Rainie said quietly. "Luke asked to lead the effort."

"And you?"

"I can't. There would be more talk."

"George Walker isn't very happy with you."

"No. A lot of people aren't. I was hoping . . . I wanted to be able to say that Danny didn't do it. Before we got to the funerals, I wanted to have so much evidence I could look George Walker in the eye and say, 'A thirteen-year-old boy didn't murder your daughter, sir. Some other bastard did it.' As if that would make a difference."

"You're not so sure about Danny anymore, are you?"

Her expression grew strained. She said softly, "No."

"Charlie Kenyon?"

She slowly nodded. "His account of what Danny told him. That he wanted to cut his father into pieces, run him through a blender. . . . So much anger. I didn't realize . . . I didn't know things had gotten that bad."

"It's not your fault, Rainie. It's hard for any of us to believe that people we personally know and care about are capable of violence. People seem to forget: Murderers don't come from test tubes. They're born into this world like the rest of us, and they also have family and friends."

"That's just a platitude. I don't *want* any more

platitudes. I'm sick of easy answers or thirty-second analyses of complicated crimes. Kids are shooting up their schools, grown men are walking into offices and mowing down their coworkers. And I understand your point that schools and businesses are still safer than driving on the highway, but that explanation is not enough. These shootings are happening everywhere, even places like here, where they don't belong. And they are happening to everyone, even to Danny O'Grady, who just three days ago seemed like a normal kid going through a hard time. And . . . and I feel like I missed something. I should've seen this coming. But then I look at it again, and I know I still never would've expected violence. Because I don't understand it, Quincy. Even I, who was raised by a woman who lived by her fists, can't imagine shooting up strangers. And I need to know why this happened to my town, because no matter how hard I try, I just can't get to sleep."

"It's not your fault, Rainie," he said again.

She shook her head impatiently. "Explain the shootings to me. I need to know. Is it because of guns? As an officer, should I be banning them from my community? Or is it video games and violent movies, and books. . . . Is it all because of that?"

"Those things are factors. On the other hand, do I think censoring Hollywood and banning guns would end all the crime? No. Some people, even kids, are that angry."

"Then it's inevitable? We've become a violent culture and there's nothing we can do about it?"

"I don't think that. There's always something we can do. We're an intelligent society, Rainie. Nothing is beyond our grasp."

"Tell that to George Walker. Tell that to the parents of Alice Bensen. I'm sure they're sitting home right now thinking about how capable society is."

Quincy fell silent. She was in a mood tonight.

"Do you want a solution, Rainie," he asked after a moment, "or do you want an excuse to be angry?"

"I want a solution!"

"Fine," he said crisply. "I'll give you my two cents, for what it's worth. Society is not filled with evil souls. But it is filled with people who are mobile, fractured, overworked, overweight, overcrowded, and overtired. That's a potent combination, particularly for people with poor coping skills and volatile tempers. And we're seeing the proof of that in the increasing number of impulsive, angry acts, such as mass murders and road rage."

Rainie sighed. She rubbed her temples. "It's a sign of the times?"

"It's a sign of stressful living," Quincy said, then shrugged. "In the good-news department, some of the solutions are fairly simple. Why not teach rage-management classes and stress-coping skills in school? While we're at it, we could emphasize good communication skills and self-monitoring. Physical care also makes a big difference. In fact, the first thing a child psychologist does when he begins treatment of a new client is address sleep, exercise, and eating habits. You think you have trouble with rage? Try getting eight hours of sleep at night, eat more fruits and vegetables, and enjoy a good workout. Ironically enough, very few people bother with these basic steps anymore, and then they wonder why they're tense all the time."

He gave her a pointed look, his gaze sliding to the untouched carton of food by her side. Rainie nodded slowly. She said, almost hesitantly, "I took a class in anger management."

"In Portland?"

"Yes. After I'd joined AA. Alcohol numbs a lot of emotions. Then you give it up . . ."

"I think that was a great thing for you to do," Quincy said honestly. "I wish more people would think that way."

Rainie immediately shook her head. "I'm not so great, Quincy. Don't admire me too much."

He didn't say anything, waiting to see if she would elaborate. The darkness still rimmed her eyes, and she was clutching her cup of tea as if she wished it were a bottle of beer. Apparently, however, she still wasn't in the mood to share.

"How's your daughter?" she asked shortly.

"The same. I called this morning."

She regarded him curiously. "That doesn't make you feel worse? She's your daughter, she's dying, and you're not there for it. A phone call doesn't seem like much in the face of all that."

"Rainie, when I said my daughter was killed by a drunk driver, I was being a little misleading."

She froze. "I see."

"My daughter wasn't hit by a drunk driver," Quincy said matter-of-factly. "She *was* the drunk driver. She loaded up at a friend's house, then tried to drive home at five-thirty in the morning. And she killed an elderly man out walking his dog before she wrapped her car around a telephone pole. My daughter is dead. The man is dead. The dog is dead. And yes, a phone call to a hospital room is completely inadequate."

"Quincy, I'm sorry."

He smiled roughly. "So am I. I'm not perfect either, Rainie. Some things, like what really matters in life, we all learn the hard way."

She nodded. Her expression was still troubled, though. She had more things to say; he could feel the words churning just below the surface. He leaned forward as if he could will the truth out of her. He hadn't lied to her last night. She fascinated him. She had worked her way into his mind, and now he wanted to cup her cheek with his hand, brush her lips with his fingertips . . .

She was a fighter, and he had so much respect for that.

Her face relented a fraction. Yearning burgeoned

in her soft gray eyes. A need to share. A need for connection. He wished he could reach out and touch her. He was too afraid she'd bolt at the first sign of movement.

"Rainie—"

"I should go."

"I'll listen."

"I don't have anything to say! I just need a little time."

"Another fourteen years? Or maybe just five, until the next homicide comes along? It's eating you up inside. Get it out! What happened with your mother? What did you do with that shotgun?"

She stood abruptly. He was stung by the fire in her eyes, the sudden hard set of her chin.

"Don't bring up my mother again."

"No dice."

"It's not your business—"

"Too late. You should've stuck with dating rednecks, Rainie. Because you have a real man now and I'm not going anyplace."

"You arrogant son of a bitch."

"Yes. Now, tell me about your mother, Rainie."

"The number one line most abused by psychologists. That's what I am to you, aren't I, Quincy? A very interesting case study. Something you can write up for the American Society of Shrinks—otherwise known as ASS—later on in the year."

"Shut up, Rainie."

"Oh, good comeback."

Quincy frowned angrily. Then he shocked them both by striding forward and grabbing her arms.

"Brute force?" she whispered, and her lips parted. He saw something dark come into her eyes.

"It's what you want, isn't it?" he countered levelly. "A pattern you recognize, a way to bring me down to the level you think you deserve. If you can keep it physical, then you'll never have to feel. Right?"

She stared at him mutinously. He brought her even closer, until her lips were a mere inch from his.

"Let me go," she muttered.

"You're only going to leave here to pace your house all night long. You're terrified of sleep. You're terrified of nightmares. You want them to end, but you still won't do what it takes to make them go away."

"Let go of my arms or you'll never sing baritone in the church choir again."

"Talk to me, Rainie. I *want* to listen. I might even understand."

She shuddered in his arms. He saw the conflict in her eyes again. Some part of her wanted to talk. Some strong, fierce part of her took good care of herself even in spite of herself. But he also saw the layers of fear and doubt and confusion. Years of baggage, accumulated every time her mother opened a fresh bottle and turned on her daughter with an open fist.

Her face shuttered. One moment he thought he might be on the brink of discovery, the next she was gone. Her jaw settled, her eyes went flat, and he knew the battle was over. He released her. She stepped back, shaking out her arms.

"Not bad," she drawled with a clear edge in her voice. "I wouldn't have picked you for a tough guy, SupSpAg."

Quincy didn't bother with a reply. She had retreated behind her brittle shell. From here on out, all he'd get from her would be attitude. Her mother had taught her well.

"I'm leaving," she said defiantly.

"Good night, Rainie."

She faltered, then scowled. "You can't stop me."

"Sweet dreams, Rainie."

"Son of a bitch," she told him flatly, and stalked to the door.

She opened it with more force than necessary. He didn't interfere. She slammed it behind her. He didn't move.

Long after the sound stopped ringing in the room, he was still standing by the bed, thinking of Rainie

Conner and all the things that could've happened fourteen years ago. He thought of shotguns and Danny O'Grady and his own daughter, whom he loved with all his heart.

The world needed more kindness, he thought not for the first time. The world needed more faith.

"Isolation is not protection," he murmured. But he wondered sometimes if his epiphany hadn't come too late.

RAINIE'S HOUSE WAS DARK when she got home. She never remembered to turn on the patio lights before leaving for work, and now her tiny house was hard to see as it sat nestled in the woods. She parked outside on the dirt driveway and fumbled with her keys.

When she finally stepped inside, no one came to greet her. This was the way she wanted her life, but tonight the emptiness deepened her mood.

She went around the two-bedroom ranch, turning on lamps. The space still seemed oppressive. She couldn't get Quincy's words out of her head or the scent of his cologne off her skin.

"Why didn't you tell me about the shotgun, Rainie? Why didn't you tell me it disappeared from evidence?"

She entered the kitchen and opened the fridge. She was the proud owner of twelve bottles of Bud Light, one pound of Tillamook cheese, and an expired quart of milk. She closed the refrigerator.

She went out to her deck.

The woods were dark around her. The moon was in its waning phase, and it was hard to see where the tops of the pine trees ended and the velvety night sky began. The bracing air brought goose bumps to her skin, and she hugged her middle for warmth.

She walked around her deck, then walked around her deck again.

"Why didn't you tell me about the shotgun, Rainie? Why didn't you tell me it disappeared from evidence?"

She couldn't. She'd been an idiot to go see Quincy in the first place. He just radiated such strength. All those lines in his face. It made her believe there was nothing she could tell him that he couldn't handle. And she was so very tired these days.

But there *were* things she couldn't tell him. She'd been naive to think it would be enough to talk around the issue. She'd forgotten that Quincy was not the kind of man who would settle for less. Damn him for grabbing her like that, making her breath catch in her throat and her stomach turn tiny flip-flops.

One more inch and her body would've been pressed against his. She could've run her hands all over the lines of his face. She could've felt the steel bands of his arms and legs. She could've been just a woman and he could've been just a man and maybe that would've been easier in the end.

She could've crept out of the room the minute he fell asleep. Some habits were hard to break.

Rainie went back inside. She found every picture of her mother that she owned. She turned them all face-down. It still wasn't enough. Tonight she didn't think anything could be enough.

She finally curled up on the sofa, fully dressed and desperately needing sleep. She was thinking of Quincy again and his intense gaze. She was thinking of Charlie Kenyon and Danny O'Grady and all the things that wouldn't give her peace.

She finally fell asleep.

And an hour later she woke up screaming. She was on the floor and her mother's body was splayed out in front of her and someone was standing on her back deck staring in at her. The man in black! The man in black!

Rainie bolted for her bedroom. She needed a gun. The CSU had taken her Glock .40. She tore through her closet until she found her old 9-millimeter in a shoebox, then went storming out into the night. But the deck was clear and the air was cold and it was all in her mind after all. No man. No intruder. Just the lingering effects of a very bad dream.

She went back inside shakily. She kept her 9-millimeter. She curled up with an afghan. And she stared at the white ceiling of her family room and willed the blood to stay away.

You're too smart to be doing this to yourself, Rainie.

But apparently she wasn't, for the night went on and on.

She finally fell asleep around five. At six-thirty, the phone woke her up, ringing shrilly. Sandy O'Grady sounded frantic on the other end.

"I have to talk to the FBI agent," Sandy said at once. "Oh God, Rainie, I don't know what else to do."

Rainie got up to face another day.

TWENTY MINUTES LATER, walking out to her patrol car, she found a note tucked under her windshield wipers. It said: *Die, bitch.*

She crumpled it up and threw it away.

TWENTY-ONE

ED FLANDERS HAD BEEN a bartender for thirty-five years. He hadn't meant to do that. In the beginning it had been just a gig, a mindless summer job that would let him hit on girls while making a ton of money in tips. He was passing down the Oregon coast on his way to L.A., where he was going to make it big. Hanging out in Seaside to catch a community play, he'd first seen the Help Wanted sign and decided what the hey.

It had been a long time since.

In the beginning, he told himself he stayed for his art. Seaside had a decent community theater program and enough tourists passing through to make it worthwhile. Each summer he'd audition for a lead role and work on building his résumé. Then, when he never moved beyond parts such as Peasant #3, he told himself he stayed for the money. A bartender could make a little dough during the wild summer months. Then he told himself he stayed for the benefits, because he'd finally hit thirty and realized the true joy of a good HMO. Truth was, he'd met Jenny by then and, stick a fork in him, he was done.

Next thing Ed Flanders knew, several decades had

passed, he was now a grandpa and pretty little Jenny was still the love of his life.

Ed Flanders didn't have any complaints.

Until two days ago. That man, coming into the bar and ordering his buffalo wings. That man, getting Darren all riled up, though God knows it didn't take much anymore.

That man, talking about those poor little girls and all the things that had gone wrong over in Bakersville.

Ed Flanders had met a lot of people in his time, and that man bothered him.

Not the questions, he decided after a bit. Everyone in town was talking about the shooting that happened just an hour and a half away. Some people claimed to know Shep personally. Lots of people had some sort of family involved.

Oh, people talked about the shooting, all right. In the bars, in the churches, in the streets.

But not that many locals, let alone strangers, went around spouting some junior officer's name. Lori . . . Liz . . . Lorraine. Lorraine Conner. She wasn't even the one on TV. That was the mayor, and some state guy named Sanders.

So how'd this guy know Conner's name like that?

And worse, why did Ed Flanders think he'd seen the guy before? Something about the eyes, or maybe it was the nose. Take away the years, maybe soften the hair . . .

Damn, he couldn't quite place the face.

That strange, uncomfortable man who had walked into his bar and made everything *wrong*.

Ed didn't like him. Didn't trust him. He just didn't know what to do about that yet.

BACK IN THE HOTEL room, the man finally allowed himself to collapse. Damn, he was tired. The pace of the last few days, the things he still had to get done . . . People who thought murder was easy had obviously never tried it.

The man fished around in his pockets until he dug up a cellophane wrapper of pills. He ripped it open with his hands and downed four herbal diet pills, one after another, then poured a glass of water. The caffeine made him a little light-headed, but he needed the pick-me-up.

Lots of things done, lots of things left to go.

Last night he'd almost botched the whole affair. Lorraine Conner had looked so wiped out when she'd finally returned home, it had never dawned on him she'd wake up. One minute he thought he'd safely made it from her bedroom closet to the back deck, the next she was flying off the couch like some banshee.

Holy shit, he'd barely cleared the deck railing in time. Even then he'd been about to crash through the woods like a maniac, when something about her movements drew him up cold. She was acting stilted, surreal, looking at things that weren't even there. A second later he figured it out. She was still asleep, chasing some phantom in her twisted dreams.

Maybe he'd triggered something. Maybe night turned her into a raving loon. Hell if he knew. He'd taken cover in his normal spot and simply waited her out. After another moment she'd gone back into the house and he'd been free and clear.

He'd gotten a little giddy after that. He even remembered laughing, one of those high-pitched sounds like you hear in movies. He'd have to watch that. Can't lose control.

Not just yet.

Today, after all, was the funeral. And then . . .

He was a very smart man. Someday soon Lorraine Conner would get to appreciate that.

Lorraine Conner, Pierce Quincy, Shep O'Grady, and little Becky.

Now this, he told his old man silently, this is how you have some *fun*.

TWENTY-TWO

"DANNY CALLED ME this morning. I know it was him." Sandy O'Grady sat on a metal folding chair in the task force's HQ, twisting her hands on her lap and trying very hard to sound calm. "I could hear clanging in the background and people talking. Institutional noises. But the caller was silent. I said, 'Danny, I know it's you. Please talk to me, Danny. I love you.'"

"What did Danny say?" Quincy asked. He was sitting in a chair beside her, impeccably dressed, which immediately made her think of Mitch, her boss. She pushed the thought to the back of her head.

"He didn't say a word. He just sighed. Heavily. Like . . . like someone hopeless. Then he hung up."

"You're sure it was Danny?" Rainie spoke up for the first time. She was leaning against the windowsill all the way across the room. Her arms were crossed over her chest. Her cheeks were gaunt. Frankly, she looked the worst that Sandy had ever seen her.

Not that Sandy was in a position to talk. She'd quickly grabbed a nearby OSU sweatshirt after receiving Danny's call, and it turned out to be stained in four different places with old yellow baby spit-up and new white patio paint. Her normally bright blond hair was dull and matted from sleep. She hadn't showered, let alone put on makeup. She didn't have the energy anymore to worry about these things.

"It was Danny," she told Rainie firmly. "Shep changed our number to an unlisted one two days ago. Only family members and Danny's lawyer know how to reach us now. We haven't gotten one of *those* calls since."

"Are you getting a lot of pressure from your neighbors?" Quincy asked gently.

"Some." Sandy kept her chin up. "Others, our good friends, are still there for us. One couple on our block—I don't even know them that well—came over last night with a plate of brownies and sat with us. There are . . . bad moments, but there are good ones too. Danny's innocent until proven guilty, you know."

Unable to help herself, she turned once more toward Rainie.

"It's official police business," Rainie said curtly. "I can't talk about it."

"Rainie, he's my son. He's upset, he's suicidal. Just yesterday he tried to gouge his wrist with a fork, for chrissakes. I'm not sure how much longer he can take being locked up in the detention center, and I don't know what to do. Shep tells me there's proof someone else was involved—mysterious shells, I don't know. Can't you do something with that? Drop the charges? Bring Danny home? Please—" Sandy's voice broke off pleadingly. She didn't know Rainie well. She would call her a friend, but more because they had Shep in common than because they'd ever spent any time talking. Still, Rainie had come to their house for dinner at least once every few months. She played with Danny and Becky. She seemed to honestly enjoy time with the kids. Surely she wouldn't forget those moments now. Surely she wasn't completely immune to Danny's plight.

The woman in question, however, remained impassive. Her uniform suddenly loomed as a wall between them, and for the first time, Sandy got it. Rainie wasn't looking at her as the sheriff's wife. This morning Sandy was in the task-force center as a mass murderer's mother.

Sandy threw out desperately, "Maybe Shep can help find out who did it."

"We don't want Shep," Rainie said flatly. "We want Becky."

"What do you mean?"

"Is she still sleeping in closets, Sandy?"

"That's not anyone's business—"

"She saw something; we all know it. You and Shep keep saying you want the truth. Let us ask for it."

"Avery Johnson would never permit it."

"It's not his call."

"Yes, it is! He's our lawyer. My God, we're going to have to mortgage our home just to pay his fees. After all that, how can we not listen to what he says? He's acting in our best interests."

"What about Becky's best interests?" Rainie pressed relentlessly. "The girl only feels safe in enclosed spaces. She's having nightmares, and Luke says she's as pale as a sheet. How long are you going to let that go on?"

"The doctor said she'll grow out of it with time—"

"We can make it sooner versus later."

"You can't have Becky! Dammit, Rainie, she's all I have *left*!"

Rainie pressed her lips into a thin line. She gazed at Sandy disapprovingly. Sandy returned the stare. Rainie didn't understand what she was asking. She wasn't a mother.

"We can prove that Danny didn't shoot Miss Avalon," Rainie said abruptly. "We can tell by the slug that was recovered and the trajectory of the shot that it was done by someone other than Danny."

"Oh thank God." Sandy sat back in the metal chair. For the first time in three days, she felt weight lift off her chest. "So there was this man in black at the scene. He's the killer, and Danny's just confused and traumatized by what he saw. Can't you drop the charges now?"

"Mrs. O'Grady," Quincy said quietly, "I think there are some things about Danny you need to know. I suspect you're beginning to wonder about them, too, or you wouldn't have called this morning."

Rainie supplied bluntly, "We're not sure he didn't kill Sally and Alice."

"But the man, the man in black—"

"Ballistics matched the slugs that killed those two girls to the .38 revolver Danny brought to school. And we have his prints on the other .38 shell casings recovered at the scene."

"That just means he loaded the guns," Sandy countered. "Shep explained this to me. The prints don't prove a thing."

"Danny's fingerprints are on over *fifty* shell casings. That means he also reloaded the guns during the shooting."

"Shep told me that rapid loaders were used. So Danny prepped the guns and the rapid loaders. This other person did all the shooting."

Rainie finally pushed away from the window. She shook her head impatiently. "Listen to yourself! Danny brought a revolver and a semiautomatic weapon to school. He loaded them, and he prepared additional ammunition. Does that sound like an innocent bystander to you?"

"He's just thirteen—"

"You don't have to be old to pull a trigger."

"He's confused—"

"He confessed multiple times!"

"He's frightened! He's angry, he doesn't understand—"

"He told Charlie Kenyon he wanted to hack Shep into twenty pieces and run him through a blender! Jesus, Sandy, we're beyond simple acting out. You didn't catch Danny smoking a cigarette or staying out after curfew. He's involved in a triple homicide. At the very least, he supplied the murder weapons. At the most, he may have massacred two eight-year-old girls. For God's sake, wake up!"

"My son is not a killer!"

"But maybe he is! Now, what the *hell* are we going to do about it?"

Rainie drew up short. She was breathing hard. Sandy was breathing hard too. She glared at her husband's most senior officer, and she thought she had never hated anyone more. How dare she talk about Danny that way. After all those dinners in Sandy's home. All those times Danny had asked to sit next to her, sweet and adoring. The cold, unfeeling—

And then she realized that Rainie's eyes were overbright. And then she realized that Rainie Conner had thinned her lips in order not to cry.

The air left Sandy's lungs in a whoosh. In Rainie's frustrated gaze she saw all the truths she'd been working diligently to deny, and suddenly she had no defenses left.

Her son was a loner. And subject to fits of rage. And he struggled with Shep and struggled to fit in at school and, dear God, he was good with guns. Learned everything straight from his father.

The world began to spin. Sandy grabbed her chair and held tight.

"Mrs. O'Grady?" Quincy asked.

"Give me a moment."

She locked her gaze on the floorboards, concentrating on making them stay in focus. Minutes passed. She didn't know how many. Time had grown slow, and she was mostly aware of an oppressive cold stealing into her body and making her tremble.

"I don't know what to do," Sandy whispered. "I don't . . . I don't know what to believe anymore."

Quincy spoke up first. "I imagine your lawyer

has arranged for a forensic psychologist to examine Danny?"

"Yes. And the court has appointed a second. They haven't started yet. He said it would be months before they delivered their reports. Maybe even six months before we know anything."

"He's your son, Mrs. O'Grady. What do you think Danny did and what do you think he needs now?"

"I can't tell you." Sandy gave a hollow bark of laughter. "That's the truth, you know. I'm under orders from my lawyer and my husband not to talk to you—an expert on these things—because you're also part of law enforcement and you could testify at trial. And my suicidal son isn't allowed to speak with anyone either. Testimony might be used against him, better not to say anything at all. Oh my God. *What am I supposed to do?*"

Quincy didn't say anything. Neither did Rainie.

Sandy's eyes filled up. She said through her tears, "I don't understand how this can be legal. They took away my son. They've locked him up for murder, but with the waiver hearings and pretrial motions it could be years before he goes to court. In the meantime, Danny has to stay in a place where he's not supposed to talk to anyone and he's surrounded by other convicted juvenile delinquents. Even if he's found innocent one year or two years later, how can he possibly be better off? I'm worried that the county is ruining an innocent boy. And I'm terrified that they've imprisoned a guilty one. Oh my God, Rainie, what if he did it? What will we do then?"

Quincy had squatted down in front of her. He had such compelling eyes. Deep, and heavily crinkled at the corners, as if he'd seen a thing or two. Sandy hadn't expected to like the man. Shep had positioned him as an enemy in their lives, to be avoided at all costs. But Sandy discovered that she was comforted by his presence. Supervisory Special Agent Quincy seemed sure of himself and the situation, whereas she felt as if the entire world were made of quicksand and she was sinking down, down, down.

He took her hand and placed it between his own. His palms were warm and rough. "It's not hopeless," he said.

"How? Our lawyer already said that if Danny is found guilty in adult court, they'll lock him up and throw away the key. No one cares that he's only thirteen."

"But the fact that he's thirteen does put him below Oregon's automatic waiver to adult court. He is going to get a hearing designed to look at his *specific* case, and thank goodness, because Danny's case has some elements worth considering."

Sandy gazed at him. Quincy ticked off the points with his fingers.

"One, we have evidence that somebody else was involved. If we can identify that person, we may be able to prove that Danny was manipulated, perhaps even threatened, into acting."

Sandy nodded faintly.

"Two, we have to look at Danny himself. The fact that he's now under suicide watch may be a positive sign. It could indicate that Danny feels remorse for his actions, that he's a troubled boy but not a budding psychopath."

"Or it could mean he's traumatized," Sandy said after a moment, her voice gaining strength. "There is someone else involved. You all agree on that. So maybe Danny was just doing as he was told by bringing the guns. Maybe he didn't understand what was really going to happen, and then by the time it was all over and done with, there was nothing he could do anymore."

"But confess," Rainie said dryly.

"That's the good news, Mrs. O'Grady," Quincy said levelly. "Now you have to face the other facts."

Sandy hesitated. She bit her lower lip. She knew where he was going to go, and she wished he wouldn't. Deep in her heart, she'd already gone there. Danny was

troubled, and it was her fault as his mother for not doing something about that sooner. That's what everyone
said when these shootings happened. Where were the
parents?

I'm sorry. I was at work.

"Danny is subject to mood swings, isn't he?"
Quincy said matter-of-factly. "He goes for long periods
of time without reacting, then explodes with rage."

"You mean the incident with the school lockers."

"He's alone a lot."

"There are not a lot of boys on our block the same
age."

"He doesn't have many friends at school."

"He's really into computers."

"Mrs. O'Grady, Danny has problems coping. His
anger is overcontrolled, which I think you realize. He
also doesn't have a good support network, and given
the issues with your marriage, he's under a lot of stress.
Then we get to the issues between him and his father.
Danny's mad at Shep but also intimidated by him. This
sets the stage for displaced rage, where Danny takes all
that emotion and turns it on someone else, someone
who doesn't scare him."

"You mean like two little girls?" Sandy whispered.

"Or a cat or dog."

"Danny has never hurt animals," Sandy said immediately. "Becky would never stand for such a thing, and
he's very protective of his sister."

"It's good that Danny's symptoms aren't that extreme. But he still exhibits some of the warning signs
we see in kids prone to do these types of shooting. For
his sake, we need to deal with that."

Sandy hesitated. "How?"

"Let's start with Danny's overcontrolled rage. He
needs to learn to vent his anger steadily and construc-
tively instead of letting it build to dangerous heights.
Most experts would recommend daily physical exercise
as a starting point."

"He's not athletic."

"What about a family walk, Mrs. O'Grady? Or some teens like martial arts."

"I . . . I could look into that."

The agent nodded encouragingly. He continued, "Also for a child like Danny, violent books, video games, and movies are not appropriate. They only fuel angry thoughts."

"Danny's never really been into violent movies. But in all honesty, I don't know what he does on the Web."

"If you have a troubled son, you need to know what he's reading or surfing on the Internet, Mrs. O'Grady. It can make a difference."

Sandy hung her head.

"Danny's issue with his father is more involved," Quincy said quietly. "He and Shep need family counseling, or Danny needs private counseling, or both. You also might want to find additional family relationships for Danny with a grandparent or aunt or uncle. That way if things are strained at home, the child still has other sources of comfort and support."

"I never thought of that," Sandy said honestly. "Our family's not that big. Shep's parents passed away years ago. My own . . . God knows they love my kids, but they aren't the warmest people in the world. It's not their way." She paused. "Do you think . . . Do you think Danny's troubles are caused by the fact that I went back to work?"

Quincy smiled at her kindly. "No, Mrs. O'Grady. Being a working mom doesn't mean you're a horrible mom. Stay-at-home parents have troubled children too."

Sandy nodded. She would never admit it out loud, but she was relieved. She hesitated, then asked, "My son was already troubled. Now at the very least he's witnessed three violent murders. What will that do?"

"He needs to get it out. Keeping the experience bottled up will only make it worse." Quincy's gaze drifted toward Rainie.

"And if . . . if he did do something bad?"

Quincy was silent for a moment. "He's going to need a lot of help," he said at last. "Chances are that he's experiencing a great deal of guilt and self-loathing. Someone needs to help him come to terms with that. Otherwise, there is the danger that he will simply shut down that part of himself. He will start actively considering himself to be a remorseless killer. And he will become one."

A knock sounded on the door. Luke Hayes stuck his head in. His gaze went straight to Sandy.

"It's time," he said.

"Already?"

Sandy glanced at her watch. It took her a moment to read the dial, for her hand was still shaking violently. Nine A.M. The joint funeral for Alice and Sally wasn't due to start until one. But the whole town was probably turning out, and people wanted to get good seats.

She had no choice but to go home. By the mayor's orders, she and her family would be spending the day under virtual house arrest. He didn't want them to upset the town, and that hurt Sandy almost more than the threatening phone calls, messages, and casseroles combined.

She slowly rose and gathered up her purse. She had hoped for easy answers this morning. Of course, there were very few such things anymore. Just more questions. And more doubts to torment her through all the long days to come.

She loved Danny so desperately. Was it right to actively wonder if her son was a murderer and still love him? Was it right to mourn for Alice Bensen and Sally Walker but still want the best for her child?

Suddenly, she felt so exhausted, she wasn't sure how she was going to make it down the stairs.

She turned to Rainie one last time. "Do you know who this other person is yet? Do you have any leads on who did this to us?"

Rainie seemed to hesitate. "Danny ever mention anyone named No Lava to you?"

Sandy regarded her curiously. "Of course he did. No Lava@aol.com. That was his teacher's account. It's Avalon, spelled backward."

TWENTY-THREE

RAINIE AND QUINCY climbed into Luke's patrol car at a little past ten. Since Luke and Chuckie were sitting in the front seat, they took the back. Chuckie immediately looked self-conscious about having a commanding officer and federal agent behind him. He kept glancing nervously over his shoulder, as if he thought Quincy might goose him at any moment. After the second time, Quincy placed his face against the patrol car's mesh divider. When Chuckie turned again, he discovered Quincy's nose up close and personal. The rookie literally squealed.

Luke sighed heavily. Rainie shook her head. Quincy sat back, contented.

"You're riling my partner," Luke said at last. He was slouched low behind the steering wheel, studying Sandy and Shep's quaint neighborhood with a deceptively lazy gaze. His hat was on the seat beside him; the brim limited his line of sight. The top of his head came to just above the dashboard; the lower vantage point expanded his field of view. Mostly, he watched the residential street for signs of out-of-place traffic, but from time to time he also perused the rooflines of the surrounding houses with his narrow gaze. Luke was an ace sniper.

"Any activity?" Rainie asked.

"Quiet as a church mouse."

"How are you holding up?" Rainie asked Chuckie. He had his baton on his lap and was stroking the handle as if it were a favorite pet.

"All right," Chuckie muttered.

He studied his lap, refusing to meet her gaze. His broad face was haggard, his hair uncharacteristically mussed. Rainie hadn't given the green rookie any thought during the last three days. Now she regarded him intently.

"Cunningham," she ordered more sharply.

Chuckie's gaze reluctantly rose to meet hers. She held it for a minute. Chuckie was messed up. He had dark circles under his eyes and a nervous twitch in his hand. Apparently, seeing real action was different from boasting about it, and it was wrong of her not to have thought about him before now.

"You did well on Tuesday," she said curtly.

"I broke a freaking door," Cunningham muttered. "Left footprints everywhere. The state technicians yelled at me. That man Sanders said I was a disaster."

"Sanders is full of shit. You acted with heart, Chuckie. The rest you'll learn with time."

Chuckie's gaze fell to his kneecaps. He still looked troubled. When he had volunteered for this job, he had probably envisioned saving lives and protecting his community. He had not expected the debilitating frustration of arriving too late or the hard truth that today his job was merely processing the damage. Rainie understood. She knew one of the reasons George Walker hated her was that she hadn't paid him the respect of personally visiting his family. She should've done that the very first day, except that she couldn't bring herself to go, sit on a worn sofa, and make small talk while a father sat hollow-eyed and a mother wept. She just couldn't do it.

Rainie turned back to Luke. He was still studying Shep's house. It was a tidy, three-bedroom ranch with an attached two-car garage. Soft gray paint. Crisp white trim. One garage door was a brighter white than the other, obviously the one vandalized on Wednesday. Rainie wondered if Shep and Sandy could look at the bright white paint without remembering what was written underneath.

"We need to talk," she said to Luke.

He nodded. He looked tired from his long trip yesterday, his cheeks not as freshly shaven as usual and his uniform rumpled. But his eyes were sharp and his hands steady. You could always count on Luke.

"How'd it go in Portland?" Rainie asked.

He frowned. "Thought we were debriefing after the funeral."

"Something came up. You can watch and talk."

"Apparently." He slapped Chuckie's leg with his hand. "Go get us some coffee, Cunningham."

"Again?"

"Three cups. The good stuff this time. We gotta impress the fed." Luke shot Quincy a look in the rearview mirror.

"I take mine black," Quincy offered.

Chuckie grumbled, but he knew when he wasn't wanted. He got out of the patrol car and started walking to the grocery store around the corner.

"Chuckie needs some personal time," Luke said the minute the rookie disappeared from view.

"I noticed."

"He's a good kid, Rainie. Just saw too much."

"What do you suggest?"

Luke shrugged. "Kid that age? We should take him out shooting a few times. Then take him drinking after that. He'll work through it."

"Stress, guns, and alcohol," Quincy said dryly. "Makes me wonder why the Veterans' Administration hasn't thought of it."

Luke grinned at him. "You're thinking quality time on the shrink's couch, huh? Yeah, uh-huh. Chuckie boy will open up to some hundred-dollar-an-hour suit the day pigs fly. Sorry, feebie, but sometimes the locals know best."

"All right, all right." Rainie held up a hand. "I want to know about your meeting with the Avalons in Portland yesterday. Tell us everything."

Luke's face immediately fell. He released his breath as a sigh, his gaze returning to Shep's house and looking troubled. "Jesus, Rainie, why don't you start with the easy questions?"

"Do you like Mr. Avalon as a suspect?"

"I spent three hours in the man's company, and hell if I know. First off, Mrs. Avalon isn't Melissa's mother. Guess she died in childbirth. So I met with Daniel Avalon and Melissa's stepmother, Angelina."

"*Daniel* Avalon?" Rainie asked sharply.

"Yep," Luke said gloomily. "Weird, Rainie. Real weird. Mr. Avalon comes from old money. Invested heavily in real estate in central Oregon and made out like a bandit in the recent boom. He and Mrs. Avalon live in an old Victorian in Lake Oswego. Nice house, I guess. It was crammed full of so much junk, I was afraid I'd break something if I sneezed. They served me tea. In real china. With Mrs. Avalon all fussed up in some buttoned-up, lace-collar, cameo-brooch outfit that I think she bought at Jane Austen's garage sale. Mr. Avalon favors tweed and doesn't permit his wife to speak unless spoken to. Need I say more?"

"Stuffy and pretentious wasn't a crime last I checked."

"May I?" Quincy intervened.

"By all means," Rainie assured him. She was sitting as far away from him as she could in the backseat. They were both pretending not to notice.

"Did Mr. Avalon wait many years before remarrying? Say twelve to fifteen years?"

"Thirteen," Luke said. He looked at Quincy curiously.

"Did he speak of his daughter glowingly, but always as a child? 'When Melissa was eight years old she was the best dancer. . . . Oh, little Melissa always had the sweetest smile. She used to charm everyone in grade school.' Little acknowledgment of her life now?"

"Yeah, as a matter of fact, he had pictures of her all over the place, but they were mostly little-girl stuff. First ballet class, ten-year-old piano recital, that sort of thing."

"No photos of her mom?"

"Not that I saw."

"Her room still a little girl's room? Lots of pink ruffles and teddy bears?"

"And clowns." Luke shuddered.

Quincy nodded. "I'm guessing Mr. Avalon had inappropriate relations with his daughter."

"Incest?" Rainie looked at Quincy incredulously. "Jesus, SupSpAg, how do you sleep with that mind?"

"I can't be sure," Quincy said modestly, "but it has all the classic signs. Domineering father alone with his young daughter for the first thirteen years of her life. Seems very doting on the outside. I'm sure if you conducted further interviews you'd find plenty of neighbors and teachers telling you how 'close' Mr. Avalon and his daughter were. How 'involved' he was in her life. But then she hits puberty and the jig is up. To continue risks pregnancy, plus she's starting to get a woman's body, and many of these men aren't interested in that. So Mr. Avalon goes ahead and takes a wife, some poor, passive woman to serve as window dressing and help him appear suitable to the outside world. Now he clings to the fantasy of what he once had. And protects it jealously."

"Does Mr. Avalon have access to a computer?" Rainie asked Luke.

"In his office."

She turned to Quincy. "If Mr. Avalon was involved with his daughter, would he have problems with her relationship with VanderZanden?"

"He'll have problems with any of her relationships. In his mind, she's his."

"That's it then. He found out, got angry—"

"And got an alibi," Luke interrupted flatly.

They looked at him sharply. He was nearly apologetic. "I tried, Rainie. I stayed in town till eleven last night trying to break this guy's story. I've probably pissed off every blue blood in the city and it still holds. Mr. Avalon was in a business meeting all day Tuesday. His secretary swears it, and two high-powered muckety-mucks agree. They were working on some resort deal from noon until nearly seven o'clock at night."

Rainie chewed on the inside of her lip. "Have you had time to run background checks on the supporting witnesses?"

"You mean between midnight and six A.M.?"

"Could be about money," Rainie theorized. "Sounds like Mr. Avalon has a lot. If they do regular business with him . . . Maybe they'd be willing to vouch for his time in return for a few favors."

"Possible. Don't know how we can prove it, though. There is one other thing. I asked Mr. Avalon if he'd ever been to Bakersville. He said absolutely not. But I ran a background check before interviewing him, and according to state tax records he owns a cabin in Cabot County, just thirty minutes away. When I pushed him on it, he said it was merely a hunting cabin. He never used it himself but kept it for business associates. His wife nodded, like that means a damn thing. I don't know. Something's wrong there, Rainie, seriously wrong, but I don't know what to make of it yet."

Luke's gaze returned to the street, where a teenage boy on a bicycle was coming into view. In sagging jeans and a loose jersey shirt, the kid seemed pretty nondescript. But he wore a green canvas backpack and he was staring at the O'Grady home intently.

"Here's my question," Luke muttered, tapping a finger on the steering wheel as he followed the kid with his gaze. "Why now? Melissa Avalon was twenty-eight years old. If Quincy's right and Daddy was going to melt down, wouldn't it have happened years ago?"

"Not necessarily," Quincy answered. He had noticed the cyclist as well. Then Chuckie came into view, carrying a cardboard box with four cups of coffee. "Was this Melissa's first time away from home?"

"Yep," Luke said.

"That would do it."

"I wonder if we're making this too complicated," Rainie murmured out loud, shifting in the backseat for a better view. "Mr. Avalon's got motive. Mr. Avalon's got money. His daughter just happens to die from a single gunshot wound to the head—"

"Assassination," Quincy filled in.

"What if it wasn't supposed to be a school shooting? What if Danny was being enlisted to create a diversion, something that looked like a shooting to disguise Melissa Avalon's death. Except—"

"Except he accidentally killed two little girls," Luke supplied dryly. He opened his mouth to argue more, then suddenly said, "Shit."

The boy was in front of Shep's house. His bicycle had slowed. His body shifted. The backpack slid down. . . .

Luke fumbled for the door handle. He shoved it open with his shoulder just as Rainie tried to bolt, realizing too late that the doors had shut and she and Quincy were trapped in the back of the police cruiser. Down the street, Chuckie saw the commotion and dropped his coffee. Rainie watched him reach immediately for his gun.

"No," she yelled uselessly, and pounded the unbreakable window. "Dammit, Chuckie, *no*!"

The boy saw Luke bearing down on him. He turned slightly and spotted Chuckie fumbling with his holster. His expression promptly shifted from purposeful to petrified.

Luke ordered, "Stop!"

And the boy shoved his backpack at Luke with all

his might and took off, while the officer staggered back in surprise. Down the street, Chuckie was still juggling his handgun. Rainie couldn't be sure from this distance, but it looked like the rookie had tears on his cheeks.

"Damn, damn, damn," Luke shouted. He regained his footing and let the backpack fall to the ground, but the kid ran from the street to dart between the multitude of houses. A second later he was out of sight. With another sigh of disgust, Luke stalked back to the patrol car and settled for bailing Quincy and Rainie out of the backseat. They gathered around the backpack on the sidewalk just as Cunningham came running up, panting heavily.

"What'd he do?" Cunningham demanded breathlessly. He rubbed his cheeks. "What's in the bag? What happened? Did he try anything?"

"One thing at a time, Cunningham," Rainie growled. She looked at Luke. He shrugged, hunkered down, and placed his ear over the green canvas bag.

"I don't hear ticking." He hefted up the backpack and frowned. "No clinking. Hell, it feels like books."

He resolutely unzipped the main pouch. Out poured two weighty volumes with fine leather binding and rich gilded edges—the Bible, Old and New Testaments: The note attached to the front said: *To the O'Gradys. Jesus forgives.*

"Oh my God," Chuckie said desperately. "I almost *shot* that boy."

Quincy said softly, "I think it's time we took a deep breath."

Luke picked up the two volumes. He carried them gently to the front porch and placed them in front of the door. Then, without a word, he went back to the wheel of his patrol car, slouched down to the level of the dashboard, fingered his hat on the seat beside him, and resumed keeping guard.

TWENTY-FOUR

BECKY O'GRADY PLACED her finger carefully over Big Bear's black-stitched mouth. He regarded her steadily with his big golden eyes.

"Shh," she told him. "We have to be very quiet."

Big Bear helped her out. Becky knew he didn't like the closet. He'd always been afraid of the dark. But now he was a very brave brown bear. He didn't make a single noise as she gently twisted the knob on the closet door and eased it open.

There was a break in the argument in the family room. Becky froze instantly. Her mommy and daddy had been fighting for a long time now. Something about some man her mommy had talked to this morning. She shouldn't have done that, Becky's daddy said. Why didn't she trust him to take care of things?

Becky's mommy wasn't happy. She told Becky's dad he was in denial. Becky didn't know what that meant, but she was sad it made her mommy so angry, because Becky was in denial too. The doctors had said so.

Maybe it was a bad disease. That would explain why Becky's best friend, Jenny, no longer came over to play. Like the time Becky had the chicken pox. No one could play with her then either. And her skin had itched so bad. She'd wanted to scratch and scratch, but her mommy made her sit in a bathtub filled with hot water and oatmeal. Becky hated the chicken pox. Of course, Grammy Surmon had made her her very own pie. Banana cream, and Danny hadn't been allowed to eat any of it unless Becky said it was okay. She'd kinda liked that.

Now the thought of Danny made Becky's chest hurt. She held Big Bear closer.

The fighting started again. Daddy was yelling that Mommy didn't care enough about Danny. Mommy was yelling that it was all Daddy's fault. "How did Danny get the guns, Shep? Tell me how Danny got the guns."

Becky slipped inside the dark hallway closet. She shut the door. The light and the voices disappeared. She hunkered down on the old blanket her mommy had put in there for her and held Big Bear close.

Sometimes, when she was alone in the dark like this, just her and Big Bear, she could almost breathe again. The funny weight would leave her chest and she would feel not so bad anymore. She was safe. She was okay. Here in the dark, nobody could hurt her.

She could close her eyes and the bad things would go away. She could float, peaceful, thinking of kittens and clouds and all the things she liked best.

Today she tried the trick. She screwed her eyes shut. She pressed her cheek against the top of Big Bear's woolly head. But nothing happened. No floating. She was just a little girl sitting on a hard floor in a closet that smelled like old shoes.

She kept seeing Sally and Alice. She saw them on the floor. Then she saw pretty Miss Avalon.

And then she raised her eyes. . . .

Becky whimpered in the closet. She turned her face into Big Bear's neck.

"Be brave," she told him. "Be brave. Be brave. Don't make a sound."

Big Bear was a very brave brown bear. He didn't

make any noise as she rocked with him on the floor while her parents fought in the living room. He didn't make any noise as she whimpered and warred with evil monsters. And he didn't make any sound as she cried and still saw too many things, like what had happened to pretty Miss Avalon.

Becky's mouth hurt from the Jell-O salad. Her shoulders sagged from too many nights without enough sleep. She didn't give up, though. She was tough. Her daddy liked to say that she was just like him, a real *trouper*.

Becky didn't know what a trouper was. But she wanted to be like Daddy, big and strong and brave. She needed to be like Daddy.

She had to be tough. She had to keep Danny safe.

THE FUNERAL SERVICE FOR Sally Walker and Alice Bensen was originally scheduled for one P.M. at the tiny white Episcopal church on Fourth Street. By noon, however, when the pews, the foyer, the lawn, and the parking lot were filled to standing room only with somberly dressed neighbors, Reverend Albright moved everything graveside. Groundsmen hastily erected canvas tents, and a fierce ocean breeze whipped the blue awnings frantically above everyone's heads.

No one complained. Cars continued to arrive. Weathered dairymen, clad in their Sunday best, escorted their wives slowly up the hill, heads bowed against the wind. Bakersville High's basketball team, which heralded Alice Bensen's brother as star forward and Sally Walker's uncle as coach, gathered in full uniform to serve as honor guard. The men of the Elks Lodge, where George Walker belonged, also wore dress colors, standing formally to one side and waiting for the service to end, when they would be in charge of transporting the mountain of flowers back to the families' homes.

The ladies of the Episcopal church gave out programs. Neighbors supplied a steady stream of condolence cards and homemade pies for the luncheon to follow.

Rainie took it in from a distance. Even from two hundred feet away, the sight of two freshly dug graves, side by side on an emerald green hillside and framed by mountains of red and white flowers, haunted her. She noticed that Quincy kept to the perimeter as well. She was surprised he'd even come. Given recent events with his own daughter, she couldn't imagine that the next hour wouldn't grab his heart and squeeze it dry.

Then again, the federal agent seemed to thrive on pushing himself to bear the unbearable.

Sanders was also present. He had taken up a post on the east side of the hill, where a side street offered cemetery access. Standing in a dark blue suit with his hands clasped in front of him, he blended with the crowd of gathered mourners.

By agreement, Rainie was the only officer in uniform. Sanders and the county men all roamed the crowd wearing traditional mourning clothes. That way they could monitor the services without intruding unnecessarily on the families.

No one expected any trouble during the ceremony. Rainie and the mayor, however, were concerned about the hours afterward, when people would leave the service with emotions running high, find a bar for a few drinks with their buddies, and work themselves into a state of pure testosterone. Alcohol and guns were never a great mix, and God knew Bakersville had plenty of both.

The county men had orders to work the crowd, listen sharp. Particularly vocal attendants would be monitored later in the evening. The mayor didn't want to take any chances, not after the recent run on rifles at the sporting-goods store.

At Quincy's suggestion, the men were also looking for "someone out of place." Maybe a middle-age white male who seemed strangely removed from the gathering of family and friends. Maybe a man who appeared to enjoy funerals too much. Any man stupid enough to look at twin coffins and smile.

Rainie didn't think they'd get that lucky, but Quincy insisted. If it was a stranger-against-stranger crime, there was a good chance the man would attend.

Rainie found herself thinking of the dream she'd had last night. Jerking awake. Tall, imposing shadow on her back deck . . . She was unnerved these days.

A hush suddenly descended over the crowd. Rainie jerked her attention back to the rolling green cemetery in time to realize that a train of cars had just arrived. The families, with their daughters, were here.

George Walker got out first. A heavyset man, his broad face flushed and his eyes bloodshot, he came around to open the door for his wife. Jean Walker was as petite as her husband was large, and she swayed against his thick arm as he led her to the grass. They waited together for the Bensens, who took much longer to climb out of their vehicle. Rainie had never met Alice's parents, Joseph and Virginia. She knew only of their son, Frederick, whom Frank and Doug avidly declared to be the best basketball player ever to pound the boards at Bakersville High. Most of the town followed his career and college aspirations.

Now Rainie was immediately struck by the Bensens' strong Nordic looks. They held their heads high as they approached the Walkers. They kept their gaze steady as they watched the honor guard step forward. They remained unflinching as their son bent his lanky legs to carry his eight-year-old sister to her final resting place.

Ten minutes later both coffins were delivered to the front of the tent and the minister formally began the service.

Rainie glanced over at Quincy. He wasn't watching anymore. His gaze was far off, where distant trees framed the blue horizon. She didn't know what he was thinking, but tears streamed down his cheeks.

The minister concluded his introduction. A young

man Rainie didn't recognize rose and helped an older woman work her way to the microphone. The wind blew hard, flattening the woman's black silk dress against her rounded frame, but she fought forward. At the front, she opened a book and cleared her throat. She introduced herself as Alice Bensen's aunt. Then she read a passage in Alice and Sally's memory. It was a selection on the meaning of friendship, from Winnie the Pooh.

That was it for Rainie. She also turned away until VanderZanden rose to give the eulogy.

He appeared somber as he stood in front of nearly eight hundred people. He had written out his speech, and the piece of paper trembled in his hands. Rainie discovered, however, that she couldn't muster any sympathy for the man. She was too busy staring at his wife, who had been patting his hand supportively for the last forty-five minutes. Abigail VanderZanden was a little plump from the years and a little dowdy in a square-shaped, navy blue JCPenney dress, but she had a generous smile and sparkling blue eyes. She also appeared genuinely proud of her husband, and that made Rainie like VanderZanden even less.

There were no winners today, Rainie thought, and that realization wore her down a little bit more. She had had hopes of big discoveries. Fantasies of standing in front of her community and telling them exactly what had happened on Tuesday afternoon and why. No more driving by the school in pained bewilderment. No more staring at your children over breakfast cereal, wondering what might happen to them that day. No more horrible questions, like why were young boys suddenly prone to murdering their classmates.

Instead Rainie stood on an emerald hillside in Bakersville's only cemetery, feeling the blustery wind against her face and listening to the haunting echo of "Amazing Grace" sung by fourteen adults while Frederick Bensen broke down sobbing against his mother, who cradled him in her arms.

Long after the final note died away, people remained standing. Reverend Albright came back up. He cleared his throat and said that concluded the services. People still didn't move.

Danny should be here, Rainie realized. Danny and Shep and Sandy and Becky, and, hell, Charlie Kenyon and the mysterious second shooter, and any boy who'd ever picked up a gun and thought about pulling the trigger. This was death. This was loss. This was the moment when everything became real. And why weren't there more children at this funeral? Most of the kids in Bakersville had the power to take a life. Why didn't their gun-owning parents think to show them what that meant?

The stillness finally broke. The first few people reluctantly trickled out of the tent. Then, like a dam breaking, the others followed suit.

Rainie looked around, trying to pick out the state men. She still saw nothing suspicious and nothing out of place. She sidled up to Quincy, whose cheeks were dry and face carefully composed.

"Ready?" he said.

She figured they both knew she wasn't. "Mann first. Then VanderZanden."

"Deal."

Rainie hesitated one last moment. Her gaze was still scanning the crowd. It finally occurred to her that she was checking out the profiles of the various men. She was studying their silhouettes. Middle of the night. The figure in black on her back deck . . .

She shook her head and forced the image away. As she and Quincy moved down the hillside, however, her gaze continued to work the crowd.

They found Richard Mann off to one side of the tent, huddled together with four other faculty members, all female. Without being asked, he stepped discreetly away from his companions, joining Quincy and Rainie behind a cluster of pine trees.

"Nice to see you again, Mr. Mann," Rainie said politely. Her bad-cop role was probably a little much for a funeral.

"Did you talk to Charlie Kenyon?" Mann asked curiously. "Was Charlie involved?"

"We talked to him." Rainie regarded him coolly. The more she tried to study the counselor, the less she knew what to think. "I'm afraid that's a dead end, though, Mr. Mann. Charlie doesn't appear to be involved."

"Really? I was so sure. . . ." Mann's face fell. He sighed heavily, then rubbed his face. That quickly, he looked haggard, and Rainie was shocked to realize that he was much more upset than she'd realized. "I'm having real issues with this," he said abruptly.

"What kind of issues, Mr. Mann?" Quincy inquired.

"I've been turning things over and over in my mind, and I just can't see Danny instigating a murder. And not just because I'm his counselor and I feel guilty. It's more. . . . Yes, Danny had rage issues." The counselor made a groping motion with his hands, as if searching for better words. "But physical action just isn't his style. Danny's a computer geek, not a schoolyard bully. If he was angry with the school or even authority figures in general, I could see him doing something sophisticated. Maybe hacking into the school's databases and giving everyone straight As. Or working his way into the DMV computers and revoking Principal VanderZanden's license. Something clever. I just . . . I just can't see him resorting to murder."

"Danny was raised with guns," Rainie said. "He's as comfortable with them as he is with computers."

"I guess." Mann, however, didn't look convinced. "What about Mr. Avalon?"

"He claimed the body," Rainie said. "It appears he's planning services for his daughter."

"Oh." Mann appeared surprised again. "I guess I heard wrong. Isn't Melissa an only child? How horrible for her parents."

Rainie nodded, but her attention was already beginning to drift. Richard Mann knew as little as she'd suspected in the beginning. No doubt he'd thought to make up for his guilt—or, hell, make up for his youth—by appearing to be some kind of expert. But in the end he was simply one more overwhelmed public servant caught with his pants down. Basically, he was like her.

"We have reason to believe someone else was involved in the shootings," Quincy said abruptly.

"Really?" Mann's brows shot up, just as Rainie gave Quincy the evil eye. She didn't see the need for him to be giving up this kind of information.

"So I was right! Danny wouldn't do such a thing. But who, then? Another student? I don't remember Danny talking about anyone in particular. He didn't have many friends in school. You know, though, there's still this Volcano person from on-line. Internet relationships can be very powerful."

"We think the contact might have been more than over the Internet, Mr. Mann. We think Danny might have also met No Lava in person. Would you know anything about that?"

Rainie nearly stepped on Quincy's foot to shut him up. What the hell was he doing? But Quincy's gaze was still boring into Richard Mann's. He looked like a hound dog on a scent.

"Oh no," the school counselor said quickly, his gaze dropping. "I never heard mention of that."

"Really? That's odd," Quincy mused out loud, "Here you are seeing this child twice a week. You know he's getting e-mails from someone, but he never mentions seeing him in person? And you never pried?"

Richard Mann began to squirm.

"Do you own a gun?" Rainie piped up, finally catching on. "How tall are you, Richard? Five-ten, five-eleven? Yep, that would fit."

"That would fit? What?"

Rainie turned casually to Quincy. "Didn't he say he's from L.A.? Chances are, he knows more about guns than you and I put together."

"I don't know *anything* about guns! Frankly, all L.A. taught me was to be wary of loud noises. Why are you two looking at me like that? What is this about?"

"Someone else shot Miss Avalon," Rainie said flatly. "We have hard evidence she was killed by someone who's at least five-foot-six. Where were you again Tuesday afternoon? And what was the exact nature of your relationship with Melissa?"

"You think I—"

"I thought you'd be happy. You said it broke your heart to think of one of your students committing murder. Well, now you can rest easy." Rainie's voice went hard. "Tuesday afternoon. Where were you, Richard?"

"In my office, like I said. This is nuts! Every time I try to help—"

"Did Danny ever mention meeting someone in person?" Quincy continued relentlessly. "A new friend. Someone from out of town."

"I don't remember—"

"No Lava, Mr. Mann. You knew Danny was getting e-mails. And you suspected more, didn't you? Danny said something that made you wonder, but you never told anyone. You never told anyone and now you're afraid. You messed up. You were his counselor and you failed him."

Richard Mann had started panting. Beads of sweat covered his upper lip. "I . . . I . . ."

Quincy leaned forward. He was firmly in control, and now he said with a trace of steel, "You're standing one hundred feet from the graves of two murdered children, Mr. Mann. You helped bury them today. You said prayers for them today. Help us solve their murders. Finally tell us the truth."

The school counselor shuddered. His gaze darted all around them, looking for escape, but there was none. There was just him and two law-enforcement officers and the secret truth Quincy had finally ferreted out from the dark corners of Mann's conscience. Richard Mann looked up. He was clearly ashamed.

"He didn't say enough for me to do anything with it," he murmured. "I swear, if I'd known what was going to happen—"

"Spit it out," Rainie ordered.

"I asked Danny once what he really knew about No Lava. I told him my concerns about him befriending someone who was only an e-mail address. What if he was really a six-year-old boy or a dirty old man—though I didn't put it quite that bluntly."

"What did he *say*, Richard?"

"He said *she* wasn't anything like that. And when I tried to explain to him that was exactly my point, she might not even be a she but a he, Danny got this funny look on his face. He blew me off. At the time I thought it was attitude. But after Tuesday I started to wonder. What if it wasn't attitude? What if he was simply positive that he knew the truth—for example, if he'd met No Lava in person, so he'd seen for himself that she was female?"

"Why the *hell* didn't you tell us this earlier?"

"It was just a theory!" Mann protested.

"You told us all your other theories."

"No Lava isn't a theory—I saw the e-mails! And I was honestly saying what I'd heard about Melissa and her father. How was I to know it was a rumor?"

Rainie blew out an exasperated puff of air. Leave it to an amateur head shrink to fuck up a critical investigation. She gave him a remorseless stare. He bowed his head.

"Anything else you'd like to tell us, Richard?"

"No," he said meekly. "That would be all."

"Do you know when Danny might have met this person? Or when they started talking?"

He shook his head emphatically, still not daring to make eye contact.

"Are you on-line, Richard? Have you ever received an e-mail from Miss Avalon?"

"I just bought my first personal computer. I'm pretty good with some of the software, but I'm not that comfortable on the Web yet. In fact, I was thinking that maybe one afternoon I'd have Danny show me the ropes. It could be a way of bonding."

"You never received an e-mail from Miss Avalon?" Rainie repeated.

"No. Why would I?"

"That's all. We're done with you." Rainie gave a little shoo-shoo motion with her hands. Richard Mann nodded gratefully, hesitated one more moment as if he thought she might change her mind, then made a bee-line back to his companions. No doubt he'd tell them he'd just been an invaluable source of help to the police investigation into this hideous crime. No doubt they'd smooth pretty boy's ruffled feathers and puff him back up to the image of the man he wanted to be. Personally, Rainie was fed up with his incompetence.

She turned back to Quincy. She rubbed her temples, where she was starting to get one hell of a head-ache. "Female, huh? Female influence, using Melissa Avalon's own e-mail address to contact Danny. We're not thinking Miss Avalon helped plan her own death with an unmarked bullet, are we?"

"No. We're thinking e-mail addresses are a very easy thing to hijack, and what better way to impress a bud-ding young hacker like Danny."

"Oh good. I'd hoped that's what we were thinking. Now, just out of curiosity, who do we think did it?"

"We don't have a clue."

"But he might be a she? I don't know. The kids re-ported a mysterious *man* in black, not a woman, and even seven-year-olds ought to know the difference."

"Unless she dressed up as a he." Quincy had a strange smile on his face. "Cross-dressing psychopaths aren't as uncommon as you would think."

"Great, more ambiguity. That's just what this case needs. VanderZanden next? Maybe Mrs. Vander-Zanden?"

"By all means. Lead the way."

Rainie had no sooner turned back toward the crowd than she ran into a man. She had just started to apologize when she looked up and realized who he was. George Walker stood before her. His beefy face was flushed red. His cheeks were covered in moisture. He raised his hand to point at Rainie, and she was struck by how hard his massive body was trembling.

Rainie's throat went dry. She tried to swallow, muster a coherent greeting. She was pinned by the ravaged look in George Walker's eyes.

"What—have you—*done*—for my—*daughter*?" he bit out.

"We're . . . We're working very hard, sir."

"You fucked up all the evidence!" George Walker roared. People glanced their way at the sudden noise. His wife saw them, went ashen, and hurried over.

"I'm sorry, Mr. Walker. I know this is very difficult—"

"That little bastard killed my daughter and you're not even trying to put him away. You think I don't know? You think we haven't heard? He killed our little girls and you're protecting him. He butchered our little girls and you're trying to clear *his name.*"

"George, George." His wife had arrived. She put her tiny hand on his arm as if she could hold him back. She gave Rainie a pleading look.

"I'm sorry," Rainie whispered.

"Sorry! You haven't even come to our house. Our children were murdered in cold blood and you didn't even pay your respects!"

"George, your heart. George—"

"Mr. Walker," Quincy tried.

"How many times have you been to the O'Gradys' house? How many times to visit that murdering little bastard? My girl, my girl. My little, little girl. He killed her and you don't care."

"We're working . . . so hard, Mr. Walker—"

"You sympathize with him, don't you, Rainie Conner? You're nothing but a murderer too!"

"George!" Mrs. Walker appeared genuinely stricken. Rainie just stood there and took it. She didn't have a good reply anymore. And she didn't have the strength to move.

"I'm going to sue your ass," George Walker railed. "I'm going to sue you and the school and Shep O'Grady. You harbored a murderer in your midst, and it's gone on long enough. Bakersville deserves justice! My little girl deserves justice! Sally and Alice and Miss Avalon. Sally and Alice and Miss Avalon. Sally and Alice and Miss Avalon—" His voice broke off. His shoulders started to heave. He turned back to his wife, wrapped his giant arms around her frail shoulders, and wept.

And Rainie just stood there and took it.

She was aware of everyone staring at them now. Hundreds of people devouring a scandalous scene, searching for each nuance, already thinking how they'd repeat the story to their neighbors later. And she was aware of Quincy watching her as well. His gaze was kind, understanding. Somehow it hurt her the most.

"You need to go," he murmured.

"I can't."

"Rainie, you aren't doing him any favors."

Rainie nodded slowly. George Walker still sobbed in his wife's arms. Jean Walker looked directly at Rainie, trying to second Quincy's motion with her gaze. *Go, get out of here, before you make things worse.*

Rainie turned away and walked down the hill with Quincy at her side. People were still staring. For the first time in her life, she didn't return their gazes.

She kept walking, and for reasons she couldn't talk about, she was ashamed.

TWENTY-FIVE

Friday, May 18, 5:04 P.M.

RAINIE, LUKE HAYES, Sanders, and Quincy assembled in the attic of city hall for the task-force meeting. Rainie had already been in the headquarters for the past thirty minutes, gathering paperwork and breaking any #2 pencil she could find. The hardwood floor was now covered with slivers of yellow debris, earning concerned looks from both Sanders and Quincy. Luke, on the other hand, barely registered the mess. He had been working with Rainie for years.

Rainie took a seat behind her sawhorse desk and briskly shuffled together her notes.

"Ready?"

The three men unfolded their metal seats and nodded.

"Let's start with updates on the suspects first, since I know we have progress there. Next we'll move on to evidence, then revisit our theories of the case. Got it?"

Everyone nodded. Rainie began:

"At our last meeting I was assigned Charlie Kenyon and Richard Mann as possible suspects. Charlie's a bust. He was out of town on Tuesday, visiting his girlfriend in Portland, which was corroborated by the girl's parents. As you'll see in my notes"—she handed out three copies of her handwritten interview with Charlie—"he hung out with Danny O'Grady on occasion, but I'm willing to believe he didn't know anything about plans to attack the school. Mostly because we have Charlie arraigned on possession charges right now, and if he did know anything specific, he'd be dealing that information to save his hide."

"Charlie, Charlie, Charlie," Luke murmured.

"Exactly. So count Charlie out. That leaves us with Richard Mann. I've run a basic background report." Rainie passed around more copies. "Mann has no record of criminal activity and no handguns registered in his name in Oregon or California. I called the L.A. school where he worked as a student teacher last year, and they rave about the guy. They're sending me a copy of his personnel file, but I'm not sure it's gonna lead anywhere. Finally, the school's secretary, Marge, confirms his alibi: She saw him go into his office with a sandwich at the beginning of the period. And she was there, right outside his and Principal VanderZanden's offices, until shots were fired. She also said that to the best of the rumor mill's knowledge, there wasn't anything one way or another between the school counselor and Miss Avalon."

"Does that seem odd?" Sanders spoke up. "They're both young, both new in town. Seems like if anything they'd be friends."

"Sure, why not?" Rainie agreed. "Or maybe VanderZanden entered the picture right away, and after that Avalon wasn't interested in expanding her social circle. Don't know. I'll keep asking around, I'm just not optimistic. On a scale of one to ten, ten being the son of a bitch we're going to lock up for life, I give Richard Mann a three, but it's a weasel factor three, based more on the fact that he's held out information on us than anything concrete." Rainie shrugged. She'd tried, but at the moment her suspects looked no good. "What about Principal VanderZanden? Sanders?"

"Still inconclusive," Sanders reported, opening a

color-coded file and also dispensing copies. Rainie noticed that his notes were typed—and he had chosen a nice font. "VanderZanden's alibi for the shooting is also the school secretary, Marge. She said she saw VanderZanden go into his office and shut the door at the end of lunch. Minutes later, when the shots were fired, he came running out of his office and joined her in the hall."

"Sounds like an alibi to me," Luke said.

Sanders shook his head. "Yes and no. When I checked out the offices"—Sanders gave Rainie a pointed glance—"*I* happened to notice that both Richard Mann's and Principal VanderZanden's offices have windows big enough for a grown man to exit. That raises the possibility of either man departing his office through the window, reentering the school through the side door, and surprising Miss Avalon in her classroom. In theory, he could've used Danny to create a large diversion by continuing the gunfire while he ran back out of the school and reentered his office through the window.

"The good news with this scenario is it would explain why some children thought they saw a man in black but none of the neighbors saw anyone flee through their yards. The bad news is that the office windows overlook the school parking lot. What are the chances of a grown man climbing in and out of that window without anyone noticing?"

"Stranger things have happened," Luke said with a shrug, but no one jumped on that bandwagon. The chances were pretty slim.

"For the sake of argument," Sanders continued, "we do have motive. According to Avalon's diary, she was starting to have doubts about being involved with VanderZanden. In her last entry she talks about wanting to find a therapist. You know, to resolve her father-figure issues."

"Had she told VanderZanden this?" Quincy asked.

"Don't know. We haven't found any correspondence between them. Plus, I can't find any close friends or confidantes to tell us more about Avalon's state of mind. According to her coworkers, she was nice but kept to herself. Her phone bills are a bust. I can't even find records of her calling VanderZanden, so they either communicated strictly in person or she did it all by computer. Of course, the computers are wiped clean."

"So we have one possible scenario," Rainie summarized. "Avalon wanted to end things with VanderZanden. He retaliated by arranging her murder, disguised as a school shooting. Which involved intimidating Danny into being his cover, wiping all lab computers clean to cover his tracks, and sneaking in and out of his office to do the actual crime." She frowned. "It's elaborate, but not impossible."

"Give him a six," Sanders said. "He has motive and opportunity. The VanderZandens only have a .22 rifle registered in their name, but it's not impossible to get your hands on an unregistered gun. I mean, as long as you're climbing out your office window, why not stop at the street corner for a black-market semiauto?"

"Point taken," Rainie observed dryly. She was about to turn to Luke when Quincy interrupted.

"What about Mrs. VanderZanden?"

"What about her?" Sanders asked.

"Any evidence that she knew about the affair? Neighbors report any tension in the marriage?"

"Umm . . ." For once the superefficient detective was caught off guard. "I'd have to get back to you on that."

Rainie was impressed. So Sanders wasn't all-knowing, after all. Who would've thought.

She returned to their rundown of current suspects. "Luke, bring Sanders up to date on Daniel and Angelina Avalon."

Luke turned to Sanders. He didn't have notes or handouts, and his expression made it clear he thought Sanders's color-coded binders were a deep-seated cry for help. "Angelina Avalon is Melissa's stepmom," Luke reported off the top of his head. "Her real mom died during childbirth. Daniel waited thirteen years to remarry, and Quincy thinks he was having 'inappropriate relations' with his daughter."

"Incest?" Sanders asked incredulously.

"Bingo," Luke said. "Daniel Avalon gets a weasel factor of fifteen, if you ask me. Unfortunately, he currently has an alibi."

"What kind of alibi?"

"Important business meeting. Two clients vouching for his time. One possibility is maybe he hired someone to do it, but I don't know. Mr. Avalon has a hunting cabin in the area, and for the record, the Avalons have five guns registered in their names, though none of them is a .22." Luke recited easily: "Smith & Wesson .357, a Glock .40, a Beretta 9-millimeter, and two Mossberg 12-gauge shotguns."

"Holy shit, what are they preparing for?"

"Y2K. The guns were purchased in the fall of '99. Mrs. Avalon probably feared for her china. Or maybe she's afraid of all those clowns in Melissa Avalon's room." Luke shuddered again.

"In other words, we can't count out the Avalons yet," Rainie concluded. "You'll push harder on it, Luke?"

"First thing tomorrow morning I'm paying a visit to the hunting cabin, then heading back to Portland and seeing if I can't finagle some bank records."

Rainie nodded. Luke planned on spending the rest of the evening guarding Shep's house. He didn't take his friendships lightly.

"That brings us to you, Quincy. Where are we with No Lava and Shep?"

"What?" Luke sat up tensely. He'd been absent during their last discussion, when Shep's actions had been questioned.

"It's okay," Quincy said, raising a calming hand. "Nothing came of it—"

"Damn right!" Luke spat out.

"According to the school staff," Quincy continued

evenly, "no one saw Shep enter the building before the shooting. Plus, his patrol log puts him at Hank's hardware store a little after one, which Hank confirmed. At that point, it's questionable whether he had the time to drive to the school and commit murder before one-thirty."

"You examined his patrol log?" Luke was still offended.

Quincy ignored him. "So we can count Shep out. That brings me to the person writing e-mails to Danny from No Lava@aol.com. I did learn a few things there. One, according to Sandy O'Grady, the No Lava address was actually Melissa Avalon's account."

"Melissa Avalon was the one writing Danny e-mails?" Sanders interrupted.

Quincy shook his head. "I don't think so. Melissa saw Danny every day, so there wouldn't be a need for her to be sending him lots of mail. Plus, I tried checking AOL's member directory on Thursday to see if I could find a record of a No Lava and nothing came up. This afternoon I followed up with an AOL technician. According to service logs, No Lava was listed in their directory until Monday at six P.M., when the account was canceled and the caller ordered all traces of the member name removed. I'm willing to bet that our shooter made that call at the same time that she was purging the hard drives of the school's computers."

"She?" Luke questioned.

Quincy pursed his lips. "According to Richard Mann, Danny had implied that his pen pal was female. It's an interesting possibility. I just don't like Mann as the sole source of information. On the other hand, that might explain a few things. We've certainly looked at a lot of suspects without coming up with any strong candidates. Maybe we are looking at the wrong gender. God knows Danny gravitates more toward women— both his mother and Melissa Avalon. In many ways, he'd be more vulnerable to a manipulative female than a male."

"Maybe Mrs. VanderZanden found out what her husband was doing," Sanders said slowly, finally understanding Quincy's earlier line of questioning.

"And maybe Angelina finally caught on to her real role in her husband's life," Luke filled in. "Can't be fun to figure out you're nothing but a place holder for a too-old daughter."

They all turned and stared at Rainie.

"What? Because I got double-X chromosomes I magically know what drives women to kill?"

Luke appeared abashed. Sanders, on the other hand, nodded matter-of-factly.

Rainie rolled her eyes. She said briskly, "Let's bring this all together. Fact one, someone else was involved in the shootings on Tuesday."

Everyone nodded.

"This person is at least five-foot-six, proficient with computers, and also gun savvy."

"And how." Sanders flipped to a gray-colored tab. Gray for guns? Christ, these state boys had too much time on their hands. "Got an update on the ballistics info. You'll like this—at least, the ballistics department is very pleased with themselves. They want to write this up as a case study. Okay, so the ME identifies one .22-caliber slug with no evidence of rifling but containing a polymer residue. Also found, one .38-caliber casing with faint traces of polymer residue. Finally, also discovered—once the crime-scene technicians were told to look for it in the debris bags—three tiny pieces of plastic, which fit together to form a single unit about the size and shape of a pen cap. Anyone, anyone? What do we have?"

"I hate riddles," Rainie said flatly.

But Luke Hayes breathed, with near reverence, "A sabot."

"Nice work, Officer."

"What the hell is a sabot doing in a school shooting?" Luke said with a frown.

"What the hell is a sabot?" Rainie asked.

Sanders looked at Luke, who did the honors. "I've heard of them for hunting. Basically you take something like plastic and wrap it around a smaller-caliber slug so it will fit in a larger-caliber gun. Then a big gun can fire smaller bullets with greater velocity and mushrooming capacity. You know, for large-game hunting."

"Oh, Jesus Christ." Rainie looked at them all as if they'd gone mad. "You mean to tell me that someone is applying techniques for large-game hunting to *school grounds*?"

"We don't think this has anything to do with hunting techniques," Sanders supplied. "The ME is the one who first thought of the possibility, and that's because she'd read about it once before—in a mob shooting in New Jersey. The other advantage of making a sabot, you see, is that it makes the slug hard to trace. No rifling marks, no matching with a murder weapon. Also, this answers Rainie's question about why only one shot to the forehead—hardly a sure kill with a .22. Well, the slug was fired by a bigger gun, meaning greater velocity, more force. Whoever we're looking for isn't dumb."

Rainie turned this over in her mind, trying to see how it was done. She spared a glance at Quincy, who had a curious look on his face, as if many things were becoming magically clear. She was happy for him. Personally, between the little scene with George Walker and now this, her temples were pounding and her hand had a tremor she hoped no one would notice.

"How do you make a sabot?" she asked Sanders.

"It's involved. In this case, ballistics has determined that the .22-caliber slug recovered from Avalon's body was actually fired from a .38-caliber gun."

"Danny's .38 revolver."

"No. Rifling doesn't match. Give me a minute, we'll get to it. Okay, so we have someone, Quincy's UNSUB, who wants to cover his tracks. He hits upon a great idea. He'll shoot a .22-caliber slug from a .38 revolver. Given the entry wound and weight of the recovered projectile, everyone will be looking for a .22 semiauto. He'll never get tied to the crime.

"But how to make a .38 fire a .22-caliber bullet? That's where the sabot comes in. The UNSUB takes a plastic rod and turns it until it's the diameter of a .38-caliber bullet. He then cuts the rod to the same length as a .38 slug and—this isn't child's play—center-drills the piece of plastic with a .22-caliber hole. He cuts the piece of plastic lengthwise in three equal pieces, then glues the pieces back together at the base. Voilà, he has made a sabot. Now he removes a .22 slug from its casing. Then he simply pushes the slug into the center of the sabot from the top, inserts the entire thing into a .38-caliber casing, and loads a .38-caliber-size bullet into his revolver. Upon being fired from the barrel of the gun, the sabot's three pieces will fall apart, leaving the .22-caliber projectile to continue on and strike the victim. And the UNSUB ejects the shell casing, then walks away with his .38 revolver, leaving no one the wiser."

"We're talking serious thought here," Rainie said.

"And knowledge of guns. Sabots have been around since the earliest firearms, but it's not like everyone's using them."

"Now that we know what it is, can we trace the bullet?"

"Not the slug," Sanders said, and got a wicked gleam in his eye. "But you can sure as hell trace the plastic. Ballistics has already reassembled the three pieces and they form a perfect model of a .38 projectile, right down to the rifling marks."

"Don't be an ass, Sanders. Tell us what we've got."

The state detective's face fell. "Yeah, well, that brings me to the bad news. So far the sabot doesn't match with anything we have. Not with the .38 revolver recovered from Danny or with any other revolvers or slugs whose rifling marks we have on file."

"DRUGFIRE," Quincy said.

"Noooo," Sanders groaned. "Not again!"

"Absolutely," Rainie overruled him. "Face it, Sanders, you can only check statewide. Through the DRUGFIRE databases, Quincy can cover the whole country for a match with another .38 slug used in a crime. The sabot goes to the fed."

"And what has he done with my computers lately?"

"It's only been twenty-four hours," Quincy said mildly.

"I'd have given you updates within twenty-four hours. Hell, I just delivered a sabot to you in fifty-six!"

"Let it go, Sanders," Rainie told him kindly. "The feds have better toys. It's a fact of life."

Luke had a perplexed look on his face. He leaned forward, planting his elbows on his knees, and peered at Sanders intently. "You're saying this person went out of his—or, I guess, her—way to make a special bullet to kill Melissa Avalon. A bullet that couldn't be traced back to . . . the person?"

"A bullet that conceivably couldn't be traced back to him or her. Yes."

"Why?" Luke asked bluntly. "Danny's there. Danny's brought two guns covered in his fingerprints and registered to Danny's father. What's with the third weapon? Isn't that *more* dangerous? Someone might see this person armed and mention it later. Or maybe something goes wrong and this person ends up dropping the gun, or dropping the sabot, or God knows what. Seems to me that the margin of error is higher with the additional .38."

They all studied one another. Sanders had brought up the question before. They still didn't have an answer.

"Symbolism?" Rainie tried after a moment. She glanced at Quincy, the resident expert in criminal behavior. "Maybe there was a personal reason behind the .22 slug as well as a practical one. The person had a reason to kill Melissa Avalon, and the choice of bullet is tied in to that."

"Christ, it's not like she was a werewolf and had to

be killed with a silver bullet," Sanders muttered. "A .22 slug is as common as it gets."

"What about the gun? Maybe the .38 revolver was a special gift from her husband, with the barrel engraved, *To the One I Love,* which had really touched her heart—until she found out he'd given it to her out of guilt over doing the hokeypokey with another woman."

"Doing the hokeypokey?" Sanders pressed with a raised brow.

"Fine, fucking. He was fucking another woman. Does that work better—"

"I think we're missing something," Quincy said quietly.

Rainie and Sanders shut up. They all turned to him. His face was remarkably composed, but there was a light in Quincy's eyes Rainie had never seen before. He was excited. He had figured out part of the riddle, and he was thrilled to death.

"Let's look at the elements of this crime," Quincy began evenly. "First, our UNSUB utilizes manipulation. He or she identifies a troubled youth—Danny O'Grady— and approaches him, probably first via the Internet but then meets him in person to cement the relationship. This person needs someone like Danny. He learns his buttons, and he begins to push.

"The UNSUB also enjoys complexity. I think Luke and Sanders are correct. Why use a sabot when Danny's .38 would've done? Maybe because he or she could. In all probability, the .22 slug would deform, making it impossible to test and leaving us none the wiser. But in case it didn't, the UNSUB left another little riddle for the police to solve. Another way for law enforcement to be impressed by his or her skills.

"Which also brings us to the computers. It would appear that the UNSUB has been using Melissa Avalon's e-mail account to contact Danny. So why erase the school computers? Any correspondence, downloads, et cetera, would only show Danny talking to his teacher. Even if the contents of the e-mails were questionable, Melissa Avalon is dead. How is she going to defend herself? But again, one level of diversion is not enough for our UNSUB. He or she also tampers with the school computers. I'm almost positive now that when data-recovery agents delve into the hard drives, they will find everything overridden by zeroes. Our UNSUB seems obsessed with being thorough."

"But what about Danny?" Rainie objected. "Once you've introduced another person into a crime, it's no longer efficient. He's scared now, sure, but sooner or later he's bound to talk. That seems like a huge loose end. If the UNSUB really wanted to be untraceable, he or she should've acted alone."

"No." Quincy vehemently shook his head. "This UNSUB absolutely *would not* do everything alone. After all, what's the point of being so ridiculously clever if no one ever learns about it?"

Rainie went still. She saw comprehension slowly washing over Luke's and Sanders's faces, and she knew they had arrived at the same conclusion she had when their eyes suddenly widened in horror.

"You mean . . . you mean this person wanted someone to admire his efforts?"

"Yes."

"And if Danny does crack, does one day tell everything . . ."

"What's one of the biggest factors we're already seeing in school shootings? Ego. Boys trying to assert their identity in a crowded world. Confused children who equate being infamous with being famous. Are you kidding? The UNSUB is *hoping* that someday Danny will crack. Not right away. Our shooter needs time to get out of Dodge. But one day he hopes to pick up the paper and read about a thirteen-year-old boy whose sole line of defense in a triple-homicide case is that the bogeyman made him do it. And all the crime experts will say this proves how today's youths refuse to take responsibility for their actions, and the legal experts will say this proves how today's defense attorneys go out of their way to confuse juries with conspiracy theories, and our UNSUB will have a good laugh. Our UNSUB will clip every article on Danny O'Grady's trial and have a ball."

"We're no longer talking a crime of passion, are we?" Rainie asked weakly.

"No. Not at all."

"But why Melissa Avalon then? The special bullet. The single shot to the forehead. Those are all signs she wasn't a random victim."

"Oh, she wasn't random. The selection process was simply different from what we thought. I should've seen it earlier, when everyone kept saying how close Danny was to Miss Avalon and how patient she was with him."

"I don't get it—"

"Danny loved her, Rainie. That's why the UNSUB chose her. Because what better way to demonstrate your control over a troubled child than to make him assist in the murder of the one person who's been good to him. The only other person he trusted."

"But that doesn't make any sense," Sanders burst out. "No one's going to turn on someone they like. You want to lead a kid over to the dark side, you play on something he already hates. You know— 'You think your daddy's an asshole? Well, so was mine. Now, let me tell you what I did about it, little boy.'"

Quincy shook his head. "You can do that, Detective, but the bond isn't as strong—not as strong as our UNSUB needs. In classic indoctrination technique, you get the initiate to turn on the things he loves the most. That's when you know you have him. In fact, a Canadian serial killer cemented his homicidal partnership with his wife by making her participate in the rape and murder of her own sister. After that, she couldn't turn against him. That would mean having to face what she'd done. The guilt's too high."

"Danny," Rainie whispered. "Already under suicide

watch. Oh my God, the things that must be going on in his mind."

"He did it? Danny did it?" Luke was rocking back and forth slightly. His face held newly etched lines, and he looked at Quincy almost in agony. "You're saying Shep's son killed those girls. And this son of a bitch made him."

"Yes. I think that's how it probably happened."

"*Who is this bastard?* Can't you tell us that? Can't you stick data in some fancy feebie database and give us something practical to work with?" Luke jumped to his feet. The tendons in his neck stood out like cords, and he looked at them all almost wildly.

None of them said anything. Rainie thought of Luke, night after night, sitting in his patrol car outside Shep's house, determined to protect the O'Gradys' honor. Little Danny, who played in their office after school. Little Danny, playing shoot-'em-up cops and robbers with Bakersville's finest. *"Bang, bang, bang. Good shooting, Danny. Way to go, kid."*

"One other thought," Quincy said in the tension-filled attic.

They stared at him, wondering how it could get worse and knowing that it would.

"Murder is like anything else. It has to be learned. The first time is messy, the second time more systematic. These homicides, they're very sophisticated."

"Oh shit," Sanders said.

Rainie closed her eyes.

"This isn't the first time this person has done it," Quincy concluded quietly. "I would bet my career on it. And if the UNSUB is using the Internet to identify vulnerable teens . . . It's a wide, wide world out there, ladies and gentlemen. God knows where he'll strike next."

A PHONE RANG. Sanders flinched in the unsettled silence of the room. Luke recovered first and picked up the receiver. He said yes. He nodded. He said yes again. He took some notes.

He hung up the phone, and there was already something about his face that made Rainie cold.

"That was some bartender in Seaside," Luke said shortly. "Some guy just walked back into his joint. He's asking a lot of questions about the shooting. And he's talking about you, Rainie. He's talking all about you and how he personally knows you shot your mother fourteen years ago."

"We got action," Sanders said crisply. Luke and Quincy nodded, muscles tensing, clearly ready to roll.

Rainie's reaction was slower in coming.

"Yeah." She sighed softly. Nodding her head. Thinking of Danny. Thinking of psychopaths. Thinking of that night, all those years ago. "Yeah," she said with resignation. "Here we go."

TWENTY-SIX

Friday, May 18, 7:12 P.M.

DUSK BLANKETED BAKERSVILLE. Homeowners flicked on porch lights, scattering pinpricks of silver illumination against the darkening hillsides. Dairy cows clustered under trees for warmth, forming rocky contours as they hunkered down for sleep.

In some houses, parents held their children close, thinking of the schools they had attended in their days and the seeming battlegrounds their children attended now. You don't want to raise your kids to be afraid. Everyone goes to school. No sense in making a big deal about it. But to button them up each morning, kiss the soft down at the top of their heads, and send them out to their day—unarmed, defenseless, terrified of the kid in the next seat . . . Oh God, oh God, what has happened to our schools?

In some bars, young men kicked back extra shots, talking about the fucking lawyers who could get anyone off and the dumb-ass juries who cried harder for the murderers than their victims. Ain't no justice in the world. Ain't nobody trying to keep our families safe. This kid will probably walk away by the time he's twenty-one, just like those boys in Arkansas. Doesn't seem right. Not like those two little girls can magically crawl out of the ground when they come of age. Why should he get better than them just 'cause he's a kid too? A murderer is a murderer. Don't do the crime if you can't serve the time. Yeah, that's it. The kid's a killer—let's make him pay!

In Seaside, Ed Flanders nervously towel-dried beer mug after beer mug and hoped the cops would show up soon.

The man's own glass was long since emptied. Ed had asked him if he wanted another. The man had declined. Ed suggested buffalo wings. The man said no. Now the man watched TV. Some news-magazine story on how a volunteer group, Cyber Angels, worked to protect unsuspecting Internet users from on-line stalkers. The man wore a strange smile.

Ed rubbed the beer mug harder. Though he wasn't the type, he was learning to pray.

Seventy miles away, Rainie tore up Route 101 with her lights flashing. Quincy gripped the dash but didn't say a word. Sometimes he would glance at her. She always looked away. Sanders and Luke were in a car behind them, Luke at the wheel and having no trouble matching Rainie's pace.

Sometimes they used to make this run up the winding coastal route just for the hell of it. To keep sharp, they told Shep. Practice their skills. Now those days seemed so far away.

The radio crackled. Suspect was on the move, dispatch relayed. Please advise.

Rainie had to think about it a minute. A crowded bar, a suspect they knew nothing about . . .

"Don't make contact. Just follow him," she said shortly, then annoyed herself by looking at Quincy for confirmation. The FBI agent nodded. She scowled, replaced the receiver, and drove faster.

An hour later they were in town. Dispatch guided them to a small hotel, and just around the corner, tucked behind a grove of trees, they encountered a ring of police cruisers.

"Looks like we found the party," she muttered.

Quincy nodded. His face appeared calm, but he still had that light in his eyes. He unfurled from her police cruiser like a boxer about to step into the ring, up on his toes and light on his feet. Rainie watched him a moment too long. The lean line of his body. His graceful, self-assured ease.

She felt a sense of doom she couldn't shake. The night was closing in on her while the others geared up for the chase. Let's get the stranger, let's get the evil man in black.

"He's talking all about you ... personally knows you shot your mother fourteen years ago."

Stranger? She didn't know anymore. She had bad thoughts about bad things that had happened way too long ago.

Quincy was looking back at her curiously. She forced her attention to unfastening her seat belt.

Sanders had already located the officer in charge. She and Quincy walked up in time to hear: "Suspect appears to be approximately forty years old, graying brown hair, five-ten, five-eleven, approximately one hundred and eighty pounds. He's wearing a long trench coat, so he could be carrying weapons. The motel owner gives his name as Dave Duncan, supposedly some kind of traveling salesman. Said the man's quiet and a nonsmoker, if that's any help." The officer rolled his eyes.

"Time he returned to his room?" Sanders asked.

"Forty-five minutes ago. We have a pair of officers interviewing the bartender, Ed Flanders, right now. I guess the guy's been in twice. The first time he seemed to be picking a fight with a few locals over whether Danny O'Grady had done the shooting or not. We'd gotten the bulletin yesterday to be on the lookout for strangers who seemed to be following the shooting, so we'd already reached out to the bartenders. Then tonight this guy shows up around seven and starts back in. Except tonight he seemed to be focused on Officer Conner." The officer's gaze slid over at Rainie. "Ahh, begging your pardon, ma'am, but Mr. Duncan was saying that he knew for a fact you'd killed your mo—um, you'd killed Mrs. Conner"—the officer seemed to decide that was a more polite way of saying it—"some years ago. He said he had proof, but when Ed tried to ask more questions, the guy blew him off.

"We haven't been able to get a good look at him yet—we were following him in the dark—but Ed swears he knows him from somewhere, just can't think of where."

"Older man?" Quincy probed. "Heavyset?"

"Yes, sir."

Quincy looked at Rainie. She shrugged. "Older man" could be several possibilities. Principal Vander-Zanden, Melissa Avalon's father. Or, what the hell, maybe even Mrs. VanderZanden or Mrs. Avalon in drag. The UNSUB was clever enough to disguise a bullet. God knows what he or she could do with physical appearance.

"Why don't we just get this over with," she said stiffly, and everyone nodded. A few of the young men had their batons out. They had a lot of experience breaking up bar fights during the hot summer months, and now they were good to go.

Officer Carr ran them through the drill. The manager of the hotel would call the room and say there was trouble with the bill, would Mr. Duncan please come to the lobby. The minute Duncan stepped clear of his room, the officers would descend. They were all wearing flak vests and were prepared to use necessary force. The goal was to be so fast and quick, Duncan would never have time to react. Once they had him in handcuffs, they could begin questioning.

Rainie nodded her consent and pretended Sanders wasn't doing the same. She could tell Officer Carr was proud of his role in hunting down a key suspect. Years later this would be one of those stories repeated over and over again in all the good cop bars.

They settled down behind the trees and prepared to watch the show.

The hotel manager nervously picked up the phone and dialed the room. Rainie could see everything through the uncovered lobby windows and was happy Mr. Duncan couldn't say the same, because the hotel manager was sweating bullets. Poor man looked like he was going to have a heart attack, while beside him a somber young officer had dropped into a crouch and had his gun pointed at the front door. Rainie understood it was just a precaution. She was less sure the hotel manager appreciated that.

The manager set down the phone. He was frowning. He said something to the officer and then Carr's radio crackled to life.

"No one's picking up," Carr muttered. "The manager can't get Duncan to answer." He appeared worried. He glanced at Bakersville's quartet for advice.

"Think he's figured it out?" Sanders murmured.

Rainie took in the half-dozen cars and sixteen milling men. "Jeez, I don't know how."

"What about having the manager approach the room in person, knock on the door?" Sanders asked. "The moment the door cracks open, we'll push him aside and force our way into the room."

Quincy looked at the hotel manager, who had sweated through his white shirt and was now swaying on his feet. "I don't think so."

"I'll do it," Rainie said.

They all stared at her. She shrugged. "I swear to God I have no real desire to be shot. But do you see any other maids around?" She gestured to the all-male crowd. "I thought not."

Five minutes later Rainie was trying to pull a too-small threadbare gray blouse over her bulletproof vest. The skirt came to mid-calf and honestly didn't do a thing for her legs. Then she thought of her mother, dying in three-inch heels.

Jesus, her head was a mess tonight. Would somebody please get her a beer?

She finally got the blouse buttoned, sucked in her gut, and walked out to the men.

"You all right?" Quincy asked promptly. Those federal agents didn't miss a thing.

"Fine and dandy." She performed a pirouette, looking for a place to stick her 9-millimeter.

"Back waistband," Sanders said.

"Can't."

"Why not?"

"'Cause the skirt's too fucking tight!"

"Okay." Sanders raised his hands and walked away. Quincy formed a pile of six clean white towels and tucked her gun in the middle, with the handle sticking out of the back for easy access. He handed it to her, his dark eyes calm.

"He makes a move at all . . ." Quincy said.

"I can't shoot him."

"If he goes for a gun, you do what you have to do."

"I can't shoot him," she repeated more forcefully. "Quincy, if I wound up killing him . . ."

She didn't have to say the rest. It simply hung there between them. The doubts, the suspicions, the rumors that fourteen years later still hadn't gone away.

"Chances are that he knows we're out here," Quincy said softly.

"Then let's just get it over with. I'm tired of his games."

She nodded at Sanders, who looked mighty curious about what would happen next, then at eager Officer Carr. Everyone assumed their positions.

Rainie didn't allow herself to think anymore. She lifted the towels high enough to obscure her face and got on with it.

March one, two, three. At the door now. Pause.

Deep breath. *Hey, mister, want some towels?* Or maybe shoot first and ask questions later . . .

She knocked on the door.

No answer.

Did you know what you were saying in that bar? Or were you making this stuff up just for me?

She knocked on the door again.

No answer.

The rest happened very slowly. She set down the towels. She picked up her 9-millimeter. She twisted the door handle, not surprised to find it unlocked, and led with her shoulder into the room.

Behind her, men yelled, Down, down, down. Others cried, Go, go, go.

Rainie tumbled into the room, bringing up her gun, though she didn't know what she expected to find—or maybe she did. Maybe some part of her knew what body she would find there on that bed. Except . . .

Empty. Empty. Empty.

Officers jostled her aside. Seaside's finest pumped into the room. "Police! Police! Police!"

Still nothing.

More scattered voices. "What do you mean, nothing? Where the hell could he have gone? I thought you said you were watching this room."

"I don't know, sir. I swear to God, *I don't know.*"

Rainie didn't look at any of them. She was staring into the bathroom at the mirror over the double-basin counter and the large words scrawled there: *Too Little, Too Late.*

A lock of hair was taped beneath the red words. It was long, black, with just a hint of curl. Rainie didn't need a lab report to guess its owner.

Beautiful Melissa Avalon, lying dead in a pool of hair.

"Too little, too late," Rainie read aloud, her voice coming out shaky. She finally looked at the men in the room. "Would somebody, anybody, like to explain this to me?"

No one replied.

After another moment Sanders picked up his cell phone. He called the CSU.

"Hey," he said shortly. "We got another crime scene."

TWENTY-SEVEN

Friday, May 18, 10:38 P.M.

TWO HOURS LATER Rainie and Quincy drove back to Bakersville. They had finally figured out how Dave Duncan vacated the room. He had cut a hole in the back of the closet, creating a small escape hatch that opened up behind a rhododendron bush at the side of the hotel. The police closed in. He squeezed out, taking his minimal baggage with him.

Quincy was right: The UNSUB liked to have contingency plans.

While the technicians dusted for prints, bagged the hair, and documented the words written in lipstick, Quincy gave them a more detailed profile of the person they were looking for. In his experience, an UNSUB of this type would most likely be male, middle-aged, and unmarried. The crime was highly organized, indicating above-average IQ and professional skills. The UNSUB also utilized manipulation, meaning he felt comfortable being around others and might even have a serious relationship, though chances were his partner often felt she didn't understand her man very well.

According to profile statistics, the UNSUB had probably tried to join the police force or the military at one time but had either been turned away or dishonorably discharged. He was obviously mobile and would still be following the case quite closely.

Common wisdom held that the UNSUB's name wasn't Dave Duncan—he'd paid for the room with cash and showed a barely legible driver's license. Perhaps he was finding a new motel even now, someplace a little more populated, where a "traveling salesman" would be hard to locate. He knew the net was closing in, and yet—they all shared the hunch—the man wasn't done. The man wouldn't flee.

Seaside would work to write up all the information they could find on David Duncan's visit to their town—description, places he'd been, things he'd said. Sanders would once more coordinate processing the evidence with the CSU.

Luke still planned on watching Shep's house for the rest of the night. Then he was heading to Portland to finish interviewing Mr. and Mrs. Avalon. This time he'd take a composite sketch with him. Maybe sit across from Mr. Avalon. Maybe push the drawing under the man's nose and see what kind of reaction bubbled to the surface.

Rainie would inherit the fun-filled task of generating lists of hotels up and down the coast. Someplace not too far from Bakersville. Someplace not too far from Seaside. Maybe even a rental room in a house run by a little old lady. Or a rarely used hunting shack.

She'd never realized how many places there were to hide around her small town. She did not envy anyone her task.

It had been a long day. They were all exhausted beyond words. Sanders and Luke hit the road. Rainie and Quincy rode back in silence.

Inside the city limits, Rainie stopped at a small convenience store for a six-pack of beer. Then, by unspoken consent, she and Quincy went to his hotel.

There was an awkward moment. Rainie stood in the doorway with the Bud Light. Quincy stood in his room, surveying the space as if realizing for the first time how small and intimate it was.

He pulled out two chairs from the rickety table. Rainie pointedly bypassed them and headed straight for the bed. He didn't say anything. After another moment he shed his jacket, drew off his tie, unbuttoned the top of his shirt, and sat on the mattress, not far from her.

It was hard to read his face from her angle. Half was lit by the lamp next to the bed, half was hidden in darkness. She didn't know what he thought after days like this. Was he still excited, thrilled by the hunt? Or was the adrenaline fading now, leaving behind the sobering realization that another monster roamed the world? One more predator on top of last month's predator and the one the month before that.

Did he get tired? She was tired. She was restless and back to the kind of mood where she didn't trust herself. George Walker's words echoed in her head. So did Officer Carr's nervous look when he tried to figure out how to mention the accusation that she'd killed her own mother. She should have a thicker skin. Tonight she didn't. She felt vulnerable and weary, sick of pretending she knew what she was doing, when she hadn't known for days and the case was only getting worse.

She was soft tonight, a little bit aching. She looked at the hard plane of Quincy's chest, the exposed smattering of dark chest hair, and she wanted to lay her head on his shoulder. A strong, capable man. She wondered how his heartbeat would sound against her ear. She wondered if he would curl his arms around her and hold her the way leading men always held leading ladies in the movies.

She had never been held. Slapped on the shoulder in good-natured ribbing. Even patted on the butt in pickup games of hoops. Lack of comforting touches wasn't something she dwelled on. But tonight it bothered her.

Rainie got out a beer. She tossed a bottle to Quincy, placed her own against the top edge of the bedside table, and whacked it once with the base of her palm to pop the top off. A cool mist rose immediately from the neck. She took a deep breath, pulling the scent of hops inside her mouth and rolling it over her tongue. Damn. What she would give for just one drink. One long, soothing, numbing drink.

She slouched back against the old wooden head-board instead and cradled the bottle against her belly.

Quincy's own bottle was unopened in his hand. He was watching her with a tight, dark look in his eyes.

"Talk to me," she murmured.

"Rainie, that display had nothing to do with conversation."

"Shut up and talk to me."

He arched a brow pointedly at that clear statement.

"What's your ex-wife like?"

"Christ, you're trying to kill me."

Rainie sat up. She gazed at him more frankly. "I mean it. What's your ex-wife like?"

Quincy sighed. Apparently he decided she was serious, for now he took the cap off his beer bottle and drank deeply. Then he settled back on his elbows in the middle of the queen-size bed. Her curled feet loosened enough to nestle against the side of his hip. She admired the line of his throat against the open collar of his white dress shirt.

"Bethie's a good mother," he said finally. "She takes wonderful care of our daughters—daughter. Daughters."

"How did you meet?"

"College, when I was pursuing my doctorate in psychology."

"Is she a psychologist?"

"No. Bethie's from a wealthy family. College was a means of meeting an appropriate husband. A shame—she has a wonderful mind."

"Is she pretty?" Rainie asked.

Quincy took more care with his answer. "She has aged well," he said at last, his voice neutral.

"Pretty, smart, and a good mother. Do you miss her?"

"No," he said firmly.

"Why not?"

"My marriage is old news, Rainie. When we met, Bethie admired my background as a Chicago cop, while fully expecting me to settle into a more socially elevated lifestyle as a private-practice psychologist. Hell, I expected the same thing. But then the Bureau started recruiting me. I didn't say no. And poor Bethie ended up with an armed FBI agent for a husband. If I wanted to be fair to her, I should've stayed a psychologist. But I was true to myself. I got into this stuff, and then my marriage faded away."

"Why don't you say anything bad about her?"

"Because she's the mother of my children and I respect that."

"You're a gentleman, aren't you?" Her voice suddenly gained an edge. She didn't plan on sounding bitter or looking for a fight, but she took a step down that road anyway. Fighting was what she did best, conflict more second nature to her than kindness. She thought of George Walker again and her eyes began to sting. She wished they would stop.

"I believe in the importance of civility," Quincy said quietly. "I see enough inhumanity in my job without needing to add to it."

"I'm not civil."

"No." He smiled wryly. "But somehow it works for you."

Rainie stuck her beer on the nightstand. Her movements were restless. He had given her a gracious out. She couldn't take it. The mood ruled her now, and she only knew how to go toward dark and dangerous places.

"You come from money, too, don't you, Quincy? The nice suits, the expensive cologne. This stuff isn't new to you."

"I don't come from money. My father is a Yankee swamp rat, born and bred. Owns hundreds of acres of God's own land in Rhode Island, works it with his own sweat and will take it with him to the grave. He taught me the importance of manners. He taught me to love fall, when the leaves change and the apples grow crisp. And he taught me never to tell the people close to you that you care." The corner of his mouth twitched wryly. "The suits I picked up on my own."

Rainie got on her hands and knees on the bed. Her gaze was locked on his. She moved closer. "I'm white trash."

He didn't take his eyes from her. "Don't degrade yourself."

"I'm not. I'm telling you who I am now, so you can't hold it against me later." She kept advancing. He didn't retreat. "I'm not civil. I hate to apologize. I have a bad temper, bad dreams, and a bad mood, and I shouldn't be doing this, but dammit, I'm going to do it anyway."

He said quietly, "Liar." Then he reached up with his broad hand, cupped the back of her head, and dragged her down to his mouth.

She'd invited the kiss, but the first contact still shocked her. She felt cool, strong lips against her own hot, angry mouth. She tasted hops, smooth golden hops, and she opened her lips greedily, as if she would gladly get drunk off him. Then his tongue pushed into her mouth, strong and commanding, and in spite of her best intentions, the old panic reared hard.

She drove her fingernails into her palms. She did her best to control her mind. Yellow-flowered fields. Smooth-flowing streams. So many techniques she'd learned over the years. Keep it simple. Keep it quick. Never lose control. No one was ever the wiser.

Quincy's palm was rough against her cheek. It tickled her and brought a flood of unexpected heat low in her stomach. She halted, a bit frightened. His lips whispered across her neck. She let her head fall back. She exposed her throat to him. His breath was warm and tantalizing across her collarbone.

He'd go lower, she thought. Must remember to

moan. Yellow-flowered fields and smooth-flowing streams. She could feel his lips, firm and skillful. But she could also feel the dark places hovering just out of sight. Yellow-flowered fields and smooth-flowing streams. He would touch her breast. She would arch her back. Get it over with. Get it *done*.

She felt suddenly, unspeakably sad. She had started this, but it would not be what she needed in the end. And she'd been wrong to do this with Quincy. He wasn't like the other men. With them it had been cheap and mindless. With this man, it would be blasphemy.

She lowered her head. Don't let him see her eyes. Don't let him see her stark and gray and thinking so hard about yellow-flowered fields and smooth-flowing streams and Danny O'Grady holding the shotgun that had blown off her mother's head.

She ached. She suddenly ached so hard she didn't know where the pain ended anymore and Rainie Conner began.

Quincy's hands came up. He feathered back her hair with his fingers. He swept the long, fine strands from her face. And then he kissed the corner of her eye where the first of her tears had gathered.

Rainie scrambled off the bed. "For God's sake, don't be so damn *nice*."

She came to a halt in front of the rickety table, holding the collar of her shirt shut with her hand and breathing much too hard.

On the bed, Quincy sat up slowly. His dark hair was mussed. She didn't remember doing that. His cheeks were raspy with five o'clock shadow. She slapped a hand against her throat and belatedly felt the warm flush of whisker burn.

Shit. She was an idiot. She just was. And now she was going to cry, and that would be adding insult to injury. How could one person be so dumb? That was it. She grabbed her coat and headed for the door.

"Stop!"

Quincy snapped the word, shockingly loud in the silent room. Rainie froze.

"Please sit down," he said more quietly.

"No." She had her hand on the doorknob and she wasn't letting go.

"Dammit, sit down!"

She sat in the hard wooden desk chair by the door.

"I'm sorry," Quincy said shortly. "I didn't mean to yell at you. I didn't mean to let things get this far. I didn't mean a lot of things tonight."

That made her feel better. Rainie pasted a smile on her face that could've shattered glass and said, "Ah, thanks, fed. Now, if you'll excuse me, I'll be on my way."

"Shut up, Rainie. And give the attitude a rest."

Quincy rose tiredly off the bed. For the first time Rainie noticed that his hands were trembling. The lines were more pronounced around his eyes. His mouth carried a fresh, grim set. The sight of him like that hurt her. She had done that to him, and she knew it was wrong of her.

She wished she was the type of person . . . She wished she could erase the grimness from his face.

Instead, she sat, like a bad pupil who'd been caught red-handed and now waited for the blow to fall.

"Don't look at me like that," he said impatiently. "I'm not your mother, I'm not some abusive husband. Sometimes I feel like wringing your neck, but I'm not going to hit you."

"Too well bred for that, Quincy? Don't know how to get down and dirty?"

A muscle leapt in his jaw. She thought she might have pushed him over the edge and she actually felt triumphant. *What the hell are you doing, Rainie? Why won't you just shut up?*

She couldn't help herself. She rose out of her chair, driven by demons she was smart enough to explain but too worn down to control. She walked toward him slowly, watching his eyes narrow again, feeling powerful because of the way his gaze fell to her lips. She undid the button at the top of her breasts.

"No more foreplay," she whispered. "Let's just do it. How do well-bred Yankees fuck? Missionary? On top? On bottom? Doggy-style? Sixty-nine? Oh, what would your daddy say?"

She slid loose another button, revealing her worn white cotton bra. Her hands weren't shaking anymore. She felt giddy. Not part of her body, but far, far away, where she could watch it all unfold as if they were merely characters in a play. How many times before? It didn't matter. There was always the morning for repentance.

Quincy caught her hand in a tight grip. She smiled and pressed her body against his, wriggling her pelvis suggestively against his erection.

"Fuck me, Quincy," she murmured in a voice she barely recognized. "Fuck me good."

And he said harshly, "What was his name? How old were you? Did your mother know, or was she too drunk to care? *Goddammit!*" He broke off contact, shoving her away and striding across the room as if he could barely contain himself. One moment she was next to his hard form. The next he was gone. She had to put out her hands to steady herself.

"You've never told anyone, have you?" he demanded. "And now here I am, and I need to be impartial to help you and there's not an impartial bone in my body. I want to hunt him down. Christ, I want to break every bone in his body. How many of these assholes can I put away, *and it still isn't enough*!"

"I don't know what you're talking about."

"Bullshit."

"Do you treat all your women this way? No wonder your life is all work and no play."

"Rainie, what happened fourteen years ago?"

"Look at the time. Clock has struck midnight. Gotta run."

"Fourteen years ago. So long, but not long enough, is it, Rainie?"

"Are you going to be around in the morning? We have a lot of work to do, but then you're not really part of this case team, are you? One phone call and you're out of here, and we both know it."

"Rainie—"

"*Let it go, dammit!* Why the fuck can't you let it go?"

"*Because I'm me!* Because I'm not stupid and, so help me God, I'm interested in you! And because some part of you is interested, too, or you wouldn't keep coming back to my room night after night, looking for conversation. Now here we are. Let's have the conversation, Rainie. You need to talk. I need to listen. Let's go. Let's get it done!"

"I don't believe this crap."

"And I don't believe that you forgot the name of the man who supposedly killed your own mother."

He delivered the words with brutal force. Rainie drew up short. For a moment she thought she'd heard him wrong. He couldn't. Nobody— How did—

Her heart hammering so loud in her chest.

But he was Quincy, of course. That's how he knew. Because he was Quincy, Quantico's best of the best, and she kept coming to him night after night, feeding him bits and pieces.

"You don't know what you're talking about," she said weakly.

Quincy just looked at her.

"I'm not going to simply stand here and take this," she tried.

Quincy set his lips.

"This is bullshit! I'm going home." She strode for the door.

He still didn't say a word.

She got the door open. She threw her coat over her arm with more force than necessary. And she realized for the first time that she wasn't looking out into the night. For all her bold words, her attention was focused behind her, in the room, on Quincy, who still stood quiet and motionless in the middle of the floor.

So help me God, I'm interested in you . . . and some part of you is interested, too.

Call me back, she thought suddenly, wildly. That's what I needed to hear; I just didn't know it at the time. So call me back. One more time. I can't do it on my own. I've spent too long keeping everything under control. And I'm tired and there was this man on my back deck last night, in black, and you don't know what that did to me.

The yellow-flowered fields. The smooth-flowing streams.

She was crying. She felt the tears trickle down her cheeks, and it shamed her. She hated tears. Her mother had told her years ago there was no use in crying, and she'd been right. Tears didn't change a thing. Oh God, they didn't change a thing.

The yellow-flowered fields. The smooth-flowing streams.

Call me back. . . .

Quincy remained silent. And then she realized she wasn't in the doorway anymore. She stood alone in the parking lot. Her coat was on and the hotel room door was shut. Once more her subconscious was working faster than she was.

The night was thick and cold around her. She looked up and counted the stars until the tears dried on her cheeks.

The vast night in the vast world. She was probably one of the only people on the planet who was comforted by feeling small.

Call me back. . . .

Rainie crawled into her patrol car. She realized there

was crap all over her window. Someone had glued newspaper over the driver's side and written: *We'll show you justis, bich!*

Rainie got out of the car. She used her keys to tear the love letter from her windshield. Night still silent. No movement from Quincy's room.

She drove home.

TWENTY-EIGHT

THE DIRT DRIVEWAY leading up to Rainie's house twisted darkly through a river of night. She'd forgotten to turn on the outside lights again and with her glue-smeared windshield she couldn't see a damn thing. Maybe she'd take a wrong turn and die in a fiery car crash twenty yards from her front door. Or hit a tree and wind up paralyzed. She could be the next Ironside.

Christ, she needed sleep.

Finally pulling up to her home, she retrieved a flashlight from the glove compartment and used it to trek around in the overgrown weeds until she found her hose. Her lawn needed to be mowed. The edges could use some quality time with a weed whacker. Her kitchen still didn't contain any food. Someday soon she was going to have to return to the more mundane matters of life.

Now she stood outside at two in the morning and rinsed sticky glue and old newspaper from her patrol car, until it gleamed faintly beneath the scrutiny of her flashlight.

Once she was done, the weariness hit her hard. She returned the hose slowly. She let the loose coil fall against the earth. She dragged herself to her front steps.

In the last few days she'd let post-traumatic stress syndrome get the better of her. She'd realized this during the drive home. She'd gone too long with too many nightmares and not enough sleep. She'd stopped eating well and started turning toward Quincy as if he could magically make it all go away. Big mistake. But what was done was done.

Tonight she had bottomed out. Tomorrow she would get back on her feet. She'd been here before and she knew how these cycles worked.

She mounted the front steps and, after a bit of fumbling with her keys, got the door open. She was struck all at once by the cross breeze that hit her face. What the—

She snapped on the hall light, her hand reaching automatically for her sidearm as she searched for other signs of danger. Her gun hand came up empty. She'd locked the 9-millimeter and her backup piece, a .22, in the trunk of her patrol car. Nothing she could do about that now. She flipped the light back off and waited for her eyes to adjust to the gloom. Still no sounds out of place. Just the breeze upon her face. She finally pinpointed its source—her sliding glass door was wide open. She could peer straight through to her back deck.

Shep?

He'd turn on a light and sit in plain sight. He would know better than to risk getting himself shot as an intruder.

Dave Duncan.

Rainie slid along the wall until she came to the open space of her kitchen and adjoining family room. Two bedrooms and a bathroom to her left, one big space to her right. No sign of life.

And then her gaze fell on her sofa, and everything inside her plummeted.

It couldn't be. Definitely not. And just after that conversation with Quincy . . .

Who would know how to reach inside her deepest, darkest nightmare and rip out her heart?

She scrambled for the light. Scraped the plaster wall with her fingernails and still couldn't find the damn little switch. Light, light, she had to see. Had to know. It couldn't be . . .

And then she had it. The single overhead light flooded the family room. Her old round kitchen table with the pedestal base. Her overstuffed chair. Her faded, comfy blue sofa. And the shotgun. Propped up against the back cushions of the sofa. Five long scratches still scarring the old wooden stock.

Time slipped backward. She couldn't stop it. She ran into the kitchen, fumbling with knives, but in her mind she was seventeen and had just come home from school.

Stop it stop it stop it. Couldn't be. The gun had gone to evidence storage in Portland. She knew. She'd looked into it. She'd consoled herself with the knowledge that she'd never have to see the damn thing again.

She grabbed the first knife she came to, a small paring knife, and yelled wildly, "Come out, come out, you bastard!"

But no one answered. Even the owls were silent, while her mother was a headless corpse in the family room and, oh God, what was that on the ceiling? Oh God, what is this, dripping down on me?

"Who are you? Who the fuck are you? Come out where I can see you!"

She tore down the hallway to the two bedrooms. No one. She ripped open the bathroom door. Empty. She raced onto her deck, trying hard not to notice the shotgun but of course staring at it, while time grabbed her by the throat and dragged her down viciously.

Her mother screaming, "You liked it, didn't you? You no-good whore!"

Herself whimpering, "I just wanted him to stop."

Shut up, shut up. She was not seventeen anymore. She was not helpless. She was a police officer. She was strong. She squared off against the towering pine trees, threw back her shoulders, and roared, "I know you're out there. I know you're watching, Mr. Dave Duncan or whatever the fuck your name is! You want me? Face me like a man, you miserable piece of shit!"

Her mother: "Liar. I should've known a daughter of mine wouldn't turn out any better."

"He raped me!"

"You're pregnant, aren't you? Well, don't look at me to help. I'm not paying for your mistakes."

"I just want him to stop. . . ."

"Then rub his balls, honey. That always works for me."

He had to be out there. She could feel him. The goddamn man from her deck, the big-mouthed stranger reviving old rumors in the bar. The stupid man in black who'd gone from manipulating mere schoolchildren to thinking he could mess with the likes of her.

Rainie ran inside. She grabbed the barrel of the shotgun with both hands, like it was a serpent ready to strike. But she was ready now. Prepared. Back outside. She hefted the gun overhead. She lofted it against the black velvet sky.

"Is this your idea of a joke? You think you can rattle me! Fuck you! I'm on to you, you son of a bitch. I'm on to you, so *fuck you!*"

She heaved the shotgun into the air. She watched it whip around and around. Heard it smack hard against a tree trunk. Her breathing was labored. She could hear faint ringing in her ears. Nothing good ever happened when she heard that ringing in her ears.

A moment passed. Then another moment. No sound in the trees, though she knew he had to be there. He'd driven a troubled little boy to murder, and now apparently he was looking for a new source of fun. What was it Quincy had said? The UNSUB would try to manipulate law enforcement for sport. He prided himself on clever acts.

Rainie would show him. Hell, she'd just thrown a shotgun at him and now stood with only her fists and her rage for protection. Oh, and a small paring knife.

She started to laugh. She didn't know how it happened. She was standing with her legs apart and her hands balled into fists, ready for a fight, and then she was laughing and thinking of what her mother had yelled at her fourteen years ago.

"Then rub his balls, honey. That always works for me."

She got it. Fourteen years later, she finally understood her mother's crude advice. And she had to slap her thighs and hold her middle as the laughter ripped out of her in savage gasps.

She was crying. Tears ran down her cheeks. Second time in one night. Jesus, it sucked to be her.

She was climbing off the deck. Knowing she shouldn't do it. It was just what the bastard wanted. Having to do it anyway.

Burrowing under the boards into the crawl space, where the soil was rich and dark and she scratched at it with her bare hands. Deeper and deeper and deeper. Still here. Still horrible. All was safe. Still here.

Oh God, she'd had no idea laughing could hurt so much. Oh God, was that her face in the mirror, with the sunken cheeks and mud splatters in the shape of tears?

An hour later she had her 9-millimeter and her flashlight. She went into the woods. She started to hunt. She had no illusions about what she would do if she found the man, and that both terrified her and left her calm.

About two hundred feet from her house, she discovered the hollow. Behind some low shrubs for cover, leaves flattened down from long vigil. Ground was cold now, but she knew he'd been there. Watching. It seemed very clear to her. A man who enjoyed manipulating children to kill. A man who was obviously angry but didn't have the gonads to do anything about it himself. Who would appeal to him more than a police officer rumored to have killed her own mother?

That was what tonight had been about. First setting

the scene at the bar, then supplying the props in her living room. He was inviting her to the party.

"Come back one more time," Rainie murmured. "Let me show you what I can do, you twisted son of a bitch. Let me show you *everything*."

She collected the battered shotgun on her way back in.

FIFTEEN MINUTES LATER the trees rustled as a figure leapt down to the ground not far from where Rainie had been standing. The man touched the dirt that still held her footprints. Then he brought his fingertips to his mouth and licked them.

And then he smiled.

Perfect.

TWENTY-NINE

Saturday, May 19, 6:01 A.M.

SANDY O'GRADY WASN'T ASLEEP when the phone rang. She was lying on her back in bed, staring at the gray shadows shifting on her ceiling. She'd been dreaming that she was a little girl again. She'd been out in fields, lounging back in the thick grass with her best friend, Melinda. They were identifying the shapes of clouds.

"Look, that one's a dragon."

"Oh, oh, an elephant!"

"A two-headed dog!"

Sandy had woken up with tears on her cheeks and the nearly unbearable need to call Melinda. Except she knew that wasn't really it. Melinda had moved to Portland nearly fifteen years ago. She'd gotten married—Sandy had attended the ceremony seven months pregnant with Danny—and she and Sandy hadn't spoken since. Their lives had moved on, the way lives did. They both had new friends who lived closer, had more in common, and required less effort to keep in touch.

She didn't honestly miss her childhood friend that much. She supposed, however, that she missed her childhood.

To be young and carefree. To be so sure that you had all the answers.

Snoring came from the living room, where Shep slept on the sofa. Rustling came from the front-hall closet, where Becky slept on the floor. And silence came from the bedroom where Danny used to be.

Six A.M. Staring at the ceiling. Wondering where her life had gone wrong. Wondering how to make sense of things. She was a mother now, and it was her job to know the way.

The phone rang.

Sandy picked it up before it completed the first high-pitched peal.

She said, "Hello, Danny."

He didn't reply. She heard the now-familiar background noises. Clanging metal, distant hum of voices. Sandy had seen some of Cabot County's facility the first time she'd tried to visit Danny. New, modern, really not so bad compared to how some youth detention halls could be. In Sandy's imagination, however, the youth center remained a grim, gray prison, and these noises fit that place.

"How are you doing, Danny?" she asked, keeping her voice light. She shifted to get more comfortable on the bed. She had him on the phone. She might as well keep him, for it seemed this would be as close to contact as she would get with her son.

"We're doing okay," she said conversationally. "We miss you. Your father is working very hard to help you. We hired a lawyer, Avery Johnson. I know you've met him. He's very good, the best of the best. Your father and I are pleased he took your case."

Still nothing.

She took another deep breath. "Becky is starting to come around. She got a new stuffed animal yesterday. A white and gray kitten. You know how much she likes cats. In fact, we might get a real cat soon. Would you like that? Your father is thinking maybe he could handle a pet after all, and Becky has sworn up and down she'll take care of everything. He'll never have to know it's around. Of course, now we need to go to the pound to pick out a kitten, and I'm not sure how Becky will handle that. She'll take one look and want to bring home every animal in the place. We could end up with a zoo. Can you imagine your father knee-deep in puppies and kittens?"

Silence.

Sandy's eyes began to burn. She blinked the tears away. "I wish I could see you, Danny," she said. "I miss you. Very much. I'll be honest. I've—I've been better. But there are a lot of folks around here who believe in you. The church has started a fund-raiser to help with the legal bills. Your grandma and grandpa, they've been by every day to help out, and they keep saying how much they can't wait to get this whole misunderstanding behind us. The neighbors have brought over food. Why, yesterday we even got a brand-new set of Bibles!

"Danny?"

Still no answer.

She sighed quietly. "I miss you. I wish I could give you a big hug right now. I wish I could kiss the top of your head. I wish . . ." Her voice had grown thick. "I wish I could make everything all right. Because I know whatever happened, you didn't do it on purpose. You're a good boy, Danny. You're *my* boy, and I love you very much."

More silence. Sandy couldn't take any more of this; her son was breaking her heart. She went to hang up, and Danny finally spoke.

He said dully, "So much noise. And this horrible smell. Not like the movies. I pulled the trigger. So much noise."

"Danny?"

"They jerked. The lockers went pop. People fell down. So much noise. I did such a bad thing, Mommy." His voice rose abruptly. *"I did such a bad thing!"*

Sandy's chest tightened. She had suspected this was coming, and still, hearing the long-feared words out

loud nearly ripped her in two. She whispered helplessly, "I'm sorry, honey. I am so sorry it came to this."

"The noise. So much noise . . ."

"Danny—"

"He's going to kill me."

"Who, Danny? We want to help you—"

"I want to die, Mommy. I wish I could lay down my
head and just . . . die."

"Don't talk like that! You're young, you made a
mistake. It's this other person's fault. He tricked you,
Danny. Can't you see that? He manipulated you. Now
tell us who it is. Please, Danny."

But Danny had pulled himself back together. She
could hear his ragged breathing quiet, then a long snuf-
fle as he wiped his nose with the back of his hand.

"I can't," he said at last, and his voice sounded surprisingly mature, surprisingly resolved. "I can't tell you
anything, Mommy. I'm too damn *smart*."

THIRTY

Q UINCY WAS ALREADY UP and moving when
the old rotary phone shrieked to life next to
his bed. At first he was startled by the
sound, then he was confused. No one called
him here. The office used his cell phone, and the locals—namely, Rainie—seemed to prefer to simply
show up. Then a new thought struck Quincy. He froze
at the bathroom sink, one half of his face still lathered,
the other half shaved.

The phone squawked again.

Funny, but he couldn't get his feet to move.

He'd been so sure that when the call came it would
be on his cell phone. God knows he lived and breathed
through its digital lifelines. But he'd also given the office the hotel number, and if Bethie had asked some
hospital assistant to please track him down . . .

The phone kept ringing. He forced himself to get
moving.

Thirty seconds later it was over and done. And it
was as horrible as he feared and as simple as he'd expected. If he would just come to the hospital. They
would unplug the machines, pull the ventilating tubes.
It could be over very quickly or very slowly. You just
never knew.

He started packing his bags. When white foam splashed his carry-on, he realized he hadn't finished shaving and returned to the sink.

He had phone calls to make. The first few, to Quantico, were easy. The last one, to Rainie, he realized he didn't know how to do. His expertise was in the professional world. When it came to his personal life, he still had a lot to learn.

The case here needed him. Things were moving fast now, and with a sophisticated killer things generally got worse before they got better. He found himself thinking of Jim Beckett and another young, beautiful law-enforcement officer whose attempt at stopping the serial killer hadn't even broken his stride. Oh God, he hoped it didn't come down to that here.

Rainie needed him. She was resilient, but she was going through things no one should go through alone. Last night, right before she turned on him again, he'd seen the ache in her eyes. One more moment, one last defense, and she'd be ready to open up completely. He wanted to be there for that moment. They had the start of something rare and special, he thought. God knows, he did not meet enough people in his life who both challenged and captivated him.

Except his family needed him, too, and as happened so often in his life, he couldn't be in two places at once. He was not Superagent or Superfather. He was just a person leading a complicated life, and sometimes he did fail the people he loved.

Rainie was tougher than Bethie, he thought. And she was trained in the field. Weak comforts, but he would take what he could get.

He picked up the phone and dialed. Rainie answered on the fifth ring, just when he was beginning to give up. Her voice sounded distant and not at all like her.

"Rainie? I'm sorry, did I wake you?"

She mumbled something that might have been yes.

He waited, and when she didn't offer anything

more, he kept the conversation simple, for there was no way to make it kind. "Rainie, I have to return to Virginia now."

Stunned silence. He'd expected as much.

He continued with more calmness than he felt. "The hospital just called me. Apparently, Bethie has agreed to shut off life support. She's already signed the forms to donate Mandy's organs, and there are people who are waiting. . . . It's . . . it's time."

Rainie didn't say anything.

"I'll come back," he said quickly. "I had the sabot couriered to the crime lab yesterday and pulled a few strings to make it a priority project. I can apply even more pressure while I'm local."

She remained silent.

"And I'd like to do some additional research while I'm back there," he added briskly. "I was thinking about it early this morning. I'm willing to bet the person we are looking for is what we call an authority-complex killer. The most famous example is Charles Manson, of course."

He thought he might be babbling. She still wasn't talking and he couldn't seem to stop.

"An authority-complex killer generally comes from a family with an extremely domineering parental figure," he heard himself say. "This parent either physically or verbally abuses him as a child. The child grows up fantasizing about facing down his parent but never has the ability to do so. Instead, his rage becomes focused on other people in power. Except rather than seek out direct violence against them, the killer manipulates others into acting. This, of course, makes him feel powerful and omnipotent.

"I need to look up additional case studies, but authority-complex killers are generally charismatic, verbal, and possess excellent socialization skills. The interesting thing about them is that they are mental. Even more than violence, they enjoy toying with people in charge, creating elaborate ruses such as we've seen. This person doesn't want things quick or easy. He wants to watch the police sweat and gloat over our seeming stupidity. In other words, the more I think about it, the more I'm sure Dave Duncan is still in the area."

"There's a chance he's still in the area," Rainie intoned dully.

"But don't underestimate him," Quincy added hastily. "He'll kill directly if he has to. Particularly established authority figures, such as cops."

There was a noise over the phone, as if Rainie was dragging something heavy across the bed.

Quincy frowned. He grew silent and for the first time heard the gulf looming between them. He had a sudden image of her sitting alone on her bed in the dark, cradling her gun for comfort. Things had ended badly last night, and now he couldn't stay to make them right.

"Rainie?" he asked.

No answer.

"I'm coming back."

No reply.

"I'm not bailing on you and I'm not bailing on this case. Isolation is not protection," he said adamantly, though he was definitely babbling now and didn't expect her to understand what he meant. "Dammit, Rainie—"

She said quietly, coolly, "Have a nice flight."

ABE SANDERS SAT DOWN to a hearty three-egg omelette in the back booth of Martha's Diner. One big advantage of working in the middle of Hicksville, U.S.A.—fresh produce. His omelette oozed with plump mushrooms, premium Tillamook cheese, and, best of all, fresh spinach. Too many places in the city ruined that. They offered canned spinach or, even worse, creamed spinach. Abe shuddered. Not even Popeye would touch that stuff.

No, Bakersville definitely offered good food, including buttermilk pancakes made from scratch. Abe loved pancakes made from scratch. This morning, however, he'd cheerfully gone with what he considered to be the healthy, high-protein choice. The case was progressing well, albeit in a different direction than he'd originally assumed, and he didn't want to slow himself down by carbo-loading.

He finished his omelette, tipped the cute waitress generously, and drove the short distance to city hall.

The attic sounded quiet as he climbed the narrow wooden staircase. That surprised him. It was nearly eight A.M., late by the last few days' standards, and he'd assumed that at least Rainie would already be in the task-force center. Seemed she was always the first to arrive and the last to depart. He definitely couldn't fault her work ethic. Now, if only she'd stop tormenting #2 pencils. He'd bought three boxes before he learned to keep them in the glove compartment of his car.

He opened the attic door, swept the small space with a quick glance. Apparently he was the first one in.

He set about brewing coffee and picked up a banded pile of mail delivered by the mailroom clerk first thing this morning. One overnighted envelope for Rainie, postmarked CA. Probably Richard Mann's personnel records from the L.A. school. One pink phone-message slip. According to a hard-to-read scrawl, Agent Quincy had to leave on pressing family business and would be gone for a few days. Most likely his daughter, Abe thought with genuine sympathy. Bad break, that. The agent didn't talk about it, but the word was all over town. Quincy's daughter had been KO'd by a drunk driver. Abe had already heard the story four separate times while eating in the diner.

The rest of the mail appeared to be junk. He threw it on the corner of Rainie's desk. She could deal with it later.

Since he seemed to have a moment to himself, he pulled out his cell phone and called home. His wife was in a state. The puppy was having trouble attending to his business this morning. She wanted to take him to the vet.

"For God's sake, feed him some bran cereal and be done with it."

She cheered up at that idea. Then, of course, she insisted on putting the puppy on the phone.

"Yeah, yeah, yeah," Abe said.

The puppy barked enthusiastically.

"You got no bladder control," Abe told him.

More vigorous barking.

"You're peeing all over my rugs."

Very cheerful barking.

"Yeah. Fine. I love you too. Now gimme back my wife."

His wife came back on. Heaven help him, he was blushing.

"How's it coming?" she asked.

"It's coming."

"Going to be home soon?" He knew she tried her best, but she sounded wistful.

His voice softened. He said, "I love you, honey. And I miss you too."

Sanders hung up the phone. He was sorry Dave Duncan had slipped through their fingers last night, but now that they knew who they were looking for, it was only a matter of time. The guy was on the run, after all. Probably panicked and scared and thinking he had no place left to hide.

Damn right. Sanders had personally issued the statewide APB late last night. If Duncan was in the area, some local eager beaver would get him in his sights.

Sanders got to work on his report. He didn't look up again until noon. Then he was startled by the time and the fact that Rainie still hadn't shown.

Something niggled at him. Something he didn't like.

Abe Sanders tried her house. Then he tried the radio

in her patrol car. And then he started to panic, because he didn't get answers anywhere.

For all intents and purposes, Officer Lorraine Conner had disappeared from the face of the earth. And even if Abe didn't care for Rainie's methods, he knew that just wasn't like her.

THIRTY-ONE

BECKY SAT ON her skinny bed, surrounded by stuffed animals and holding Big Bear against her tummy. Her parents were talking unhappily in the family room. They were trying to keep their voices down, the way they did when they were mad at each other but didn't want anyone to know. Becky thought that her mommy had been crying. And her daddy was in one of his Very Bad Moods. He'd boarded up the hall closet when Becky got up this morning. He'd told her that little girls were supposed to sleep in beds, so by God she had better get used to hers.

Becky didn't think her mommy agreed with that. Becky didn't care. She had a closet in this room too. She'd picked the hall closet only because it was closer to where her daddy slept. And as much as Becky liked Big Bear, she didn't know if he'd be any good in a fight. He was only made out of stuffing, after all, with a button for a nose.

Her mommy and daddy were arguing about Danny.

"He needs help, Shep! Serious help that he's not going to get from a youth detention facility."

"I know that! But we have to be patient, Sandy. You heard what the lawyer said. If Danny talks to the wrong person, it could wind up in court. Then what kind of help would he get? We have to wait until the forensic exams are done. We'll know more then."

"In six months to a year? For God's sake, he's already under suicide watch—"

"They're taking good care of him."

"There's no one for him to talk to. You had to hear him this morning. He was begging to die. Goddammit, this is our *son*!"

Becky slid off her bed with Big Bear. Careful not to make any noise, she crept closer to the family room and pressed herself against the hallway wall.

"There is nothing more we can do," her daddy was saying roughly. "We gotta just . . . trust him to get through this."

"No."

"Sandy—"

"There is another option."

"Like hell there is!"

"He did it, Shep! Oh for God's sake, don't cover your ears like a child. This is Danny, and he called me at six in the morning to tell me that he'd pulled the trigger and he can't get it out of his head. He's only thirteen years old. I don't know how it all came to this. I wish I did. But somehow . . . He went in that school, Shep. And he did what he did, and now it's tearing him up inside. And we can sit here in denial or we can climb into the trenches with him. I think . . . I think that's all we have left."

"Trenches? There are no trenches. There is prison. And he goes in alone and he dies there alone. Christ, haven't you been following the other cases? There aren't any second chances for mass murderers. Not even for a thirteen-year-old. Danny goes away for more multiple life sentences than years he's got left to live. End of story."

"Avery Johnson said that if Danny was willing to plead guilty, the county would probably be willing to work out a deal. It would spare everyone the anguish of trial."

"My son is not a murderer."

"Yes, he is."

"I'm warning you, Sandy."

"Danny shot two little girls! Danny killed Sally Walker and Alice Bensen. Those parents have to walk by empty bedrooms for the rest of their lives. Because of our son. What about that, Shep? *What about that?*"

"Goddamn you, Sandy—"

Shep's voice broke off savagely. Becky peeked into the room and saw that her daddy's face was swollen and ugly red. He had his hand drawn back, like he was going to hit something. Except it was her mommy who stood in front of him. She had her chin up and was staring at him like Danny did when he was daring someone to do something bad.

Becky was frightened. She wanted to yell stop, but just like in the school, she was too scared to make words come out of her mouth. She didn't recognize these people, with their flushed faces and mean hands. She wished they would go away so her real parents could come home. She missed when they all used to eat dinner together, even Danny, who would sneak his peas onto her plate.

"If you beat your wife, will that make you feel better, Shep?" Sandy said quietly. "Or maybe, right at this moment, are you getting some idea of where we went wrong?"

Shep shuddered. His hand slowly came down.

"I'm trying," Sandy continued softly. "I'm trying harder than I've ever tried in my life to make this family whole. But I can't do it anymore. We failed, Shep. Somewhere we went wrong, and Danny went wrong, and poor Becky—God knows what's even going on with her anymore. But the way I see it, we have two choices. We can pretend it never happened and not act too surprised when we get the call someday that our son is dead, or we can give up on what we wish had happened and start dealing with what did.

"Danny was involved in the killings. Danny has

problems dealing with his rage. Danny is a deeply troubled boy. But he's a good boy, too, if that makes any sense, and the guilt is tearing him up inside. If we don't let him talk, and talk soon, I don't think he's going to make it. He'll either finally find tableware he knows how to use or, worse, he'll shut out his emotions. He will become cold and remorseless.

"He's only thirteen, Shep. I want him to have a chance to become the man we dreamed about, not a newspaper headline. I don't know about you, but for me that makes our choice pretty clear."

And Becky's father said tiredly, "What choice, Sandy? Danny's not ours anymore. He belongs to the legal system, and I know that beast. The minute he says he's guilty, he'll be locked away for life. And even if he gets counseling and becomes our good boy again, what the hell is our good boy going to do locked away with violent felons for the rest of his life? Why don't we just buy him a T-shirt that says RAPE ME NOW and let him wear it at the fucking trial?"

"Shep!"

"Sandy, what do you think is going to happen? *Why do you think I'm so scared!*"

Her mommy fell silent. Becky thought she looked like she was going to cry. Becky was crying. She had tears all over her cheeks.

"There must be other options," her mommy said at last, but she no longer sounded so certain. "We need to talk to Avery Johnson, raise the possibility. See what can be worked out. . . ."

"He can't go to prison, Sandy. I won't let that happen. I won't."

Sandy rubbed her arms. "I don't know what to do anymore," she murmured. "I feel . . . like the worst is still to come."

"I'll think of something, Sandy. He's my son. Give me time, and I'll come up with something."

Becky's mommy finally nodded. Becky clutched Big

Bear hard and slid away from the doorway. Her heart was pounding hard in her chest now. She had the heavy feeling, where she could barely breathe.

She wanted to run into the family room. She wanted to throw her arms around her daddy's legs and beg him to leave Danny alone. But just like at the school, she was too frightened. Her mouth wouldn't work.

She went back to her bedroom. She started throwing blankets and clothes in her closet for cover. Big Bear would need a place to hide. And Mrs. Beetle and Polly the Pony and her new kitten.

Becky had a lot of work to do.

Bad things were gonna happen if people pushed Danny. Very bad things. The monster was still out there, and if Danny wasn't smart, if Becky wasn't smart, he'd kill them all.

He had promised.

RAINIE STARTED HER PREPARATIONS the minute she got off the phone with Quincy. First she mowed her lawn. Then she took care of the edging. The high grass would make the tracks too easy to see for what needed to happen next.

She put on a mask. She grabbed a shovel. She ignored the ringing phone and went to work, not letting herself think about what had to be done. Afterward she raked the grass back up to cover the marks. Then she took a long hot shower and steamed the rich, moist earth from her hands.

Another hour, toiling with the shotgun, just in case.

A little after two, as she returned from the trunk of her patrol car with her substitute 9-millimeter and backup .22, her phone started ringing again. She didn't answer but then heard Luke's voice on the machine.

She picked up the receiver as he was still calling her name.

"I'm here."

"Jesus, Rainie. Where the hell have you been? Sanders is going nuts trying to find you."

"I mowed my lawn. How are things in Portland?"

"Muddled." Luke sounded confused. She could hear the sounds of traffic, so he must be using his cell phone. "You took the morning to do yard work?"

"The grass didn't seem to realize murder was a good excuse not to grow. Why are things muddled in Portland?"

"Daniel Avalon has disappeared. We were supposed to meet at his office this morning, but his secretary's been stalling me with one feeble excuse after another. I finally tried his wife. Looks like Mr. Avalon didn't come home last night. And, get this, I drove by his hunting cabin on the way to Portland. It's definitely been recently used."

"You think he's Dave Duncan."

"Well, with the right disguise . . . Hell, anything's possible." Luke sighed. "I put out an APB with his 'normal' description, plus a description of his car and the cabin. It's the best I can do for now."

"I'm sure he'll turn up shortly," Rainie said neutrally. Her eyes had already gone to her back deck.

"Rainie . . . I made Angelina show me the gun cabinet. One of the shotguns is missing. I don't think that's a good thing."

"Fire with fire," Rainie murmured.

"I'm coming back to Bakersville, okay? There's nothing for me to do here anymore and I'd feel better if I were back in town."

"Whatever you think is best, Luke."

"Good." He hesitated. She could hear the unspoken questions still in his voice. She and Luke went way back. He would come if she asked him to. He would die for her if it came to that; he was that kind of man.

But she was who she was, too, and she couldn't ask anyone to pay for her sins.

He said, "Rainie . . ."

And she said, "I'm a big girl, Luke. I know what I'm doing."

She recradled the phone. The hour was growing late and she didn't have much time to waste. She went with a simple white cotton shirt, covered by a light jacket, perfect for concealing her handgun. She paired the top with long jeans that flared at the ankle. Perfect for disguising her backup .22.

She took her ID. She would need it to get into the Cabot County Youth Detention Facility. After that, however, she considered herself on her own. Not Officer Lorraine Conner but simply Rainie, doing what she should've done days ago.

She prepared one last surprise in her family room, just in case. Then she glanced at her watch. Danny was due to be moved at five P.M. Shep had decided he wanted Danny to be examined at the nearby psychiatric hospital. That didn't give her much time.

Rainie hit the road in her own beat-up Nissan. An hour later she sat across from Danny O'Grady, whose thin, gaunt face was a close match for her own.

"Danny," she said quietly, "I think it's time we talked."

She didn't leave until he'd told her everything.

QUINCY WALKED TIREDLY down the hospital corridor toward the room he'd hoped never to see again. He'd had to pass through Chicago on his way to Dulles, and his damn flight from Portland had landed forty-five minutes late, forcing him to run for his gate. He'd been terrified of missing his connecting flight, terrified of being stranded at O'Hare. Terrified of having to call Bethie and tell her he was missing another momentous occasion in his daughter's life. This one, though, would definitely be the last. Ha ha ha.

His thoughts were raw. He felt both exhausted and wired, the way he did when he approached a fresh crime scene, and that unsettled him even more.

A few nurses saw him walking and nodded in greeting. He recognized their faces but didn't remember their names.

Finally he was at the door. That damn smell again. And the overwhelming sense of white. He had been raised to believe that death wore black. He felt needlessly betrayed.

He put on his game face, for he knew no other way to enter the room, then briskly opened the door.

Bethie was curled up in a chair next to the bed, sound asleep. Her dark hair had lightened in the last few years but curved gracefully around her shoulders. With her taupe slacks and fine silk sweater, she looked much too nice to be spending her days in a hospital room. Quincy felt instantly guilty, his most common emotion when it came to his ex-wife.

He cleared his throat. She woke up slowly, blinking her blue eyes and looking startled to see him.

"Pierce? Done saving the world already? I figured it would take you at least another week."

Quincy ignored her sarcasm and gazed upon his elder daughter. Amanda's face was still covered in white gauze. Tubes and needles bristled across her prostrate form and nearly obscured a body that had once been defined by slender grace. The violence of keeping her alive shocked him once more. It slowed his steps.

"I came as fast as I could," he told Bethie as he picked up Mandy's hand. He squeezed gently. There was no response. He studied her small pale fingers against his palm. He marveled at her fingernails, dutifully growing long and pink while the rest of her withered away. It seemed like only yesterday those were baby fingers, gripping his thumb tight.

"I don't understand," Bethie said from behind him. "I thought you'd had enough."

"I wasn't going to miss this, Bethie. I'd always planned on being here, once you were ready."

"When I'm ready for what?"

Quincy turned around. He was still holding Mandy's hand, but now he was registering the genuine confusion on his ex-wife's face. His stomach plummeted. Someplace deep inside him had just gone cold.

"Someone from the hospital staff called. You're ready to turn off life support—"

"I most certainly am not!"

"Bethie—"

"Is this some kind of trick of yours, Pierce? Do you think this little melodrama will force my hand? Because it won't work. I am not killing my daughter just to convenience your schedule."

"Bethie—" But he didn't say anything more. She had no idea what he was talking about. He'd been set up, and he'd walked into the trap as meekly as a mouse.

Oh God, Rainie.

Quincy replaced Mandy's hand on the sheet. He kissed her temple. His hands had started to shake.

"No changes?"

"No changes," Bethie said stiffly.

"And Kimberly?"

"Settled back in at college, I suppose. Not that she bothers to call."

Quincy nodded and tried not to appear too hasty as he headed for the door.

"Thanks for visiting," Bethie called out sarcastically behind him. "Do come again."

Quincy stopped for just a moment in the doorway. "It's not your fault," he said honestly. "What happened to Mandy, it was not your fault."

"I don't blame myself," Bethie said thickly. "I blame you."

Quincy headed down the hallway. The minute he was in the parking lot, he flipped open his cell phone. His first call was to his friend in the crime lab, who had received the sabot late last night.

"Did you enter it into DRUGFIRE?"

"Jeez, Quincy, nice to hear from you too."

"I don't have time, Kenny. Where are you with the sabot?"

"Well, if you'd bothered to check your voice mail, you'd know I worked on it all friggin' night. The rifling matches with two other shootings, Quince. Two other *school shootings*. And both those cases are considered closed, with two kids in jail. So if these crimes are still happening . . . Get your butt to Quantico, Quincy. You're kind of in demand."

"I'm going back to Oregon. Fax everything to the Bakersville number as soon as you can."

"Are you nuts? We have the same gun used in three separate school shootings in three separate cities over a ten-year span. What do you think is going to happen next?"

"He's going to kill Rainie," Quincy said simply. "It's part of his game. Drive her over the edge, then attack when she's down. And I didn't see it coming. Shit, I didn't see it coming, and now I'm *all the way across the fucking country*!"

And then he was off the phone and in a taxicab, where he yelled at the driver to go fast, fast, *fast,* while he thought of his daughter and all those moments in his life when he hadn't done enough.

THIRTY-TWO

Saturday, May 19, 4:48 P.M.

DANNY WAS EXHAUSTED. Long after Rainie left, he lay on his bed, curled in a ball, staring at the same spot on the floor. He had told her everything. He shouldn't have, but he had, and now he was drained.

She had told him that secrets made things worse. She had told him that secrets gave the man power over him. Danny didn't know anymore. He had so many pictures in his mind. He wished he could turn off his brain and make everything go away.

This morning his hands had started trembling, and now they wouldn't stop. This morning the cold had left him and now he was filled with a burning pain. He hated the feel of his own skin. He hated the sight of his face in the mirror. He wanted something sharp so he could slice away his fingers. Then he wouldn't have to see them holding a gun or pulling a trigger. Then he would hurt outside the way he hurt inside, and somehow that would be more right.

He was tired. But he couldn't sleep. He was worried about Becky. He should make himself move, do something. He didn't know what.

Footsteps came down the corridor. One of the guides appeared. He was smiling, jolly, like a clown. "It's that time," he said cheerily.

Danny looked at him blankly.

"You're going on a field trip, Mr. O'Grady. Your parents are sending you to the funny farm." Mr. Jolly laughed at his joke.

Danny curled up more tightly on the bed.

Two men materialized behind Mr. Jolly. They wore uniforms and looked vaguely familiar to Danny. They held up shackles. If you left the walls of the detention center, you had to be shackled. There was no point in avoiding it anymore. They would take him one way or another.

Off to the funny farm. His insides burned. He wished he had something sharp.

Danny stood as ordered. He held up his arms. The younger guy did his ankles first. He didn't make it very tight. Not as tight as the last guy had done. That guy had cut into Danny's skin and left welts. Danny had known from the look on the man's face that that was what he wanted.

Danny kept quiet. The younger guy had the belt around his waist now. His hands were chained in front of him to the belt. He was done.

The older man nodded. "Danny," he said roughly, familiarly.

Danny figured he must know the man. Maybe a friend of his father's. Good old Shep loved the brotherhood of the uniform. Couldn't be easy to be a cop now.

The patrol officers led him out to a Cabot County police cruiser. They stuck him in the back, then climbed into the front. The two men kept looking at each other but didn't say much.

Danny didn't ask any questions. He didn't know why he was going to the funny farm or for how long or what happened when he got there. He still didn't ask any questions. He just wished he had something sharp. Cut away his fingers. Never have to gaze at his hands anymore. *Miss Avalon, Miss Avalon, Miss Avalon.*

"Run, Danny, run!"

The car started moving. The older man studied

Danny in the rearview mirror. Danny didn't like his look. He hunched his shoulders and tried to be small.

Ten minutes later the older man said to the younger man, "What do you think?"

"I guess it's as good a spot as any."

"Hey, you," the older man said to Danny. "Hold on, kid."

Suddenly, the car swerved. One minute they were on the road, the next the car went bouncing down the embankment. Danny thought the man would try to brake. Instead he hit the gas. *Boom.*

The impact slammed Danny forward into the divider. He blinked his eyes. It took several seconds more for the dust to clear. When he finally had his senses together, he realized the patrol car was smashed against a tree. Steam came from beneath the hood. The two cops looked bleary, and the younger one had blood on his forehead.

"Shit," the kid cop murmured, touching the cut and wincing. "Shit, that's gotta be authentic."

"Get out," the older man was saying. His lip was bleeding and his cheek appeared bruised. He spoke with more urgency. "For God's sake, kid, grab the keys and get the hell out of the car. Didn't your dad tell you anything?"

Danny finally realized that the back door had opened. Had one of them done it, or was it from the crash? He couldn't remember how things had happened, and already his feet were moving, though through no will of his own.

He got out of the car. Both cops were moaning. Someone squawked over the radio. They pretended to moan louder while the older one pointed at the keys dangling from his utility belt.

Danny took the keys and undid his shackles. Now he saw another police car coming, except this one wasn't from Cabot County. It was from Bakersville, and Danny knew immediately who was climbing out of the front seat.

Danny threw the keys into the grass. He leapt forward, catching the older cop by surprise, and grabbed his sidearm.

The man's eyes turned white with fear. He started to babble; Danny didn't stick around to hear. The fog had lifted. He had no more doubt in his mind.

He ran. Straight into the ravine, crashing through the underbrush. He heard the cops yell and his father yell. *"Wait, wait, we're just trying to help." "Son, please . . ."*

Danny ran faster.

He had a gun now, and he knew exactly what he had to do next.

He was *smart*.

AT A LITTLE AFTER five-thirty in the evening, Principal Steven VanderZanden turned his car up the rounded driveway to his house. Abigail was sitting beside him, holding his hand. Ever since the shooting, she'd had a need to touch him. She stroked his cheek more often, cajoled him out of his recliner onto the love seat, slept with her body pressed up against his.

It had been years since she'd been so affectionate, and right after the shooting Steven hadn't known how to feel about that. His sadness and guilt over Melissa left him needy, grateful for the contact. And yet the nicer his wife was, the worse he felt.

Today he had realized he needed to tell his wife the truth. Just get it all out in the open. Then see what she did to him.

Except this morning his wife had suggested that they drive to the beach, get away for a little bit. The days had been long since the shootings, so many people who needed his guidance and so many doubts to keep him up late at night. It would be months before he sorted through the aftermath. Months before he understood his role as a principal and guardian of students again.

His wife wore a new sundress she'd apparently

bought yesterday at Sears. The bright blue made her eyes vivid, and he found himself watching her, noting the way she smiled. She was flirting with him, he'd realized finally. Gently, subtly, in order to give him plenty of space.

And he found himself thinking about other times, when the marriage was new and they thought nothing of spending hours giggling on the sofa. He thought of the way he'd always appreciated his wife's common sense and how she made him feel strong, when he'd spent his whole life as a five-foot-eight runt who was never the hero on the football field. He remembered the way he liked his wife, particularly in the days before Melissa Avalon had arrived in Bakersville and stunned him with her smile.

By five this afternoon he had made his decision. He'd made a mistake, an error in ego and judgment. He hoped his wife would never have to learn how much he'd hurt her. And now he just wanted his old life back.

They approached the house.

The first sign of trouble was just a flicker of movement out of the corner of Steven's eye. The next minute the back window of the car exploded in a hail of glass.

"Oh my God," Abigail cried.

"Duck!" Steven yelled.

He floored the gas pedal on instinct and overshot the driveway. The car tumbled down the side of the hill and came to a halt in a tangle of underbrush. He fought for reverse. No such luck. He tried to shoot forward. They were stuck.

Another gunshot. The side window exploded.

Steven looked at his wife of fifteen years. He thought he knew what was going on. There would be no escape. Melissa had warned him.

He said quietly, "Run, Abigail. Run as fast as you can."

And then he got out and prepared to meet his fate.

• • •

IN THE ATTIC of city hall, Sanders was restless again. Six-thirty. Christ, for how long could one woman take care of her yard? That was a local for you. Perfectly good as long as the case was exciting. Once it got down to the grunt work, bailed out through the closest window.

He grumbled some more, strolling around the tiny attic and rolling out the knots in his neck. Luke Hayes had checked in briefly, but he was now back in the main office of the sheriff's department, writing up the day's worth of paperwork under Sanders's orders. Sanders didn't know how they generally did things around here, but in cross-jurisdictional investigations you needed up-to-date written reports or things fell through the cracks.

Speaking of which.

Sanders picked up Rainie's mail from the California school. Since she wasn't here, he'd just have to take matters into his own hands.

He opened the flat envelope and began to skim the contents.

"Oh shit," he said thirty seconds later. "Oh *shit*!"

And then, in the corner of the room, the police scanner crackled to life with the first reports of gunfire.

THIRTY-THREE

H ELLO, RICHARD."

Rainie stood on her back deck in the gathering gloom. It was late, nearly eight o'clock. She'd stopped on her way back from Cabot to grab a sandwich and turn things over in her mind. She hadn't eaten much, but things had become clearer to her. Why the shadowy figure of a man on her back deck? Why some stranger spouting off about her mother in a Seaside bar? Why the shotgun on her sofa? Because, somewhere along the line, this had become about her.

And having found her, the killer would not magically go away. Quincy was right. He wasn't done yet.

Rainie had parked her car at the bottom of her driveway. She'd already known who she was looking for. When Danny had finally, brokenly uttered the name, she'd realized she wasn't even surprised.

She had carefully made her way up through the woods to the back of her house. Her efforts were not disappointed. Mann sat calmly on her back deck with her mother's shotgun cradled in his arms.

She boarded the stairs, then leveled her 9-millimeter at his chest.

"Hello, Lorraine," he said conversationally. "Hope you don't mind, but I'm tired of foreplay."

"Fine. Stand up and I'll shoot you."

"Lorraine." He gave her a chiding look. "Didn't you learn anything fourteen years ago?"

"Yes," she said honestly. "Don't wait so long. And confess sooner—it does a body good."

Richard Mann grinned at her charmingly. He wore black jeans and a black turtleneck, making him harder to distinguish in the falling night. His brown hair was different. He'd bleached it blond and touched up his eyebrows and lashes. The effect was startling—from conservative young professional to aspiring rock star. Rainie understood what that meant. Richard wasn't planning on continuing his starring role as Bakersville's school counselor. In fact, he was merely attending to one last loose end before he rode off into the sunset.

"I went under your deck," Richard said. "Why did you move him?"

"I had my reasons."

"You visited Danny today, didn't you? Surely by now you know you can talk to me. In fact, I'm probably the only person in town who can truly understand."

"You're a sick, twisted bastard, Richard. I'm a cop. There's nothing you understand."

He laughed with genuine amusement. "You honestly believe that, don't you, Rainie? How clever. You've manipulated your conscience into allowing yourself to live. But I'm curious. This beer thing. I've been watching you for months now, and I just have to know. When you dump the beer over your deck railing, what is it you say?"

"None of your business."

"And once again you disappoint. I had such aspirations for you in the beginning, but then you became prickly and dull. I'm not sure I like you anymore."

"It's probably the gun," she told him. "Stand up and surrender. We'll see if that improves your feelings at all."

He smiled. "No, thank you. I'm more comfortable the way things are. I'm good at my job, you have to admit that. A good school counselor should be able to lead and inspire. And boy, did I lead and inspire. You should've seen Melissa's face at the end. She really hadn't a clue."

"Is that why you came here? To gloat?"

"You know why I came here."

"I'm not as easy to manipulate as a thirteen-year-old boy," Rainie said stiffly.

Richard stood abruptly. "No. You're even easier."

He took a step forward.

"Stop or I'll shoot."

He threw the shotgun aside. "But, Lorraine, I'm an unarmed man."

"Don't call me that!"

He took another step forward. "You know you want to do it. Killing gets in the blood. Hard the first time, so much easier after that. I've read it releases powerful chemicals in the brain. No other high quite like it. Believe me, I know."

"Freeze!"

"Come on, Lorraine. Just pull the trigger. You've been talking to Danny, you know how good it feels. You hate me. You hate me for manipulating the boy. You hate me for helping him kill those girls. You hate me for putting him in your dreams. Yeah, I've watched you sleep. I know it's all back in your mind. So pull the trigger, Lorraine. Do it one more sweet, satisfying time. Remember the power. Celebrate your rage."

"Goddammit." She dropped the handgun to his kneecap, and when he took another step toward her, she fired.

And the automatic weapon uttered a hollow little click.

Richard laughed. He picked up her mother's shot-gun, holding it loosely in his arms. "Keeping a gun in a shoe box in your closet? You don't even make my life that difficult."

Rainie was still staring at her Beretta. "How? I just cleaned it, loaded it . . ."

"The firing pin. Filed it down a fraction of an inch, just enough so it can't hit the firing cap. That was the night you woke up, but I was already outside by then." He held up the shotgun to her gaze. "You removed the firing pin. I know, I checked. Take it from me—too obvious. Never do a lot, Lorraine, if just a little will get you by. It's grand deceptions that always come back to haunt you."

"I wouldn't be polishing up your lectures just yet," Rainie countered. She let the 9-millimeter fall from her fingers, then eased back, trying to giving herself more time for her next move. Her ankle holster. She'd kept the .22 locked in a box in the trunk of her police cruiser. She couldn't believe he'd been able to get to that. "You're not doing too well this time. The clean shot to the forehead for Melissa Avalon—"

"Have done it three times now. Always the informa-tion teacher, always a single shot to the forehead. No one's ever put the pieces together. Once a mass mur-derer is in custody, who starts comparing his work to other homicides? Ask your friend Quincy. Shooting rampages are considered one-off crimes."

"But we knew you were involved—"

"Please, the sabot was a calling card. Sooner or later I needed someone to pay attention in order to have any fun. For God's sake, I gave you No Lava. I even invited you to personally visit my office so you could stare at the window I used to exit the building and rendezvous with Danny outside. You could've at least considered the possibility."

"We did. It seemed far-fetched."

"Yes, well, cops have singularly linear minds,"

Richard conceded with a shrug. "It's where you go wrong. Violence is a creative act. It requires patience and care. I've been nursing Danny O'Grady along for over a year, you know. Slowly making him feel comfortable on-line. Letting him know his feelings of rage and inadequacy are common and acceptable. Then it was easy. Met him in person. Showed him I'm a legitimate guy—his own school counselor, in fact. How can you doubt what the school counselor is telling you? 'You need to stand up for yourself, Danny. Show everyone, including your father, who's boss.'

"Of course, I never mentioned Melissa Avalon. I left that as a last-minute surprise. He just had to bring the guns and his backbone; I'd help him take a stand. When we walked into the side entrance of the school, the boy was shaking like a leaf. But you should've seen the look of determination on his face. Man, I was proud. Ironically enough, I kind of felt like a father. And then I walked into the computer lab and drew down on pretty Melissa Avalon."

Richard's voice lowered. He leaned forward conspiratorially. "The trick is to hesitate," he confided. "Let the kid apprise the situation. Let him understand he has the chance to intervene. And then, while he's still shocked and dazed and trying to find his conscience, *bam!* Pull the trigger. Down goes the precious little teacher. And the kid is all yours. He didn't stand up for good. Now he's gotta be evil. I told the boy to let it rip, and he bawled like a baby, but he didn't disappoint. Not bad shooting, really, considering he was too frightened to leave the doorway of the computer room. Shep might be a decent teacher after all—at least when it comes to guns."

Mann rocked back on his heels. He sighed and finished up contentedly, "Danny killed himself two little girls. And as soon as everyone left the building in a wave of mass confusion, I calmly exited stage right. Piece of cake, just like the times before."

"Not quite. Becky saw you."

Mann merely shrugged. "Guess she tried to play hero and find her brother. Bad break for her, when she ran down the hall and discovered her own brother and school counselor holding the proverbial smoking guns. But not so bad for me. I simply threatened to kill Danny if Becky talked, and threatened to kill Becky if Danny talked. Voilà. If people would raise children who were *more* callous, my job might actually be difficult. Without a guilty conscience, of course, there is very little to manipulate."

"And is that why you created Dave Duncan, some stranger running around Seaside? More need to manipulate?"

Mann smiled wolfishly. "Come on, Rainie. A murder has been committed—what do the brilliant cops do? They line up the locals. Now before, that was my whole advantage. I had no apparent ties to what happened, so no one ever thought to even question me. But that got boring. This time I became a local—quite nicely, if I do say so myself. But now I will be subject to questioning, and I kind of stole an identity, which might come up if somebody pushes too hard. How to cover? I know. I'll create some out-of-town stranger for you to chase. Clever and ironic. Someday I'm gonna have to write a book."

"Not to burst your bubble, Richard, but if you're so good, why do I know you're the shooter? And Danny's admitted that you are. For that matter, I've already called and left messages for the others about you. Face it, the jig is up." Rainie was lying about having left messages for Sanders and Luke, but Mann didn't seem to care.

"They aren't coming, Lorraine. Don't you understand that yet? Your hero Quincy is rushing into the arms of his ex-wife. And your friends Detective Sanders and Officer Hayes are dealing with another shooting across town. Or didn't you hear? It seems that someone sent Daniel Avalon a copy of a private tape his daughter made of her and her new lover, in flagrante delicto. I guess it was a little much for Mr. Avalon. He looked up good old Principal VanderZanden. He brought his favorite shotgun." Richard covered his lips delicately. "Oops. It's just you and me, Lorraine. Let's talk."

"Why? You had your fun. What do I have to do with anything?"

"Tell me how it felt that afternoon. Tell me how much you enjoyed killing the man who shot your mother."

"Go to hell."

"It felt great, didn't it? You don't like to admit it, but it gave you a secret thrill. And you like to relive it, don't you, Lorraine? Every time you step onto your back deck. Every time you raise your beer in a silent toast to the man you blew away."

"Richard, I changed my mind." Rainie sat down on a nearby bench. She watched him still. "I will tell you what I say each time I dump out a beer."

"What?" He was honestly breathless.

"I toast my mother." Her fingers trailed down to her ankle.

"You tell her off? You send her a giant, postmortem fuck you? Oh, I like that. I do the same thing once a year."

"No." Her hand closed around the small handle of her gun. "I don't tell her, Fuck you. She tried to stop him, you asshole. She was slow to believe, but she finally told him a few choice words. And then he blew off her head. So no, I don't tell her, Fuck you. I tell her I'm sorry. I tell her I should've killed him sooner. And then I tell him I hope it's hot enough down there in hell."

She whipped out her .22. "Bye-bye, Richard."

"Too late, Rainie. Danny's right behind you."

Rainie heard a board creak. She turned reflexively, saw Danny's shocked, pale face. Too late she realized her mistake. She tried to turn back around. She squeezed off one wild, desperate shot.

Then Richard savagely slammed her mother's shotgun into the side of her head.

RICHARD STEPPED FORWARD QUICKLY. He leveled the unfirable shotgun at Danny and said, "Gimme the gun."

Danny looked at Rainie's crumpled form. The boy handed over his firearm.

Richard smiled. Like candy from a baby. He tucked the gun in the back waistband of his jeans and left Rainie's shotgun on the deck. "Your daddy sprung you, didn't he?"

The boy didn't say a word. He simply gazed hungrily at Richard's gun. Richard wasn't worried, however. Danny was too browbeaten by his father to ever do something bold. That had been half the fun.

Now Richard bent over and, with some difficulty, hefted Rainie onto his shoulder.

"You squealed on me, didn't you, Danny? Didn't I tell you that smart boys don't squeal? Smart boys stay quiet, if they want to keep their families safe."

Danny remained wordless.

"Well, there's only one thing to do now," Richard said with a sigh. "We're going to have to kill your sister. Rules, Danny. Just ask my old man. You gotta live by the rules."

QUINCY'S FLIGHT DIDN'T touch down in Portland until nine P.M. Luke met him at the gate and started briefing him as they both half-walked, half-jogged to his illegally parked car.

"Her neighbor reported hearing a gunshot a little after eight P.M.," Luke was saying. "Frankly, we didn't get that call until nearly nine P.M."

"Why so late?"

"Because we had our hands full with another shooting, and dispatch got confused. Daniel Avalon had disappeared as of yesterday afternoon. Today he surfaced in Bakersville, trying to blow off Steven VanderZanden's head."

"Casualties?"

"Not yet. VanderZanden ended up bruised and battered, but fortunately Avalon's a lousy shot. On the other hand, VanderZanden's wife figured out what it was about from all the cursing and swearing. I don't know yet how VanderZanden will fare with her."

"Hell hath no fury like a woman scorned," Quincy murmured. Someone came barreling toward them with a cart filled with luggage. They both swerved wildly and kept running. "When did officers arrive at Rainie's house?"

"Fifteen minutes ago. So far there's no sign of Rainie, but there are blood splatters on the deck. Sanders thinks he got her."

"Any phone calls, any gloating? He loves games. This whole thing has been one giant adventure for him."

"Yeah, well, we're trying to cut off his amusement ride. In the good-news department, Sanders opened up the personnel file for Richard Mann around six-thirty. First thing he saw was a black-and-white photo of the real Richard Mann, which certainly didn't match our favorite counselor. He'd already called for a couple of uniforms to descend upon Mann's house when the shooting started at the VanderZanden residence."

They arrived at Luke's patrol car. Quincy threw his bags on the floor and climbed in. Luke flipped on the sirens. Off they went.

"What did they find at Mann's house?" Quincy asked, gripping the dashboard as Luke took a corner hard.

"We found one computer. A cop hit the space bar. The monitor came up with a screen that said: *Love you too, Baby.* Then the whole thing blew up. Luckily, it was a small charge and no one was hurt."

"Fuck!" Quincy slapped the dashboard. "We've spent this whole dance two steps behind."

"Yeah, and now the dance floor is getting crowded. In other news, Danny disappeared at five-thirty this evening. Two Cabot County cops were transporting Danny to a mental facility when they ran off the road. Supposedly when they regained consciousness, he'd already stolen the keys to his shackles and disappeared into the mist."

Quincy looked at Luke. He said, "Shep."

Luke said nothing, which coming from him was a yes.

"Is he in custody?"

"They're still questioning him. But there's no sign of Danny, and I know Shep. He'd do anything for his son, probably even this. But something's gone wrong. He looks like a giant bowl of jelly. If I didn't know any better, I'd say he's scared out of his mind."

"You think Danny ran off on his own?"

"I don't know."

"You think he went to Rainie's house?"

"We're dusting for prints. Ask me when the reports come back."

"How well does Danny know the area?"

"He's hunted here all his life. He'd do all right."

"Get your hands on Shep. Have him meet us at Rainie's place."

Luke didn't bat an eye. "Okay."

"Ask Sanders to send two state troopers to the O'Grady house. I want Sandy and Becky under full police protection. According to the preliminary information, Richard Mann—or whoever he is—has done this three times. On each occasion it's been a mass shooting. And on each occasion there have been no witnesses. I don't think he's going to start now."

Luke paled but nodded soberly.

"Luke, do you have a vest?"

"Yes."

"Put it on. Make sure everyone puts theirs on."

"You don't think he's left town."

"I know he hasn't left town. It's the nature of the beast. Each time, he has to raise the stakes in order to get the same thrill. And, heaven help us, he's tired of being bored."

THIRTY·FOUR

Saturday, May 19, 10:05 P.M.

ABE SANDERS RAN UP to meet Quincy the minute he arrived at Rainie's house. The CSU was tearing up floorboards, dissecting the deck in search of trace evidence. Giant floodlights illuminated the grounds, while men in navy blue windbreakers swept the premises inch by inch with bobbing flashlights. Quincy had seen this scene hundreds of times by now, and it still struck him as surreal.

He'd never even been to Rainie's home. There should be nothing here to connect to her in his mind. But when he saw the back deck framed by soaring trees, he could picture her at once, and pain socked him in the gut. Her vulnerable eyes, her stubborn chin. So much unfinished business.

He had to reach out a hand to steady himself. Then he got on with the matters at hand.

"What have they found?" he asked Sanders.

"It's under the deck."

Quincy followed Sanders around. Shep was back there as well, hunched with his chin tucked in the top of his coat against the night's chill. Luke was right. Shep looked on the verge of being ill. If he'd been behind the jailbreak, things had not gone as planned.

Then Quincy noticed that men were furiously

working the dirt beneath the deck like a promising archaeological site. They dusted, fluoresced, and categorized. They carted away piles of dirt.

"It looks like a fresh grave," Sanders was saying. "Right under the deck. But all we've found so far are some old threads and gravel. They're still working on it."

Quincy looked at Shep. The sheriff had thinned his lips. Quincy understood. They were looking at the final resting place of the man who had killed Rainie's mother. And Quincy also understood who had put him there.

"Anything else?" Quincy asked.

"We found an old shotgun," Sanders said. "Shep already identified it as the gun that was used to kill Molly Conner fourteen years ago. In theory, it's an open case, so all evidence has been held in the state police's storage locker in Portland. Then two days ago a young man claiming to be from the Bakersville sheriff's department checked out the evidence. He gave Rainie's badge number, which the doofus officer in charge never followed up on. And gee, Bakersville's newest police officer just happens to match Richard Mann's description."

"He gave this some thought."

"No kidding. We got a ton of fingerprints from his house, but it's going to take a while to work through the system. We've been calling him Mann, though apparently the real Mann is teaching in some remote village in Alaska and has no idea someone stole his identity. When he gets back to civilization, he's in for a little surprise."

"Mann's still around here," Quincy said.

"He'd be an idiot to remain in the area. We got guys everywhere."

"He's an adrenaline junkie. He's taken it this far. He'll see it all the way through."

"What do you think he's doing?"

"I'm not sure anymore. In the beginning, I think he

was planning on business as usual. He identified a kid who was troubled. He found an identity he could use as a ruse. It's not rushed. He's executed three complicated crimes in the space of ten years. He takes his time. He's cautious. Think of what we talked about earlier: He operates with a double contingency plan. So even if you penetrate the first wall, you simply encounter the next layer of defense.

"My guess is that he was too good. Two spectacular crimes and no one came close to figuring them out. Where's the thrill in that? Where's the rush? So this time he started to take more chances. He lingered after the shooting. He gave us more hints, but I just didn't see them. His whole little diatribe on what makes a good father. He was referring to his own issues with his father, of course. Then that little speech at the funeral on how he'd decided Danny couldn't be the shooter. Danny was too smart, too sophisticated to use blatant force. He wasn't talking about Danny. He was talking about himself.

"And then we get to Rainie. He brought her the shotgun, the gun most of the town believes she personally used to kill her own mother. That must have captivated him. Here's a woman who is rumored to have done exactly what he fantasized about every day of his childhood. She probably seemed glorious to him."

"You think he wanted her to run away with him? Become his partner?" Sanders asked incredulously.

Quincy shook his head. "No. I think he made the same mistake everyone else in this town has made. She didn't shoot her mother. And that deeply, deeply disappointed him."

Sanders could fill in the rest. "And if he's disappointed . . ."

"If we don't find them soon," Quincy said quietly, "I doubt she'll live through the night."

A voice suddenly came from deep in the woods. "Over here, over here," a technician cried. "I got something!"

They ran. There on the ground, a tiny piece of white cotton, as if torn from a T-shirt.

"They went into the woods," Sanders said triumphantly. "Quick, somebody get some dogs."

"Adjoining roads," Quincy said immediately. "Logging roads, rural routes, dirt roads, anything. Get your men on them, because he didn't come all this way on foot."

Abe excitedly began making the calls, and then they were plunging into the underbrush, desperate to find a trail, desperate to find Rainie.

"SHIT!" RICHARD MANN SAID for the fifth time in about as many minutes. He staggered to a halt, wiping the heavy sweat from his brow and giving Rainie a look that was rapidly growing ragged.

She pretended to ignore his hatred while lowering herself gingerly to the ground, not the easiest thing to do with her hands tied behind her back. Her head hurt. She had regained consciousness quickly, but that hadn't done her any favors. When Richard had smacked her with the shotgun, he'd done a good job of it. Her jaw throbbed; she suspected it was broken. Her eye had swelled shut; she thought the socket might be fractured. She was starting to see double with what vision she had left, and the pain was becoming less constant but more acute. Hemorrhage, maybe? Blood clot? The possibilities were endless.

At least she was having the last laugh. Her wild shot had caught Richard Mann in his right buttock as he'd swiveled around to swing the shotgun. He'd dismissed it as a mere flesh wound, but after hiking up the steep mountain for a bit, he'd taken to favoring his right leg. His walking was no longer steady; his face had become flushed. They were taking more and more breaks and stopping for longer periods of time. It was hard to tell in the dark, but she suspected he was bleeding heavily.

He'd stuffed his windbreaker down his pants to bandage the wound, but he must have begun to doubt that system, for he kept pausing now to check the ground for signs of blood.

Mess with me, get shot in the ass, Rainie thought. She smiled at her own dark humor, then promptly winced in pain.

Danny was still with them, now sitting quietly beside Rainie. He had yet to say a word. He simply walked, his head ducked low and his hands stuck in the pants pockets of his blue surgical scrubs. The night was cold. He kept fidgeting with his white cotton undershirt as if trying to get warm. Rainie wished there was more she could do for him.

Hell, at this point, with the trees swaying sickeningly in front of her eyes, she wished there was more she could do for herself.

How had Danny gotten out of the detention center? And why had he come to her back porch? Had he suspected Richard Mann might show up there? Had he wanted to help her?

Or was he still Richard's accomplice? She thought of what Quincy had said yesterday. Once the dominant partner got the other to kill, it became too difficult for the weaker one to walk away. And Danny had killed. He had told her about it today in a thin, high voice that sounded as fragile as a reed.

She didn't know anymore. She was trying to hold the thoughts together in her mind, sort through them, come up with a plan. Her face was on fire, and the pain was becoming more intense.

Mann staggered back to his feet. His flashlight swung wildly. It illuminated two dark spots on the dusty trail and made him curse. The man was bleeding quite nicely. He kicked up dirt over the blood, grabbed a tree limb to rake over their trail, and gave Rainie a look that was downright feral.

"Up," he snarled.

"I think I'm going to vomit," Rainie murmured.

"*Up!*"

"Okay," she said. She leaned forward and threw up on his shoes.

"Fuck me!" Mann leapt back two feet, kicking furiously at bushes and needles in a vain attempt to get the puke off his shoes. His arms flailed. His face had gone purple. Rainie didn't hesitate. Maybe it wasn't a pretty plan, but it was as good as it was going to get.

"Run," she yelled at Danny. "*Run!*"

And then she hurled herself at Mann.

They went down in a tangle of bodies, the gun flying from his grasp. She heard Mann thrashing and swearing. It seemed his legs and feet were everywhere, and she instinctively tried to protect her head. Her eye, her eye. Oh God, her cheek was exploding on her. But she couldn't bring her hands up. They were tied behind her back, leaving her churning on the ground like a helpless worm.

Richard went after her with a vicious kick. She barely rolled out of the way; then he abruptly backed off.

Shit. He was going for the gun. She rolled back and kicked him as hard she could in the back of his knee. His legs folded beneath him. She went after his shot-up hip with her pummeling feet.

She couldn't see any sign of Danny. Please let him have run. If she could buy time, give him a chance to get farther away . . .

Richard was trying to get to his feet again. She saw his gaze go to the handgun he must have snatched from Danny, which was now lying just four feet away in the dust. He gritted his teeth and lunged. She rolled to the right as quickly as she could and managed to kick him in the side of the head.

"Damn bitch," he swore. Then he suddenly got a curious smile on his face.

He reached out and curled his hand around a big helping of pine needles and dirt. Rainie ducked her head. She closed her eyes to protect herself, but she had no hands to hide her bloody face as he flung the dust and needles at her head.

She spluttered, blinked reflexively, and buried eight tiny needles in her one good eye.

"Goddammit!"

It hurt. Hurt worse than she'd imagined pain feeling. Hurt even worse than all those years ago, when she'd been so small and helpless. Fuck that. She would not be small. She would not be helpless.

She went after Richard Mann with her pummeling legs and realized for the first time that he was laughing. He was standing now, not even going after the gun. He just stood there, watching her writhe on the ground and finding it funny.

"Going someplace, Lorraine?"

"Bastard!"

He laughed again.

She rolled toward Richard Mann with a kamikaze yell, and he calmly kicked her in the damaged side of her face.

Lights exploded. She saw blazing, fantastical colors, followed by a white-hot blur. And then the corresponding agony ripped a scream from her lips.

"Had enough yet, Lorraine? Want to taste a little more?"

She started rolling again. She couldn't see. Just felt him coming after her and knew what kind of pain he'd like to inflict next. She wanted to be fierce and brave, but the pain was too much and now she fled in the dirt. Rolling, rolling, rolling, seeking some desperate way out.

Her kneecap smacked into a tree trunk. She howled. Mann laughed. Footsteps coming closer. Faster, faster. She switched directions suddenly, working on memory only, and ripped her way across the earth. The gun, the gun, the gun. Somewhere around her, the gun.

"No!" Richard Mann yelled suddenly.

And then she knew she had him. She rolled on top of the 9-millimeter and grabbed it with her bloodied fingertips.

"What are you going to do, Lorraine?" Mann taunted breathlessly. "Shoot it with your kneecaps?"

She said hoarsely with her back to him, "Halt. Police."

"Hand it over, Lorraine. Be a good girl, and I promise I'll kill you quickly."

Footsteps coming closer.

Her wet, slippery fingers frantically trying to orient the heavy pistol, find the trigger.

The sound of Mann's ragged breath, bearing down on her. She couldn't see him, had little hope of aiming. Just try to find the trigger. Pull it back. Do something, even if she only ended up winging his big toe. The gun slipped again. She was doomed.

Mann bending over her. Mann rearing back his leg to kick her in the face—

"Halt! Police!"

Flashlights suddenly flooded the area. Rainie tried to focus her dirt-filled eyes. The lights were too bright, the voices too far away. Her fingers reclaimed the gun as she turned her head and saw Richard Mann gazing toward the lights. He was breathing hard. So was she. His face was ugly and mottled with rage. And hers?

"Fuck them," Richard Mann snarled. He reared back to wallop her in the head—

And Rainie pulled the trigger.

Richard Mann dropped to the earth, just as three other officers opened fire. Rainie rolled over. She lay three feet from Mann's body and watched the hate slowly dim and die out in his eyes.

A moment later, Quincy came forward. Rainie knew him by his smell as he bent down and cradled her against his chest.

"I came as fast as I could," he murmured. "I told you that I would."

She could see the others now. Abe Sanders. Luke Hayes. Shep O'Grady. And Danny, standing with his father's arm around his thin shoulders and tears on his cheeks.

"How did you find us?" she asked.

"Danny left us a trail with pieces of his T-shirt. He's been ripping them off and dropping them down his pants leg."

Danny said simply, "I'm smart."

Rainie turned her face into Quincy's embrace then. His arms were warm. His heartbeat strong. He felt so nice.

I'm finally being held, she thought.

And then she started to cry. She wept for Danny, who had caused so much death, and she wept for herself and what she knew she must do next.

EPILOGUE

Two weeks later

THE SUN WAS OUT when Rainie descended the stairs of Cabot County's courthouse. She wore jeans and a simple white T-shirt, tucked in and belted at the waist. The days were already warm with the promise of summer, and after four hours in the office, she enjoyed the feel of spring on her still-healing face. In the good news department, the swelling in her jaw and eye socket had finally gone down. In the bad news department, her face was now approximately eighteen different shades of yellow and green. At least Richard Mann had not inflicted as much damage as she'd originally thought. Her doctor assured her that she'd be fine within another few weeks—after he muttered that this proved once and for all that she was thick-skulled. Wiseass.

The Bakersville task force had been busy in the days since Richard Mann's shooting. Abe Sanders had gotten his wish—formal jurisdiction over the case. He'd also gotten more federal agents breathing down his throat than any one man could handle.

The fingerprint results had been stunning. Richard Mann was really Henry Hawkins of Minneapolis, Minnesota. Born to a domineering army lieutenant and his meek librarian wife, Hawkins had moved a dozen times in his childhood. He'd grown up hard, according to his journal, steeped in guns and his father's quick fists. He'd mastered a chameleon personality as he'd shuffled from town to town, school to school. And he'd honed his rage. At his father's harsh ways. At the other children who always saw him as an outsider. At his mother, who never stood up for herself or him.

At the age of twenty, Hawkins's parents died unexpectedly in a car crash, robbing him of any chance for retaliation or forgiveness. And his homicidal rampage began.

At this point, the FBI had linked him to two other school shootings. They were revisiting those cases now, interviewing the boys who'd craved notoriety so badly they'd gone to prison rather than admit someone else had been involved. The feebies were also looking into a handful of other shootings, where children had lashed out unexpectedly while Hawkins was living in their town. No doubt some cases were coincidences. They weren't sure, however, that would be true for them all.

Hawkins still owned his parents' house in Minnesota. He had armed it with a number of pipe bombs and booby traps to make the investigators' lives more interesting. It slowed down efforts but did not stop them. Sanders was leading that raid, and Hawkins had met his match in the state detective's meticulous nature.

It would probably be months, maybe even a year, before the last of the evidence was processed. Not that it would matter to Henry Hawkins. With no one to claim his body, he had been laid to rest in potters' field.

Danny's case was also being revisited. Shep and Sandy were now working with Charles Rodriguez on a plea arrangement. There was still a long road ahead for Danny. He had killed two little girls, and even understanding that he had been influenced by a savvy outsider didn't change that fact. There should be barriers in all of us, the DA had argued this morning, lines we should know better than to cross. And one of those barriers should be resistance to taking human life. Danny hadn't possessed that barrier, and that had to be addressed.

In the end, it appeared that Danny would enter an admission to the charge of aggravated murder in return for a guarantee of remaining under juvenile court's jurisdiction. There he would receive a disposition of serving at a youth correctional facility for a period not to exceed his twenty-fifth birthday. The Oregon Youth Authority would formally assume custody over him, conducting a new mental-health assessment and providing resources for his treatment. It would be up to the OYA to determine when he was ready for parole.

Sandy and Shep put their house up for sale. Chances were that Danny would end up at the Hillcrest facility in Salem, so they were looking to relocate there. Shep was interviewing with various security companies. Though most suspected that he'd engineered the "car crash" that allowed Danny to escape, there was no proof of wrongdoing, so his record remained clear. Sandy wanted to focus on her children and become more active in reforming juvenile law. Technically, they remained married, though the last time Rainie had seen them, she'd witnessed few moments of intimacy. She had a feeling they'd reached a point of living together but separately. Maybe they thought it was better that way, for Becky.

Rainie reached the bottom of the courthouse steps. She was trying to decide whether to head immediately to her car or spend the rest of the sunny afternoon walking around town, when she heard a voice behind her.

"Hello, Rainie."

Rainie turned and spotted him immediately. She smiled before she thought to stop herself, and then it was too late to take it back.

Quincy leaned against the stone wall, wearing one of his expensively cut suits and a conservative blue tie.

It had been two weeks since she'd last seen him. Following the scene on the mountainside, he'd flown immediately to the sites of the other Hawkins school shootings to handle the reopening of those cases. She imagined he'd been flying all over the country since, interviewing youths and juggling more crime-scene photos.

Now he was in front of her, and she no sooner looked at him than she realized she'd missed him. He was smiling at her. Maybe he'd missed her too.

"Hey," she said.

"Shep told me you'd be here."

"I didn't know he spoke to federal agents."

"Neither did he."

Quincy motioned to the empty spot beside him. She made a big show of wandering over, trying not to move too fast. He smelled good. Someday she'd have to ask him about his cologne, because, damn, she liked that scent.

"How are things going?" she asked.

"That was going to be my question."

"Things are looking up for Danny," she offered. "A lot of people have come out to support him. Not that they condone his actions, but Henry Hawkins/Richard Mann/Dave Duncan fooled the entire town, including the school district. After that, it's easier to understand his impact on one troubled child."

"And Becky?"

"Better. The minute Sandy told her Richard Mann was dead, the weight lifted off her shoulders. Apparently in the confusion of the shooting, she ran to find her brother. Unfortunately, she spotted him and Richard together in the computer lab, not far from Miss Avalon's body. Richard told her if she talked, he'd kill Danny. And if Danny talked, Richard would kill Becky. He was right, you know. Simple strategies can be highly effective."

"Well, now he and the devil can debate the matter to

their hearts' content." Quincy's smile lifted the corner of his mouth. The familiar expression tugged at her. She wished she didn't feel so awkward. She wished she could touch him.

"Rainie?" he asked quietly. "How are you?"

She shrugged. There was no point in lying anymore. This was the new and improved Lorraine Conner. Telling the truth until it hurt. "I've been better."

"Is the DA going to press charges?"

"Don't know." She jerked her head toward the courthouse. "My attorney and I just had a meeting to hear our options. Funky thing, Oregon law. I thought since I shot Lucas when I was seventeen, it would fall under juvenile jurisdiction. Nope. In Oregon, it's the age I am when it comes to the attention of the court that matters, not the age when I committed the crime. That means Man One, up to five years' jail time. The DA said that 'given the nature of the extenuating circumstances,' he might be willing to deal down to less than a year, served locally. All I have to do is plead guilty to a felony murder charge. I wasn't—I wasn't expecting that."

Rainie didn't have to say anything more. Quincy understood. A felony charge would bar her from law enforcement for the rest of her life. She wouldn't be able to get a job working security. She wouldn't even have the right to carry a gun.

"Can't you fight it?" Quincy asked after a moment. "Plead not guilty due to diminished mental capacity. Or argue you acted in a dissociative state, brought on by the trauma of your mother's murder."

"You sound like my lawyer. She doesn't think the state has a leg to stand on. Frightened seventeen-year-old girl. Rampaging suspected murderer with more tattoos than morals. She considers this case a slam dunk."

"So you're pleading not guilty," Quincy said.

Rainie merely smiled. She peered up at the blue sky, turning over facts that were still new and troubling to her. "I think I want to plead guilty and give full allocution," she said quietly.

"Why? You have a need to eat jail food?"

"I think I just need to tell, Quincy. I need to get it out in the open. What I did fourteen years ago was horrible. And you were right: no matter how long it has been, it will never be long enough."

"He raped you, Rainie."

"Yes."

"Did you try to go to your mother?"

"Yes."

"But she didn't believe you."

"No. And then I went to Shep."

For the first time, Quincy was surprised. "He knew?"

"I wanted to press charges, but Shep didn't believe me. He was just starting out, and I was a seventeen-year-old girl from the wrong side of town. No one gets out of life without a few regrets."

"So you went back to your mother," Quincy deduced.

"No. I just went home. I didn't know what else to do. But I guess she just needed time to think about it. I'm not sure. Later that night Lucas came over. Drunk—what else was new? They had a huge fight and she threw him out, yelling at him to keep his stinking hands off her daughter. I think that's the first time I felt proud of my mother. The first time I had hope that things might be better.

"Then I came home the next day, and Lucas had shot off her head."

"And Shep was remorseful?"

"Not when he arrested me. But Bakersville didn't have any female officers, so he had to take me to Cabot County for processing. There a woman made me strip so she could bag my bloody clothes as evidence. And I . . . And I was pretty damaged from what had happened. When she left the room, I heard her tell Shep that either my boyfriend really liked it rough or I'd spent a long night with the Hell's Angels. Poor Shep. It couldn't have been fun to realize what a mistake he'd made."

"Did he give you the shotgun, Rainie?"

"No. At that point, I think he simply saw the error of his ways. Between my condition and the neighbor's report on the time of the gunshot, they put out an APB on Lucas. They figured he'd flee the scene, but I wasn't convinced. He didn't have a lot of money, he specialized in being a mean son of a bitch. I think . . . I think I just knew he'd come back. That had been the point. My mother was dead. Now he could do as he pleased.

"I didn't have any more weapons. I wasn't old enough to legally buy a gun. The shotgun was the only thing I knew about. So I went downtown. I waited until six o'clock when the sheriff locked up the office for the night. I knew the volunteer officers were out on patrol. If any other business came up, the department's answering machine told you how to reach the sheriff at home, so everything was deserted and safe. I broke into the sheriff's office."

"There wasn't an alarm?"

Rainie raised a brow. "In Bakersville? Who's dumb enough to break into a sheriff's office, anyway? Even now, one of us forgets to lock up half the time. It's not like we have a decent coffee maker to protect."

"You have evidence, though."

"In a separate evidence locker in the back. These days we use a safe. Very solid, hard to penetrate. Fourteen years ago, however, it was a basic lockbox. I picked it open with a hairpin. And I took my shotgun home."

Quincy sighed, rubbed the bridge of his nose. He obviously knew where things were going from here. "Lucas showed up," he said.

"He walked right up to the sliding glass door before seeing me. And then . . . he smiled, like this was going to be even more fun than he'd thought. He slid open the door. I shot him at point-blank range in the chest. Wouldn't you know it? He died with that same goddamn grin on his face."

"Why didn't you call the cops, Rainie? You could've claimed self-defense."

"I was a kid. I didn't know the legal system. I just knew my heart, and in my heart it wasn't self-defense. He had hurt me. He had taken away my mother. And I wanted him dead. I wanted him wiped from the face of the earth. And I'd taken my mother's shotgun home, just for that."

"You buried him under the deck."

"Took me all night."

"And then you ran away," Quincy concluded.

She nodded. "I took off for Portland and spent the next four years trying to drown every image in my head."

"What about his car, Rainie? What about any neighbors reporting the sound of a gunshot—"

"My neighbor had left for a fishing trip. There was no one around."

"Fine, what about the fact that one minute Lucas was in Bakersville and the next he disappeared? What about the fact that your mother's shotgun just happened to disappear from the evidence locker one night, only to magically reappear sometime later? This doesn't sound like rocket science to me. Shep should've been searching your place by the end of the week, tops. You didn't even hide the body well."

Rainie didn't say anything.

After a moment Quincy sighed. "He let it go, didn't he? No harm, no foul. Remind me never to let Shep feel as if he owes me a favor."

"It's a small town, Quincy. And small-town policing . . . The rules are sometimes different. What goes around comes around. It's not always just, but it can be right. For the record, to this day Shep and I have never spoken of it."

"Of course not. That would make it conspiracy."

"I was prepared to pay for what I'd done," Rainie countered immediately. "In many ways, that might have been better. I could've gotten it out in the open. I could've faced it, put it in perspective, paid my dues. Instead . . ." She faltered for the first time. "Lucas had a wife and a kid. I took him from them. For fourteen years, they haven't even known what happened to him. I should've known that. Even if I hated him, I shouldn't have forgotten that he was human. Rodriguez is right: there are certain barriers we shouldn't cross, and one of them is the willingness to take a life."

"He would've gone after you that night," Quincy said gently.

"But that's the point, Quincy. I'll never know. I killed him first, and that makes me no better."

"Rainie—"

She held up a hand. "No platitudes. I did my deed. Now I'm going to get to pay for that. Responsibility and accountability. They're not such bad things. You know why I dug him up that night?"

"Why?"

"Because I was afraid Richard Mann would take him away from me. When we first got the call about a man bragging that he had proof I'd killed my mother . . . I don't know. I just flashed to Lucas, under my deck, and this strange dream I'd had the night before of a man standing there, the man in black. Suddenly, I was terrified. That it had been the killer on my back deck. That he had discovered the body and when I walked into Dave Duncan's hotel room, that would be the first thing I'd see—Lucas's corpse waiting to greet me. But then I walked in, and the room was empty, and . . . I realized I wasn't relieved. In fact, I was even more anxious. What if he still knew, what if he'd taken the body, and then . . . then I'd have no proof of what I'd done, and I needed that proof. I needed to confess what happened. Danny had made that clear to me."

"So what happens now, Rainie?"

She had to take a moment. In spite of her best intentions, the answer to that question made her throat close up. She worked on clearing it. She still sounded husky as she said, "The mayor asked me to resign last week."

Quincy looked immediately pained.

"You know," she said more briskly, "there's just something about a cop with a corpse under her deck that people don't like. And here I'd finally managed to impress a tight-ass like Sanders. But Luke's in charge now. He'll do a good job."

"You could move, start over someplace else."

"Not if I plead guilty. Things like that are hard to explain away during a job interview. 'What do you feel is your biggest weakness?' 'Uhh, last time I was pissed off and under stress, I shot a man.'" She shook her head in disgust.

"Is that why you want to plead guilty?" Quincy asked levelly. "To punish yourself further?"

"I *killed* someone!"

"Who raped you and shot your mother, all within forty-eight hours. Post-traumatic stress syndrome. Dissociative state. These aren't magical terms psychologists have come up with to confuse juries, Rainie. They are genuine syndromes, well documented and well known, as your lawyer can tell you. You were seventeen years old. You were frightened. And Lucas came back to get you. Your lawyer is right—there isn't a jury in this world that will find you guilty. Now how can twelve strangers have more faith in you, Rainie, than you do?"

Rainie couldn't answer. Her throat had closed up again. She looked down and resolutely studied the cracks on the sidewalk.

"If you really want to move on with your life, Rainie," Quincy said gently, "move on. Forgive yourself. Go to trial and give the jury a chance to forgive you as well. You're a good person. You're a great police officer. Ask anyone in Bakersville. Ask Sanders. Ask Luke. Ask me. I'm an arrogant federal agent, and I would be honored to work with you again."

"Oh shut up, Quincy. Now you're making me cry." He was. She dabbed at the corners of her eyes and sniffled roughly. Damn fed.

"What are you going to do?"

"You might have a point."

"Of course I have a point. I'm the expert."

"I still have so much to learn."

"Rainie—"

"No, don't say it."

"How do you know what I'm going to say?" He tried to reach for her. She stepped out of his grasp, already shaking her head.

"Because I do! Because for a man who's been to so many crime scenes, you still have a romantic view of life. But it'll never work, so just don't say it." She made a firm no-crossing signal with her hands.

"I want to take you out to dinner," he said calmly.

"You are such an ass!"

"I'm promising lo mein, with green tea. I'm hoping this time we'll both eat."

"For chrissakes, you're not staying, Quincy. You're an agent. You love your job. You're good at your job. I'm just a stop along the way."

"I could stop a lot. It's the advantage of being a big shot."

"Why? To watch me cash my unemployment checks?"

"Rainie—"

"It's true and we both know it! You're . . . you, Quincy. You know who you are and where you're going and that's great. But I'm me. And me is a mess. I liked being a cop. God, I liked being a cop. I don't . . . I don't know what comes next. I have to figure it out. And I guess I have to go through a trial. And I can't do that with you watching. I liked being your coworker. I won't be your charity case."

"Rainie." He sounded exasperated. Then he simply sounded sincere. "I *missed* you these last two weeks. I drove myself crazy thinking about you. People said only civil things to me, and I honestly resented it. I wanted you instead."

Rainie shook her head again. He was not making this easy for her. She felt longing. In all honesty, she felt pain. The scent of his cologne haunted her. It made her want to lean into his hard frame. He would hold her. He had done so that night, and it was one of the few precious memories she had.

But she still knew better. He had a hero complex, and she was too proud to be a damsel in distress.

Another minute passed. Quincy's shoulders finally slumped. He shook his head, and it was his turn to stare at the ground. Rainie stuffed her hands in the back pockets of her jeans.

"I gotta go," she said after a moment, looking at everything but him.

He didn't say anything, and she figured that was that. She started walking back down the cheery street, and the sun was so bright in her eyes, it brought on tears.

She turned at the last minute. She shouldn't do it. She did it anyway.

"Quincy."

He quickly, hopefully looked up.

"Maybe . . . maybe someday, when things are going a little better. Maybe I could come visit."

And he said honestly, "I can hardly wait."

ABOUT THE AUTHOR

LISA GARDNER is the author of *The Third Victim, The Next Accident,* and *The Survivors Club,* all *New York Times* bestsellers, as well as *The Perfect Husband* and *The Killing Hour.* She lives with her husband and daughter in the New England area, where she is at work on her next novel of suspense, *Alone.*

Visit her website at www.lisagardner.com.

Dear Reader,

I hope you loved THE THIRD VICTIM, and now I'd like
to share with you a sneak peek at my next novel, ALONE.
I'm very excited to be working on such a dark,
twisted tale, this one featuring a homicidal cop, a
manipulative widow, a vengeful father, and a happy-go-
lucky psychopath. I like to think that it's psychological
suspense at its finest, where the person you love the most
should be the person you trust the least. . . .

Lisa Gardner

A L O N E

by

Lisa Gardner

**Read on for a thrilling preview of Lisa Gardner's
latest novel of suspense, ALONE,
coming in hardcover from
Bantam Books in January 2005!**

ALONE

LISA GARDNER

ALONE

ON SALE JANUARY 2005

CHAPTER ONE

HE'D PUT IN a fifteen-hour shift the night the call came in. Too many impatient drivers on 93, leading to too much crash, bang, boom. City was like that this time of year. The trees were bare, night coming on quick and the holidays looming. It felt raw outside. After the easy camaraderie of summer barbecues, now you walked alone through city streets hearing nothing but the skeletal rattle of dry leaves skittering across cold pavement.

Lots of cops complained about the short, gray days of February, but personally, Bobby Dodge had never cared for November. Today did nothing to change his mind.

His shift started with a minor fender bender, followed by two more rear-enders from northbound gawkers. Four hours of paperwork later, he thought he'd gotten through the worst of it. Then, in early afternoon, when traffic should've been a breeze even on the notoriously jam-packed 93, came a five-car pileup as a speeding taxi driver tried to change four lanes at once, and a stressed-out ad exec in a Hummer forcefully cut him off. The Hummer took the hit like a heavyweight champ; the rusted-out cab went down for the count and took out three other cars with it. Bobby got to call four wreckers, then diagram the accident, and then arrest the ad exec when it became apparent the man had mixed in a few martinis with his power lunch.

Pinching a man for driving under the influence meant more paperwork, a trip to the South Boston barracks (now in the middle of rush hour traffic, when no one respected anyone's right-of-way, let alone a trooper's), and another altercation with the rich ad exec when he balked at entering the holding cell.

The ad exec had a good fifty pounds on Bobby. Like a lot of guys confronted by a smaller opponent, he confused superior weight with superior strength and ignored the warning signs telling him otherwise. The man grabbed the doorjamb with his right hand. He swung his lumbering body backward, expecting to bowl over his smaller escort and what? Make a run for it through a police barracks filled with armed troopers? Bobby ducked left, stuck out his foot, and watched the overweight executive slam to the floor. The man landed with an impressive crash and a few troopers paused long enough to clap their hands at the free show.

"I'm going to fucking sue!" the drunken ad exec screamed. "I'm going to sue you, your commanding officer, and the whole fucking state of Massachusetts. I'll own this joint. You hear me? *I'll fucking own your ass!*"

Bobby jerked the big guy to his feet. Rich exec screamed a fresh round of obscenities, possibly because of the way Bobby was pinching the man's thumb. Bobby shoved the man into the holding cell and slammed the door.

"If you're gonna puke, please use the toilet," Bobby informed him, because by now the man had turned a little green. The rich executive flipped him off. Then he doubled-over and vomited on the floor.

Bobby shook his head. "Rich prick," he muttered.

Some days were like that, particularly in November.

Now it was shortly after ten p.m. The rich ad exec had been bailed out by his overpriced lawyer, the holding cell was washed down, and Bobby's shift, which had started at seven a.m., was finally done. He should go home. Give Susan a buzz. Catch some sleep before his alarm went off at five, and the whole joyous process started once more.

Instead he was jittery in a way that surprised himself. Too much adrenaline buzzing in his veins, when he was a man best known for being cool, calm, and collected.

Bobby didn't go home. Instead he traded in his blues for jeans and a flannel shirt, then headed for the local bar.

At the Boston Beer Garden, fourteen other guys were sitting around the U-shaped bar, smoking cigarettes and nursing draft beer while zoning out in front of flat-screen TVs. Bobby nodded to a few familiar faces, waved his hand at the sixty-year-old bartender, Carl, then took an empty seat a bit down from the rest. Sally brought him his usual order of nachos. Carl hand-delivered his Coke.

"Long day, Bobby?"

"Same old, same old."

"Susan coming in?"

"Practice night."

"Aye, the concert. Two weeks, right?" Carl shook his head. "Beautiful and talented. I'll tell you again, Bobby—she's a keeper."

"Don't let Martha hear you," Bobby told him. "After watching your wife haul a keg, I don't want to think of what she could do with a rolling pin."

"My Martha's also a keeper," Carl assured him. "Mostly 'cause I fear for my life."

Carl left Bobby alone with his Coke and nachos. Overhead, a live news bulletin was reporting on some kind of situation in Revere. A heavily-armed suspect had barricaded himself in his home after taking potshots at his neighbors. Now, Boston PD had deployed their SWAT team, and "nobody was taking any chances."

Yeah, November was a funny kind of month. Wired people up, left them with no defenses against the oncoming gloom of winter. Left even guys like Bobby doing all they could do just to hold the course.

He finished his nachos. He drank his Coke. He settled his bill, and just as he had convinced himself it really was a good idea to go home, the beeper suddenly activated on his belt. He read the screen in one instant and was bolting out the door the next.

It had been that kind of day. Now it would be that kind of night.

Catherine Rose Gagnon didn't like November much either, though for her, the real problem had started in October. October 22, 1980, to be exact. The air had been warm, the sun a hot kiss on her face as she walked home from elementary school. She'd been carrying her books in her arm and wearing her favorite back-to-school outfit: knee-high brown socks, a dark brown corduroy skirt, and a long-sleeved gold top.

A car came up behind her. At first she didn't notice; but dimly she became aware of the blue Chevy slowing to a crawl beside her. A man's voice. *"Hey, honey. Can you help me for a second? I'm looking for a lost dog."*

Later there was pain and blood and muffled cries of protest. Her tears streaking down her cheeks. Her teeth biting her lower lip.

Then there was darkness and her tiny, hollow cry: "Is anyone out there?"

And then, for the longest time, there was nothing.

They told her it lasted twenty-eight days. She'd had no way of knowing. There was no time in the dark, just a loneliness that went on without end. There was cold and there was silence, and there were the times when he returned. But at least that was something. It was the sheer nothingness, endless streams of nothingness, that could drive a person insane.

Hunters found her. November 18. They noticed the fresh

dirt, poked around with their rifles, and were startled to hear her faint voice. They dug her up triumphantly, unearthing her four-by-six earthen prison and releasing her into the crisp fall air. Later she saw newspaper photos. Her dark eyes oversized, her head thin and bony, her body curled up on itself, like a small brown bat that had been yanked harshly into the light.

The papers dubbed her the Thanksgiving Miracle. Her parents took her home. Neighbors and family paraded through the front door with exclamations of "Oh, thank goodness!" and "Just in time for the holidays," and "Oh, can you really believe . . . ?"

She sat and let people talk around her. She slipped food from the overflowing trays and stored it in her pockets. Her head was down, her shoulders hunched around her ears. She was still the little bat and for reasons she couldn't explain, she was terrified of the light.

More police came. She told them of the man, of the car. They showed her pictures. She pointed at one. Later, days, weeks—did it really matter?—she came to the police station, stared at a lineup, and solemnly pointed her finger.

Richard Umbrio went on trial six months later. And three months into that, she took the stand in her plain blue dress, polished Mary Janes, and pointed her finger once again. Richard Umbrio went away for life.

And Catherine returned home with her family.

She didn't eat much. She liked to take the food and put it in her pocket, or simply hold it in the palm of her hand. She didn't sleep much. She lay in the dark, blind bat eyes seeking something she couldn't name. Often, she held very still and saw if she could breathe without making a sound.

Sometimes her mother stood in the doorway, her pale white hands fluttering anxiously at her collarbone. Eventually, Catherine would hear her father down the hall. *"Come to bed, Louise. She'll call if she needs you."*

But Catherine never called.

Years passed. Catherine grew up, straightening her shoulders, growing out her hair, and discovering that she possessed the kind of strange, potent beauty that stopped men in their tracks. She was all pale white skin, straight black hair, and oversized navy eyes. Men wanted her desperately. So she used them indiscriminately. It wasn't her fault. It wasn't their fault. She simply never felt a thing.

Her mother died. 1994. Cancer. Catherine stood at the funeral and tried to cry. Her body had no moisture and her sobs sounded papery and insincere.

She went home to her barren apartment and tried not to think of it again, though sometimes, out of the blue, she would picture her mother standing in the doorway of her room. *"Come to bed, Louise. She'll call if she needs you."*

"Hey, honey. Can you help me find a lost dog?"

November 1998. The Thanksgiving Miracle curled up naked in her white ceramic tub, her thin, bony body trembling from the cold, as she clutched a single razor in her fist. Something bad was going to happen. A darkness beyond darkness. A buried box from which there would be no coming back.

"Come to bed, Louise. She'll call if she needs you."

"Hey, honey. Can you help me find a lost dog?"

The blade, so slender and light in her hands. The feel of its edge, kissing her skin. The abstract sensation of warm red blood, lining her skin.

The phone rang. Catherine roused herself from her lethargy long enough to answer it. And that single call saved her life. The Thanksgiving Miracle rose again.

She thought about it now. As the TV blared in the background: *An armed suspect has barricaded himself in his home after taking numerous shots at his neighbors. Boston SWAT officials consider the situation highly volatile and extremely dangerous.*

As her son sobbed in her arms. "Mommy, mommy, mommy."

And as her husband bellowed from below: "I know what you're doing, Cat! How stupid do you think I am? Well, it's not going to work. There's no way in hell you're going to get away with it. Not this time!"

Jimmy stormed up the stairs, heading for their bedroom.

The phone had saved Catherine Gagnon before. Now she prayed it would save her once again. "Hello, hello, nine-one-one? Can you hear me? It's my husband. I think he's got a gun."

CHAPTER TWO

BOBBY HAD BEEN a member of the Massachusetts State Police Special Tactics and Operations Team (STOP) for the past six years. Called out at least three times a month—and generally every damn holiday—he thought very little could surprise him anymore, but tonight he was wrong.

Roaring through the streets of Boston, he squealed his tires taking a hard right up Park Street, heading for the golden-domed State House, then threw his cruiser left onto Beacon, flying past the Commons and the Public Gardens. At the last minute, he almost blew it—tried to head up Arlington straight for Marlborough, then realized as a guy who generally drove around Boston and not through it, that Marlborough was one way the wrong way. Like any good Masshole driver, he slammed on his brakes, cranked the wheel hard, and laid on his horn as he cut across three lanes of traffic to remain on Beacon. Now his life was tougher, trying to pick up the right cross street to head up to Marlborough. In the end, he got it right the first time—he simply followed the white glow of floodlights and the flashing red lights of the Advanced Life Support Ambulance.

Arriving at the corner of Marlborough and Gloucester, Bobby processed many details at once. Blue sawhorses and

Boston PD cruisers had already isolated one tiny block in the heart of Back Bay. Yellow crime scene tape was strewn across several brownstone houses and uniformed officers were taking up position on the corners. The ALS ambulance was now on scene, and so were several vans from the local media.

Things were definitely starting to rock and roll.

Bobby double-parked his Crown Vic just outside a blue sawhorse, jumped out the door, and jogged around to his trunk. Inside he had everything a well-trained police sniper might need for a party. Rifle, scope, ammo, black and urban camo BDUs, Ghillie hood, body armor, changes of clothing, snacks, water, a bean bag, night vision goggles, binoculars, range finder, face paint, Swiss Army knife, and flashlight. Local police probably kept spare tires in their trunk; a state trooper could live out of his cruiser for days.

Bobby hefted up his rucksack and immediately started assessing the situation.

In contrast to other SWAT teams, Bobby's tactical team never arrived en masse. Instead his unit consisted of thirty-two guys located all over the state of Massachusetts, from the fingertip of Cape Cod to the foothills of the Berkshire Mountains. Headquarters was Adams, Mass., in the western half of the state, where Bobby's lieutenant had taken the call from Framingham Communications and made the decision to deploy.

In this case, a domestic barricade with hostages, all thirty-two guys had been activated and all thirty-two would arrive. Some would take three to four hours to get here. Others, like Bobby, made it in less than fifteen minutes. Either way, Bobby's lieutenant prided their team on being able to get at least five officers anywhere in the state in under an hour.

Looking around now, Bobby figured he was one of those first five officers. Which meant he needed to hustle.

Most SWAT units were comprised of three teams—an

entry team, a perimeter team, and snipers. The perimeter team had the primary job of securing and controlling the inner perimeter. Then came the snipers, who took up position outside the inner perimeter and served as reconnaissance—appraising the situation through their scopes or binoculars, and radioing in details on the building as well as all people and movement inside. Finally, the entry team would prepare for last resort action—if the hostage negotiator couldn't convince the suspects to come out, the entry team would storm in. Entries were messy; you prayed it didn't come to that, but sometimes it did.

Bobby's STOP team brought all those bells and whistles to the table, but they didn't specialize. Instead, given that they arrived piecemeal, they were cross-trained on all positions so they could get up and running the moment boots hit the ground. In other words, while Bobby was one of the team's eight designated snipers, he wasn't looking at taking up sniping position just yet.

First goal—establish the inner perimeter. The inner perimeter was the area looking in at the scene. Establishing a good inner perimeter solved 90 percent of any tactical unit's headaches. You controlled and contained. It took at least two guys to form a perimeter, each standing on opposing corners, monitoring the diagonals.

Bobby was one guy. Now he was looking for a second. He spotted two other state police cruisers parked across the way, then noticed the white van set up as command center. He hefted his rucksack on his shoulder and resumed running.

Bobby climbed into the command center. "Trooper Bobby Dodge," he announced, setting down his gear and thrusting out a hand.

"Lieutenant Jachrimo." The CO took his hand, handshake tight but quick. The thin-faced lieutenant wasn't from the state police, but from BPD. That didn't surprise Bobby; the scene was technically BPD jurisdiction, plus his own state police commander was probably still two hours away. The state police often assisted other jurisdictions, and secretly prided themselves on playing well with others.

Jachrimo already had a white board up in front of him and was making a Gant chart in the upper left-hand corner. "Position?" the man barked.

"Sniper."

"Can you hold a perimeter?"

"Yes, sir."

"Great, great, great." A Boston uniform was walking by. Lieutenant Jachrimo broke away from the white board long enough to stick his head out of the van and yell, "Hey, hey you." Jachrimo flagged down the uniform. "I need the phone company. Understand? Use your radio, call into dispatch, and get the goddamn phone company, 'cause nothing in this van is working, and you can't really have a command post if it doesn't command. Got it?"

The uniform went flying, and Jachrimo returned his harried attention to Bobby. "Okay, so what do you know?"

"Domestic barricade, male subject believed armed with a gun, wife and child also on the premises." Bobby repeated the message he'd received on his pager.

"Suspect's name is James 'Jimmy' Gagnon. Mean anything to you?"

Bobby shook his head.

"Just as well." Jachrimo finished his Gant chart, then started an overhead sketch of the neighborhood on the lower part of the white board. "So here's where we're at. Woman called nine-one-one shortly after eleven-thirty. Claimed to be Catherine Gagnon, Jimmy's wife. Said her husband was drunk and threatening her and their son with a handgun. The nine-one-one operator tried to hold her on the line, but there was some kind of disturbance and the call was disconnected. About four minutes later, nine-one-one received a call from a neighbor reporting sounds of gunfire.

"The call came into headquarters, but our guys are already out on a situation in Revere, so I kicked it to Framingham Communications, who contacted your lieutenant. Your unit's serving as the primary, maybe for the whole show, maybe until our guys wrap up the party in Revere. Don't know. As of this moment, we have uniforms already securing the external perimeter. There are men posted here, here, and here, and cars positioned here and here to block off the connecting streets." Jachrimo made a series of X's on his sketch, and that quickly one block of brownstones was cordoned off from the surrounding neighborhood.

"The Gagnons occupy the top three levels of unit number four-fifteen. Uniforms have already evacuated the residents below their unit, as well as the residents of the brownstones on either side. We haven't had contact with anyone inside the residence yet, which frankly doesn't make me happy. As far as I'm concerned, we should've had the inner perimeter secured ten minutes ago, and the hostage negotiators here eight minutes ago. But hey, that's just me."

"Manpower?"

"Troopers Fusilli, Adams, and Maroni are already on scene. They're scoping the building now, looking to form a very tight perimeter, probably inside the building. I got one officer tracking down blueprints and another—hopefully—getting me the goddamn phone company."

"Intel from the neighbors?"

"According to the downstairs unit owner, the Gagnons did significant work on the place in the past five years. Top level was converted into cathedral ceilings, eliminating the attic. There's one main elevator, serving three floors. Stairs go all the way to the top, one set inside the building and one set of fire escapes on the side. He's not sure about crawl spaces or how many rooms per floor. It's an old building, though, so there's bound to be a few surprises.

"It would seem that the Gagnons keep to themselves and

whatever parties they've had, they haven't invited too many of their neighbors. Couple has a reputation for its fights and we've been called out here before for domestic disputes. First time there's been mention of a gun, though, so that's a fresh kick in the pants. Is it her? Is it him? Hell if I know. Mostly, I'm sure it just sucks for the kid. So that's where we are and that's what we got."

The lieutenant's spiel ground to a halt just in time. Phone company had arrived. Another one of Bobby's teammates as well.

"Perfect," the lieutenant declared. He stabbed one finger at the new trooper. "You, inner perimeter. And you"—the finger moved to Bobby—"find a position. I want intel on that house. Where's the husband, where's the wife, where's the kid? And better yet, is anyone still alive? Because it's been over thirty minutes now, and we haven't heard a thing."